Praise for the novels of Jacquelyn Mitchard

The Deep End of the Ocean

"A wrenching first novel…. Wonderfully written."
—*New York Times Book Review*

"Masterful… A big story about human connection and emotional survival."
—*Los Angeles Times*

No Time to Wave Goodbye

"A bold, brilliant powerhouse of a novel. I read it in one sitting, unable to walk away until I'd come to the startling and unexpected end."
—Kristin Hannah, #1 *New York Times* bestselling author

"Gripping, suspenseful and downright good; a beautiful reminder of why the world loves Jacquelyn Mitchard."
—Karin Slaughter, *New York Times* bestselling author

Second Nature

"Timely…provocative…. [Mitchard's] distinctive voice is strong throughout…. Her latest will not disappoint."
—*Washington Post Book World*

"Mitchard's latest ought to come with a warning: make no immediate plans, because this book will take over your life… A high-profile novel destined to galvanize fans and new readers alike."
—*Booklist*, starred review

"A riveting tale."
—*Publishers Weekly*

"There's a newsy urgency to this story."
—*Chicago Tribune*

Two If by Sea

"Suspenseful…nearly impossible to put down."
—*People*

"Soulful and emotionally arresting… Mitchard masterfully mines the place where catastrophic loss meets near-impossible hope and healing… This book will open your mind and heart in equal measures."
—Paula McLain, *New York Times* bestselling author of *The Paris Wife*

"A thoughtful, sweeping read."
—Jodi Picoult, *New York Times* bestselling author of *Leaving Time*

"Mitchard returns with another heartbreaker."
—*Library Journal*

"A troubled protagonist, beset by disaster and malefaction, is touched by magic."
—*Kirkus Reviews*

Jacquelyn Mitchard

The
Good
Son

mira

ISBN-13: 978-0-7783-1179-9
ISBN-13: 978-0-7783-8642-1 (International Trade Paperback Edition)

The Good Son

Mira
22 Adelaide St. West, 41st Floor
Toronto, Ontario M5H 4E3, Canada
BookClubbish.com

Printed in U.S.A.

For Henry the First and all very good sons

The
Good
Son

"The dead cling to the land. The living cling
to a story that, like currency, changes hands."

Laura Van Prooyen

"Now that my ladder's gone,
I must lie down where all the ladders start
In the foul rag and bone shop of the heart."

William Butler Yeats

"Though lovers be lost love shall not;
And death shall have no dominion."

Dylan Thomas

BOOK ONE:

Release

1

I was picking my son up at the prison gates when I spotted the mother of the girl he had murdered.

Two independent clauses, ten words each, joined by an adverb, made up entirely of words that would once have been unimaginable to think, much less say.

She pulled in—not next to me, but four spaces over—in the half circle of fifteen-minute spots directly in front of the main building. It was not where Stefan would walk out. That would be over at the gatehouse. She got out of her car, and for a moment I thought she would come toward me. I wanted to talk to her, to offer something, to reach out and hold her, for we had not even been able to attend Belinda's funeral. But what would I say? What would she? This was an unwonted crease in an already unaccustomed day. I slid deep into my down coat, and wished I could lock the car doors, although I feared that the sound would crack the predawn darkness like a rifle shot. All that Jill McCormack did, however, was shove her hands into the pockets of her jacket and lean against the back bumper of her car. She wore the heavy maroon leather varsity jacket that her daughter Belinda, captain of the high school cheer team in senior year, had given to her, to Stefan, and to me, with our names embroidered in gold on the back, just like hers.

I hadn't seen Jill McCormack up close for years, though she lived literally around the corner. Once, I used to stop there to sit on her porch, but now I avoided even driving past the place.

Jill seemed smaller, diminished, the tumult of ash-blond hair I remembered cropped short and seemingly mostly white, though I knew she was young when Belinda was born, and now couldn't be much past forty. Yet, even just to stand in the watery, slow-rising light in front of a prison, she was tossed together fashionably, in gold-colored jeans and boots, with a black turtleneck, a look I would have had to plan for days. She looked right at my car, but gave no sign that she recognized it, though she'd been in it dozens of times years ago. Once she had even changed her clothes in my car. I remember how I stood outside it holding a blanket up over the windows as she peeled off a soaking-wet, floor-length, jonquil-yellow crystal-beaded evening gown that must, at that point, have weighed about thirty pounds, then slipped into a clean football warm-up kit. After she changed, we linked arms with my husband and we all went to a ball.

But I would not think of that now.

I had spent years assiduously not thinking of any of that.

A friendship, like a crime, is not one thing, or even two people. It's two people and their shared environs and their histories, their common memories, their words, their weaknesses and fears, their virtues and vanities, and sometimes their shame.

Jill was not my closest friend. Some craven times, I blessed myself with that—at *least* I was spared that. There had always been Julie, since fifth grade my heart, my sharer. But Jill was my good friend. We had been soccer moms together, and walking buddies, although Jill's swift, balanced walk was my jog. I once kept Belinda at my house while Jill went to the bedside of her beloved father who'd suffered a stroke, just as she kept Stefan at her house with Belinda when they were seven and both had chicken pox, which somehow neither I nor my husband, Jep, ever caught. And on the hot night of that fundraising ball for the zoo, so long ago, she had saved Stefan's life.

Since Jill was a widow when we first met, recently arrived in the Midwest from her native North Carolina, I was always talking her into coming to events with Jep and me, introducing her to single guys who immediately turned out to be hopeless. That hot evening, along with the babysitter, the two kids raced toward the new pool, wildly decorated with flashing green lights, vines and temporary waterfalls for a "night jungle swim." Suddenly, the sitter screamed. When Jill was growing up, she had been state champion in the 200-meter backstroke before her devout parents implored her to switch to the more modest sport of golf, and Belinda, at five, was already a proficient swimmer. My Stefan, on the other hand, sank to the bottom like a rock and never came up. Jill didn't stop to ask questions. Kicking off her gold sandals, in she went, an elegant flat race dive that barely creased the surface; seconds later she hauled up a gasping Stefan. Stefan owed his life to her as surely as Belinda owed her death to Stefan.

In seconds, life reverses.

Jill and I once talked every week. It even seemed we once might have been *machatunim*, as they say in Yiddish, parents joined by the marriage of their son and daughter. Now, the circumstances under which we might ever exchange a single word seemed as distant as the bony hood of moon above us in the melting darkness.

What did she want here now? Would she leave once Stefan came through the gates? In fact, she left before that. She got back into her car, and, looking straight ahead, drove off.

I watched until her car was out of sight.

Just after dawn, a guard walked Stefan to the edge of the enclosure. I looked up at the razor wire. Then, opening the window slightly, I heard the guard say, "Do good, kid. I hope I never see you again." Stefan stepped out, and then put his palm up to a sky that had just begun to spit snow. He was twenty, and he had served two years, nine months and three days of a five-year sentence, one year of which the judge had suspended, noting Stefan's unblemished record. Still, it seemed like a week; it seemed like my entire life; it seemed like a length of time too paltry for the monstrous thing he had done. I could not help but reckon it this way: For each of the sixty or seventy years Belinda would have had left to live, Stefan spent only a week behind bars, not even a season. No matter how much he despaired, he could always see the end. Was I grateful? Was I ashamed? I was both. Yet relief rippled through me like the sweet breeze that stirs the curtains on a summer night.

I got out and walked over to my son. I reached up and put my hand on his head. I said, "My kid."

Stefan placed his huge warm palm on the top of my head. "My mom," he said.

It was an old ritual, a thing I would not have dared to do in the prison visiting room. My eyes stung with curated tears. Then I glanced around me, furtively. Was I still permitted such tender old deeds? This new universe was not showing its hand.

"I can stand here as long as I want," he said, shivering in wonderment. Then he said, "Where's Dad?"

"He told you about it. He had to see that kid in Louisville one more time," I told him reluctantly. "The running back with the very protective grandmother. He couldn't get out of it. But he cut it short and he'll be home when we get back, if he beats the weather out of Kentucky this morning, that is." Jep was in only his second season as football coach at the University of Wisconsin–Whitewater, a Division II team with significant chops and national esteem. We didn't really think he would get the job, given our troubles, but the athletic director had watched Jep's career and believed deeply in his integrity. Now he was never at rest: His postseason recruiting trips webbed the country. Yet it was also true that while Stefan's father longed equally for his son to be free, if Jep had been able to summon the words to tell the people who mattered that he wanted to skip this trip altogether, he would have. But he couldn't quite bring himself to say it's a big day, our son's getting out of prison.

Now, it seemed important to hurry Stefan to the car, to get out of there before this new universe recanted. We had a long drive back from Black Creek, where the ironically named Belle Colline Correctional Facility squatted not far from the campus of the University of Wisconsin–Black Creek. Stefan's terrible journey had taken him from college to prison, a distance of just two miles as the crow flies. I felt like the guard: I never wanted to see the place again. I had no time to think about Jill or anything else except the weather. We'd hoped that the early-daylight release would keep protestors away from the prison gates, and that seemed to have worked: Prisoners usually didn't walk out until just before midday. There was not a single reporter here, which surprised me as Jill was tireless in keeping her daughter Belinda's death a national story, a symbol for young women in abusive relationships. Many of the half dozen or so stalwarts who still picketed in front of our house nearly every day were local college and high-school girls, passionate about Jill's work. As Stefan's release grew near, their numbers rose, even as the outdoor temperatures fell. A few news organizations put in appearances again lately as well. I knew they would be on alert today and was hoping we could beat some of the attention by getting back home early. In the meantime, a snowstorm was in the forecast: I never minded driving in snow, but the air smelled of water running over iron ore—a smell that always portended worse weather.

Once outside the gates, we headed for the highway and a restroom where Stefan could change outfits.

He had asked me only one thing—to bring shoes and clothes and a coat. And I had. But although over the course of more than a hundred visits it should have been obvious to me, I had never fully realized until now how, when he went in, he was only a boy of seventeen, five-ten, a hundred and sixty pounds. And by now he had grown three inches taller. The flight parka that seemed so huge on him the last Christmas he spent at home wouldn't even close over shoulders hardened by intervening years of obsessive solitary exercise. His feet were probably a size bigger, too. In my eagerness to bring Stefan things that were his own, familiar shirtsleeves I had rubbed between my hands when the days and nights were too long, I had not stopped to consider just how ruthlessly time had passed. Maybe I didn't want to know that.

"It doesn't matter," he told me.

"Sure it does," I said. "What else does?"

It seemed right to offer every teaspoon of conferred civility that I could. So I pulled off at a nearby Target, and apologized for this being the only choice for haberdashery. But Stefan loved Target, he always had; he thought of it as a bazaar of consumer delights. Target, not homemade dinners or a proper bed, was what always headed the list of things he missed. His excitement was poignant. He appeared in the dressing room door, posing in a striped pullover, then a bright Green Bay Packers hoodie. I thought helplessly of Stefan as a little boy, wearing matching shorts and sailor tops from The Children's Place, so expensive and foppish that Jep complained his son looked like one of the dolls in a Victorian child's bedroom on *Masterpiece Theatre*.

He was my only. What could I do? Then and now. It is far easier to hate yourself than to hate your own child.

We bought jeans and a sweatshirt, flannel shirts and Carhartt boots and a light down parka, and he threw out the stiff black prison-sewn shirts and the two pairs of mended chinos, as well as the coat that stank of sweat and cigarettes that had once belonged to some criminal—though, of course, Stefan was a criminal, too. The only thing he kept was the pale blue sweater he had knitted himself, just in the past year when he'd been trusted with plastic knitting needles. Cheerfully disdaining the new jacket, he wore the Green Bay Packers sweatshirt out of the store, the way a child would do. When he grinned and pointed to the gold Packers logo, I took a picture and messaged it to Jep, who texted back, Yes! He then texted me privately, Is he okay? And I answered, So far so good. Who would have imagined that this was how I would communicate that news? In this new universe, the most critical exchanges—between parents, between a long-married husband and wife, new sweethearts, or a stalker and his victim—were shared on a four-inch screen, with emojis of hearts and smiley faces. This was probably a metaphor for something but I could not fathom what.

Newly outfitted, Stefan and I headed back toward the highway.

We'd driven only a few miles when the blizzard leaped upon us. We edged our way into a hotel parking lot. I couldn't even see the sky. A check of the local weather on my phone promised hours of possible whiteout conditions.

"Did you get a good night's sleep?"

Why was I talking to Stefan as though he were my great-aunt?

"I never slept a whole night the entire time I was in there," he said. "The last couple of nights, I didn't go to sleep at all. I was afraid I'd die before I got out."

I'd never been a good sleeper, but the previous weeks— enduring Christmas, the winter break at my college, New Year's Eve with Jep, my best friend Julie and her husband, Hal, and a few other couples, all with my mind arrowed toward this moment—had been impossible.

"Let's just stay here until the storm eases up," I told Stefan.

"I'll get us hotel rooms. You can…relax, have a nap or watch a movie. Later on, we'll get a fancy meal."

I was, as always, too optimistic. I had in mind a steak house like Bee's and B's, the place I took him to for birthdays when he was a kid, with the whole family, grandparents and cousins and aunts and uncles and a couple of neighbors at a table nearly as big as the room. Who knew? Three solid college campuses and a sizable airport were within fifty miles. Maybe there would be at least one luxurious hotel, with flat-screens and plunge tubs and blackout shades and a pricey, chef-owned eatery on the first floor. As it turned out, our options were limited to Pizza Hut and Panera Bread. Apparently boutique hotels were scarce near a prison. How had I not known this before?

Well, for all my weekly visits, I had never spent an overnight in Black Creek. Nor had any of Stefan's aunts or grandparents who visited. When I came alone, which was most often, I would hit the road again right after visiting hours, bombing my way home along the back roads in the summer, the highway in the winter. Then I would slam into the house straight upstairs to sit in a tub filled with scented oil and hot water for over an hour, adding more hot as needed, an almost holy observance after the stench of the place where Stefan lived. I would sit there and cry. I cried so hard each week it seemed impossible that I did not actually lose water weight.

We were already in the parking lot of a Residence Inn on the frontage road, so we followed a smudge of light that seemed to be the lobby and parked under the portico. I booked a two-bedroom suite, but that quickly seemed like an iffy idea so I changed it to a room for Stefan to give him privacy and one for me, not even on the same floor, because why would you want to share a suite with anyone, even your mother, especially your mother, on your first night out of jail? The rooms were generous vistas of downtrodden brown tweed carpet and the kind of overly pebbly white walls that could rip an elbow out of a sweater. Down the hall from Stefan was a woman herding three little girls and three miniature greyhounds, all of them yipping up a storm. A slight, pretty girl in a crop top and squeeze-tight leggings, her extensions coiled around her regal skull, gave us handfuls of emery boards and press-on nail kits as we passed her, sweetly sharing her fear that her home-salon event was going to be snowed out. I saw her heavily-kohled dark eyes sweep appreciatively over Stefan, saw him notice how she looked at him, and wondered if anything would have happened had I not been there. I almost regretted that I was.

Fluttering around Stefan's room, I said, "This is awful."

"Not to me," Stefan said. "It's heaven."

The hotel had a sort of little convenience store in the lobby that carried a few things we would need to stay overnight, toothbrushes, bottles of water, the most cursory kinds of comfort food. Although it was only late morning, Stefan wanted the kind of meal he would have craved as a teenager. He flopped on the bed with a spoon and a carton of ice cream, Häagen-Dazs Rum Raisin, his favorite, which he had not tasted in years, and a microwave cheese pizza. As I sat across from him, drinking black coffee stirred up from the hot tap water and stingy little packets, he ate the whole pint of ice cream and three-quarters of the pizza and, and then, to his humiliation, threw it all up.

"I've been hungry for years," he said. "I'm so sorry."

He looked so young. I thought of him on his first day of preschool, when he gravely explained that he no longer wanted his fried eggs flipped over. When he finished breakfast that morning so long ago, he said to me, "You know what, Mom? You're my sunny-up egg."

Now he told me, "In AA, they say the whole thing is to trust the process. You just do one thing at a time."

"You went to AA? But you had regular group counseling."

He was silent. Then he said, "No."

"What? Stefan!"

"I had a half hour a week in the hospital, right after, right after Belinda. This doctor, he looked a lot worse than most of the patients, his face was all red and chewed up, like he had a sunburn, and he smoked in this windowless room, they all smoked like it was vitamins. And all the doc would say was, are you taking your medication? Are you having nightmares? Are you having thoughts of suicide? I said yes sometimes and I said no sometimes. He didn't seem to care what I said. But in jail, there's no therapy in jail, Mom. Not unless you're in a maximum security nut place, like Mendota."

"You said there was."

"No, I never said there was. You just thought there was and I never told you anything different."

"Is there other stuff like that?"

He said, "Yes."

"You can go to counseling when you get home."

"Okay. But not yet. I just have to sit here right now and be grateful I'm free. Like, I can go to sleep right now, and it will be dark and quiet all night." He didn't seem to notice the woman shouting at her kids and her greyhounds. There were many worst parts of prison, but one of the worse worsts he had shared with me on visits was the sobbing and screaming and rustling and laughing that went on all night, under lights that were never dimmed.

There was a surreal quality to this middle passage, neither here nor there, neither morning nor night. After we had purchased the clothing, picked up food and checked in to the hotel, the blizzard enclosed us like a glittering tower. Just as a big storm can feel comforting when you are safe in your own nest, this one felt isolating, hazardous, as if we were stranded at sea. Stefan ate and got sick and then the both of us were suddenly, simultaneously, exhausted. He wanted to nap, the cheap square laminate bedframe looking to him like a tropical paradise.

"Are you okay if I leave? Do you want to watch a movie or something together?" I said.

"I'm good. I'll probably just sleep."

I went to my own room. For some reason, you had to walk out into a courtyard to go up a floor. The snow fell steadily around me, more a column than a cloud, light and dark, metal and gem. Once inside, I sat on my bed, damp and shivering with nerves. I got out my phone and dialed up my Kindle and tried to read something, but by the time I got to the end of a sentence, I couldn't remember the beginning. Finally I lay down, pulled the hood of my coat over my eyes like a tent. I must have fallen asleep myself, because later the knocking at the door hit me in the chest like a fist, and I gasped awake, rolling off the bed and stumbling onto the floor. I opened the door and Stefan stood there, snow spangling his hair.

"I can go out in a blizzard anytime I want," Stefan said.

"Most people wouldn't consider that much of a privilege," I told him.

And he said, "Mom, it's letting up. I thought I could sleep, but I can't."

"How come? Are you still sick to your stomach?"

"No, but there are all these crazy…noises. The heater keeps going tick tick tick like a bomb or something. You just settle down and then somebody slams a car door."

A car door? How could that bother him after years of men wailing and banging on the pipes?

"I'm also just shaky. I still feel like I'm too close to The Hill."

I flinched at the convict talk: The Hill was what prisoners called Belle Colline. *Going down the hill,* they said, when someone was freed. *Jack and Jill went up the hill,* they said when a convict got married. "What I really want is, I want to go home. Mom, please. Right now."

I put on my shoes and jacket, unplugged my phone and charger, grabbed my purse and we left.

The blizzard wasn't really letting up, but I thought the weather might get better the farther south we got. So we inched along the 320 miles at twenty miles an hour.

I will never be able to think of that nightmare trek as a "ride."

A "ride," even a long one, seems to me like something you do with cheerful purpose, like a biking event to raise money to defeat a disease—just as a "drive" is something you do with your grandparents on a summer Sunday.

This felt like a sort of rolling brawl, studded with strange thoughts and incidents.

At first, Stefan was chattering, apologizing over and over for wasting the hotel room and the food, me reassuring him, promising to make chicken noodle soup and homemade rye bread when we got home, although I could think of nothing more than lying flat on clean sheets when we got there. We stopped every torturous twenty or thirty miles, and I fell into frantic short bouts of sleep, then wakened to find snow mounded like bolster pillows against the windshield. We would get out and push the accumulation away with a plastic windshield brush until that soon broke. Then with the corner of a cardboard box I found in the trunk, and then when that got soggy, with our hands, because somehow, no one ever prepares for such a storm. The dashboard indicator read two below. So much for it being too cold to snow.

Start, then stop. Start, then stop, from noon until six that night.

Once, on a break at a truck stop, Stefan fell asleep too, and it was when a semi gave out a long blast on its air horn that we sat upright, sweating in our winter coats, spooked by how easily we could have slept on forever, our car a potential crypt flooded with carbon monoxide, banked in snow and etched with filigrees of frost. We set out again, and I told Stefan to go ahead and nap. It was only with all that suspended time that I let my mind drift back to Jill McCormack. The victim's mother, as she was always referred to in court and on news broadcasts when she gave all those wrenching interviews about domestic violence against young women, when she first founded the organization SAY, Stop Abuse Young. I thought about what she was doing there this morning, how she must have known about the timing of Stefan's release, wondered if she meant to speak to him or to me, then ended up driving all that long way for nothing.

I wondered what Jill did now. She was one of only two women pros at Little Wood Country Club. Was SAY a full-time job for her by now? I thought back to our meeting the first time, that athlete's posture and ease, the kind of woman who would never loosen the top button on her pants. How years later, Belinda, then a high school sophomore, giggled when she confided how horrified her mother was that her daughter would decide to give up varsity tennis for cheerleading. It had been a rebel move that united us—Belinda, Stefan and me. Jep was equally nonplussed when Stefan, a running back who as a junior was already being scouted, let it be known that he wasn't interested in making a film reel of his best action because he was not going to play college ball. In fact, he had decided that junior year would be his last season. I remembered the night that it all came to a head: Stefan finally said, "Dad, I love football. But I don't love it enough. Guys in college, they're going to be bigger and stronger not to mention meaner than me, and I don't even want to think about getting hurt or hurting somebody else. I just don't have that killer instinct."

Those last words would echo back to us in the years that followed.

I thought more about Jill. If my prayers were answered and the attention to Stefan's case melted away with time, would the purpose of Jill's life melt away as well? Belinda had been her only. Her husband, a minister, died years ago when Belinda was small in a skiing mishap just after a big financial scandal broke at his church. For every hour I'd cursed my literature students as spoiled illiterates back when I was a newly-minted PhD, I now blessed my teaching position that had at least given me a handhold in the ordinary world. I still had that job and my son, still had my husband and my family, mostly nearby, however fraught the circumstances. So I still had cause for hope. And when it came to hope, I was hopeless. Optimism was my opiate. Obsession was my default. I would will things to go my way. I would muster every known force to make it so.

My husband called it the First Law of Thea-dynamics: I could take anything and transform it into energy that could then never be destroyed. And he was right. I would never admit it, but my personality was such that once I got involved with something, it was like hearing a fragment of a song you knew and having no choice but to sing the whole thing in your head, over and over, for days, until something blessedly intervened and bore it away. I'd once raised three baby robins from turquoise eggs no bigger than the tip of my thumb to fledglings that took wing to the sky behind our garage. When I couldn't find a couch I liked, I built one and upholstered it. I would turn that tenacity to Stefan now. I would apply it to the future, and to the past. If it had been the drugs for Stefan, well, then, he didn't use them anymore. If Belinda's death had truly been an accident, well, even the most wretched accidents are accidental, and they happen in the world.

I never fully realized that others lived like I did, and that some of them were people I knew, people who would never give up unless the choice was death or ruin. Months after Stefan's conviction, after I gave a talk, I was approached by a woman who said that the belief that things would somehow always get better was a character flaw particular to Americans and American culture, and especially to American parents. They stand shivering in the dark forest but insist the sunny plain is just ahead, she said. Why, I asked the woman, do you think? She was Chinese, a pediatric hematologist, and she smiled sadly when she told me: Why, what else would you expect when their own parents ruined them for reality by raising them on the sweetened milk of hope?

My thoughts were interrupted when my cell phone sang out, Debussy's *Clair de Lune*. It was a local Madison number, not that this meant anything. Stefan was asleep in the passenger seat. Even though I had to take a quick glance away from the road, I picked up.

"You don't know the real truth," said a young female voice. "But I do."

"What truth is this?" I asked. Unless I was much mistaken, her answer would have God in it.

"I saw what happened that night," she said. "The night Belinda was killed. I was there."

"You weren't," I said.

"I was."

"And you waited until now to reveal this."

Then the voice on the other end of the phone started to cry and cried so hard that for a moment, all I could hear was the bellows of her breathing. "I had to! But I can't stand it anymore. Nobody knows the truth except me." Then she hung up.

Did I recognize her voice? I thought I did. But I still got crazy calls all the time from psychics, psychologists, and, for all I knew, psychotics, most of whom had something urgent to tell me—or sell me. Sometimes, it was burial insurance, or pet insurance, or a new mortgage rate. Sometimes, all I could hear was a growl or a scream or a sigh before the receiver on the other end crashed down. Sometimes strangers wanted to excoriate me for having given birth to a demon. But often, they had a message from Belinda or from Jesus and it was just for me, for $120 only to cover their time, and ZipCash would be fine. I'd given up trying to figure out how they got my cell-phone number. It was probably published in some dark web chat forum.

But this one...this was the repeat caller who would usually

ask, How is Stefan? Then she'd hang up almost before I finished my answer. Last year, I stopped hearing from her. Now, here she was again. There was something naked in her voice that made her seem valid and caught my attention. For the hundredth time, I thought I would get a new phone number. For the hundredth time, I decided why bother—why confuse the people who actually knew me for the sake of crazies who would somehow find me anyhow?

We inched off the road to a rest stop, and Stefan woke up. He got out to fill up the car and buy more plastic window scrapers.

I won't ever know why I took that call. The way the girl sounded, so desperate and young, lit some tuft of kindling in me. It reminded me of Belinda's voice. The girl called again and I answered. I said, "Who are you? Do you need something from me?"

"I know everything she did. I know everything they did," she said. "And I know about the drugs."

She meant the drugs Stefan used on the night Belinda died, a combination that could have killed him and, indirectly, killed her. The paramedics told me later my son might easily have suffered a heart attack from all those toxins, but he was rescued by his own youth. But the other thing the girl said was a fishhook that snagged. Whoever she meant by "they," could it possibly matter, today of all the days? Then it occurred to me, and a hot stout taste forced its way up my throat when I wondered if Stefan realized, because of course he did know, that this glacial January day, was the three-year anniversary of Belinda's death? How, in the accumulation of all the incidents and images, the words spoken and suppressed, the events seen or sensed, from the dank meaty stink of the prison visiting room to the peachy aura of Belinda's cologne that floated around her everywhere she went, from my son's blood-crusted palms to my mother's white gloves beside her on the bench in the courtroom, from the harsh voices of the protestors, Stefan's hoarse shouts for me from the locked ward, Jep's strong hands under my elbows when I stumbled the morning we returned from a walk to find the word *MURDERER* scrawled in red paint on our garage door, to the heft of the loaf of homemade bread I pushed through the car window as Stefan set out to join Belinda at college, all towed behind me like shells and weeds in a huge strange net through a tidal flow. How, through these years to this glacial day, had I managed to forget the anniversary of that singular event?

"I was right there," she said.

"You were not there. I know who was there."

"Nobody saw me." The caller said crazy things, but she did not herself seem crazy. What awful event could have made someone so young act this way? What life circumstances would shape a person to make such calls to strangers?

"Okay, okay," I said. "I'll listen. Not right now. I'm driving in a blizzard…"

She said, "I know."

Of course. It was suddenly obvious. This person, whoever she was, knew Stefan was getting out today. She was a prison crank, a crime junkie.

"How about I call you some other time?"

"I should tell someone," she said, sobs gargling through her words. "I should tell everyone."

"Tell me."

"I can't. But listen. Tell Stefan not to talk about that night. Would you do that? That's the important thing. Tell him not to say anything about that night. And tell him I'm sorry."

I thought she would hang up then. But she did not. Once more the damp sound of her crying filled the void. Maybe she was one of the groupies who'd never met Belinda but who identified with her, as they should, as they must.

"Maybe you just want to feel important. Like you want to pretend you're part of some big sensational story because you don't have a real life of your own," I said. Might a little squeeze of lemon over my words draw her out? I thought so, but I repented when she cried even harder.

"You could help me have a real life of my own," she finally said. "But you'd just hate me for what I did."

"Why would I hate you? I don't even know you. In my experience, people who come close, then run away, want someone to run after them."

Stefan was back now, struggling with the door that had frozen shut in mere minutes. I pushed with all my weight against the inside door panel.

"No," she said. "I'm not like that. You'll never find me." She hung up.

Ah, I thought. *You underestimate me.*

2

We weren't even halfway home when the snow kicked up harder. I slowed again to a crawl, the world a featureless dazzle. I was digging my fingernails into my palms to keep alert. We were the only car on the road, or so I believed, until I glimpsed a bright blue smudge gaining on me faster than seemed possible. A break in the cloud around us showed me the river bridge ahead where the road rose high over the sandbars below. Even though it was a four-lane highway, the strange vehicle seemed to take up all the space, and then it swerved, nearly sideswiping us. I jerked the wheel quickly and felt the sickening float of a doughnut spin. Because time seems to drop into slideshow slowness at moments like these, I was able to observe everything—Stefan's clenched jaw, him not talking because you wouldn't, you couldn't, the face of the driver of the other car, which I thought, in some crazy reach, might be Jill. But it was some Unabomber look-alike, a figure in a huge hoodie, a ball cap and mirrored sunglasses, hunched over the wheel. Tense, my arms coursing with electrical prickles, I let him gain the distance, then when he was out of sight, I picked up speed just a little.

"Take a picture of his license plate," I told Stefan, pointing to my phone.

"I can't even see the car much less the plate," he said.

But then we did see the car. Out of the veil emerged that same blue glow, that same vehicle, clearly a newer car with those odd, too-bright headlamps. It was not moving, but parked under an overpass just ahead. I slowed down, scanning quickly for an exit or even a death-trap rest stop. Nothing. Stefan said then, "There is no license plate." I had to go on, so I sped up; but as I passed the driver, he spun the car around and hit the gas, this time aiming straight at us. I switched to the far lane and dropped back. He made a fast stop...what did he have on that car? Tank treads? I had no other way to go but to pass him again. Why would some person I never saw before in my life try to run my car off the road? I proceeded slowly, but the lone driver gunned it. This time he actually did clip my bumper, and our car skidded, spinning around once, twice, then ploughed a backward path across lanes and the shoulder into the snow, toward the edge of the river bluff. Stefan and I slammed against our seat belts as our car finally lurched to a stop, both of us afraid to glance to the right, as if that glance would dislodge us. Finally I looked down, down the sixty feet or more to the riverbed. Our car had stopped just short of going over the ledge. Just beyond us, the phantom vehicle had pulled over on the shoulder, and the driver stood there beside it and stared down at us through his mirrored glasses. He wagged a warning finger. It seemed an older man's gesture, but this guy looked young, around Stefan's age. Then he got back in his car and pulled away.

I opened my mouth. I shut my mouth. "We're okay," I finally said. "We're okay, right?"

"We're good." He said, "Do you think he's going to be waiting for us up ahead?"

"I'm going to call Triple A," I said. But the thought of the two hours it would probably take for them to reach us yawned like a cave. "I'm going to call the police."

We stared at each other. No police.

"I'm going to call Dad," I said.

"It will just worry him," Stefan said and suggested, "Maybe we can get ourselves out." He managed to carefully shove the door open then edge his way out safely, bless his new boots. For a brutal, soaking half hour, he pushed against the car bumper as I kept the wheel turned tightly toward the road until, in a miracle of four-wheel drive, the car finally gave a little jump and struggled up, lipping the shoulder. My hair was plastered to my face with tears. I hadn't realized I was crying. Stefan hopped back in and we drove on.

"Who do you think that was?" Stefan finally murmured as he warmed his hands on the dashboard vents.

"Some lunatic. Right?" I glanced at him, terrified even to blink. "Right?"

Right, but neither of us felt remotely assured, instead we were certain that a madman sat, nudged up behind a big highway sign, eyes shrunken to dark points, lying in wait for no one but us. But the blue car never reappeared. My body remained on high alert. Even the collar of my parka was damp with sweat. We came to an exit, stopped to examine the crumpled fender, drank burned coffee and ate cellophane-sealed doughnuts. Then we headed on in silence, unable by then even to bear listening to an audiobook, the stale news loop or sports talk, hypnotized by the sound of the wind and the crunch of the tires.

It was then that Stefan said, "I'm so sorry, Mom."

"Is this about the hotel room again?" I sounded sharper than I meant to.

"No. Everything, everything."

I glanced at him. He was crying, his fingers pressed against his eyes. "I screwed up your whole life. You probably wish I was never born."

"Never," I assured him.

Letter after letter from prison echoed the same strains:

Happy Birthday, Dad. I feel like an idiot even saying, hey, have a great day, because I should be there being someone you could be proud of as you turn the big four four, not somebody you have to be ashamed of...

Dear Mom, Happy Mother's Day. Kind of ironic, right? Here I am congratulating you on something you probably wish never happened...

His words reeked of self-pity, but then again, who could blame him for feeling sorry—for us and for himself? We wrote back each time, alternately reassuring and admonishing him. When he was down on himself but could at least write to us, we could be pretty sure he was marginally okay. It was when he didn't write that fear consumed us.

While Stefan was in prison, the time came to renew his driver's license, which set off a firestorm of emotion for him. When Stefan first got his license, Belinda, a few months older and already in proud possession of her own license, accompanied us to his road test. She lectured him sternly: *You better do this the first try, Christiansen, is all I can say.* He did. And his laminated driver's license lasted longer than the girl.

"I miss her so much already," he said to me that fatal night at the hospital. "She's the one who told me that I should mark the organ-donor box, just in case. Nothing would ever happen, but just in case..."

I thought of myself, that night three years ago, speeding the long distance nonstop, running into the hospital so frantic I forgot to close the driver's side door, after a call that told me only that there had been "a serious accident." I pictured his car accordioned against a tree. Studying the impassive faces directing me to the fifth floor, I found a detective named Pete Sunday who told me Belinda was in surgery. He told me what kind of surgery she was in, and my legs began to wobble. It was the kind of surgery that happened when you were a good girl and marked the organ-donor box... Then he led me to Stefan, in the hospital's locked ward, chained to a bench behind a grill and sobbing, only half-conscious. His body was turned away from me, the pelt of dark hair at the back of his head matted with blood.

"He needs a doctor," I said. "He's bleeding."

"It's not his blood," Pete Sunday told me.

I sat down, hard, on the floor. Stefan turned. He saw me. He didn't know me.

Willing that vision to recede, I glanced at Stefan now and he turned to me as if I'd called his name. "What?"

"I didn't say anything."

"I just heard you," he said, and then added, "Is Dad scared about me coming home?"

"Sure. Scared, happy, confident, nervous." *Scared for you, or of you?* I looked at the muscles bunched in Stefan's forearms. My boy. My child. My only.

"It's when people come out that they get in trouble. They realize that the whole world has passed them by. That's why they end up back inside," he said.

"But you're not worried about that."

"Committing a crime? No. Jeez. Does Dad think I can have a real life? Do you think I can have a real life? Do you think the whole world has passed me by?"

I had considered this, oftener than I wanted to admit. If only we could leave, all of us, move away...anywhere... But Jep had his career. I had tenure. And without special permission, Stefan couldn't travel more than fifty miles while he was on parole. So I made a careful abstract of my words before I answered. "No. You're twenty years old. Life hasn't passed you by. Maybe it's going to be harder than we'd like to believe, though, at first. Maybe a lot harder than we think." Maybe harder than I think, I admitted, and my heart began to tap-dance. "Getting out is supposed to be the beginning of the good part, the part we've all been waiting for. But some people may be against you, Stefan. I've told you that some people still stand outside our house. Talking about that isn't the same as it's going to be to really see that. It can be scary. And you know Jill's position."

"It's not true. I mean, the worst part is true. But about Belinda being abused...no. Never. I never would."

"Well, not everyone believes that. If it were just me and Dad, we'd say, only look ahead. But you're going to have to keep fighting the things other people may say, at least for a while. That's probably why people get in trouble when they come out of jail. The things people say get into their hearts."

"All I can do is try. Right?"

"You can't not try. I'm not Dad. I'm not a coach. But Dad says that there's only one way to succeed in anything, and that's to give it everything."

"Dad didn't say that. Vince Lombardi said that."

"Well, Dad said it, too. I thought he was a genius."

We stopped for another break. Another cup of foul coffee. My guts felt like I was coating them with some sort of engine cleaner. How did people drink shit like this and live past the age of forty? Stefan drove when we got back into the car, his first time behind the wheel.

"How I feel is, she died, but it should have been me. I have no right to be alive."

"I'm thrilled that you're driving then."

"I think you worry that I'm going to kill myself. I don't think Dad does, but you do."

I said nothing. The wind shoved the car back and forth like a bear rocking a cradle. "Mom, think. If I wanted to kill myself, I could have killed myself in prison. They say they do all kinds of prevention, but they don't. A guy I knew did it when I was in there."

"He did? Why?"

"A weird reason. His cellie said it was because the sister of the woman he shot forgave him. He couldn't handle it." Stefan stopped talking for a moment and looked into the middle distance. "He was a nice guy. I know what you think, Mom, but he wasn't the one who pulled the trigger. It was a robbery, and he said he didn't even know his friends had a gun. Yeah, I also know everybody says that shit. Everybody in there is an innocent man. His name was Nightclub Owens. He had a beautiful voice. He sang this old song called, 'Up on the Roof.' It made hard guys cry."

"Did you ever consider it?" I hated myself for asking, but to stop myself from asking, I would have had to stop breathing.

"I thought about it. It's not that hard, if you hang yourself. It's getting over the fear. Belinda lost everything, all because of me. Belinda wanted to do something in the world. And what am I ever going to be in the world? I'm no genius. I look like every other guy. I'm another ex-druggie. I've never figured out what I want to do. It would be easy, just to give it up, just to let it go."

"Pull the car over," I said.

"What?"

"Pull the goddamn car over."

"I'm not going to wreck the car, Mom." But he pulled over slowly anyway. I got out, and a cyclone of snow burst into the vehicle as Stefan scrambled over the console. When I was strapped back into the driver's seat, with the zipper on my coat lowered to let my arms move more freely, I reached out and grabbed Stefan's arm. I felt that huge muscle tense, and for a moment I was afraid. I glanced down at his hands, remembering those hands when they were tiny starfish with dimples instead of knuckles.

This is your child, I thought. *You are his mother.*

How dare he even hint at taking himself away from me?

"Listen, you melodramatic little jerk," I said. "I get the worry and the regret. That's natural. But if you think I drove up and down this road to that shitbox prison in that shitbox town every week for two years, when half the people I knew thought I was nuts, and I didn't ever stop believing it could be better, so you could come out and kill yourself, you are sadly mistaken. If you think you have the luxury of killing yourself, after the worst is over, with all the people you'd be letting down, then get out of my car and get out of my life."

"Did I say I was going to? I thought I was saying that I never would, hello!"

"Because of that guy you knew who killed himself?"

"Well, sure, that's part of it! It's over for him. He wasn't some hardened criminal. He had a chance for it to be better, and now he'll never know how it all comes out."

"What's the other part of it?"

"Because it has to be better to live. And the other part...the other part is you. You don't have a backup child. I don't have a better brother."

There was only one thing I could say to that.

Just before we got off our exit on the highway, Stefan spotted the all-night mom-and-pop pancake house where my father used to take him before dawn on the mornings they went fishing. "Can we stop, Mom?" he said.

I worried that he'd get sick again, or that we might run into someone. All I wanted now was to be inside our own home. But I agreed, even though my own stomach almost gave it up when he ordered waffles with whipped cream and strawberry jam. By then, however, I realized that I was ravenous, and dispatched a bowl of oatmeal and two orders of buttered wheat toast. As I gobbled, the server shied from me in a way I didn't understand until I looked down at my hands and was shocked by how filthy they were, one nail sheared off in a gory grin. In the bathroom mirror, my face was similarly streaked with dirt and even some blood: I had apparently bitten through my lip at some point. I wanted to apologize to the woman, but what would I say? I'm a college professor... I don't usually have blood on my mouth.

"Why didn't you tell me how I looked?" I asked Stefan, when I sat back down.

"You look fine," he said, rolling his eyes and nodding when I gestured at my face. "For real, nobody in here looks that good." In the booth opposite us, two enormous farmers, in overalls of an incalculable size, were eating identical breakfasts. In front of each one was a plate of French toast with ham, two plates of bacon, and four fried eggs.

One of them waved shyly to the waitress. "Could I get a decaf skim cappuccino?" he asked.

We laughed then. Forgive me, we laughed. I hadn't heard Stefan laugh in years.

He smiled at his waffles, as if they were little children. "I can eat anytime I want. And the food is clean," he said. My stomach processed what he meant by "clean," and its opposite, about the ghastliness of the way food might be prepared in a place where punishment was the first goal.

I cast my mind back to everything Stefan had said about his life in prison. It wasn't much. Twice, early on, he showed up in the visitors' room with an angry bruise on his cheek; once, he was limping; another time, his arm was in a sling. But he wouldn't talk about that. He might, he said, someday, if there was a reason. All he would tell us was, "They don't like people who hurt women."

For almost three years, he'd done almost nothing beyond his assigned jobs, except reading and working out, hours of running in place, of push-ups and sit-ups and leg presses. Always more interested in sports and movies and Belinda than in school, Stefan found it comical when people inevitably called him "Professor," because he had started college there in a place where most people hadn't finished high school. ("I read all your books, Mom, all the Russians, all the Victorians, all the American Romantics...") The associate's degree he'd earned was in English Lit.

In a single grim sentence, he explained that exercise helped keep your body and your head working, so you, in turn, could keep people away from you. I'd seen those people, bulging, pebble-eyed men, squirming with tats. A couple of them apparently "jumped up" for him—protected him—after he taught them to read. He was gabby only about that, the thrill of seeing the world open to people when they could read.

That was the one good thing. The rest of it at least was over.

We were still laughing, in bursts, when we walked out into the parking lot. The snow slacked off to a sprinkle, as it sometimes does toward evening, and spires of light pierced the clouds. The yellow eyes of the snowplows came prowling in convoys. Stefan saw the flyer under the windshield wiper before I did, but I noticed that there were no other, similar ones under the wipers of other cars. He grabbed the paper and turned to me, his eyes drained. It was a photo of us outside the prison, when Stefan put his hand on top of my head. Through it was drawn a slash, in thick red marker. Stefan said, "What?"

Suddenly I felt we were no longer in the parking lot of a pancake house on a darkening late winter afternoon, but instead in a blind dark alley where heavy footsteps scraped from corners we couldn't see. I forgot that I wasn't talking until Stefan prompted me, "Mom? Aren't you going to say anything but, well, well, well…?"

Ever since Stefan went to prison, I had a recurring dream, not quite a nightmare but a grim fantasy of sorts. I was at his arraignment and the judge pointed at me and asked me to explain how all this had happened. I was willing to do that, but every time I tried to speak, I had to stop to remove handfuls of gravel from my mouth. I'd try again, only to find myself spewing little pebbles that chunked onto the table in front of me.

"Well," I said. "Jill was there."

He dropped the sheet of paper, hunched his shoulders and jerked, gazing behind him. "Where? Where is she?"

"Not here. She was at the prison, before you came out."

"Why didn't you tell me that?"

"It seemed like too much. I'm sorry."

"Jill was at the prison and you didn't tell me because it seemed like too much?" Stefan reached up and grabbed a handful of his hair.

"She left before you even came out!"

"What if she had a gun or something?"

"A gun? Jill?"

He picked up the sodden paper. "Well, who did this?"

"I have no idea. Who knew we were here, I mean, here at this diner?" We both scanned the edges of the parking lot then. Who was here just moments ago? Who was here now? With a camera? With maybe a gun? I scrabbled for the keys. "And who had access to a photo printer so quickly? Somebody took this, like with their phone, and then must have sent it to somebody else."

"That's pretty elaborate."

You really have no idea, I thought. And he really did have no idea. I'd never told Stefan in any real detail about how persistent the protestors had been in front of our house. He watched television, I knew, but he'd never mentioned seeing any local coverage of SAY. I got the impression that the tastes in the prison common went more toward action movies and game shows than news from the small town where we lived, hundreds of miles away. How would he feel when he saw the protestors live on our doorstep?

As we got closer to Portland, the town where we lived, the snow was tapering off and Stefan was all but leaning out of the window like a golden retriever. I thought he would jump out and start to run. "Did Dad text? Did he get home?"

"I'm sure he'll be there."

Stefan was no fool. His dad's visits and calls numbered two to my ten. But he must have wanted badly to assume that Jep's lapses owed more to scheduling and his personal pain than anything larger. He longed for his father. If the relationship of fathers and sons is always turbid, how much more was theirs? Rightly or wrongly, though he loved him truly, Jep considered Stefan more "my" child, a mama's baby, not the rough-and-ready little man's man that he'd always dreamed a son would be. I would see Jep's involuntary grimace when Stefan worked harder on his dance floor moves than his field moves, when Stefan nodded off in front of the TV during sacred Sunday Green Bay Packer games. Stefan was physically talented but lacked the interest. A man who could not take solace in athletic passion was an alien life-form to Jep. Unspoken was the vapor of a suggestion that none of this might have happened to a boy who had given himself fully to the integrated life of body and mind. When Jep said he was a simple man, he usually meant only to disarm. Sometimes, though, he meant to reproach. To be fair, he would have been surprised to learn that anybody thought that.

Stefan and I briefly looked at each other. For the past few hours we had been slouched like passengers on a cross-country bus. Now both of us sat up straighter, as if to make ready for battle.

We turned onto Washtenaw Street. A last curve, and we were there.

"My tree!" Stefan said, looking down the road. "It's taller. Is anything else different?"

We'd planted an apple tree in the yard when Stefan was born. As an intrepid eight-year-old, he used to open his second-floor window, hang by his fingertips from the sill, drop into its branches and climb down. Once we thought that there might be a little grove—another apple, perhaps, or maybe a pear tree for a little girl. But Jep found himself overwhelmed by the day-to-day reality of fatherhood and the ways it changed me, changed us, changed all our priorities. I was barely twenty-one when Stefan was born, twenty-three when I lost my next pregnancy. Plenty of times, even very recently, I brought up us having another child. Jep never quite said no, and he never quite said yes.

The time for a pear tree came and went. Our family tree remained tiny, all our hopes on one branch.

But…wait…was someone sick? I expected the protestors. But
why was there also an ambulance in front of the house? I thought
immediately of our neighbor next door, Miss Hennessey, easily eighty now. Stefan's childhood babysitter, she'd mailed him
pound cakes that the authorities at Belle Colline confiscated
(although Stefan wrote to her praising their delicate lemon fla-
vor). Lights were spinning; trucks and cars were angled up on
the curb.

No one was sick.

We would find out later that the ambulance was there because
one of the demonstrators had forgotten to eat and had fainted.

As if to open an exhibit, the snow then completely stopped.

There, on the sidewalk, standing impeccably in a long white
coat and hat, was Jill, a Stop Abuse Young banner draped across
her midriff like a shield. All around her, people crowded in the
anemic glow of the streetlights. Among them were Stefan's fifth-
grade teacher; his T-ball coach; a priest from St. Michael and All
Angels Anglican Church down the block; Luda, from the Russian bakery; and Frank Timms, who taught creative writing at
my school, Thornton Wilder College, his office just across the
hall from mine. And there were young women, college-age,
high-school age, all rhythmically hoisting SAY signs and chanting, "Say, say, say her name. Belinda! Say, say, say her name!"
The trucks were news vans, from WMOO, WLAK, all the
network affiliates, and a few radio stations with musical notes
sprinkled over the van doors.

I rolled the window down a crack and heard an earnest young
man say, "We're here in Portland, Wisconsin, where even in
single-digit weather, activists against domestic violence are pick-
eting the home of convicted killer Stefan Christiansen, who got
out of prison just hours ago. While they say everyone deserves
another chance, these people believe that Christiansen's chance

should not be so close to home, specifically to the family home, only a block away, of Belinda McCormack, the girl he admits to beating to death."

This must have been why Jill had been at the prison, to make sure today was the day, to be sure of the timing. How, I thought, as we pulled past the people and into our snow-banked driveway, as I fumbled for the garage-door opener, did she know we would come back here tonight, in a snowstorm, when I had not even known that myself? Next to me, Stefan cringed back against the seat, his feet braced as if he were stomping on the brakes.

"What's all this? What's going on?" he asked.

"It's usually not this bad, honey. It's probably because you got out today."

Stefan was no fool; he heard the syntax. "How bad is it usually?"

"Well, they generally gather and chant and wave their signs."

"When?"

"A lot."

"How much?"

"Every day pretty much."

"Jesus Christ." Stefan stared out the car window at the group of young women, older women and a few men, Jill moving among them, stopping to speak to each one or to bestow a hug. On the seat between us, my phone pinged a text message, and Stefan snatched it up before I could stop him.

It was all in capitals, like a tabloid headline: TELL HIM TO KEEP HIS MOUTH SHUT OR IT WILL BE BAD FOR HIM.

"Mom, is this about me? Keep my mouth shut about...?"

"It's some crank, Stefan. It happens all the time. Different cranks with different messages."

"Are these people, are they going to kill me?"

"Stefan, no, it's only..." Something slapped hard against the passenger side of the car and Stefan screamed, crouching and curling his arms over his head. It was just Jep, still in his travel uniform of sport coat and khakis, his grin breaking apart as he saw what he'd done.

"I'm sorry. I just got here," Jep said.

"Dad, oh, Dad, no, you just shocked me a little," Stefan said as he rolled down his window and Jep reached through to cup the back of Stefan's head in his hand. He kissed him on the forehead, and then stood back. The marchers shouted, "Say, say, say her name!"

"*Awww*, Dad," Stefan breathed, barely a whisper. "I can't get out."

"I'll be right here. You can do it," Jep said.

Her claws clattering on the door, our dog, Molly, came rushing out the front door, then tried to hoist herself through the window to get to Stefan. He opened the car door to pull her in and stroked her gray muzzle, his tears spilling. "Molberry, you got old." As she always has, Molly brought in calm along with a sifting of dusky gray fur.

I gave the top half of the driveway another try, but the car slipped and skidded on the mush. I couldn't make it up the incline to the garage. We had to park right there.

Then they were on us.

3

When I was a young mother, I believed that if Stefan was ever in danger of choking to death and the Heimlich maneuver didn't work, I would snatch up a paring knife and perform a tracheotomy to save him. I had no training. I had no idea how it was done. Did I think there'd be an online video? I was later to learn that I wasn't the only woman crazy enough to have nurtured this kind of fantasy. The fury of mother love is so formidable that it seems to scoff at the limits of known reality and confer abilities befitting a god. Now, the arrow of my own future was aimed at a fight for Stefan's future. What good would it have done Stefan—or Belinda, or the world?—for hard times to destroy him? No good. I hadn't reckoned on how shattered Stefan was. I thought he would feel safe once he was home, as though he'd finally reached dry land. But he seemed instead to be drifting in dark water.

His first days were a revelation.

He wouldn't even consider walking across the living room

where he might be glimpsed through the bay window. He knelt on his bed and watched through his bedroom porthole window the marchers and the comings and goings of traffic. Sometimes, he did nothing but stare out of that window for two hours. He asked me if I thought they could see him, telling me that they seemed to be pointing their signs at him directly. I said that was impossible: his window, like all the bedroom windows in the house, had a lower pane of thick, frosted glass. The next day, he asked me again. Once he had something in his mind, he couldn't put it aside. He reminded me of me.

One morning, Stefan was coming out of the upstairs bathroom when Jep, exiting our bedroom a few paces in front of me, affectionately clapped him on the back. Stefan whirled and dropped into a crouch, fists up. From the snarl on his face, I knew that whomever he was seeing, it wasn't his father. Within a couple of seconds, Stefan's eyes cleared and then filled with the tears that always seemed ready. "Jesus, Dad, Jesus, I'm so sorry," he said, creeping back into his room, locking the door. Another morning before 6:00 a.m. Stefan had gone outside and was picking up the newspaper from in front of the house when he heard the roar of the garbage truck pulling up to the driveway. He advanced on the poor guy, shaking the paper and threatening to call the city on him for disturbing the peace. I couldn't imagine what the fellow thought—and what Jill's troops would have thought had they been there.

Stefan had trouble eating, often saying his throat was blocked by something. Jep arranged for Elliott Andreekov, the doctor who doubled as the team physician, to see Stefan for a physical, double-quick. With Stefan's permission, Elliott assured us that while Stefan was losing weight, this would improve when his anxiety settled down. The sensation of being unable to swallow was mostly psychological, for which he prescribed an antidepressant and a low dose of Xanax short-term. What Stefan had gone through, Elliott said, felt like the stress of wartime: In other words, he had symptoms of PTSD. Until he got this under control, we had to understand that his brain was telling him that every noise or motion could be a threat. We should understand that the outbursts weren't personal and to avoid anything that would aggravate the humiliation he already felt. He used the word *fragile* four times. I thought again of Nightclub Owens.

Medicine and time alone wouldn't restore the factory settings. I had to. That was that. For the past three years, I'd made his mood and survival my personal goalpost, with daily letters and weekly visits, first to the prison hospital and rehab, then prison, refusing to miss once, not even the time that I had a fever so high I hallucinated a herd of elk crossing the road. I just needed a lever and a place to stand.

Getting what you wanted, I always thought, was just a matter of setting your eyes on the prize and refusing to surrender. The fictional women of romantic literature that I taught in my classes never seemed particularly over-the-top to me. Emma and Cathy and Lily Bart just didn't take no for an answer. Of course, I understood intellectually that ambitious people could sometimes make a very hard landing. But I didn't feel that. What I felt was insulted even at the idea of accepting defeat. I guess that came from my father, who bucked the odds all his life.

My parents gave us a good life, as owners of a successful stationery store in Arcadia, a ritzy little suburb north of Milwaukee. But there were few extras for my sisters Amelia and Phoebe or me. I worked in the store from the age of fourteen and then, during summers in college, I worked the overnight shift at a local paper factory, cleaning the slurry out of the machines. It was disgusting, backbreaking work, and probably dangerous despite the mask and protective suit I wore. But the factory paid well, although it took what seemed like a month every fall for me to get the paper residue out of my hair. In truth, I probably really didn't need to work those jobs. But both my folks were disposed to think of diligence, even a little desperation perhaps, as good for building character. As tired as we got of hearing his origin story, our dad never got tired of telling it.

Until I was born my father, against all odds, was a respected photojournalist. He freelanced all over the world, often with my mom along (who now had to be cajoled into leaving her screen porch), exploring Antwerp, Nairobi, Delhi and Saigon. Over the years, he had gifted each of us with a few discreetly-framed copies of the photos he made for *Life* magazine and the holy grail, *National Geographic*. One of mine, of a little Afghan boy laughing in a field of opium poppies, had won my dad an international award. But when he became a family man, my mother let it be known that it was time to stay put. He got a position working for the state, then privately. Later, together, they opened Demetriou's Papierie. My father still took photographs, of course: Photos of us growing up and the ones he took of us with our own children were far beyond anything we could have commissioned.

He also gave each of us daughters copies of two photos he had not taken himself, but which he prized. They represented the two sides of his life—the Greek side, the arrivers, and the American side, the strivers.

The first pictured my father's parents on their wedding day, walking home from church through the narrow streets of Nafplio, outside Athens. Papu wears a dark blue suit; Yaya, a white dress embroidered in red and gold with a thick white veil that falls from a golden band. Not long after that day, my grandparents and their brothers and sisters all came to the United States. Friends of theirs lived in Milwaukee, and there was a strong Orthodox presence there. My father grew up in Arcadia, Wisconsin, a suburb, but his father and uncles worked in a run-down rim town near the Milwaukee airport where Greeks ran all the restaurants, even the food trucks, and where Papu and his brothers built the best hotel. When my dad moved to Madison to study photography at the state university instead of working his way through all the stations of the cross at Cosimo's Restaurant, Papu probably expected him to fail. But Dad did just the opposite, in part because he grew up well-connected, although he would not ever have said that.

That was what the other picture was about. Taken many years after the first one, it symbolized my family's American side.

In the gauzy bokeh foreground, my mother and Wisconsin's former first lady, Alma Romero Hodge, are tossing handfuls of petals into the air at a victory celebration for Malachy Hodge, a two-term governor and my father's closest friend since high school. But the focus isn't on the jubilant adults. Instead, it's on me and the Hodges' eldest daughter, Alice, called Alzy, peeking out from under a long table. Aged about five, both Alzy and I were guarding the laps of our white dresses which we had filled with dozens of small wrapped chocolate bars.

When he would later lecture my college-girl self, my father would point out that, for the men and women who worked beside me on the line of vats and molds at the paper factory, this was their life, but for me it was only my start. On the other end of that scale were the Hodges, his best friends, and we were not the same as them, either. If I envied the Hodges too often or too openly, it made my father stern. In any event, while I never listened to my father's litanies as devoutly as he wanted me to—what girl does?—I did grow up with the awareness of being both things: I was a full college professor now, but I was still the teen who worked at the paper factory whose parents had paid a teacher to teach Greek to us and our cousins from kindergarten through high school so that we might never forget who we were.

Now I look at that photo of me and Alzy and reflect on how the destinies of those two little girls are intertwined in a way I never could have imagined. Alzy's life, and perhaps especially her death, would be a major turn in the road for me and for Stefan, but it would be months before I would discover exactly how.

What I learned at the end of my first week back at work after the holiday break was how rough at least some of that road would be. Keith Fu, my department chair, dropped by my office. He brought me a latte. I'd just found a fortune cookie in my pocket and I showed it to Keith. It said, *I cannot help you. I am only a cookie.*

He said, "No wonder people think the Chinese are inscrutable."

"Stefan used to say 'inscrewable.'"

"That, too," said Keith, and laughed, albeit weakly. "My name in Chinese means master teacher."

"I never knew that was what 'Keith' meant," I said.

Keith attempted another laugh. "How is Stefan? How are you?"

"I have no idea how I am. I just feel so guilty because I have this other world, my respite, and he has nothing." I sipped my coffee. It was foamy and cinnamon-y. "Thanks for this."

I told Keith how diligently Stefan was working since he came home to find a job. He made lists of *A* employers and *B* employers, so that he wouldn't wreck his mood by trying all the top places first, in case he was rejected. His parole officer had given Stefan the names of employers who proudly hired the formerly incarcerated; and in a Twitter chat about Stefan, one vocal community influencer wrote that no one ever prospered without help. But, strangely enough, that man didn't have a job for Stefan, nor did anyone else the man could think of. Stefan tried a painting company and a moving company. He tried the French patisserie, the Russian deli and the New York bagel bakery. He tried the garden supply, the pool supply, the art supply, the pancake house, the steak house, the Omelet House and Gandalf's House of Games. As soon as he identified himself, people standing right next to Help Wanted posters said there were no openings. His mood sank deeper with every rejection. I would pass by his door sometimes in the early morning and peek in if it was open a crack. He often slept on the floor, curled like a shrimp with no pillow, always fully dressed in a sweatshirt and sweat-pants and socks, as if he might have to spring up at any minute. I guess the floor felt more like the shelf in his cell. It seemed so cruel, but I dared not bring it up with him, for which humili-ation might be the endmost one?

I was afraid to leave for campus this past week, afraid that I might come home to find him hanging by an electrical cord from the garage door opener. I would waste time staring blankly out the window as protestors gathered; then push past them to my car with a sheaf of folders in front of my face. I tore into my classroom door a few times at twenty after, perhaps ruining the morning for my students who had just begun to dream that the two-hour seminar would be canceled. Like some woman in a sixties comic strip, one day I was still wearing my Minnetonka bedroom slippers when I arrived.

Not my finest pedagogical hour. But that was why they called it "tenure." I was popular, published, respected. Mourning Be-comes Her: Bereft Women of Fiction from Olivia to Olive Kit-teridge and my other seminar, Ghost Stories: Shades in Short Fiction, turned away students every semester.

I told Keith, "I shouldn't bend your ear."

He said, "Ah, Thea. Someone from *Dateline* called me the other day. And she called the dean, too."

I said, "Ugh. Sorry."

"Well, the thing is, Thea, maybe this is an opportunity for you." His voice went official. "No one would blame you for taking a year or so leave of absence. Call it a sabbatical. You've been wanting to write *Women of Obsession* for years. Given the circumstances, why not turn lemons into lemonade?"

"Did you just make that up?" I asked. "If I did that now, it would look like I was running away. And Stefan is probably going to enroll in summer school next semester."

Keith said, "Here?"

"Where else?" I got free tuition for family members at Thornton Wilder. When Stefan decided against the football route, we re-evaluated. He was young in years, almost a full year younger than many of his classmates, and he was no scholar. So my institution became the plan for him, after he'd taken some community college courses to start. Now the latte in my hand looked like my cup of hemlock. I set it down, too hard. They didn't want a murderer matriculating at Thornton Wilder College; they didn't want a murderer's mother teaching there either, especially my new seminar, which would be about fictional women and obsession. Tears blurted from the corners of my mutinous eyes. Keith looked wretched.

"I told them, she's a great teacher," he said. "She's my friend. If it were up to me…"

"It *is* up to you. You should defend me and Stefan. Doesn't everybody deserve a second chance? Isn't that one of our cultural precepts? Or does all that righteousness go bullshit when you really have to double down?"

"Come on, Thea."

"Come on, Thea, what? I have a right to my job."

"I have a right to protect this department's…"

"What? This department's reputation? I thought its reputation was for excellence in teaching, not blandest-personal-lives promised?"

"It's a long way from blandest personal lives to…"

"To what? Okay, Stefan's situation is one thing, maybe. But me? I've done nothing. I've done nothing but do my job well for fifteen years, Keith." I asked him, "Why didn't people ostracize me when it happened? Why now, when my son's done his time?"

"That's the thing. To some people, it doesn't seem like much time."

So I wasn't the only one. Shame only intensified my anger. "He wasn't charged with murder, Keith. The most he could have been sentenced to for involuntary manslaughter was about five years. He didn't mean to kill Belinda. He didn't even mean to hit her. He was seventeen, Keith. He had never even had a speeding ticket…"

"The fact remains that a girl is dead. And she died violently… with her skull smashed in." He fixed his eyes on me defiantly, as if no one had ever dared to say the words before.

"As if I don't think of that every day of my life." I wanted to tell him how, for the past few years, my sole refuge was the first moment of each morning, before I was fully awake, when I could hear the tapping of sweet rain or the trill of a cardinal and think, *it's Saturday at last,* or *only two weeks until spring break,* the kinds of thoughts that a person has who lives a small life populated by small dreams. But then the reality of Belinda's death would rise up like a miasma.

"Back then, he was only seventeen. And he *was*…well, lots of people have had kids get caught up with drugs, and the feeling has usually been, there but for the grace of god…"

"He *was* what?"

"He was going away then, Thea, not coming back."

"Okay," I said, absorbing this. "Okay. But it's different now, how? Do I seem insufficiently miserable?" I was on my feet by then. I didn't know where all this hostility was suddenly coming from, but there seemed to be no way to stop it. "Wouldn't anyone be at least relieved that her child was out of prison? Wouldn't you?"

"I don't know, Thea. As a parent, I don't know honestly how I would feel. I don't know if I could feel such righteous anger. A lot of people would say that your anger is misplaced."

"And would you be one of those people?"

"I'm torn. But I see where others are coming from."

"Well, maybe we should get started right away then. Maybe my TA can teach my classes, *given the circumstances,* and we'll just give all the students an A. How would you like that, huh?"

"I don't see any huge problem with that, Thea. Of course

your salary will continue during your leave as well, if that's your choice."

My breath snagged in my chest. I thought I was being wronged. But I was only being wrong. I had meant to call his bluff, and he called mine. Grabbing up my big leather tote, I barreled past Keith, then past a wide-eyed Frank Timms—Frank Timms, protest marcher!—who leaned against his office door frame not even pretending detachment—past Robin, the department secretary and Jolly Ames, the security guard who'd worked in the building since I was an undergraduate there. Out the door I ran, painfully grateful that I had disobeyed policy and parked in the emergency lot. I tried not to look around me, tried to ignore the peal of the carillon, which randomly alternated between songs by Mozart and songs by Madonna, and the bright bursts of laughter and voices as kids streamed out of the cafeteria into cold sunlight, their eight-foot-long scarves wrapped around their faces, their slouchy suede boots chumbling the new snow.

Ferber Humanities Hall was my home, my safe haven, sometimes even more than my house. I gave myself a few minutes to bawl out loud in another parking lot, where I was sure I wouldn't run into a colleague. Crying was such a trope now. Crying was an occupation, a daily constitutional. I didn't know if it was anger or confusion: A few years ago, during the trial and all the news coverage of Belinda's death, they had all been so supportive—or if not supportive, I thought now, at least silent.

Out of nowhere came a memory of Belinda. Her first weekend home from college, she came over to see Stefan and showed me some of her poetry, all about a girl, a persona, called Esme. *Longing Esme/hair of weeds/eyes of starfish/teeth of seeds.*
Longing Esme/broken grace/passion buried/under lace.
Such a sad poem for such a happy girl, I told her back then.
Who says I'm happy? she asked me.
Now the enormity of her death rolled over me once more. I saw her in preschool, the day she and Stefan met; Belinda, no

bigger than an acorn, already lecturing a taller, gangly Stefan about how people did not play tennis with Ping-Pong paddles... *"If you do that, they'll think you're a Stoopie Magee."*

How purposefully had I spent so much of each day trying to forget why all this was happening... *Say her name...* how wrong that was, how morally perverse? Belinda, Belinda. Stefan was alive. Life was hope. Hope offset setbacks. Keith was correct: My anger was indeed misplaced. I had no right to any anger at all. Anger was for the wronged.

I called Keith and left a contrite message: Yes, I would ask for a sabbatical. Could we make a lunch date? Suddenly I couldn't wait to be away from my campus, my second home.

That was when I saw him.

The hooded figure from the highway, who looked smaller outside a vehicle, was standing across the street from my car on the path to the lake, as students swarmed around him like water around a boulder. I might have hoped that I was wrong, that he was just some freshman in a hoodie and sweatpants twinned to my troubles by my fevered mind—except for what he did next. He raised one hand and pointed a finger at me, wagging it in that same admonishing gesture he gave us on that nightmare drive. I quickly unlocked the car doors, sure that when I looked up and blinked, he would be gone. But he wasn't. He was standing there when I peeled out of the lot, and he was standing there as I drove away.

When it comes to emotional sturdiness, I have pretty big shoulders. But all this was too much. I was so rattled I couldn't think in sentences. By dint of muscle memory, I found myself in my own driveway. Just then Jep texted me, reminding about the dry cleaning. So I didn't even go inside. I backed out and drove away without looking back. I did stop to pick his jacket up at the cleaner's but was so anxious by then that I accidentally left it on top of the car where I had placed it as I rummaged for the key, then wondered what was that big flapping package flying around on the road that I saw in my rear mirror? When I finally realized what it was, I had to backtrack again along my route to look for it, until I saw a kid maybe ten years old holding it and waving at me. I jumped out and took it and gave him the only bill I had in my purse, a twenty. He said, "Lady, do you know that this isn't a dollar?" By then I was already back in the car. At least, it was a good day for somebody.

I pulled up and sat at the curb in front of my house, shaking and gripping the steering wheel like a life jacket. What did that figure want? Why did he follow us all the way from Black Creek that day? How did he know where I worked? Where we lived? (This last wasn't a shock: He could have found that out from the SAY website, which featured photos of our house with the messages painted on the garage door and the sidewalks, like the Lourdes of domestic abuse protest.)

Grabbing my phone, I scrolled to the number for the girl caller with the little voice, then pressed Call.

When she answered, I said without preamble, "Is the one stalking us, a thin kid in a hoodie? Is he the same person who was on the road?"

She said, "I... I don't know."

"But you know who I mean."

"Yes."

"He's still after us! What do I do?"

She seemed to drop the phone and then recovered it. "Just... just do what I told you. Tell Stefan not to talk to anyone about that night and nothing will happen."

"How can you be so sure? Are you the one behind this?"

"No!" she said. She sounded genuinely aghast. "Of course not. It's complicated."

"Well, should Stefan be in... I don't know...in witness protection or something?"

She said, "Don't be dramatic."

Suddenly my mind made a connection. "Are you Esme?"

She paused so long I thought she'd hung up. Then she said, "I don't want to say anything else. I've already said too much. Don't call me again. I'm changing this number." I heard the phone click. When I tried to call back, the phone just rang and rang, without even the option for a voice message.

Thankfully only a few weary-looking marchers were standing there in front of our house, so I rushed out and grabbed the dry cleaning from the back seat and then the mail. I didn't even notice the red-haired woman with a shy, sweet smile waiting on the porch. "Hi, Thea," she said. "They're giving you a little peace today, huh?"

"Yes. So what's up? Do I know you?" I said and reached past her to put my key in the lock, a lock I'd never bothered with until a few years ago. The way she spoke, distancing herself from the protestors and press, I thought maybe she was from the local Democratic party or something. So I wasn't ready for what came next.

"Just give me thirty seconds and if you don't want to talk to me afterward, I'll leave." She held out a press pass from the local public TV station. "No one else is going to give you the time to tell your side of it."

"Oh, come on! I don't have a side of it that anyone could ever care about!"

"Let's make them care," said the woman, looping her thumb and index finger around her long hair and pulling it back, the way some women do. "And if you try and they're still like this, you're no worse off."

"People would blame me even for talking," I said.

From the street, someone jeered, "Do a little shopping on the way home, Mrs. Christiansen? Get some nice things for Stefan?" Then from nowhere, a tomato came splatting against the porch pillar, then another one hit the bay window.

"Sorry," I said. "Tomatoes are a favorite. The police tell them not to do it, but they do anyway. They hit my husband in the back of the head once. He thought he'd been shot."

"Just take my card. You don't have to call me if you don't want. We are looking to do a series that highlights the social issues impacting our communities. Not an exposé. We'd come here and talk, and you could explain what good can come out of something bad. It wouldn't just be about Stefan. It would be about what can happen to people as a result of their being involved with drugs. Other guests would be profiled, too. We envision it being multi-part."

I took her card just to get rid of her then slipped inside, glad to have the safety of the door against my back, protecting me from them. It was such a small thing, an inch of wood that could probably be dislodged with a single kick. A small wastebasket sat just to the right of the door, and I flicked the card into it. Over the years, I had thrown dozens of messages of hatred there that had been taped to our garage door and porch railings before I took the time to throw them out. Messages like: *STOP STEFAN* and *LOOK BEHIND YOU...*

Stefan was up in his room and Jep came home early, so I decided to postpone talking about what happened at work and try for at least the appearance of a normal night. That seemed to work.

Next morning, I kept busy with one thing and another until after eleven. At last, I went up and knocked on Stefan's closed door, my breath coming in gasps when there was no sound. I finally heard a rustle as he got up. He had been setting up a new study space and taking down some of his teenage things we'd enshrined. We'd given him a new Mac laptop with all the trimmings to make up for the Christmases we'd just had to give him money for the commissary.

"I know I should be up by now," he said. "But it's easier to sleep."

Then he put his hand over his eyes. He told me that he felt

haunted. Every front door and light post on the street reminded him not—as I expected—of the carefree child he had been, but instead of Belinda, at fourteen, at sixteen, dropping by, inviting him to her pool to swim, trying to talk him into coming along and getting on a horse when she took riding lessons, posing in a tulip of satin for the prom. He had taken out one of the framed photos of them on graduation day, of Stefan tipping her mortarboard over her eyes while she laughed.

She left for school that August. We knew before then that Stefan wasn't ready to go away to college just yet; he was a young seventeen and not a particularly good student. Belinda was nearly a full year older. So we convinced him to enroll in a few classes locally for at least a semester and then re-evaluate, and he did. But that fall turned out to be a torment for all of us. When he left to drive up to Black Creek every Friday night, driving back exhausted every Sunday night, when he begged Jep and me to let him quit the stupid junior college classes and just move up there to work in a pizza place or a grocery store for now, to be near Belinda; when he grew gaunt and monosyllabic as he pushed himself harder during the weekdays at home, falling asleep over his books at two in the morning, to get the grades he needed for a college acceptance starting in January. My plan had been for him to transfer to Thornton Wilder. He had another plan. I thought he would be jubilant when he was accepted at UW–Black Creek, but he wasn't, and it would be years before we would really understand why. The only suggestion we dared was that living with Belinda might put too much of a strain on their relationship, so we offered to pay for a dorm room. All of them were already filled. But Stefan found a room in an old house that was affiliated with the college and we agreed to pay for that. It was on the fourth floor and Stefan, always fastidious, recoiled from the discolored sink in the shared kitchen, the crust of grime on the refrigerator shelf where he would have to store his milk and his juice. But it was only a mile from Belinda's apartment.

As it turned out, he occupied that room for five days. He signed up for classes that he never attended. My sister was the liaison to help us get our money back; Jep and I couldn't even bring ourselves to care, but Amelia decided wisely that this wasn't the time to start throwing away cash. Those were the kinds of things our family did for us in those helpless months. They brought us food; they asked for our bills and the checks and debit cards we used to pay for them; they stood between us and the voracious press.

Long before Belinda's death, we were already on high alert. When Belinda came home for Christmas, Stefan complained bitterly about her two-day visit to her grandfather's house in North Carolina, and about all the seasonal observances she and Jill cherished together. "It's just a bunch of church crap," Stefan groused.

One night Jep, usually the most gentle-spoken of fathers, glowered at Stefan. "Sit down and listen for a minute, son. You know what? You're obsessed with this girl."

Stefan threatened his father then, saying that if he lost Belinda, he would never forgive himself and he would never forgive us. He would hate us until he died.

Now Stefan said to me, "So, instead, I lost her forever, Mom. She's more real to me here than she was when I was inside." Stefan wanted to go over to Belinda's house, to look at the backyard pool where they swam together, the kitchen where they made cookies. He wanted to tell her mother Jill how sorry he was, every day.

"But you can't," I reminded him as we went downstairs. "You can't have any contact with any member of Belinda's family. That's a condition of your parole. Think if it was the other way around, if it were you who'd been killed and the person came to me."

"I just want Jill to believe me! I was never really that guy who would hurt Belinda."

"Drugs change people," Jep said. He was packing his lunch in the kitchen. For a flash moment, because I needed a rest from all-Stefan-all-the-time, I hated my dearly beloved husband for still being able to eat like an eighth-grader—two sandwiches, some leftover rice, an apple, a slice of cake.

Stefan said, "I never even had a beer before I tried coke, Dad. I never smoked a joint before I did meth. Did you know that? Dad? Huh?"

"Well, we spent a shitload of money on rehab bills for you in the hospital for a guy who was never really that guy," Jep said, his voice dangerously low and even. "Don't you think you should at least go to a meeting? To AA?"

"I guess maybe. I don't know."

"Try it and see?"

"People who go to AA in real life, some of them are probably more normal than I am."

"Some of them are probably doctors and lawyers and schoolteachers and cops," Jep said. "What do you mean?"

"In jail, they weren't."

"That was jail."

"Well, some of those guys would have sold their kids for drug money. I'm not putting them down. For them it's like being high is probably the only time in their lives they get to feel like everything is all great and fine, and they're really smart and sexy and all that. Most of them never got good stuff in real life."

"But you did."

"I did, before things got really hard. I mean with prison, sure. But also with Belinda. Before she died."

Jep put one hand over his eyes and pressed. "Things are hard now, Stef. What makes you think that you won't want to take them to escape again?"

"That should be obvious," Stefan said.

Not for the first time during these discussions, I thought that if I lifted my brain out of its carapace, it would smell like burnt hair. As far as deterrents for taking up drugs go, Stefan probably owned some prime horror real estate, even for having weathered the denizens of prison. From some of my students who stayed in touch with me after they graduated, and who'd gone on into high-pressure careers like advertising, I knew that cocaine probably had a long reach and a short memory. For a while, their blazers were Blank Check; the skirts were Ravishment. The parties were throwbacks to the millennium, at urban cloud-house condominiums in Chicago and elsewhere where sculpturally thin young women and men lived on the dime of bigwig benefactors thirty years older and where on every flat surface sat a Murano glass salt cellar brimming with coke. They told me that they controlled their use…right up until they woke up to pillowcases that looked as if they'd been used to swab off the slabs in a butcher shop and had to admit coke controlled them.

But I had never personally met anyone who used meth before I learned about Stefan. I didn't even know how Stefan took it. Was it in pill form? Did he use a needle? He was terrified of shots; he fainted twice when he had blood drawn when he was younger. All I knew was that meth was an ugly, scraping door to dopamine. A lawyer we met during those days after Belinda's death once called it, "diamonds for the downtrodden."

Now Stefan said, "They should make high school teachers sample the stuff so they know what it's like."

"That's a spectacular idea."

"Dad, half of the kids I met in Black Creek, they didn't think they were addicts; they believed you could take it or leave it. The other half were terrified. Me, I thought they were just trying to scare me," said Stefan. "You know how I got addicted to cocaine real fast, Dad? I tried it. I tried it once. You know how I started using meth? I tried it, once. And then if I would have had all the money in the world to spend on stuff like that,

I would have spent all the money in the world on it. It made me feel that good. Especially the coke. But that cost too much."

"I don't know why you needed to do it in the first place," Jep said.

"I couldn't keep up," Stefan said.

"With school?"

"With everything. I would be so wound up all week and then all I'd want to do was sleep when I got up there on the weekends. I would get up and take a shower and then I'd want to go back to bed. Bindy would complain that half the time, all I did was fall on her couch and start snoring. Drugs saved me in a way, or so I thought then."

Stefan could, and did, stay up for a couple of days straight. He said he felt he was bionic. He didn't need food. He would bang out an online quiz before he left to drive up, then he'd go straight out with Belinda to the town's one gay bar to dance all night. Druggies, he would tell us later, called the sensation ringing your bell, because it was exactly like that, as if everyone in a restaurant was tapping their spoons on their wineglasses. "So if I wasn't really doing that great, I still felt like I was doing great. Then when I moved up full-time it all changed." His gaze fastened somewhere out of the frame, as if he were seeing again his crummy room, the size of a VW van, in a campus house so derelict that it would be demolished a year later. "Just like I told the judge."

The other shoe swung softly in space.

"What did you not tell the judge?" I asked.

He made a helmet of his hands, over his scalp. "I couldn't keep up with Belinda. In other ways."

"What other ways?"

"It doesn't matter. All that matters is now, and I can't even keep up now! People hate the sight of me."

As it turned out, that would be proven within the next twelve hours.

The following morning, early, after another snow tapered off, the three of us took advantage of a break in the weather to finish the path Jep was shoveling to the shed where we kept giant bags of birdseed and snow melt. I was scooping out seed when I heard Stefan talking to someone. Peeking through the crack in the shed door, I recognized our neighbor Charlie Ribosky. Charlie was a retired firefighter in his seventies who'd been Stefan's T-ball coach fifteen years ago.

"I've known you all your life," Charlie said, interrupting Stefan's glad greeting. "And I know you're trying to say this was all a tragedy caused by drugs. But I happen to know that nobody does anything on drugs that they wouldn't do otherwise…"

"But they do, Mr. Ribosky!" Stefan protested. "Especially, the drugs I was on. They're really linked to violence. I didn't know. I'm never like that naturally."

"So you expect everybody here to just say, well, heck, that was too bad, but it's all over now." Charlie poked his index finger at Stefan. "You ruined this neighborhood, son. I say, good for Jill for starting this movement of hers after losing Belinda in that way because how many other girls are living in terror like her poor daughter was?"

"Mr. Ribosky, no. Listen a minute. Just listen. I wish I could change places with Belinda. I don't remember what happened that night. I blacked out. I take responsibility. But I never hit Belinda before. I swear. It's like it was someone else."

"Well, it was not someone else. It was you! I just feel sorry for your poor dad, a finer man I never knew."

Stefan threw down his shovel and jogged back to the house. Jep rushed past him, picked up the shovel and headed out into green space behind the backyards. Once he was outside our fence, and directly in Charlie's line of sight, he raised his voice: "Hey, Charlie, you want to start something, how about you start it with me?"

"I can't believe you people. Acting like it's all going to be fine."

"What would you do?"

"It's nothing to be proud of, is all."

Jep hurled the snow shovel at the base of Charlie Ribosky's neatly buzzed privet hedge. Charlie jumped back, then swore softly and stomped off into his house. I had never seen Jep so angry. When we argued, he was always the one to call time until we could both get a good night's sleep. He wasn't the coach who called his players sissies or told them that if they weren't puking, they're weren't really playing. He treated them like what they were—boys—and coaxed forth their agility and toughness with humor and patience. They revered him. Now he bent over, hands on his knees, red-faced and panting. He finally picked up the shovel, came back into our yard and shut the gate behind him, banged the shovel against the trunk of a tree, just once but hard, and went inside. Feeling exposed, I followed both of them.

Jep was making a cup of tea in the kitchen. When he was sure that Stefan was out of earshot, he said, "Charlie shouldn't have said that. But a part of me agrees with him."

"What do you mean?"

"It was almost easier when Stefan was in prison. Now I have to look at him every day and wonder, what are people thinking about him? And, Thea, what am I thinking about him? I love my son, but I don't know how I'm supposed to feel."

He wasn't the only one. I finally told him about Keith's reaction, which I had so far avoided. I told him about my enforced sabbatical too. He kept his face neutral, but John Paul Christiansen and I were hardly newlyweds. While he could still surprise me, most of the time, if I couldn't tell the gist of what he was thinking before he said it, it was because I didn't want to know. He and the neighbor were anything but the only ones. I recalled uneasily my own trill of fear when I glanced over in the car at the size and strength of Stefan's hands. My own mother kept

calling and telling me about how Jill's stance against dating violence was undeniably inspiring, and how, now that Stefan was
finally home, her own friends were looking at her in a funny
way. I wanted to be furious, but I wasn't. When Stefan was in
prison, I put myself out there, almost defiantly. Now, I found
myself hesitating. Before today, was it because deep down, despite my stance to the contrary, I was ashamed of my son? Yes.
A part of me resented the way his wrongdoing had muddied
up my security, my serenity, my own space on earth. And now,
the door to our front porch suddenly looked like the portal to
hell. I felt I had lost my defenses. What was out there, and how
much worse was it than the worst I'd already imagined?

Some people, despite knowing us, definitely wanted the worst
for Stefan. Some people believed he'd doffed the past like an
old coat and was now indifferent to the families of victims. Jill
had her cause; but no cause existed that could help people like
Stefan show their contrition to those suffering families, and to
the world; contrition that might give them, if not forgiveness,
if not an open door, at least a crack in the black glass wall of absolute denial. There were organizations that provided a means
for crime survivors to offer forgiveness, but not the reverse.
There was no way forward for offenders who were remorseful
to make amends if the survivors were not interested. Was that
reverse even defensible? Or was the best that people like Stefan
could hope for a life of marginally-productive obscurity? Even
if he never did anything wrong before this, and he never does
another wrong thing after this, would Stefan's life always be defined by his one brutal act? Would it always be the only thing
people thought about him? Even his own parents?

The landline in our house rang. I picked up and listened to
nothing but cavernous gusts of breath. Then the caller hung up.
I put the phone down. It rang again, the display a local number.
I picked it up again. The caller breathed more slowly.

"Leave us alone," I said.

The girl's voice I recognized said, "May I speak to Stefan, please?"

"No, you may not speak to Stefan. Leave him alone! You said you weren't going to say anything else. How about you stick to that?"

"I want to. But I can't. I have to do this."

I hung up. The phone rang again immediately. I grabbed the receiver like a weapon. But this was a new voice, honeyed, almost musical, a Glinda-voice. "You know, Thea, your son really should die."

I reached down and unplugged the phone. The bland rabidness of such ordinary folk, people with mortgages and microwaves, who ordered pizza on Friday nights, frightened me even more than the fanatics.

"Never pick the phone up again, Thea," Jep said then, again in that calm, dangerous tone.

"It's just such a natural response, like a baby crying..."

"Please don't pick it up anymore. Let it go to voice mail."

"Okay, okay," I said.

I waited for him to say more.

"Jep?" I said then. "Do you still love me?" Jep leaned over and kissed me. We hadn't even kissed, much less anything else, since Stefan had come home. Just the recognition that I had a physical body and emotions above the level of survival flowed through me, shivering deep in my abdomen. "I know it's not just him. It's us, too. But I can't do all of this at once."

"You don't have to do it all at once, Thea. I'm not... You know, whatever doubts we have, we're the counterweight. Against what anyone else says. We have to be the one thing he can count on. The thing is, how?"

We went our separate ways, me to my upstairs office, Jep to a coffee shop, where he was meeting a running back from Jesus the Only Light of the Universe High School. I thought then about Stefan when he was young and begging us not to send him to this terrific prep school, because he did not want to go through life after Portland saying, "Yes, I played for Jesus the Only Light of the Universe." Jep got annoyed finally and said, "You'd just use a short form."

Stefan complained, "What? I play for Jesus?"

Unable to concentrate on my emails or writing, I realized after a while that I'd been sitting at my desk for nearly three hours without doing one single useful thing or even prosecuting a complete thought. Jep was already home from his meeting, scrubbing the pile of vegetables I'd set out for stew. Not even four in the afternoon, it was already nearly dark, the kind of late afternoon in winter that coaxes people to eat heavy food and retire early to their caves, like bears. Stefan came into the kitchen and started rummaging in the refrigerator. Like Jep, he had an odd habit of taking out the ingredients for different options—the makings for scrambled eggs, some leftover pizza, cold chicken, a fruit salad, cheese and crackers—before choosing one thing and leaving all the rest on the counter island. Especially as an expression of his freedom, this didn't usually unduly irritate me. Right now, I wanted to pinch him.

Sharper than I meant to be, I said, "Don't you see we're making stew? You don't need another meal now."

"I'm starving. I'll still have the stew. And anyhow, how did I know that stew wasn't for tomorrow?"

"Put all that stuff away when you're finished."

"Well, okay, Mom! What's eating you?"

Instead of answering directly, as if I were in a TV movie about people like us, I took out an unaccustomed bottle of wine and poured myself a glass. I stared at it. People on TV drink so much—at every meal, at every upset—that I'm surprised they can hold down jobs. On BBC shows, they down a glass of whiskey and a pint four times a day. I finally said, "Well, I lost my job not long ago…well, no, that isn't true. I didn't lose my job, but I'm taking a sabbatical I didn't know I was taking."

"Is it because of me?"

There was no point in lying. "It's because of you...this...but it isn't your fault."

"I should just take off, go to Montana or someplace where nobody knows me, just be somebody else."

"Wouldn't that be great! If you left the only place you know and the people who love you the most and just disappeared into the wild like Christopher McCandless? That would help us all out! Besides, your parole won't allow it."

He exhaled sharply. "Okay! Sorry! I just really feel bad about all this. Do you think it would help if I talked to your boss?" Then he said, "Who's Christopher McCandless?"

Stefan was so young.

"No, honey. That's a gallant thing to say but no, it wouldn't do any good. Stuff doesn't happen every day. This is a sort of flash point. It's all new. You're starting over. We'll get through this."

We stood there, me leaning my head on his shoulder, him awkwardly patting my back. Jep came in and put his arms around both of us.

There was a knock at the front door. Jep opened it, and there stood Annalee Ribosky, Charlie's wife. "Jep, let me apologize for what Charlie said. I'm sorry, and the fact is, he's sorry as well. We're not the only people who've said things, and that doesn't make it right." Jep shook Annalee's hand. "But we will not say one word behind your back. So I'm sorry, Jep. I'm sorry, Thea. Tell Stefan, too. Charlie made a mistake. Please forgive an old man. Those people out front, they get to you. Whatever you need, Jep, we are right here."

Jep turned back to the room then. "Stefano, if you could get people like them to believe one thing about you, what would it be?"

"That not everyone is the same," Stefan said.

If he hadn't been speaking about himself, and he had not been flesh of my flesh, I would still have been fascinated by what Ste-

fan had to say next. While we stood in the kitchen, he talked to
us about what he thought was the real reason that most people
reoffended after they got out of jail. He believed that it's not because they're intrinsically evil and not because they're any more
susceptible to their peers than anyone else. He pointed out he
had watched how the whole concept of being a team relied a
lot on what people thought of you—the coach, the other team
members, the fans, the school, the community, even history. If
you did wrong, or even if you didn't do all you could, it was a
betrayal to all those people, seen and unseen. But habitual criminals, he said, don't usually have somebody who really wants
them to do their best, who motivates them, just people brokenhearted or enraged because they *didn't* do their best. Which is sad
and awful, but also very ordinary and human. The most common thing that he and his friend Roman, the only real friend
he ever made in prison, observed about his fellow criminals
was surprisingly how easily they got bored. Most didn't have
the patience for going through a process, trying and failing and
trying again. Maybe the first time they had to do that was in
prison, but it was a whole new thing for them. "Like, in their
brain. Their brain isn't usually used to that," Stefan said. "Trying and failing and trying again is not exciting. Doing a crime
is really exciting—not, like, me, comatose, but doing a robbery
or a burglary, it had to feel really exciting…living on the knife's
edge, anything could go wrong, it's like a race against time, the
Olympics of being bad."

    It was his own opinion, but Stefan didn't think that crimi-
nals usually committed crimes for money. Most of them just
went through it all quickly anyway, he said. He believed they
craved the excitement, the adrenaline, the heightened sense of
existence. Advocates were so let down when the criminals who
were really bright, big readers say, for whom they found good
jobs, would get out and either then reoffend, repeating almost
exactly what they'd done before, or sometimes kill themselves.

Having a good job, that can be pretty much the same routine every day; that's boring if your brain is trained a certain way. Being sober is slow and boring if you're used to being high.

"So what do you think's the answer?" I said.

"Roman believes you have to find a way to make doing good feel just as exciting, the same as when you're doing bad, the same rush," said Stefan. "Like Robin Hood. There has to be a thrill."

Other criminals he met were as smart as he was, he said, a lot of them even smarter. They had talents. But what set him apart was what he had before…because of that advantage, he had time to think about a different future for himself because he knew he had a safe place to come home to.

Jep took it all in quietly, then told his son, "You've given us a lot to think about, Stefan. But honey, you know, you don't need to worry about changing the world today or tomorrow. The day after would be fine. What you need most right now is what soldiers used to call R&R, rest and recreation, as much as you need clear purpose. Give yourself some time to recover from prison. As the doctor told you, it's almost like you went to war."

That night, I heard a commotion at the front door. Julie, my best friend, had been traveling when Stefan first came home. She was often traveling for an international dental outreach she sponsored, while her husband, Hal, manned the home front for their boys, who were eight and twelve. So I hadn't seen her more than in passing. Now she had arrived in full benefactress mode, bustling through the door with packages and bags. Presents were her delight, and she wouldn't let you feel guilty. Until last year, Julie had merely been wealthy. Trained as a dentist, she had worked for her father, who'd invented some widget that caused what Julie called "an orthodontic revolution." That still made me laugh, picturing legions of white-coated marchers, all carrying flags emblazoned with retainers. After her father retired, she and her older brothers helped him sell his business for what she called, in her way, a "silly amount" of money. Even more would come when he died. There were times when I was struggling trying to rob from the lawyer's bill to pay the electric bill, when I knew that if I asked Julie, she would pay both, then buy me a Max Mara silk-and-cashmere coat, on top of that. When I admired just such a new coat a few years back, she took it off and gave it to me.

So I never asked.

"Hey Jujubees," Stefan said. It was his nickname for his honorary aunt. "My mom wants to trek on a camel across the Sahara Desert. Can you take her? She was thinking a couple of months, maybe. She needs a break from me and, oh boy, do I ever need a break from her."

"You've been home for like, ten minutes. What, did you hit the ground hard?"

"What you think is the end is really the beginning."

"That's deep, man," Julie said.

"I know, man."

"I think you need to seek solace in nature, Stefan," Julie said. Nature was Julie's prescription for everything short of an arterial stent, and she was full of suggestions. She could give Stefan the keys to her family's cabin. (Her "cabin" was a ten-bedroom flagstone pile in Door County with four cub cabins on the same woodland site, where all of us had stayed many times.) Or he could go to Mendota County Park and find a soldierly stand of trees that, even in the leafless deeps of winter, would shelter him.

"This is a great winter camping tent right here," she said. "You can test yourself by sleeping out a few nights. By morning, you'll appreciate your mom and your humble bed." She brought a digital thermometer on a leather cord that set off an alarm when your body temperature got too low—"In case you don't realize you're freezing"—stormproof matches—"So you don't end up like a Jack London story"—a red sleeping bag of Everest caliber and an inflatable down-filled camping bed that packed down to the size of a wallet "for meditating in the holy wild." She brought him cave-aged cheddar, pumpernickel bread, homemade truffle risotto from our favorite snobby diner, Racine Kringle, chocolate chip cookies with walnuts and coconut, and the largest jar of Nutella I'd ever seen.

Stefan said, "I accept these spectacular gifts from your spectacular self. And I promise to take my Nutella to the cathedral of nature."

Julie always had a better everything. When Stefan told her that the list of therapists he got from his parole officer hadn't been updated in fifteen years, she promised to email him some recommendations. I was glad he trusted her, but it made me wistful too. I wasn't Julie, representative of the new and more efficient universe. I wasn't a fixer with treats and answers. I hugged her. She'd brought me ten novels, five sweaters and the kind of lounging pajamas she imagined French writers wore while they composed.

Later that night, after I'd placed my phone on its charging station, the screen lit up with a text. It was so late that I knew it was the girl with the little voice.

How is Stefan? Did you tell him about my calling? Did you remind him not to talk about that night?

I hadn't yet. I didn't know how. And he would ask why. I turned the phone off.

4

It had been over a month since Stefan came home. If I didn't ask my extended family to come celebrate his homecoming soon, it would look to him and to them as though I were ashamed. "You're overthinking this," Julie said the next time she stopped by. "We'll just have a party with lots of food. We can have it at my house to avoid the usual 'greeters' who tend to camp out at your doorstep." I agreed, especially when Jep pointed out that hosting a coming-home-from-the-penitentiary party at a house with picketers was like hosting a pool party with piranhas.

Julie even tied a yellow ribbon around a tree in her yard that Sunday afternoon. We set out platters of pastitsio and dolmades and huge bowls of salad salty with olives and feta for parents and my sisters and Jep's sister, all their husbands and children. We all gathered at the table-for-twenty in Julie's huge dining room, which reminded me of the kind of hall where a sixteenth-century king would have hosted a warrior banquet. Hal set up card tables for the kids.

Once we were serving dessert, I spoke up.

"Guys, all of you, Stefan has been having the worst time trying to find a job. He's tried everywhere, and he doesn't seem to get anywhere. Even the people who say they're committed to hiring people like him, you know, with his status, say that they don't have any openings. Please, Andy, Amelia, will you see what you can do?" Amelia's husband Andy owned three lumberyards. Stefan had worked at one of them every summer in high school.

"Don't put your sister on the spot!" my mother said.

"I'm not!"

"You are a little," Stefan said.

"Let me think about this," Andy said.

"Unkie, take your time."

Andy studied his slice of almond-coconut cake. "Okay, I had enough time. Stefan, when can you start?"

"Are you sure?"

"Of course. You're a good worker, you already know the ropes, and you're family."

"Is the yard open tonight? I can start right now."

"Well, all these announcements, I have to get mine in," my sister Phoebe said. She was expecting her fourth child, a boy, in just three months. She was so fit, our sister Amelia said with no small amount of rancor, you couldn't even tell. Everyone cheered. Phoebe was the youngest of the three of us sisters, just about to turn thirty-six. She graduated the Art Institute in Chicago and was actually a very good sculptor, big bold figures in stone like Sylvia Shaw Judson, and an even better photographer, but she only took the rarest commission. Her husband, Walker, was an architect who made plenty of money and their three girls had the full panoply of enrichments. I was shocked by my jealousy. This could have been our life, a lot of sunshine, a little rain, the years of the green corn turning to gold.

Stefan said, "Since we're all saying this big stuff, can I just say one thing to you, Tia Phoebe? I mean, congratulations, but something else? The photos you sent me were the best thing anybody ever did for me." What Phoebe mailed to Stefan every month was a lifeline into our lives, the Christmases and picnics and birthdays and baptisms, the chocolatey smiles, bursting golden turkeys and kokkina avga, red Easter eggs, he would never see, in envelopes of four-by-six photos. I thought it would be too painful for him. But Phoebe, like my father a gifted photographer, and also the tenderest of women, insisted, and prevailed.

"We would like you to be our baby's godfather, Stefan," Phoebe said then, and Walker nodded, taking Phoebe's hand.

"Me?" Stefan's face strobed surprise, puzzlement...and pride. "Really?"

"If you can bring yourself to drive three and a half hours in four and a half months!"

Stefan regarded his splayed hands. "I can't do that, Aunt Phoebe. I'm so sorry. I can't go to any other state or anywhere more than fifty miles from here, and then I would have to get special permission from my parole officer and do a check-in every three hours."

"Oh, Stefan, I'm sorry, too. I didn't mean to say anything that would hurt your feelings!"

"Of course you didn't!" my mother said loudly and unhelpfully.

"Mother, do you have to make it worse?" I said to her. "Why are you being a pain?"

"We'll do it by Skype," Walker said. "Or we'll bring the baby here. I'm sure he'll still be pretty small and portable. A church is a church."

"You don't have to do that," Stefan said. "But it would be great if you want to. I'd really like that. I'll be a godfather! Then a job, then a college degree, a *Sports Illustrated* swimsuit model who's also an orthopedic surgeon and a millionaire..."

He meant to be funny. Just funny.

He was a twenty-year-old guy who had every right to make a comical wish to fall in love with a beautiful girl.

This time, not even Phoebe spoke. Finally, the only sound was my father's long sigh. My father could sigh for Greece. "That will really take time," my dad finally said.

I could feel myself begin to combust. Julie quickly marshalled the kids to clear the table, then fired up her espresso machine and began taking orders. "Can you come out here and help me, Thea? This one is new, and it's got more knobs on it than a nuclear reactor!"

"I'll help, Jujubees," Stefan said, attempting to cut the tension with his childhood nickname for her, after the candies she once told him she liked as a child. A few moments later, Stefan emerged. "Another announcement! I have just drawn my first latte art! Mom, this is called the tree of life, but I think it looks more like a blowfish." Everybody got interested in the hearts and leaves and panda faces he made with successive cups.

A half hour after coffee, we left. As Jep drove, I glanced at my phone, a few student messages and one from a friend who'd moved to Boston but was coming back to town for a conference.

And then there was this: Longing Esme/hair of weeds/eyes of starfish/teeth of seeds. Longing Esme/tears of rain/hands of sea glass/song of pain.

That night I called the number. The phone was no longer in service.

But two hours later, just after I had fallen asleep, I saw my phone light up on the bedside table. I picked up. She was on the line, her breath catching like a crying child. It was a new number.

"Is this…you? So you changed your number?"

"I didn't want you to find me until I was ready to tell you more." Then she added, "It has to be this way. Is Stefan okay?"

"Not really," I said. "Why did you send me Belinda's poem?

Did you know Belinda? If you have something to say, just say it and stop tormenting me and yourself."

"I can't," she said. "It's too late. I did things. If I said what I did, I would be all alone."

"It sounds like you're pretty alone right now," I said, relenting.

"I am. Don't ask why."

"Well, you need some help. Seriously. Professional help. I know you weren't there. I know exactly who *was* there. So please stop playing this game."

She sighed and said, "You don't know. You think you do, but you don't. No one can help me now. Please just do what I asked. Just tell Stefan."

But I still couldn't tell Stefan about the caller, and I still didn't. I had wanted all my life to practice restraint, and this seemed like the time. Let each day's evil be sufficient unto that day. I weighed the caller's warning against the positivity Stefan was beginning to feel around his return to the ordinary world. The warning felt threatening and absurd, fashioned from dark alarm. The prospect of Stefan settling down felt sunny and sensible, more like normal life.

Stefan started work at the lumberyard a week later. I don't care what anybody else says, I think almost everyone who can work, wants to work. Everybody wants to feel good and be able to talk about work—to talk at work, to have a place to show up at regularly where you're expected and at least minimally respected. At the lumberyard, Stefan made friends. As the winter wore on, he joined the basketball league and bowling team, pursuits he once would have considered ludicrously geezer. Stefan talked all the time about his coworkers Cal and Casey, twin brothers just a year older than he was, who'd started working at the mill the weekend after high school graduation and had already earned so much, living at home and living frugally, that they wouldn't have one cent of college debt. There was a woman named Katie who sewed team sweatshirts for everyone and an old guy everyone called Pearl, who built harps on the side. Especially, he talked about his uncle, Andy, whom Stefan considered the stand-up guy of the universe.

It was Andy who called our home phone from the hospital emergency room that glowering afternoon. I picked up.

"Stefan is in surgery...now wait, he's not in any danger. He's not going to die. He's not hurt like that. But there was an accident, an incident."

"Tell me, Andy."

"I'll meet you here. I'll explain." He hung up. Jep was already walking in the door; my sister Amelia had called him.

"No," I whimpered.

"Let's just get there, and then we'll figure everything else out," Jep said.

At the University of Wisconsin Hospital in Madison, we made our way through the maze. When it was built, the hospital was billed to be a marvel of modernity, but instead turned out to be something out of *Alice in Wonderland*, a place with no evident plan or sense. We ran to the first door we saw and then down one of the corridors that branched away like the halls in a cruise ship, past abandoned wheeled carts loaded with medical supplies. A rainstorm had started, and a sudden darkness turned the windows to opaque mirrors where I glimpsed my own face coursing rainwater tears; my shocked, rumpled hair. It was only the third time in twenty years that I'd been in any hospital—the first, right here when Stefan was born, the second, that night in Black Creek when Belinda was in surgery.

We finally came upon a woman at a long counter, all alone. A novel sat open facedown in front of her, along with a bowl of tomato soup and a sleeve of crackers.

"Hello," I said. "Hello, please, we need help." With a sigh, the woman glanced up. "I'm looking for Stefan Christiansen. He's in surgery."

"Surgery for what?"

"He was in an accident."

"Then that would be emergency surgery. That's in another building. You can get a map in reception." She dipped her spoon into her soup. Both the woman and I jumped when Jep slammed his palms down on the counter.

"We're not going to try to find our way to reception to get a goddamn map! Get off your duff and take us to the right place immediately."

She was a massive woman, but one of those people who astounded logic because she shouldn't be able to heft even one of her pillared thighs, but who instead moved like a cheetah. I had to run to keep up. We jogged for what seemed miles until we came to a room bordered in stiff, foreshortened green sofas. "Wait here," she said. Then Andy and Amelia were with us.

"He's still in surgery. There are two ophthalmologic surgeons. They got here right away. It's his left eye. It's pretty bad. But they said they would give it their best. The nurses said these guys are amazing."

"His eye...? What?"

"It will be a while yet."

"What happened to his eye? Did something go wrong with the machinery?"

"Thea, there was a fight."

We listened as Andy pieced together what had happened. From what he heard, a kid not much older than Stefan hit him in the back with a two-by-four, knocking him down. Stefan stood up, waiting for the guy to say something, but the kid just walked away. Andy heard Stefan say, "Man, what's up with this?" The kid's reply was something like, you don't want to get going with me, I'm not a girl. Stefan asked him to say it again, to his face. In reply, another guy charged him. Stefan knocked that guy down. There was a melee, six or seven people scuffling, some on Stefan's side, some on the other guy's. A few of them, not Stefan, picked up boards and swung away. Evidently, one board had a nail in it and the nail went into the outside corner of Stefan's eye. "Which was good, I guess, that it didn't go right into the middle..."

"Which is the good part?" I said. Andy's face was all concern and kindness, and I knew enough to see that a workplace injury with possible criminal charges was going to cost him time and money, not even reckoning the cost of Stefan's surgery. "That board with a nail in it, that was no accident."

"Let's deal with all this later," Amelia said. "Let's just wait until we can talk to the doctors."

Conversation ran out before the end of the first hour. I wanted to ask Amelia over and over, do you think he'll be all right? Do you think he'll lose his eye? She was the sister most tolerant of my anxieties. But it would have driven her and Jep nuts. So I got up and took a long walk. Another hour went by. I checked my phone when I got back and saw a text from Julie, on her way, and one from my mother—Please call and let me know how he is. A third text was from the girl with the crying voice, ever a presence. It was as if she had some kind of uncanny ability to catch me in moments of maximum stress.

I have to tell someone, she wrote. I deleted it. Then I prayed.

Now, I was never really a believer. The sounds and scents of the Orthodox Church in which my parents raised me were precious childhood images, but I had never felt the presence of God. Still, helpless, I now prayed to the blank, impassive universe, offering my sight in exchange for Stefan's. That night in Black Creek three years ago, I had offered my life in exchange for Belinda's—but not Stefan's life in exchange. Perhaps that was the turn of the key. Maybe they don't listen on high unless you offer up what is most precious to you.

After three hours, one of the doctors emerged, looking just as an eye surgeon should look—thin, ascetic, gentle. "I hope we got lucky," he said. "I hope so. We won't know how much of a genius I am until the healing is complete, and that's going to take a while. A good while." Briefly but not unkindly, he explained that Stefan's eye socket and nose were broken and that the nail had pierced the eye. There had been some muscle damage, which the surgeon was reasonably sure he had addressed. The worries were function and nerve damage. The best was a full recovery, which the doctor thought we could honestly hope for. The worst was diminished vision and lingering pain. The eye would not "look funny" long-term, he explained, adding that young people cared about that, and they were right to care. Either way, Stefan would be able to drive and do most things and if there were lingering nerve pain, that could possibly be addressed with another operation. "For now, let's hope that's something you folks never have to consider. Tell him to stay out of bar fights after this!"

A bar was where we all went after Stefan was moved from recovery to a private room. We looked in on him, but he was sound asleep, lost to the world for the moment, gauze covering both his eyes.

Andy explained his quandary. Somebody knew who'd actually wielded the board with the nail in it. Somebody knew just how the whole event was planned to injure Stefan. Somebody knew why now, instead of six weeks or a month ago. Andy had no idea who that someone was, and he was certain that the group would never give up the individual who planned it all. Andy's was not a union shop, so that was one worry off his plate. I didn't like the sound of that. His concern was about whether to report the incident to the police.

"What possible reason would you have to not report it to the police?" I asked.

Andy and Amelia exchanged looks. "The big reason is that Stefan could be blamed too, and he threw the first punch."

"You said somebody hit him from behind first with a board."

"But Stefan didn't just walk away when someone made some

comment afterward. He went in hard. Angry. He got physical, too."

"What should he have done? Do you think anyone would
have had any respect for him if he just walked away? Do you
think they wouldn't have come after him just the same?"

Andy leaned back and closed his eyes. He acknowledged how
terrible the situation was, and that Stefan didn't really have any
choice. It was a lumberyard, not a hair salon. But he pointed
out that while the setting wasn't unique, the situation was. If
something like this could happen in a workplace run by Stefan's
own uncle, with that uncle standing just a few yards away, what
could happen in another place?

"So, you're saying wherever he goes, somebody is going to
try to hurt him?"

"Basically, the people who work for me are good guys."

"Good guys? Good guys that put a nail in my son's eye?"

"Younger guys, Thea. Hotheads with something to prove."

"They're hotheads, but when Stefan gets angry, that's different?"

"A few of them actually knew Belinda. The past Stefan has,
it's with him right now. Maybe five, ten years from now, people will forget. They'll know him for other reasons, ten years
from now. Right now, they only know him for one reason."
Andy paused and took a sip of his beer. "This was an assault. Of
course it was. Did they plan to hurt him? Will they admit it?
The point is, it was an assault. Possibly on both sides. Open to
interpretation. Yes, Stefan was attacked. He was provoked. But
who knows what side the police would come down on? Do you
even want to risk the chance of Stefan, just out of prison and on
parole, being involved with a violent crime?"

When Andy put it that way, I had to take a long breath. And
then I had to take another long breath. *A few of them actually
knew Belinda.* Was one of them the kid in the sunglasses and
hoodie? Would the menace always be this close? How could I

live in such a world? How could my son? It wasn't as though I
was one of those wives who had some kind of honor promise
to tell her husband everything. I was annoyed by women like
that and how fulsomely they boasted about being one soul in
two bodies; I wanted full custody of my own soul, thank you
very much. But I had never wanted to confide in Jep about the
hooded stalker more than I did right now. He would be outraged, and rightly so, that I had not. I was leaving Stefan wide
open to any threat.

Meanwhile, Andy was saying that he would give Stefan six
months of full pay beyond his disability time. And he would
give Stefan some clerical work to do at home once his vision
recovered to give him enough work time to qualify for unem-
ployment so he could have extra time to consider his options. It
occurred to me to ask why he couldn't just give Stefan work to
do at home until he could actually find another job, but I didn't
dare. My brother-in-law had done everything right. This wasn't
his fault or his wish, but I was still aggrieved.

"So, he can't come back to work at the lumberyard. But everyone else is forgiven."

"I didn't say that everyone else is forgiven. I'm going to do
my own investigation and there will be consequences, and not
just losing a job, when I find out who did this. The fact is, Stefan is not safe there. What if it had been worse, Thea? Your sister and I could never live with ourselves and neither could you."

Stefan came home two days later. He and Jep hatched a plan
in the hospital about how he would help Jep out informally at
some local football camps for high-school players, but the eye
surgeon had nixed that idea. He said while he couldn't put Stefan in a bubble, he would if he could, since the slightest speck
or inflammation of the injured eye could deep-six the whole
intricate effort of repair he had undertaken. Stefan was looking
at least more than a month of downtime. By the time he was
fully healed, it would be nearly summer.

★ ★ ★

One morning a week or so later, on the kind of glorious morning that makes you wish you could live forever, Stefan wanted to visit Belinda's grave. I was surprised to realize he had never been there. But of course he wouldn't have gone.

"I thought I'd get arrested or something," he told me. "I don't know how this works. I don't know if I'm allowed."

For a fact, I didn't know either. The etiquette for this particular mourning eluded me.

"Do you want me to come with you?"

"I'm still not supposed to drive until my eye heals more," he said. He seemed angry, for some reason. Lately he seemed angry all the time, which I put down to his frustration with his injury and its aftermath. "Of course I could, but I'm not supposed to."

"When do you want to go?"

He said, "Soon. I'll let you know when."

So I waited for his request.

I busied myself with my manuscript, on which I was finally making some progress. The editor at the publisher of my previous book had written me several emails, calling herself "really quite eager."

One day, I came home from getting groceries to find Will Brent, Stefan's best male friend from growing up, sitting in the kitchen. The two had played football together and remained close throughout high school. Will had been, in fact, Stefan's one true buddy. So complete had been Stefan's absorption with Belinda that he had never seemed to require other friendships, and though Belinda had more friends—I'd seen her with groups of girls—her first loyalty always was to Stefan as well. They spoke to each other each morning even before they had breakfast; they told each other good-night, last thing before turning out their bedroom lights.

"Ho, Stefan's mom! Long time no see!" Will said. They were eating a pizza. Will was drinking a beer. I thought that it was the first time that anyone Stefan knew from before had actually reached out to him, but Will later said he had tried to visit Stefan when he was inside, but Stefan had turned him away. Family was one thing, but Stefan had no interest in friends seeing him that way. I remembered Will as a handsome mischief maker, but now he was in a combined BS and master's program in nursing.

"Hey, Will!" I said, and then, hating myself, added, "You can't drink, Stefan." Even if he had been of age, his parole forbade him to touch alcohol or drugs.

"And I'm not. Will can drink though. He's twenty-one." To Will, he said, "Parole condition. Not that I was ever a big boozer."

"Leave that to me," Will said.

They were going out to play bocce ball by the lake with some guys Will knew from college, and for some reason, this cast me into a panic. What if someone who knew us saw him? What if someone who saw the local news coverage spotted Stefan? Not that they necessarily would recognize him, in the baseball cap he donned, but what if they did? What if some busybody snapped a picture of Stefan frolicking with friends while Belinda lay folded cold in earth at Angel Oak Cemetery?

Stefan looked, if too wary to be eager, then at least willing to go, glad of a break from the endless days he'd spent alone since his surgery, hours watching detective shows and cold-calling prospective employers. He did go with Will. He was careful of his eye but still yelled and sweated. He had fun, got exhausted, went for fried perch with the guys, left his sneakers by the door so he wouldn't track in dirt. Luckily no one was out front to harass him when he came home. Will was busy that spring with finals and planning for a summer nursing internship, but he went out of his way to make time for Stefan.

Stefan marveled at this, and the expression of wonderment on his face turned my heart.

"Nobody treated me any different," he said. "I could tell the others were curious, but Will was direct and just said, this is my boy Stefan. We go way back. He was responsible for a bad accident, and he went to jail. That's over now. So we're good. And they were good. It was like I was a regular person."

"You are a regular person."

"You know I'm not, Mom."

After that Stefan saw Will often, most weekends, sometimes going over to campus with him to see a movie or shoot pool at the Union, sometimes just hanging out at our place and playing games on the PlayStation console my parents had given Stefan as a belated Christmas gift, which Stefan had never taken out of the box. Stefan didn't really have the same hand-and-eye coordination since the accident, but he was happy to play electronic games with the others now. Even touch football and lifting weights were off the table for him for the time being. Still, Will introduced Stefan to a group of guys and girls who welcomed him. The group of them went to a ball game. They went to the movies. They went out to hear music. Stefan mentioned that he was interested in Will's plans for a combined degree. He talked about getting a master's in English, maybe teaching someday and though we knew that was probably unrealistic, at least the teaching part, we didn't say so. He talked to his therapist, sometimes in person, sometimes on the phone. It seemed sometimes that things were beginning to fall into place.

I got used to the rhythms of a louder, more expansive Stefan rushing down the stairs, slamming the doors, growing to inhabit the space that belonged to him, but that he could not quite bring himself to trust, in the same way that, at first, he couldn't quite believe he could stand out in the snow for as long as he wanted.

But still when he was at home on his own, Stefan usually remained withdrawn. He seemed perpetually restless, obsessed with the possible outcomes of his surgery, even though he knew that when the patch came off, the full extent of his eye healing would take weeks more still. Perhaps because he understood his uncle had no choice, Stefan seemed to accept Andy's decision to let him go from the lumberyard. Still he muttered about the eventual fate of the guys who'd jumped him. Jep overheard Stefan and Will once discussing plans that included following cars to local watering holes with baseball bats and eggs in the back seat. We hoped that was no more than aggressive preening. Jep said he would have a word with him to remind him what was at stake, but he understood Stefan's simmering fury.

No part of this process was easy, no part was going the way I had hoped it would. But I had no choice. I had to slow myself down, pace myself, follow Stefan's lead. No way was I giving up on my son having a normal life again someday. I was realizing it really would take time.

Jep and I thought at first the best way for Stefan to move forward would be for him to get a job. So we were hopeful that the lumberyard would be that step. But clearly it was not. Still there had to be something. Something had to work. Jep wasn't a patient man by nature, but he was enduring. And also a bit naive. Stefan wasn't. Every time I turned toward a new hope, I scraped my face against that particular wall. But what was my option? Neighbors could turn away. Employers could turn away. Even relatives could turn away, but I could not. I made him. He was my only.

Spring comes and goes in Wisconsin like a gifted illusionist, revealing a little more each time. Still, at this point, it was making a boisterous display, every day another blazing blue sky, a bonus that seemed to shout, *get out here and recreate.* The last of the ice broke up. Boats began their familiar skim across nearby Lake Mendota and tourists couldn't wait to start throwing themselves at the art fair and the farmer's market, buying crocheted ponchos and hen-shaped oven mitts they would never take out of their closets, and more jam than a family could eat for a generation. We who lived here knew enough to keep our parkas handy.

One Monday morning toward the end of May, Stefan said this was the day; he was ready to go to the cemetery.

We bought two dozen pink roses, Belinda's favorite, on the way there. When we got close to the place, Stefan mumbled thanks to me, something about being scared of facing a real grave, the grave where Belinda's body was, all alone. He was also scared somebody might see him. As we drove through the black iron gates, I was reminded of the pattern of leaves wrought into those iron gates of the prison, right next to the acres of razor-topped wire. Stefan could drive out of these gates as we had driven out of the other ones; but Belinda could not. She was a permanent resident.

Despite its quaint name, Angel Oak was the biggest cemetery in the area, by far. We had to stop at the office and get a map of the grounds to find the place where she lay next to her father, the Rev. Lowell McCormack, and Belinda Lowell, the great-grandmother for whom she was named. I'd never met Belinda's father before he died in an accident; but the family was originally from Wisconsin. After divinity school in North Carolina, where he met Jill, Lowell was "called" to become assistant pastor at Temple Baptist Church, not far from where we lived. Jill hated the brutal Wisconsin winters, and often spoke of how Lowell had "broken his vow" to take her Smoky Mountain home where the black-eyed Susans and cardinal flowers grew wild in the backyard of her childhood. And yet, she was a minister's wife who knew her duty. Athletic and strong, she said she followed Lowell into winter pursuits with the church youth group: It was, in fact, on a ski trip up to the Porcupine Mountains in Michigan that Lowell died, with Jill at his side. Later, and cruelly I thought, doctors would tell Jill that Lowell might have survived his spinal injury if she could have reached the ski patrol in time. Belinda told me that her mom's mobile was fully charged but the surrounding hills evidently blocked the signal. So Jill held his hand and sang his favorite hymns to him, Belinda told me. When he died, she was not quite three and she barely remembered anything of her father, but the conjured image of her brave mother, her voice a pure pipe in the fastnesses of those cold and darkening hills, always made Belinda cry.

How much Jill had suffered.

How much more than I she had suffered.

I could not even imagine my way into Jill's deracinated world, stripped of everyone she loved, even her musical cousins, her aging father, a minister who, well into his seventies, still rang the bells himself, evenings and Sundays in a green, fog-shrouded North Carolina hollow where Jill went to church three days a week and never suspected there were little girls who only went once—if at all.

For a moment, I wondered if Jill might not go back to the South now; but I put that speculation quickly aside. Her advocacy against dating violence—and, if I am honest, I thought as well, her hatred of Stefan—were the beacon in her life now.

At the cemetery, I was astonished at the number of cars on a weekday until I realized with a shock that this was Memorial Day.

The caretaker advised us that we'd see a flowering redbud tree and then a small wrought-iron fence on a knoll far back, not visible from the winding little road. We parked the car at the curb near that section and slowly walked up the gentle hill. The fence wasn't as small as I imagined. It was waist-high and about four by six feet. Inside it rested a few bedraggled teddy bears and a few tiaras, and a large SAY sign laminated against the weather. We stood there quietly, and then, impossibly, simply not possibly, I heard, and I hoped that Stefan didn't hear, a treble voice say, "It is so him! I saw him on the news."

Stefan tried to shrink. He would have loped back toward the exit if it didn't mean passing the members of a small family group who were now all frankly staring at him.

"Maybe they didn't even mean you." I cast around for a possible loophole.

"Sure, Mom. There are probably a lot of people in this cemetery right now that somebody saw on the news." His lip jutted and his elaborate slouch was almost risible, a cartoon of disgruntlement. "You know, this is bullshit."

"What is?"

"My coming here today. Trying to make anything better. What am I, an idiot? A child? No one's ever going to believe a word I say ever again. Nothing is ever going to change. Everybody will always think I'm a stone-cold killer who likes to hit girls. I'm a real model for rebuilding your life, huh? Broke and now, wow, probably half-blind, no future, living with *my parents* and sleeping in the bed I slept in when I was twelve?"

"Stefan, half the people you know your age are still living with their parents. Give it time."

"Give it time! More time! More time! More time won't change anything. I've been home months now."

"I get how hard it is to keep starting over."

"Do you? I don't think you do. All you ever had to do was be the good girl and life just unfurled in front of you."

I struggled to breathe deeply and stay quiet and just let my son vent. I pictured my stomach like a beaker into which an incendiary acid fell drop by drop, until the bubble quickened to a boil. He was wrong, of course, in part because he was young; to any kid, it might seem that life for his parents fell easily into a smooth sequence. What I couldn't say, wouldn't say, was that our path, Jep's and mine, was probably smoother because we didn't stop to get hopelessly screwed up on drugs and kill somebody.

"Stefan, it probably seems that way. But don't make us out to be the bad guys. We've been your biggest fans."

He sank down to his haunches in the grass outside the fence and put his hand through the black spikes until he could just touch the soft pink stone, in the shape of a heart, that read:

BELINDA LOWELL McCORMACK
BEAUTIFUL DREAMER

"You're my only fans," he said, after a moment. "The thing is, you really don't get it. Dad doesn't get it. The only one who would get it was her. Not how she ended up here. Can you imagine her, Bindy, all bright and shiny like she was, here? Under the dirt? I don't mean that. But she would get how I feel. I shouldn't say that, right? But you know what? I don't even care. Bindy, sleep tight baby. You were all I ever wanted."

I reached for compassion. What came instead was scorn.

I said, "Maybe you should have wanted something more than only her. Maybe you should want something more now, in fact."

"Gee, thanks." He said then, "That's what the therapist says. He says I have faulty thoughts and I acted on them in the past, and I still act on them." In cognitive behavioral therapy, Stefan went on, you learn to question irrational beliefs and try to up-root them. One was that he could only be happy with Belinda or someone just like Belinda. Another was that he could never do anything he really wanted to do.

"Well, that much is true. Whenever I ask you what you want to do, you say you don't know."

"A lot of people don't know, at my age. That's why they're living with their parents."

"They know what they're interested in."

"I actually want to be a firefighter," he said.

"It's an honorable profession."

"But I can't, because I'm a felon."

"I'm sorry."

"So I guess I'll just work at Target the rest of my life if I can get hired there."

"This is going nowhere. I don't want to fight with you. We didn't come here for that."

As I walked over to gently place the roses on the grave

through the fence, Stefan suddenly pointed out that a chunk of the headstone had apparently been broken off and simply set back in place. When he reached in to touch it, the piece fell to the ground. "They're going to think I did this," he said.

"No one will think that," I told him. "I can't imagine how it happened. We'll let the caretaker know." I knelt down, and then, to my surprise, I couldn't straighten up. Leaning on the fence, I began to cry, hard. I had never cried for Belinda, in part because her death engendered so much shock and horror that it shouldered grief aside. Time, however, had done its work, and I thought of her picking Stefan up to play tennis or go biking when he, of course, was indulging his lifelong romance with sleep. I could hear her voice, loud and deep for such a tiny thing, as she stood throwing gravel from my rose garden at Stefan's second-floor window and calling, "Get up, you're wasting your life!"

"Whatever you did, and whatever she did," I said, "she loved you, and she wouldn't have wanted you to waste your life. That sounds like a guilt trip, but it's true."

Stefan leaned down and half lifted me up, putting his arm around me and awkwardly shushing me, as I had shushed him hundreds of times in our life together. Huddled, we walked past the gawkers, back toward the car. When I turned to look back, the figure in the hoodie was standing under a tree watching us, as still as one of the monuments. With a jerk, I stumbled forward quicker, virtually hauling Stefan along. "Get in and lock the doors," I told him as I took the driver's seat.

As we pulled out, a sharp wind burst out of nowhere. Stefan huddled inside against the passenger door and the gust swept petals everywhere and the birds shrieked in the trees.

After that morning, Stefan seemed to sleep most of the rest of the week. Then one night he knocked at my bedroom door and said, "Mom, I'm sorry about the cemetery. I was so rude to you."

I didn't assure him that it was okay. I just accepted his apology.

In due course, Stefan's surgeon announced he was pleased with the progress of his eye repair. It would still be some weeks before its complete functionality could be assessed. Until then, Stefan would continue to wear a patch. For the next six weeks at least, he was still to avoid heavy lifting, like bench pressing (or humping lumber, although that was no longer on the table). But he could return to some type of ordinary work.

It was still early in June when Stefan spotted an ad for a job as a janitor at the newly completed Orthodox church, our parish church, a lavish structure five years in the planning and construction. He called right away and arranged to stop by within the hour. But once he was there, Reverend Kanelos balked, at least at first, perhaps using Stefan's eye patch as an excuse. He templed his fingers and said there were so many factors to consider, which sounded like him. Stefan didn't tell me the next part, but I had gone to high school with the reverend's now wife Vivian who later told me that Stefan spoke up for himself: "Father, this is not just a church, this is my church. If my church will not forgive me, who will forgive me?"

Challenged to the foundations of his ministry, the priest relented. He had known Stefan since he baptized him twenty years ago; there was no retreat.

Stefan worked his janitorial duties alone at first and just part-time. He cleaned the church and took pleasure in massaging beeswax into the newly carved benches and using an extended pole to polish the extravagant stained glass of St. John the Wonderworker with vinegar and water. But he grew transfixed as he watched the local florist Fancy's Florals wheel in urns and pots of seasonal flowers. Stefan told Father Kanelos, "I can do the floral arrangements for you for less money." He had no idea what the church was paying Fancy's Florals; he just assumed he could do it cheaper, even if he had to scavenge flowers from the dump behind University Hospital to start. He knew that's where patients' flowers were discarded. When he was in rehab at Our Lady Queen of the Universe Hospital in Black Creek before he was incarcerated, he spent hours gazing through the narrow, barred windows at all the mounds of flowers and plants left behind by hospital visitors; many of the arrangements still lush, healthy, extravagantly potted. Either hospital personnel already had their fill or some bizarre policy was in place to prevent workers from taking the stuff home. Sardonically, I suggested he might peruse the funeral homes as well; but he told me that the funeral homes donated their flowers to the hospitals.

Whatever Stefan said, it worked, and soon, he was heading up a small crew of church volunteers, mostly grandfathers, planning then planting a series of new gardens and choosing the ornamental plantings for the interior. Despite my record as a lapsed churchgoer, I knew the minister well, and so I went over there several times to see what Stefan was doing.

He was as proud as a new father, giving me a tour of the grounds. "You try to match the plantings to the architecture and the colors. I mean, what do I know about that? But, like, if you had a modern, industrial building, you would have lots of evergreen and sturdy red geraniums. This structure is modern, but it's also got the feeling of the old Byzantine church, so you can have more elaborate flowers that are still delicate."

Clematis arched over raised beds filled with fuchsia, catmint, campanula, delphiniums, foxgloves, hardy geranium, herbs and lavender. My son had recently found a pair of old stone birdbaths with hooplike trellises over their tops and he persuaded two of the men to bring them to the garden in one of their trucks. Then he wound these with pussy willow stems and filled the bath hollows with cliff roses and crocuses, both native plants in Greece.

"Listen to these names: Russian sage, ice cap, lady orchid peony," he said to me. "The names are like perfume." He pointed out how the lavender and rosemary scented the air around the gardens, and explained the sequences in which the plants would flower. The raised beds were edged in artemisia and green boxwood, and through them were veins of gold and purple stone. "The shrubs and the little trees add structure, like the frame on a painting," he told me.

"How did you learn to do all this?" I asked him.

"I looked it up on the internet. Then I started streaming gardening shows at night on my computer. I figured out how to hit garage sales and where the cheapest places were to buy stuff and get the church a big discount. I find a lot of it from people's trash, too, frankly."

He said he was now maybe thinking about studying landscape architecture the following year. "It's the perfect blend for me. You get to think and move your body around. You don't get as much of a chance to be depressed because you have to go outside all the time. And you can start your own small company and bid on jobs. People's houses. Small businesses. You can get a riding mower. People don't care who the guy is who shows up to do the landscaping. They don't say, hey, have you got a record? Then maybe someday, I can get contracts for whole subdivisions and parks. There's this woman online who only designs garden seating. She only designs park benches. And she's famous." Once the gardens were completed, he said, he would maintain them as he did the interior of the church.

He starting working longer hours at the church, sometimes close to forty hours in one week, and wished he could work more. Soon he even had a company car. My sister Amelia sold him her old Mitsubishi Eclipse for $500—which I thought was charity until I found out that those cars hadn't been manufactured since 2008. Still, it got him around. He first stuck rakes in the back, but soon he got help to mount a tow on the rear and was pulling an old boat trailer around onto which he added some planks and a pretty snazzy donated riding mower (apparently, like the waterbeds of a previous era, they were a much-repented purchase). Then one evening he came home with a very old but very theatrical pickup truck on which he had stenciled the image of a globe spilling over at the top with tulips and sunflowers and the words THE WHOLE BLOOMING WORLD, along with the words ★ Plant Environments ★.

"I figured that environments covered everything," he said proudly.

"It seems like it might be a lot to take on."

"Just this truck and the mower, and maybe I'll add a part-time high-school kid to work for me."

"What about bonding and insurance and all that?"

"Mom, for real. Do you think everybody who drives past here with some rakes and a mower on a pickup truck is bonded and insured?"

"Probably not. But if you are going to advertise, you'll need to at least look into it."

"I'll get to that if this is a go. I'll be very, very careful. If it isn't a go, then, oh well."

It seemed to be a go, however. Within the month, through ever-resourceful Julie and through word of mouth, Stefan had six regular landscaping clients, then ten. Stefan's eye had been healing nicely and so he was gradually able to lift and tote things safely. The crowning achievement of those initial efforts was being hired to landscape and caretake The Luck Institute, a beautiful building in town with an indoor atrium that housed offices, a jeweler, a bakery and a high-end luggage store. One of Stefan's jobs would be to create a rotating indoor display that reflected the season. The idea thrilled him. Stefan pitched the theme of boats and sailing for the midsummer season and po-sitioned a derelict old row boat in the middle of the plaza that foamed with dusty-blue buckets of coneflower and particle hy-drangea, while sailboats planted with orange and red and blue sedum marched up the outside of the staircase. An old fish trap was festooned with small pots of gerbera daisies and veronica. Strategically hidden clip-on grow lights, set on timers, switched on at night to give the flowers an artificial drink of sun.

He took me to see it one morning, melodramatically insisting I cover my eyes. When he gave the word, I stared, then gasped.

"It's stunning."

"Most of this stuff is salvaged," Stefan said. "I literally got it free and cleaned it up. I'm going to rent a storage shed when the season changes and keep the decorations there, so I can reuse them."

"The grow lights must have been expensive."

"They were, but Luck Sergenian approved them since I can use them again for the fall display!"

"Luck is her real first name?"

"Yep. She told me she was born three months early and her parents were superstitious." He added, "I wondered how many people she's had to tell that to. She actually said the same about me, asked me how many people did I have to tell that yes, I am that guy, and no, I am not dangerous."

I thought about why Luck, a local celebrity in her own right who at the age of thirty-one was a home-grown legend as a businesswoman in Madison—first this, wealthiest that, youngest-ever the other thing—was not only trusting when it came to my son, but sufficiently urbane to be able to crack wise about it. "She told me she actually had to do some community service herself for possession with intent when she was in college," Stefan told me. "Ten months. It was cocaine. The amount she had, it could have been prison time."

"No wonder they call her Luck…"

"That's exactly what she says."

So maybe, this…this chance, this piece of luck, as it were, finally, would be the opening door. Stefan could walk through; we would stumble after him. We would try not to look back. An addict for hope is like an addict for anything: It only takes a taste to get a jones going. And so I let myself think that maybe my son had really turned a corner.

There were still two sides to the life he lived. I would hear him trading playful insults on speakerphone with Will as he got ready for a night out, and he would sound like every other guy his age—bombastic, silly, lobbing testosterone grenades into the air.

But even when I would hear his low voice coming from his room late at night, the sound of his crying, I let myself bless those noises, too. Even grief is feeling, I thought. And feeling outflanks numbness. It is a start: An embryo is an egg is a chick is an eagle. I let myself bless those sobs, awful as they were to hear.

Sometimes I would also hear him talking into his laptop microphone.

"It was her favorite ice cream, but I just throw it up, like how can I eat it if she can't eat it?"

And...

"I think about it and, if I was sure I would get to be with her, but I don't believe that way about after you die."

And...

"I wish I could be a kid, like eight years old. You don't know about the pain of love yet, and you just want a puppy or something."

And...

"It's the first thing you think of when you open your eyes, then you can't stop thinking about it, I lost her, I hurt her, it's all my fault."

And...the worst...

"If I was sure that there was really a heaven, and she would be there, and everybody there was all happy, maybe I would end it. But I have to give this world a chance. I have to give my future a chance. That's only right."

If women waiting for their number to be called in purgatory would be talking about shoes, men in purgatory would definitely be talking about sports. I remembered how, for an anniversary long ago, I had given Jep a list I had made when we were just dating, which I'd kept in an old cigar box of letters.

PLUS	MINUS
Smart, but good looking	Sitcoms
Enthusiastic sex	Not a reader
Polite	Churchgoer
Actually likes kids	Meat every meal
Unselfish/Patient	All sports, all Sundays
Sense of humor 78/100	Hates conflict
Loves his parents and sibling	
Wants to be somebody	
Good traveler	
Hates conflict	

After Jep stopped laughing, his comment was, "Enthusiastic?"

I'm sure Jep never imagined struggling to try to bond with Stefan after some traumatic estrangement. Never imagined struggling to try to bond with Stefan at all—or with anyone else. For Jep, the world threw open its arms. He never fretted his looks or his style or his goals. My father called him "Everybody's All American," with just a slight sizzle of sarcasm, although my family embraced Jep as their own from day one. Jep's own parents, John and Paula Christiansen, lived in England for most of Jep's adult life, where Paula taught at the London School of Economics, and the Demetriou family became his default clan. My sister Phoebe always said that if Jep hadn't been a coach, he should have been a priest, like in an old Bing Crosby movie. People who came into his harbor felt graced. He had so many Coach of the Year plaques from his different schools, he could have built a shed out of them. He kept every single one. Over the years, many times, he turned to me at night and said in a tone of wonder that he still couldn't believe that he had the great privilege of doing what he loved for money.

It surprised me how keenly I missed the crisp, sharpened-pencil focus of my own classroom and campus home. But this would be a year spent on tilling my own garden—in a number of different ways. I was right where I needed to be, or so I consoled myself, and every day that passed only seemed to emphasize that truth.

One night a few weeks into the fall semester, Jep came home, gave me a kiss on the forehead and said to Stefan, sitting at the table, "Well, if it isn't Father Nature." He got a beer out of the fridge, put it back, and extracted the jug of orange juice. "I can't let myself have a beer tonight. I'll never stop. I'll end up hopelessly drunk. One of my players told me today that he wanted to ask his sociology professor a question, but he didn't know who she was or where the class met. The tutor just does all the assignments for him. Isn't that a great system? But if I pointed out the irony, my player would just stare at me and say, What's up, Coach? It's his norm. Like he's been treated like royalty all his life."

Stefan got up, walked into the living room and stood looking out the window at the tree he'd climbed as a child. Without turning around, he said, "Dad, it's funny you brought up that whole deal with your players. Because I've been thinking about that, not exactly that, but how that whole dynamic applies to me. I have some news for you guys. Not like earth-shattering big news. Just news."

My mind was a thumb flipping pages: Everything went by. *He had AIDS. He had cornered and attacked the guy from the lumberyard. He was on drugs again.* When I finally remembered to breathe, my inhale hurt my chest.

"I had an idea," he said. "I've been thinking about it for a while now. Ever since I got hurt, actually. It could be stupid. But it's about those things I was telling you a while ago when I first came home about people who end up in prison... About how you need to change the things people believe about you.

About how doing something good has to be a thrill. It's sort of a program. Julie thinks it's a good idea."

That made me smile.

He'd confided in Julie before me. Again.

Well. On the other hand, I had to admit, "If she thinks it's a good idea, it probably is."

And it turned out to be a very good idea. It would end up changing my son's life, and all our lives, in ways that seemed to mean that the possibility of redemption was real and in reach. We didn't know that then. At the time, I just surrendered to hope, because why not? Hope was always my default setting.

BOOK TWO:
Renewal

5

The germ of the idea came to Stefan when Jep spoke to him one day about how rest was an important part of his healing, about putting off trying to save the world until the day after tomorrow.

"You have to make healing yourself a project," Jep had told Stefan. "You have to let yourself feel the healing." His father's words didn't have the intended effect, Stefan later told us. Instead, the sound of the words rolled over and over in his mind, healing, feeling, healing, feeling, urging him to do something, to offer something, to realize something that would really matter to someone else, but would excite and delight him at the same time.

He thought about what he still felt…grief, shame, frustration, remorse. He thought of what he wanted to feel, especially since his eye had healed so well…a second chance, a new life, a different outcome, a positive point of view. It was a project.

The Healing Project. Those three words.

"Look, Stefan," I told him. "That day we went to the cemetery, I wasn't trying to use your obsession with Belinda to guilt trip you. I was just reminding you how she always would say to you, don't waste your life, and how, as awful as it is, you now have this second chance to make something meaningful of your life."

"Which your landscaping company is doing," Jep said. "You're making a lot of people happy, some who you'll never even meet. You're giving people beauty to appreciate. And you're healing. You're healing from your injury and from prison."

Neither of us knew how to say to our son, you don't have to be president of the United States. You don't have to be president of a bank... But what if he *did* want to be a bank president, or a computer designer or an architect? Were we suggesting somehow that his sights should be limited? That he somehow wasn't smart enough?

"It's just that what I do doesn't really matter," Stefan said. "Oh sure, I could just go on making people happy with all the pretty flowers and arrangements. Making myself feel temporarily happy."

I put in, "Honey, no one's ever happy every minute, and there's never anything wrong with happy."

"Except I feel I'm like one of those guys, those athletes of Dad's. I've had it all handed to me. And I didn't live up to it."

"Honey, you've worked as much as most people for what you got. And you paid for what you did wrong."

"Well, I suffered. I suffered a little. I should have suffered a lot more. Because what I did was horrendous. I know I owe more. I want to use what I went through for something positive, not just have it be the dark place I go to in my mind."

His therapist, whom he'd been talking with every week now, would agree with us, Stefan went on. The psychologist didn't think that The Whole Blooming World was a trivial endeavor, especially given how it had opened Stefan's eyes to his joy in something he'd never considered before—color, design, the living world. The therapist further didn't believe Stefan's quest to make amends needed to be commensurate with the relative size of the wrong he had done. Even Stefan knew this challenge was his own magical thinking. (He just wanted us to know that he knew.) And yet, if some sort of redemptive action, some sort of atonement, could shield Stefan from the deep despair he felt at times, even the psychologist admitted it would be as effective as the antidepressants and the pills he prescribed for Stefan to calm down and sleep.

Gradually, especially with the physical nature of his work, the ratio of Stefan's sleeping to waking had started to regularize, and he no longer jumped out of his skin every time one of us walked up behind him.

"Do you have time right now for me to explain my idea?"

We had time.

Setting up one of the ubiquitous easels Jep used to map out his team's plays, Stefan brought down flip charts he'd been working on in his room, drawing them on Jep's huge pads of paper. My son was taking on the role of the teacher; we were his students. He would share the bones of implementing his idea. But he wasn't ready to do that yet. He needed to give us background first. We sat in the breakfast room, Jep and me on one side of the table, Stefan facing us.

"We're starting with the premise that my life is worthless," Stefan said.

I personally had no use for that premise. I knew that Stefan was still haunted by Belinda's death, by what happened to Nightclub Owens and by a hollowed-out feeling of unearned forgiveness. The latter was a subject he told us he'd chewed over with his therapist, then tried to explain its burden to Will. Everybody else could forgive you, he believed, but if you felt you didn't deserve it, you might lose your will to live.

"Will got the whole thing," Stefan told us. "He's an ordinary guy. He's never been in any real trouble. He's like I used to be. And he saw my point. He said if it were him, he would do whatever it took to give life a solid try."

"A solid try?" I said. "Just a try? You're not fully committed to living?"

I remembered again the words I'd overheard my son confide into his laptop late at night. Again, I thought of a shadow cast against a door, the impossible slow swing of tennis shoes with the toes pointed down. I turned to face my husband and son just at the moment that Stefan's face literally slid out of the happy-boy lineaments he'd clearly been putting on for us. What we saw instead was similar to one of those optical-illusion drawings of an Edwardian lady that, when you study it, reveals a skull.

"Of course," Stefan said. "Sure I am."

Then he explained the evolution of his thinking.

"The repentance you do in prison doesn't really signify anything," he said. In prison, people who did wrong still felt wronged themselves. The confinement was awful. The smears on the wall were awful. No matter how hard he scrubbed the experience from his memory, vestiges of his being another person, probably a much worse person, remained.

"The sight of even one cockroach in my cell panicked me," he said. "If I saw more than one, I couldn't sleep. I wanted to work more hours than were required, but that made me stand out, and I didn't dare stand out." ("If you figured out that working harder passed the time, you probably wouldn't be in prison.") Stefan thought that working in the laundry might make him feel cleaner, too, but the sight of other prisoners' sheets roused in him almost a disgust. The prison kitchen was mostly appalling, too, although he liked baking bread and even unpacking canned goods.

"So I got permission to work outside. And that was great. I loved being outside, like I do now. You would never think of mowing the grass and shoveling the snow as a privilege, but it felt like that to me. I wasn't free, definitely not free, but when I could look up and see the sky above me instead of a metal grate, that was everything. It could get me through the fear. It could get me through those nights of no hope." So he mowed and weeded and watered until one of the other prisoners working with him ran away.

"It had nothing to do with me. I was just standing there when the guy took off running. I almost puked because I thought the guard in the tower was going to shoot at him, but the guy wasn't a violent guy, just a petty burglar. The sirens, like, exploded, and I couldn't tell if the sound was inside me or outside me. Guys literally crouched on the ground with their hands over their ears. And suddenly, this big porker guard is dragging me inside like it was my idea and they're asking me, what did you know about this escape and when did you know it? I said, nothing! Nothing! Not a fucking...sorry, Mom. Not a thing! I don't even know that guy! and they believed me but it was still ruined for me. I had to be inside all the time except for rec time."

So Stefan made the best of that. At recreation, he started organizing guys who had any concept at all of team sport. He realized he had become a coach by osmosis from his dad; within a few months, he had trained a prison football team that was the envy of the Great Lakes region. ("These are very aggressive guys, you know. You had to watch them like they were attack dogs. It was called touch, but it was really tackle," he told us.)

Eventually, it got too cold even for Stefan to do more than take a brief jog about the yard every day.

In the kitchen now, he drew two large ovals on the flip chart.

"So I thought, what do I want? What can I get other people to want?"

He drew an arrow from one oval to the other.

"I knew I wanted to eat good food once in a while. Basically, they feed you slop. I was living on canned carrots and bread."

Once a month, the inmates got the chance to use hot plates and toaster ovens to make some of the food they remembered from home. So Stefan called restaurants and talked chefs into coming in and teaching a cooking demonstration. The cooking demonstrations soon became an institution, every couple of weeks, which even the most hardened guys loved. As the organizer, Stefan had his pick of everything—from linguine and bracciole to homemade tamales.

"I want you to know that the potatoes and carrots and stuff were cut up by the trusties in the kitchen. They most definitely did not give us guys knives. And you would have to be pretty crafty to hurt somebody with a hot plate. I was shocked that nobody tried. The worst was the guy who threw hot pepper sauce in the eyes of his sworn enemy. That was way worse than it sounds."

Stefan then got permission, he told us, to call public libraries to ask them to donate their oldest used books. He stamped and cataloged hundreds of books and organized dozens of library shelves and a big roving book cart.

"But even that didn't fill up all the time there was," he said.

Stefan stood up then and squeezed his temples. I had never seen his expression so sad, not even on the day we left him at rehab on the psych floor.

"Dad, you never realize, in real life, how much time there is in the world. In real life, you're always wondering how can you cram one more thing into this day that is already crammed full of stuff you have to do? But I guess that's why they call it doing time. Time is all you're doing. Time is passing. Your life is passing. Time is terrifying if you can't be useful."

He did all his college coursework in a couple of hours each day, spreading it out over several days between classes so that it would sustain him. He wrote ten letters every week, at least two pages to us every day—the ones he wrote to my sisters were virtually a diary, but, probably wisely, he didn't share as much with us. When he could no longer write or type because his hands cramped, he "became a cliché," doing hundreds of pull-ups and push-ups. He practiced yoga. He broke up Snickers bars to feed a sparrow that lived inside the cell block, thrilled when it hopped onto his palm, believing the little bird was somehow more alive than all the men who snored and sang and screamed all around him. At night, he prayed to die in his sleep. He prayed not to die in his sleep. He was afraid that the prayers, on the way to heaven, would get mixed up. In the mornings, through a kind of meditation, just as he awakened, he could imagine himself a child again, curled in his bed with puppy Molly snuggled against his back, where she now snuggled again each night, although now he had to lift her elderly body up. She had abandoned her spot at the foot of our bed the first night Stefan was home.

Every morning in prison he wished everyone he saw a good day and said not one other thing.

"I had to be strategic. I had to bar myself from the bad guys, the real scary guys. That's what you call it. They respect that you want to bar yourself from white supremacists and black supremacists and the real nutters, like rapists."

He made sure to be the last one leaving the block or leaving any room so that no one was behind him. He made sure to stand at the end of the shower and complete his ablutions in two minutes.

"I have to tell you the worst thing I ever did."

"No," Jep said, crossing the room in two steps. "You don't have to tell us that."

"I do so I can get clean of it," Stefan told him.

There was this kid not much older than he who was a child molester. The little boy this prisoner raped was six or seven; for his sin, the molester was labeled a "chomo."

There was the word that went around that this was the day they would beat the chomo down. "And the deal was, for me, I was fresh fish, and you beat him or you join him." Stefan could still make himself throw up he said by thinking of what happened that day, behind one of the metal shelves in the library, that young man's empurpled eye and ripped lip, the pallor of his cheeks and the back of his neck as he cowered in submission. "But it was worth it. It was worth it for me because then I could say my own terms, I mean, without ever really saying anything. I could be an indy. There were a few dozen. Not part of anybody's gang. Just yourself."

He lived all his prison days in either boredom or fear or both, unable to even conceive of how it must have felt for those who faced twice, three times, four times as long a sentence. The aggregate of all of that extreme emotion would be that, sometimes for hours at a time, he would feel sorry for himself. And feeling sorry for himself was how he knew, he told us, that something was changing in him for the worse, and that he would need to change it back to become whole again.

Hence, the plan my son had conceived and was ready to embark on now.

Back at the flip chart, Stefan said, "I owe something to the world. I'm also scared to death of the world. I'm more scared of ordinary people these days than I was of scary people in prison. I'm always afraid they're going to see right through me. But I'm fighting it. So I am hoping that through this path and through my everyday work and just living right, plus my friends, plus you both, I'm hoping it will all be enough...enough to redeem myself."

He went on, "I think of it as a kind of renewal, for myself, and for other people. And just maybe, it will work on my head. And I'll really believe that I deserve to live."

Right then, I wished my son were in a locked ward at our local hospital, stripped of belts and shoelaces and sheets, and I was sitting there with him, saying, please no, please don't leave. Death is not a fanfare or a tunnel terminating in beautiful light, death is the balm of hypotensive shock. That's why people who survive near-death experiences say nothing hurts, not because there is really a life hereafter, it's just a few seconds of biology, a little parting gift from your good brain. It's hearing maybe one trill from a bird, remembering how good it was on a summer night, through an open window, to hear music from the radio in somebody's car going past, but by then it's too late, sound is all there is, a last rasp of fluid settling in your ears, and then nothing at all.

I was reminded of riding up in the hospital elevator to the locked ward that fateful night, how that elevator was fitted with an odd series of outside-looking windows, like an amusement park ride, so that inside I could watch the parking lot drop away and glimpse the distant hills with their muddle of red clouds forecasting dawn. Then, and now, the image reminded me of being at Disney World with Jep and Stefan; how, at eleven, Stefan was still unselfconscious enough that he gladly held both our hands. Ten years ago. Only ten years ago. How could I fit that boy into the boy in the locked ward, and both of them into the man he was now?

There is in every incident a lesson, said Father Kanelos, even if the lesson is not immediately apparent; this is true even if it is never apparent.

The lesson in my experience seemed to be that, in whatever present circumstance you happened to find yourself, there was not necessarily a seed of the inevitable.

How would Stefan ever get past the place he had arrived at where taking his own life was always the default? Shit, it was probably possible to commit suicide even at Disney World, if you wanted to badly enough.

Maybe this new plan of Stefan's, this plan of renewal he was about to reveal, this plan of how to move forward, would become his new default. At least I could hope.

But first, we had questions:

What could this Healing Project achieve?

How would the process work?

Who would be involved?

Remorse was the inspiration. Hope and renewal would come through the project. The project plus the inspiration equaled healing. At least, it equaled the beginning of healing.

To participate, you had to have remorse. But you weren't ready to move forward if you didn't have a plan of action to make amends.

The plan you created to make amends had to be something real, something to act on or teach or try to change, Stefan said. Not everyone would succeed. But everyone would be required to commit to a plan of action and a way to make it happen. Some participants might get a financial subsidy—money enough to see their plan through, if they incorporated that into their strategy. So that for instance someone could run a bike repair shop for a year, or buy tools, or complete a year of the culinary course at a junior college, or buy a laptop, or get one's teeth fixed or take driver's ed. Money would never be directly given to a participant. It would flow through a sponsor who would help find a funding source, then document every transaction involving funds or services. The sponsor could be from AA or be a minister or a social worker, one of the tutors in prison, or a former supervisor. Just not a relative.

Each participant would receive a folder: Stefan and Julie had already created a prototype, two dozen of which were donated by a local printer. The illustration on the front was an arrow, half embossed in silver, half in gold, that arched like a rainbow from the word *Healing* to the word *Project*. Inside was a brief history of the program and its rules, which were very specific: The expression of remorse had to be one page or less, handwritten and hand-signed, although there could be help with revising it—no excuses, no exceptions, no evasions. This was key. Describe the nature of your offense or offenses in detail. Name and describe the person or people to whom you wish to express remorse. Sug-

gest the manner by which you will express remorse. Describe in
detail the plan for your renewal. The letter had to be written on
the notepaper provided; each page was embossed with a wing.
This was Stefan's belief that making something beautiful of the
letter would solemnize the effort. Other forms had to be filled
out as well, including a brief history of the participant's inspiration behind his or her project. Each would also make reference
to Stefan and his crime: He had insisted.

Merry Betancourt, the youth minister at Julie's church, had
volunteered to be the clergy face of The Healing Project. For
two weekends when we thought Stefan was busy with landscaping jobs out of town that Luck Sergenian arranged for him,
Stefan and Merry had attended a training in Fox Lake, near the
women's prison at Taycheedah. It was for the nationwide Forgiveness Project, which gave victims and families the chance to
initiate forgiveness of the bad guys; it was the only organized
program that approximated what Stefan wanted to do. "One
thing different from the familiar tradition of the Forgiveness
Project," Stefan said, "is there would be no scenes of families from both sides embracing and crying together. Volunteers
would meet separately with the crime victims and their families
and with perpetrators and their families. But the injured families would never have to lay eyes on the wrongdoer—at least
under the auspices of the program."

"This program you've come up with is damned impressive,
son," said Jep.

"A lot of it was with Julie's help," Stefan told him. "And we
don't know yet if it will work." He added, "But it's what I can
do now. If it does gain momentum, we might get some publicity for it, newspapers and TV and stuff. They like so-called
good news. My story could become good news."

My antenna shot up. *No news*, I thought.

Stefan went on, "Like all I can do to protect myself—and also
to redeem myself really—is to prove myself, my worth. What

else can I do? Buy a gun illegally? Lock myself in the closet? I know probably a lot of people still have it in for me who aren't going to text me to send a warning. Maybe they'll come for me, like the guys at the lumberyard. Like the marchers outside our house."

Stefan's words made it clear that even though the protests in front of our house were fewer after the lumberyard incident, and the hoodie guy had vanished for now, Stefan still felt a sense of personal threat. And so did I, on his behalf.

That certainly wasn't just because of the protests or because of what the little-voiced caller had said during our few conversations. I didn't know any better way to express it but this: I was beginning to have a deep sense that something was missing. Something was missing from the bigger picture of what had happened to Belinda. Some information. What was it? What about that particular night had combusted an ordinary lovers' quarrel into a petroleum fire raging out of control? What? Was there another person involved besides Stefan? Was it this girl? Was there an earlier argument? Had someone used Stefan's wildly over-the-top possessiveness to get at Belinda? Why would anyone ever want to hurt Belinda? No one was ever so seemingly stainless. It was beyond the bounds of imagination.

But nobody's life was one-dimensional. Nobody's life was the life she showed the sunny world. What was it this caller wanted to say? Was she part of this? Was she guilty also and afraid to come forward?

The wondering itched at me. At times in the past few months, I did try to reach out to the girl phone caller, but she was a kaleidoscope of phone numbers. The longer the silence stretched between her calls, the more fixated I became on finding her and extracting what she thought she knew, as if she alone held the key to that night. My brain ran up and down the possibilities like a dog at a chain-link fence: Did she really know Stefan? Did she really know the hoodie guy? Was he trying to intimidate Stefan into silence, or was he waiting for his moment to strike? Surely, he wasn't brazen enough just to kill Stefan—or was he? Maybe he'd done it before. Why did the caller keep saying she knew who was there that night—and that I didn't? I knew everything about that night. From what Stefan could remember. From the police report. Then it occurred to me that I had never set eyes on the actual police report, but our lawyer received information from the police about the crime scene. And at that time, I left it all in the lawyer's hands. I didn't have any desire to know one single detail more about the night that crashed into our lives like a burning car. But given the possibility that the caller might actually know something else, what was my excuse now? Maybe I wouldn't be so frightened and blindsided by some creepy little death hag if I could make my own assessment of what happened at Belinda's that night. And who might be after Stefan. Did ordinary citizens get to look at police reports? I assumed so. Why not, weren't they public records? Reporters looked at them all the time, didn't they?

Suddenly my protective instincts were fully engaged. I said to Stefan, "Look, you should avoid the media. Reporters are not your friends."

Stefan shot me a confused, angry look. "So the only thing I am ever going to be known for in my life is something horrible?"

"I didn't say that," I told him.

But when Stefan walked away, Jep said, "That's exactly what you said, Thea."

I spilled it all to Jep then, about the caller's messages and the in-person threats, and what Stefan had glimpsed on my phone. I couldn't believe I'd held it back from him for so many months, despite the threat I often felt. That I had done so was a measure of how fully ensnared I had become in this web of menace. It was only responsible, I suggested, to warn our son now that he could be in real danger...but Jep cut me off.

"No, Thea," he said. "I'm not going to let you put that fear in him. As it is, our son is like a piece of glass, he's so tense. This project is the first thing I've seen him talk about that seems to make him feel like he can take control of his past. I'm not going to let you interfere with that by putting one more layer of angst on that."

"But he needs to know the calls still come."

"He does not need to know. Not at all. That…person is probably just one more crazy from your stable of crazies…"

"Just how are they *my* stable of crazies?"

"Because you answer them! You give them agency. You should just ignore them. Then they'd get tired of the game and go away."

"This one is different, I know it is…"

"Thea, I love you and I've always loved you. But this is what you do. Stefan is trying to build a new life. Don't put him in a bubble."

I knew there was something to what Jep said.

And so, I decided I might as well go along, blow the horn, too, about Stefan's new endeavor. Why? Sigmund Freud's receptionist would have been able to explain it: If Stefan had something to prove…so did I.

Stefan had made plans that were meant to redress wrongs beyond his own needs, and this meant that Stefan wasn't all bad, which meant, therefore, that I wasn't all bad.

The following Sunday, when we gathered with my family to celebrate all the seasonal birthdays, including my father's seventieth birthday, I knew it was time to share what Stefan had been up to. After my father, with Phoebe's youngest on his lap, blew out the candles and everyone accepted "just a sliver" of Amelia's magnificent coconut cake, I jumped in and described Stefan's idea for The Healing Project. I knew that he wouldn't do it himself; my family was too cherished an audience to risk their disapproval. I would need to open the curtains and then let him take the stage.

"So if there's anyone you know who might know someone who'd like to be involved, that person could volunteer, especially as an intermediary. He already has a representative from the clergy giving the project support."

"Where will the money for all this come from?" my father said.

"Stefan got a very generous start-up grant," I told him. "From an anonymous donor."

"Miss Moneybags," my father said, guessing rightly that Julie was indeed the bank behind the plan. But he smiled. The first year Julie had offered to divert a small portion of the foundation she had set up with her husband, Hal, and one of her brothers. It was now being fully used to fund Global Smiles, a dental version of Doctors Without Borders, which sent teams of dentists and hygienists to impoverished sites to do emergency services and train locals to run small clinics for routine care.

"So what do people get out of this? A certificate or something?" my dad went on. "What if a person has a plan and it doesn't work? Doesn't it make doing this like those participation trophies? What's the meaning of it?"

"You have to believe in it for it to have meaning," I told him. I pointed out that marriage, for example, was symbolic, just a few words and a piece of paper, but that it changed people's status. And it didn't always work out.

"Everybody who participates has to create a plan that could work out," Stefan said. "The variable will be how much the person is committed to making it work out. And sure, it could still fail."

"And someone like a minister or a social worker will be the go-between? Those are busy people," my dad said. He sighed and I could feel that sigh run right down my spine. I wanted to break a window.

Meaning to joke, I pointed out, "Merry is a Unitarian minister. So she has plenty of time. And she's also a prison chaplain part-time. And they don't have to be clergy or a social worker."

"So, Stefan. What is *your* plan?" Dad sighed again.

After a moment during which anyone with eyes could see him gather up his dignity, Stefan said, "Well, Papu, getting The Healing Project up and running is actually my plan."

Mostly everyone nodded.

"And how will you find people who would want to be part of that sort of thing?" my mother asked. "I don't think anyone in our family knows anyone like that. Or my friends."

"You'd be surprised," my sister Amelia said then. "Now, is this just for people who've been through the justice system, like they're in jail or they used to be in jail, or could it be for people who want to express remorse for something nobody knows about?"

Stefan said, "Something nobody knows about? That's pretty wild, Tia Amelia. That's a good idea, though. I think it could be."

Then Amelia told us about a woman she knew who'd been tormented for years because when she was a teenager, she and her friends were on a family vacation in the north woods and they trashed a beautiful cabin that belonged to some neighbors down the lakeshore. They vandalized it when no one was there; they threw paint and ketchup on the newly-papered walls; they ate whatever food they found, although they didn't break or remove anything. When the other family arrived, though, Amelia's friend was brokenhearted. She saw the people's despair and wanted to confess. She was fifteen. She thought juvenile detention would wreck her life and break her parents' hearts. She had written them letter after letter and torn them all up. "It's not just her peace of mind," Amelia said. "Those people were freaked out. They were scared for years after that it would happen again. They felt like they'd been assaulted."

Another woman she knew, Amelia added, had shoplifted tons

of makeup over the years, all from a little mom-and-pop drug-store. "I always wanted to apologize and give it back," Amelia said, and then blushed. "I mean, this woman I know wanted to apologize, not me! Could she be part of The Healing Project? Does the crime have to be big?"

We all sat there quietly for a moment, all the adults probably thinking what I was thinking: Amelia the admirable, the straight arrow, was talking about herself. She had lugged this guilt around all these years.

"It only has to be big in your mind," Stefan finally said. "Not everything has to be the bombing of the World Trade Center."

I looked around the table. Could silence get quieter, I wondered?

Stefan went on then, as if he, a felon, hadn't just referred to the bombing of the World Trade Center, which, to be fair, in his mind was something that had happened before he was even born. He explained that any trusted person could be the intermediary and do the outreach, and also deliver the apology with its promise of service. We would receive referrals for participants from ordinary families, or people who read about The Healing Project in Merry's nationwide Unitarian newsletter, or in the press if it got any attention, or from the families of the felons, or the felons themselves, from parole officers, and from community-based organizations that helped people start over after jail, like our local Fresh Horizon, "which sounds like cereal to me," Stefan added.

Every person who went through The Healing Project had to promise to try to find two more participants and to mentor at least one of them. That was the deal…to pay it back and forward. The grant from Julie would be in a trust that would renew itself, and he hoped that others would also contribute funding.

Then Stefan said, "So, Tia Amelia, those old people who ran the little store?"

"Yep," said Amelia. "I thought they were old people at the

time, but they were probably in their early fifties... Do the people who participate have to use their real names?"

"That's the idea. But I guess the person could just send the victims an anonymous check," Stefan said.

"That wouldn't be the whole deal though, would it? It's hard. It's a hard thing. It would be easier to just go on and not think about what one had done."

"Except you do think about it," Stefan said.

Amelia did become the first participant in the program. She took the time to write the letter and formally made amends to the store owners and the people with the cabin—Amelia, the quietest sister and the biggest sinner. So we all saw that this could work for offenders of all types. In the world, this was a very small thing. In my sister's life, it had wings, and I was proud of her for it.

Before that happened, I tried to ignore most of this, spending days on my scholarly book, while Stefan and Julie and Merry did the spadework for the first "real" iteration of The Healing Project. It would entail a fair amount of preparation, part of the reason why it would only be possible to carry through with one renewal project at a time, at least for now.

Stefan finally settled on the next penitent after his aunt.

It seems quaint now that I never expected that one of the Healing Projects would center on a family we actually knew. Portland, Wisconsin, was a small town, and Madison, just nearby, a small city. Even Stefan would have remembered them from the photo in our living room. Perhaps memory, however distant, guided Stefan's hand.

There were three contenders, all worthy; but one was particularly poignant, in part because the woebegone penitent hadn't done anything wrong but had been dragging a weight for a long time.

One morning, Stefan handed me a file. "This is the next project, Mom, and I'm meeting with the woman who reached out. She's coming here today. I thought you should know."

I started to read the file. Seconds in, I was stunned. "Stefan, we know these people. They're the Hodges."

After his time as a globe-trotting photographer, my dad kept just one main client, his best childhood friend Malachy Hodge, former governor and senator of Wisconsin, brother and son and grandson of governors and senators and heir to a timber fortune. I pointed at the large black-and-white photo on our living room wall taken at one of Mal's victory celebrations where two little girls peeked out from the cloth that covered the speakers' table. One was Alzy Hodge. One was me.

"I know that!" Stefan said, with a hint of a scoff. "I know all about it."

"No you don't," I told him. "Not everything."

As I began to talk about those days, my sunny childhood burst upon me, weather vanes spinning on the tops of boat-houses, the snap of hot dogs sizzling on a giant grill, the smell of a fresh-cut fir tree, jumping off the raft into the green water, breathless with cold.

"Papu and Mal played soccer together," I said, "and they went to the prom with girls they later married. When your grandpa was working for the Hodges, he took photos for them all over the place, of the good things they accomplished, like these gorgeous ecologically restored lakes in Minnesota and at this old logging camp in Maine where any family who asked could stay a week for free."

We often went along. Just like my parents, the Hodges had three daughters, about three years apart in age. They were named sentimentally for an old Longfellow poem that Governor Hodge's mother read to him and his sisters when they were small. "Your aunts and I grew up with Alice and Allegra and Edith, more like cousins than neighborhood friends. They were all beautiful and accomplished, blond like their father and dark-eyed like their Puerto Rican mother. We went swimming at the governor's mansion and slept over, thrilled to order hot-fudge sundaes from the kitchen at midnight."

The Hodges' retainer was generous. When the time came, my parents used that income to buy the block-long building where Demetriou's Papierie would be located. But my dad reminded me, all the Hodges' advantages had not insulated them from tragedy. As a triumphant post-doc working on strategies to help single mothers own their own houses, my dear childhood friend Alzy died in a terrible way, from exposure on a winter night in circumstances that were never entirely clear.

"I know it's hard for you to think of me as being your age," I said. "But I was once."

"It's really not that difficult, Mom. I'm not ten years old. And you're pretty young for having a kid my age."

"Well, now that you say that, I'm going to have to tell this in a pretty old lady way. Because this is a story that has to do with your family history too."

He stifled a sigh, in that moment, but a few minutes later, he was urging me on: "What happened next?"

"Well your project has to do with Alice Hodge, the oldest girl, the one we called Alzy. There was nothing she couldn't do. Math? You bet. Field hockey? A star forward. Cello? Good enough for the Wisconsin Symphony. After we were in college, the families didn't hang around together so much anymore, but I would still see Alzy and we would fall into the language we spoke together. She called me Threepy."

"That fits you."

"Not that we had much in common any more. Her friends were these sort of campus legends, the intense kids, the brainiacs." Alzy's friends graduated in three years and became Rhodes scholars. "And that's essentially what she did too. After she earned her Master's in Law and Diplomacy from the Fletcher School, she was chosen to be a fellow at UW's Maraniss Institute of Journalism and Public Policy, her focus on media bias as it pertained to economically disadvantaged single mothers. Her wedding, to another similarly gifted academic whiz kid, was on a bounteous Midwestern October afternoon."

"Wait, Mom, back up," Stefan put in. "You forgot to tell me about your friends."

"Well, I had friends," I said. "Julie was always my closest friend. But I hung around with some people."

"Lit geeks," he said. "People in black turtlenecks who would break into a frenzy of quoting Yeats at the drop of a hat."

I said, "No!" And then, I added, "Well, yes. Somebody has to be the one to say, but one man loved the pilgrim…"

"Pilgrim soul in you," Stefan finished the line.

"How do you know that?"

"Geez, Mom, some kids heard 'The Itsy Bitsy Spider' over and over, but I heard 'Now and in time to be, wherever green is worn…'"

"I'm embarrassed."

"Don't be. I'm sure it will impress girls someday." He prompted me, "So Alzy sounds like the perfect child. I'm guessing that wasn't all true."

By the time of that beautiful wedding, I told him, Alzy was already an alcoholic with two failed stints in rehab behind her. "She was so dazzling that no one would ever have believed she was stopping to buy a pint of vodka on the way to work and another on the way home."

"Jesus. And she must have been, like you."

"What do you mean?"

"Like small. Like that much booze. Guys in jail used to make pruno, they called it pruno, from fruit cocktail and oranges. They would guzzle it, these big skinheads. But if you had one swallow, you saw stars. Even me."

I ignored that.

Instead I told him about Alzy's wedding reception in the barn at her father's farm, about how I, already a wife and mother for several years, thought I was too old, at only twenty-five or twenty-six, to be a bridesmaid in a wedding party, but how I ended up having the time of my life.

"To begin with, I looked so beautiful after the stylist got done with me that your dad did a double take when he saw me," I said. "He didn't recognize me." The twelve bridesmaids were dressed like orchids in strapless wine-red velvet dresses, the bride and groom in a horse-drawn cart filled with pumpkins and sunflowers. "The setting was as close to a fantasy as there could be in real life." Sun spangled the red-dappled trees and golden sheaves of hay, and the fences festooned with grapevine wreaths twined with dried dahlias and eucalyptus and lavender. "I have a picture of them in that cart somewhere, that your grandfather took. He would not consider letting anyone else take the photographs.

"The meal would not have looked out of place at the court of Henry VIII, and it certainly would not have been confused with cucumber sandwiches at a wedding in Connecticut. Slabs of meat and platters of delicate trout were flanked by pyramids of late sweet corn drenched in butter, followed by six kinds of cheesecake. Then the tables were dismantled and the planks used to set up a platform for the band and a smooth dance floor. Alzy spinning and spinning in her dad's arms to 'The Lullaby Waltz.'

"So then go forward, what? Seven years? Eight years? Alzy was divorced. The drinking was out of control. Her husband loved her, but he had no choice, I guess. Their little girls were probably only four and two. He asked for full custody and he got it, even though Alzy took him back to court, more than once, and even though, obviously, the judges all knew Malachy Hodge."

"Did you see her then, Mom?"

"I didn't," I said. "Obviously, I feel guilty about that. Not that it would have made any difference. Alzy had the finest care that science knew about, whether it was here or in New York or California. Her family left no stone unturned. But I was busy with you and I was starting my own graduate school. It seemed like there would always be time. When you are as young as I was then, time seems like a renewable resource, constricting in the moment perhaps but burgeoning in the abstract.

"When Alzy fought back, she lost. And it wasn't much more than a year, maybe it was a couple of years, after the last custody hearing, that she was dead."

"That's crazy. And she was your age? So early thirties then? That went fast."

"I remember they played that same waltz at her funeral. The two little girls wore matching blue sweaters and black-watch plaid skirts. I thought that those clothes were so tiny they looked like they were made for a doll. The younger one slept in her father's lap. This was when you were about twelve. Right. I didn't want you to come to the funeral, although your grandfather did. He thought it would be a good lesson. I'm not sure in what."

Stefan said, "I am."

"Well, but there's a lot of room between…" I was going to say the way you drugged and the way she drank…but there wasn't. What is worse, to lose your best beloved or to have your best beloved do the very worst thing? I was a beggar at the same door of fate as the Hodges.

"That's what this application is about, Mom," Stefan said. "It's one of the saddest stories in the world. Your friend fell so far."

"I have to tell you the last part, Stefan," I said. "It will help you do this project. Governor Hodge got up to read a part of 'The Children's Hour':

"From my study I see in the lamplight
Descending the broad hall stair,
Grave Alice, and laughing Allegra,
And Edith with golden hair.

I have you fast in my fortress,
And will not let you depart,
But put you down into the dungeon
In the round-tower of my heart.

And there will I keep you forever,
Yes, forever and a day,
Till the walls shall crumble to ruin,
And moulder in dust away…

"When he finished, he looked out helplessly at the crowd that filled every seat and overflowed out the doors of the church. As if he had just noticed all of us, he said, 'I want… I hope that…' He tried to summon his politician's firm posture. But his legs wobbled and he could not walk away from the lectern. It was Papu who finally helped him back to his seat in the front row and even your grandmother was crying on my shoulder like a child."

"Now, I'm messed up," Stefan said. "And I have to be strong and calm for this person."

There was a knock at the front door.

On my porch stood the dark-haired young woman I'd just seen in my memory, sobbing in the church pew at Alzy's funeral—older now but undeniably the same person.

"Mom, this is Rebecca Broom," said Stefan.

I held out my hand. "I was just talking about you," I said. "But I didn't know I was talking about you. It's the strangest feeling. Like I woke up from a dream, but the dream was actually happening in real life."

"We've met before."

"I know you were…"

"I was Alice Hodge's helper. I worked for her family."

How long ago had the funeral been? Was it eight years ago? Alice and Malachy, all of the family, occupied the Beforeland: where I lived before Belinda's death and Stefan's incarceration, where I once looked down on a welter of messy tragedies that only befell other people. I hadn't talked to any of the Hodges since Belinda's death. Too much shame. Too much of the same shame.

"I remember now. Rebecca, I hope my son Stefan can help."

"Oh, I hope so, too," she said. "It's about Alzy... I killed her."

For a moment, my back burst with electrical prickles, because I thought we were about to hear a criminal confession.

Then Stefan said, "Becky, you know that isn't true. You didn't..." But he stopped, respectful. He knew all about magical thinking.

"Tell us," I said.

Stefan thinned his eyes at me: Becky's letter of remorse had already been written, the file prepared.

"I'm sorry, Stefan. I want to know about the night Alzy died. This matters to me in a personal way."

"But you do know."

"I don't know the details."

Why had I never wanted to know, to know everything, before? She had been my friend. We'd once been as close as cousins. Now, I recognized that I probably never wanted to know everything about my friend Alzy's death. At first, it seemed too far from my own reality in life. Now, it probably seemed too close.

"Do you think it's your karma or something?" Stefan asked.

I noticed that Rebecca, whom I'd met formally only five minutes before, was looking at both of us like she needed to be closer to the nearest exit.

"I don't believe in karma, but it's something," I told Stefan.

"You guys, it's really okay!" Becky said. "I don't mind telling you. It's not an imposition. It will probably help me along this road, if anything."

Stefan suppressed a sigh, and so did I. They were different kinds of sighs.

So Becky began with the start of her relationship with Alzy.

She answered an ad.

As a new college grad, she answered a lot of them.

But one was particularly intriguing. *Intelligent Resourceful Companion*, read the headline. The ideal candidate would work for a young professor who had been sick in the hospital for a while. Those words raised an alarm.

"It was the combination of the word *young* and the word *hospital*. I thought, what kind of hospital would a young person be in? The mental kind? But then, I thought, who cares? So what if it was? Did it really matter if the young professor wasn't homicidal? I looked up clinical depression. I looked up schizophrenia. I looked up bipolar illness. I had no idea what any of it meant. I studied English and library science! I needed a job."

The terms of employment were attractive, she said: A private carriage house off the main house, all expenses paid; use of a car and a weekly salary. The work was mostly nights and weekends; no lifting or physical care. The professor was fully employed during the day. It sounded like something out of a Jane Austen novel.

"Then I met Alzy," Becky said. "That was it. You know how she was."

Yes, I knew how she was. Alzy made everything look easy. She fought for poor single moms, her writing and advocacy meant to expose the subtle ways in which even well-intentioned media painted them as the architects of their own disaster. She worked around the clock. When she was literally sick with exhaustion, three shots of vodka taken rapidly perked her up. Impeccable and composed, Alzy would have starter cocktails over lunch with colleagues, drinks with influential friends for dinner, and afterward continue with folks in bars until closing time. Despite all her accomplishments, however, Alzy had the warm heart and politician's timing of a Hodge. When she sat down with you, it wasn't just looking at her, how beautiful she was, her ringleted blond hair from Mal's side of the family and the

soft but sturdy dancer's figure she inherited from Alma, like Er-
hart's *Mary Magdalene* carved from linden wood, it was also the
way she treated you. She would get so enthused about whatever
you were doing that you would feel as if you'd just lost twenty
pounds and defended your thesis. Becky said, "An old friend of
hers told me once that he was burned out by his research into
synesthesia when Alzy said, what if there was a restaurant in
Paris where all the chefs could see taste in their minds, so that
the color yellow tasted like braised carrots and the color purple
tasted like plums?"

The guy ended up finishing his degree but also writing a
novel about that restaurant.

So why would such a woman, accomplished and adept, loved
and lauded, already in possession of all the gifts life could offer
to the body and the spirit, trade those blessings for a couple of
inches of firepower at the bottom of a glass with a twist of lime?
Why would she do that, with not a single hint of any addiction
in her ancestry, to the tip of the last branch of the family tree?

As Rebecca posed those questions, I thought to myself,
indeed...why would Stefan?

I let my eyes slide over to him then, and I saw that he was
already looking at me, looking at me as if my skull were made
of window glass and he could read every thought on my brain.
He knew the answer. There was no clear answer. There was no
dot-to-dot that, traced, would set forth a clear route that could
be studied, understood and avoided.

"Pretty soon, I figured out that the very attractive money was
combat pay," Becky said.

When Alice was sober, she was diligent, generous, painstaking
and charming. When Alice was on a bender, she was devious,
defiant, sometimes cruel...and charming. "It was like taking care
of a baby who never got older but could filibuster like a senator, which she could, it was her birthright, okay? Lying was to

Alzy like the cello to Yo-Yo Ma. She had a gift. It was almost something you could admire."

With a reproving look that asked, how could you suspect anything else, Alzy would sometimes tell Becky, "I'm just getting my briefcase out of the car." But minutes would pass. Alzy would not return. Then the grim hunt would begin. Friends' houses, restaurants, libraries, parks, bars, bus shelters along the lakeshore, the Civic Center parking lot.

Becky would be afraid to call Alice's sisters or her mother and father or her ex-husband, afraid that they would put Alice back in rehab and Alice would lose her good job or never see her children again. Becky would also lose her good job. The Hodges trusted Becky and treated her like family. And Alzy was ever gallant, loving, contrite, when she was sober.

"I loved her," Becky told Stefan and me. "I wanted to save her. But I was only one girl."

Alzy loved Christmas.

The first Christmas after the final salvo of the custody battle with her ex-husband, she was to have the girls with her starting that Christmas Eve. Not a drop of liquor passed her lips. The days were tender and festive. But when they went back to their dad several days later, her mood plummeted.

That New Year's Eve was gorgeously counterfeit: The sun was so high and bright it was impossible to believe that the high temperature, in late afternoon, was minus four. In the evening Alzy sat and gazed into the fireplace and drank huge mugs of what Rebecca believed was tea. Becky recalled Alice turning to her and saying, "I love my little girls. And I love my husband. I had everything. I ruined everything."

"It's not all your fault, Alzy," Becky told her. "You have a disease. You just can't have booze, is all. It'll kill you."

"Then I might as well be dead."

"Not even a little. Your girls need you. Your husband probably needs you. You can see how much he loves you. So many people love you and admire you and count on you."

As I listened to Becky, Stefan made tea and brought each of us a mug. Becky thanked him and went on.

"Finally, I calmed her down enough to put my arms around her and help her get settled in bed," Becky said. "I thought, well, here I am, twenty-one years old on New Year's Eve! The glitter times just never end." But she was too worn out to even consider any of the invitations to go out dancing that friends had left on her voice mail. In the coach house, Becky took a long bath and made a deep dive under the fat goose-down comforter her grandmother had made for Rebecca's last birthday. When she woke, it was past midnight.

"I knew something was wrong," she said, tears filling her eyes as she took a deep draught from her mug of tea.

For just that reason, Rebecca never put her coat or boots away; she kept them next to her bed "like a farmer or a vet" so she could shove her feet and arms into them and run down the stairs and through the passage from the coach house to the main house. The main house was freezing, the front door wide open. When she looked outside, she saw that Alzy's car was gone, although Becky had parked her own car behind it and had no idea how Alzy had maneuvered her own car around it without being able to make a Volvo station wagon fly.

"I pushed the door closed. Snow was drifted onto the floor. The door had been open for a long time. And I saw how crafty she was. Her keys were gone but so were mine. And her winter boots were missing from the hallway mat."

Upstairs, she said, Alice's nightgown lay curled on the floor of her bedroom. Outside, there was not a sound in the neighborhood if you didn't count the creak of the ice on the lake. She would have to call Governor Hodge or get into a cab herself and start to search. But where first? She felt cold and sleepy.

"And I thought, I just can't tonight. I have done this so many nights. I just can't."

So she went back to her still-warm bed and pulled the covers over her eyes. When she woke again, the sun was up full. It was after eleven, and Becky relaxed when she shrugged into her robe and crossed back into the big kitchen at the main house, to the smell of coffee and the subtle sounds of a morning kitchen.

"Happy New Year," she called out, but no one answered. Not Alice, but a man was standing hunched at the sink, Alice's husband. He looked as though he'd been beaten up, his face red and blotchy, his white fisherman-knit sweater covered with black smudges, his pants wet to the knee. He asked Becky to sit down, then gave her a cup of coffee before he recounted what happened.

And after that, Becky just finished her tea without saying a word.

Stefan and I sat there waiting.

"What happened?" Stefan finally asked her. "I know what happened, but now I have to hear the rest, even though I really don't want to hear..."

Becky interrupted him. She said, "Please give me a minute." She added, "Some things get easier. This one doesn't."

At about eight that morning, police had spotted what appeared to be a red blanket on top of a snowbank a few hundred yards from Mickey's Fishbowl Tavern. On closer inspection, it was a red wool coat. Alice had probably died a few hours before in cold so extreme that she had all but frozen solid. She almost certainly didn't suffer at all: She would have been drunk and passed out. As I listened, I thought unavoidably of the lines from Emily Dickinson... *As freezing persons recollect the snow, first chill, then stupor, then the letting go.* The bartender had called Alzy a cab at closing time and watched her leave. He remembered her saying that, by this time next year, everything would be merry and bright. Those were the words she used. Who knows what

happened next? It would not have taken very long for Alzy's
body temperature to plummet. At that point, the brain would
no longer care. She would not have been thinking about all she
was losing.

"Jesus," Stefan said. "The words she said make it worse."

The Hodges family invited Becky to stay on for a while,
to ease any of the fallout, she said. They knew how much she
loved Alzy, how dedicated she was to her. Their big hearts were
cracking too. Eventually Becky found a new job, as a research
librarian. A year passed, and then two and then three. Slowly,
unable to forgive herself for her role in Alzy's death, Rebecca
began to look for an emotional way forward, a way to pay hom-
age to her friend. She was still living in the carriage house; the
main house remained empty. But she was determined not to
ask the Hodges for anything more. Then recently, from Merry
Betancourt's newsletter at the Unitarian Church, she learned
about Stefan's Healing Project. And her idea for a way to make
amends took form.

She would ask the Hodges if she could convert Alzy's main
house into a residence for women who were profoundly addicted but committed to recovery. She would house and treat
ten at a time. She would call it The Alice Hodge Safe Home.
For two years, each resident would have to perform every task
of their day in partnership with another. Once these teams of
two were in place, they could not be changed unless someone
left the program. They would have no choice but to support
each other. They had to go everywhere together, even to work.
They would share cooking, cleaning, doing laundry. The rules
would be absolute, a single offense would trigger a ban for both
members with no possibility of reinstatement.

Becky would continue to live at the carriage house, in a supportive role, but the women would have to sustain each other—
an experiment in healthy codependency. Their motto would be:
No One Goes Alone. Rebecca had brought Stefan her plans for

a pilot Safe Home program. What she needed was the where-withal to finance the first two years while she actively sought public and private funding. After she received word of accep-tance for her program from The Healing Project, Becky con-fided her plans to Alice's family. She didn't know if they would even approve of the idea. If they did not, she would withdraw her application and never raise the subject again.

They *did* approve.

"In fact, they gave me both the main house and the carriage house, outright. They even set up a foundation to pay the taxes. At first, I refused to take it. I said it wasn't right. They said it was. I said it wasn't. They said it was. Finally, Alma said, it's the only right thing. I guess that convinced me. And now, I have to live up to it."

When she stopped talking, Stefan read her letter out loud.

It said in part:

"My remorse is everlasting. When I could have saved Alice Hodge, I let selfishness rule me. I was literally asleep on the job on the night that my employer and my good friend froze to death in the snow. If you give me the chance, my renewal will be to try to help save someone else, someone who is fight-ing addiction the way that Alice Hodge fought. Although she lost, not everyone loses. Not every bright light has to go dark. I don't flatter myself that it will be because of me that another bright light continues to shine, but if I can feel responsible for the smallest part of that light, maybe I will not feel so respon-sible for what happened to Alice."

And as he read it, pity washed over me. Rebecca didn't do something terrible. She just didn't *do* something, and something terrible happened.

Suddenly I thought of the mysterious caller Esme's claim, *No one can help me.* I was fed up with the caller's games, but what if this person really did have no one else to trust? Rebecca's proj-ect had opened a vein of empathy toward this troubled soul and a renewed wonderment at why the caller reached out to me, rather than to Stefan or to Jill. Even if I didn't believe what she said, she still seemed tormented by it.

I excused myself for a moment. On the porch, I sent a text from my phone. This is Thea, Esme. Please call me or text. I do want to know what you know.

But I heard nothing from her. And there was nothing I could do.

A few weeks later, Stefan and Jep and I stood with the assembled Hodge clan, including Alice's mother and her two daughters, her sisters and their families and my own parents, in front of the sign, hand-carved from Wisconsin red cedar, that read The Alice Hodge Safe Home. Rebecca was standing with us, a departure from the rules. Although she was technically the person who had done wrong and she was making amends to the Hodges, they were having none of it. They asked for her to be with them. They wanted the chance to publicly thank her for her sacrifice and ingenuity in deciding just what she—and by extension, Alice—would find meaningful for this big lakeside house that had already seen so much joy and grief. Not only did they gift The Alice Hodge Safe Home an operating budget that would be reviewed after six years, including a salary for Rebecca and money for home improvements as they were needed, they also independently gave a substantial sum directly to Stefan's The Healing Project to be used at his discretion.

Just before the end of the ceremony, Alice's mother, Alma, usually quiet in big groups, spoke up. "We accepted your letter, Rebecca, but I want you to know that none of us accepts its basic premise. You did not let our Alice down. No one did. Some people will fight and win. Some people fight and lose. Alice had a choice between the dark and the light of her nature. It seems cruel to say so, but she did have that choice. Your choice means that people will always be reminded of the best part of our Alice. You have brought a part of Alice back to us. And we thank you."

Stefan, Jep and I stood there in the brave sunlight, moved by the free mingling of emotions that chased across those changed, familiar faces. I leaned heavily on Jep's sheltering arm. As we walked back to the car, Stefan mused about how both things were true—Alma's explanation and Becky's account. Her inaction was an action; she was not guilty, but in a way she was responsible.

6

After his experience with Becky's project, Stefan told me, "I feel lifted up by this. I think it's helping."

His conditional enthusiasm alarmed me, but I tried to paper over my misgivings. Life was not going to offer him a sustained emotional high. I wanted to talk to him about this, but I didn't want to so pointedly burst such a fragile bubble.

One night, Stefan was getting ready to pick Will up; they were going out to a club to dance and Stefan was really looking forward to it.

"I used to love to dance, when I…well, before," he said to me. "I almost said when I was young. Do you think I'll remember how?"

"The way people your age dance, no," I said.

"Geez, Mom, disco queen, do you have to be such a ger?" He'd called me this before, short for "geriatric." In a withering parody of my own voice, he said, "Why, the way you young people go on, you never get a haircut, you never save a nickel…"

He took a fork from the silverware drawer and sat down with me at the table, expertly plucking first the tomato peppers and then the Greek olives and salty cheese squares from my salad. Finally, I jabbed the back of his hand with my own fork. "Nice," he said, and drifted to the refrigerator. "Oh! There's another whole one in here!" He went silent and I belatedly realized he was making short work of the other salad.

"That's for Dad!" I called.

"Well, where's mine?"

"I didn't make you one. I didn't know you wanted one."

"I worked all day!"

"So did I."

"I mean, I really worked all day, lifting bags of potting soil, dragging hoses around…"

"So did I."

"Yeah, dragging…verbs around."

I told him, "You have no idea how heavy a verb can get. Go ahead and make yourself a salad."

"It's okay. This one's practically gone… I'll just stuff some more lettuce and olives in the bowl. He'll never know the difference."

"Well, you're certainly saving some nickels."

Stefan's silence breathed affront. "Hey, I've got an idea. It's Friday night. I'm looking forward to going out. You make some belittling remarks about my generation and then bitch about me eating fifty cents' worth of iceberg lettuce. Now I'm in a great mood. You're a real antidepressant, Theaitsa," he said, using the Greek endearment for my name. When he was little, we called him "Stefanakis mou," or my little Stefan. My mother still did.

I thought of that, and I felt bad, and asked him to sit with me for a moment.

"I know you feel great about the last project," I told him. "But you know, you're not going to get everything to wrap up so elegantly every time, right? Such a neat package? Not everybody is going to be as smart and decent as Rebecca or Tia Amelia. They're not going to be people you know or feel comfortable with. These have been postcard moments but..."

"What's your point?"

"Well, just that you can't expect a big emotional payoff every time..."

"Why not?"

"Because life isn't like that, Stefan. Life is sometimes you win, sometimes you lose. Sometimes you take five steps forward, but sometimes you take two steps forward and three steps back."

"Really?" he said. "I didn't know that. No wonder all the great philosophers were Greek. Excuse me for feeling enthusiastic."

"You should be. I just don't want you to get so flattened if something goes wrong that you give up or..."

"Or what? Kill myself? Mom, how many times do I have to say I'm not going to kill myself? I could kill you, though," he said.

I gasped. When I looked at him, I could see tears welling up in his eyes.

"I didn't mean... I meant the way you say, I could just kill you..."

"Stefan, I know that. I didn't think for a second that..." And I didn't think for a second that he was actually threatening me. But I did think, for a second, of the way those words sounded, in his mouth.

I wanted to tell him that I got it, that I saw that he was trying to find a new way forward, to a sense of parity with other people, a way of being as normal as he could in the world. In a way, I think he was working his way up toward his own reckoning over Belinda.

I got up and tried to put my arms around him, but he stiffened.

"Let's rewind this," I said.

"We can't."

"We can. Let's rewind this. Before you go, tell me about the next Healing Project."

He snorted, contemptuous. "Well this next one, even if I wanted to, I couldn't be part of it directly. You'll see why. But it could turn out to be another one of those postcard moments."

How far off the mark that description was would be evident only in hindsight.

By the time he got back with the latest letter that he and Merry had chosen, I'd made him his own salad with a few pieces of garlic bread. ("Thanks, Mom," he said of refusing the bread. "That's not exactly minty fresh for a nightclub. Why don't I carry a mirror and a crucifix too?")

The letter was from Roman Villera, Stefan's only real friend in prison.

"You know Roman was a teacher, right?" he said and I nodded. "He taught sixth grade and it was a passion for him. He was always winning these best-teacher awards and stuff."

I remembered meeting Roman, talking briefly with him and his family at the prison's Christmas dinners. He was almost cartoonishly handsome, like the drawings of Prince Valiant in the old comics sections my parents used to pull from the Sunday newspapers. Sweet, soft-spoken, he was married to a girl he'd known all his life, who meant what she said about better and worse and stuck by him after Roman, who was also a binge drinker, mowed down a mother and daughter, killing the daughter, who had two children of her own. Roman's little boy, Joey, was at one of those dinners. Roman told us that Joey was the same age as one of his victim's children.

Stefan said, "You guys only met him a couple times. But I saw Roman and Trina and their little boy all the time because they had those special visiting hours for families to have some private time, but you could invite another inmate in if the guards and the family approved of it."

While Roman and Trina held hands and talked privately, Stefan used to play with Joey, making puppets out of strips of paper and playing endless rounds of Chutes and Ladders. Trina told Stefan later that whenever he wasn't around, Joey would ask, where's that big boy? Does he want to play? "She was just the nicest person. She raises Neapolitan mastiffs as a business and her breeding pair, Churchill and Tosca, they're champions, worth ten thousand dollars each." He said she had emailed him when he got out, and I remembered him talking about it at the time. "Trina said that Roman was seriously depressed when I left. I used to keep his mood up a little. We played chess and talked about movies. Now I'm not even allowed to write to him."

Stefan's parole conditions stipulated that he could never associate with another former inmate.

While I quickly volunteered to act as the intermediary on behalf of Stefan this time, the next day, I confided in Julie my anxiety about doing this. She stepped up and offered to help me. I lied when I told Stefan I was ready. The Healing Project was way more appealing to me in concept than in actuality.

Julie was always made of sterner stuff than I. You don't think of oral surgeons as having to be gladiators, but Julie showed me pictures of mouths with grotesquely mislocated teeth impinging on the person's eye sockets that turned my stomach. In ordinary life, to be fair, Julie's sterner stuff had not been tested quite as vigorously as mine had. But I owed Stefan for dumping ice water all over his zeal. This would be my amends; and to quote Thea Demetriou, it wouldn't always be pretty.

It wasn't Roman who answered our knock when we arrived at his home, but his wife, Trina. When she swung open the door, I nearly jumped onto Julie's back. The dog creature who stepped into the space resembled a living gargoyle the size of a pony. "Say hi, Churchie," Trina instructed the beast. Julie knelt, and a hundred and fifty pounds of muscle melted into her arms like a newborn lamb. Nervously, Trina invited us in. "I would

really like to give Stefan one of our puppies as a thank-you."
Another huge dog, trailed by a slight blond boy, rounded the
corner into the front hall as we entered. Tentatively, I ruffled
the several yards of grizzled skin that draped the dog's neck.

"These are very expensive dogs," I said. "You shouldn't just
be giving them away."

"Well, Thea, I can call you Thea, right? My husband might
not be alive except for Stefan."

Roman came to greet us, and I remembered his abundant
waves of hair and eyes so big they almost looked upside-down.
He was still jail pale, only fifty days out.

"Stefan and I talked about everything," Roman told us, as
Trina and Joey carried plates of sandwiches into the living room
where we gathered. "Sure, I hated that Stefan was there. I hated
what he did. But he seemed like just a kid, not that much older
than my students. And your son was just consumed with regret.
Helping him find a way to go on, it helped me find a way to go
on. I never pictured myself in prison. Not that anyone ever does."

Roman asked if I had a picture of Stefan with me. Then he
laughed. Why would you? Stefan wasn't a child whose mother
carried school pictures in her wallet. But he wondered, had Stefan gained some weight? I assured him that he had, that Stefan
was stronger in every way, working outside, planning to go back
and finish college and that he sent his regards. Roman seemed
relieved by this. Stefan often told him what we already knew,
that if he'd ever really cared about anything beyond Belinda,
maybe none of this would have happened. Roman preached the
salvation of school. Nothing about education would ever go to
waste, he told Stefan, although they acknowledged that nothing about education had made either of them smart enough to
avoid his fate.

"Guys like Stefan and I, we had a lot more breaks than most
of the others in there. But we were murderers," Roman said.
"Stefan often said, why did people always tell you to get past

feeling guilty? And I agreed. Guilt is probably one of the most complicated of human feelings, but one of the most useful. It makes you think." Roman laughed nervously at himself now, tugging at his mat of blond curls I noticed now were going gray.

Sun spattered the perfectly alphabetized spines of a library straight out of old-timey *Boy's Life*: *Treasure Island, Great Expectations*...and it did seem absurd that we were sitting in this safe, silent space talking about unspeakable horrors. I knew from Stefan that Roman had been a model prisoner, breaking up fights, hosting book clubs, but nothing eased his shame. He told us now, "I can never get past the wounded bafflement on the face of my own mother and father, a vegetable farmer from Del Rio, Texas, who put his four sons through college." He added, "I am the youngest of them and, especially for my mother, I was a shining light, the promise of the American dream made real. The only time I feel suitably punished is when I think about never being able to teach again." He remembered his father, too, exhausted, his faded blue shirt still salty with sweat and grassy from the smell of the tomato fields, reading to them at night about Thor Heyerdahl's epic voyage aboard *Kon-Tiki*. Now, encouraged by his wife, Roman was going to complete a second degree that would allow him to work as an alcohol and drug abuse counselor.

"The purpose of this Healing Project is just that, to start you on a new road," Julie said. "But even more, it lets you do some real good for your victim's family." As we spoke, I noticed a door to the room open and close quickly. A small, attractive woman, maybe in her late sixties, poked her head in for an instant. The look on her face as she took in the scene was as if she were watching a knife fight. *This is his mother*, I thought. I wished I could sit alone with her and talk about all of this.

Roman's proposal for renewal was that, as a drug counselor, he would pledge part of his salary to an education fund for the children of the young woman he had killed. Merry Betancourt would help him set up the fund, which would start with an initial grant from The Healing Project until he finished his training as a counselor.

He read his letter to us:

"If I were you, I would probably throw this letter out. I would be thinking, he got away with murder and now he wants to say he's sorry? I can't change the past. I have no right to think of the future. But I have to find a way to go on, for the sake of my wife and child. My son is innocent. I have to consider his future and the future of Rowena and Rosalind Wild. I had a great life, great job, great wife, great parents. I threw it all away. I liked to drink. I loved to drink. A little relaxation but then hours of being a buffoon, staggering all over. I always thought I was fine to drive. A lot of drunks think this and they are never fine to drive. But I was such a fool that I kept it up. It took ninety seconds. It took ninety seconds to wipe out a family's dream. I got ninety seconds in court to apologize. I got six years to repent. Okay. Wise people say that forgiveness means giving up all hope of a better past. I can't repair the damage I did. I was drunk when I hit Maggie Slaney and Jessamyn Slaney Wild with my car. I took away Maggie Slaney's only child and I took away Rowena and Rosalind Wild's mother. This is my remorse, expressed in writing. Here is my renewal. I pledge to contribute to the education of Rowena and Rosalind from every paycheck I earn until they are eighteen years old, because this is what their mother would have done for them. I can't bring her back, but at least I can offer this. It is up to you if you want to accept it."

Afterward we shook hands with Roman, then with Trina and Joey and said our goodbyes. Wondering where all this emotion was coming from, I turned back and gave Roman a hard hug—from Stefan. He stood and watched as we drove away.

"Those are some serious dogs," Julie said in the car.

"People who have dogs are happier," I reminded her.

"Then they must be very happy."

My phone abruptly pinged, a few times in sequence.

How did it go? Stefan wanted to know. Tell me how Roman is. Did you see the dogs? And five seconds later, before I could answer, Are you done yet? Is it going to work out?

But just after Stefan's were two other text messages from a number I didn't recognize.

Will you still talk to me?

And then.

I don't blame you if you never answer this.

I answered her before I answered my son. Why? She was the shell around something I sensed I needed to know.

I texted her, I will still talk to you. I promise. Just not right now. Give me a couple of days.

Stefan was literally standing in the doorway when I got home. I told him everything, even about exchanging glances with Roman's silent mother. Then I called Maggie Slaney, who had been alerted previously about the mission of The Healing Project and about Roman's offer, and, thanking the universe for answering machines, left a message proposing a time for our visit, asking her to call back if it was inconvenient.

I hoped she would change her mind. I hoped she would say, just leave a letter in the mailbox. But no call came.

The next morning, Julie brought me coffee.

"I hope this goes as well as it can go," Julie said.

We both knew this would be harder. How much harder, neither of us had any idea.

The big farmhouse where Maggie Slaney was raising her two granddaughters on her own was just a few miles outside Madison. Spontaneous raw "neighborhoods" sprouting crops of one-acre mansions shared the countryside with traditional family farms. I had all but ordered Julie to go with me. I knew this encounter would not be the same kind of lovefest that transpired for Rebecca. Still, we had high hopes.

When we knocked, a woman opened the door unnervingly quickly, but then made no move to admit us. "I am Thea Demetriou and this is Julie Bishop." I held out my driver's license and a page of The Healing Project letterhead. "I called yesterday. We're from The…"

"I know who you are," Maggie Slaney said. She was probably sixty, maybe a little younger, nobly tall, her pretty face framed by messy whorls of thick, dove-colored hair.

"So you know why we've come," Julie said.

"Yes."

"May we come inside, please?"

"I'm not sure."

Julie had the ability to stand in one place and maintain a quiet dignity. I shuffled around as if my silk shirt was lined with red pepper. Finally, Julie said, "This is a beautiful place." The apron of lawn around the house rolled down to a quilt of neat, hedged fields.

"My family has lived on this land for six generations," Maggie Slaney said. "We thought that Jessamyn and Connor, that was her husband, would raise their family here. He was literally the boy next door. But they chose the city instead. Then Connor died, he died in a Jeep crash a few days into his first tour in Afghanistan. Another car wreck? Who says lightning doesn't strike twice? Jess was thinking about moving home here, with the girls. Rowena was only a newborn then. Maybe one of the girls will raise her family here." She raised her hand in a wave to the girls, who were playing badminton on the lawn. "They're only nine and eleven now. They spent all their summers here with me before, so it wasn't like my girl died and they landed on another planet. I'm thankful for that one thing. But that's a long time into the future from now. A lot could change. It's more likely they'll want to move back into the city than out here in dullsville."

Julie said, "They'd be lucky to have this."

"I wouldn't call anything about our situation lucky," Maggie said. She nodded downhill toward one of the fields. She still owned eighty acres. One had been planted in saffron by a hardworking hippie: It looked like an expanse of pale purple butterflies at roost.

Julie was undaunted. "But it is beautiful. And we want to try to change a tiny part of the luck."

Maggie Slaney looked at me then.

"You must be proud of your son," she said.

For a moment, I almost agreed. But there was something avid in her glance that warned me off.

"I'm sure you think he's a fine young man who made a terrible mistake and now he's trying to make amends." She smiled at me, but her eyes glittered.

"He's trying to do the best he can," I finally said.

"My Jessamyn is dead, and Belinda McCormack is dead, and the scum who killed them can just go on like nothing happened. Maybe they served some years as guests of the state. But then they get to go cut down a Christmas tree and have a future. And they have all these special programs to help them make a nice smooth transition back into society."

Julie said, "Maggie, I can understand how you hate hearing about anything good that would help people like this. But do you really think it's better for them to make a bad transition back into society? Wouldn't you rather that they at least tried? That they used their remorse to do something good?"

Maggie Slaney cocked an eyebrow. Then she opened the door all the way. We walked in and sat down in the tidy breakfast nook she pointed to. A few moments later, she brought a cake stand crowned with a brown sugar and pecan coffee cake and coffee so strong that my fingertips tingled after a single swallow. She smiled slightly as if reading my mind. "I figure why bother if you don't want to fill your tank? Coffee doesn't taste good enough to drink it decaffeinated. I generally have about ten cups a day. My husband used to say I could put my finger in a socket and light up the whole house." She shook her head. "He left me after the accident, when Jessamyn died. He couldn't handle the loss."

"I am so sorry," I said.

How would it have been if we had split up? From what little reading I had done about the families of criminals, I knew that the sundering of the family was a common consequence. I had been spared that. Unbidden, I thought of Jill, locked in her solitary cocoon of grace.

After offering us thick slices of cake—I stuffed mine down in about forty seconds and accepted a second, with coffee chasers— Maggie leaned back with her own mug, and she wasn't lying, it was the size of a beer stein. She said, "Just so you don't get the wrong idea. I have a rule that I don't let anyone into my house without offering them something. Don't think that because I have manners means I care about you or your son's project or Roman Villera. He's a waste of oxygen. I wish he was paralyzed. Every night, I wish on the first star that his wife and child die. Does that shock you?"

Neither of us could say a word.

"The only reason I let you come here is the money. I'm not sure I am going to accept it, but I owe it to Rosalind and Rowena to consider it. So what's the catch?"

"There is no catch," Julie said. "The Healing Project will set up a bank account into which Roman Villera pays a portion of his earnings into a savings account for Rosalind and Rowena. It can be used for their college education, or whatever else they decide. Our organization administers the account. Roman Villera will have no contact with you or your family."

Maggie waved at us as she'd waved at her granddaughters, and continued as if Julie had been speaking Mandarin. "Just so you know I'm not going to go public and talk about how grateful we are that this man wants to make restitution to Jessamyn's children. I'm not going to go on Dr. Phil and hug him. We'll take his money, and I might tell the girls what he did, I haven't decided that yet. It would only be to teach them that there's some good even in the lowest of the low. But we don't want anything to do with him."

"That's exactly what we're offering."

"And I will never forgive him." She held up a finger. "I will never. They gave me all these pamphlets at the grief support group. About how forgiveness is really not for the criminal, it's really for your own peace of mind, and how we're all human and we're all sinners, and there but for the grace of God. Now, I may be a sinner, but I don't give a shining shit if I am. I wish Roman Villera died in that crash, too; actually no, I wish he was paralyzed, because he's nothing but a useless piece of meat. It's not fair. I hope that us accepting his so-called renewal is the best thing that ever happens to him for the rest of his life."

She went on then to say that she wished she could forget Villera, but she was reminded of him every morning, the moment she got out of bed. Abruptly pulling up one cuff of her soft trousers, she displayed her prosthetic lower leg, the shape of an immersion blender but three times the size. Then she opened a manila folder that sat on the table the whole time, which I failed to notice. It was clearly there for her to show us.

"This is Jessamyn on her wedding day," she said. We gazed at the demure girl with her short crop of brown curls caught back in a band of crystals and pearls. "This is Jessamyn after the wreck." Her face was sheared in half, as if the top of her head had been opened like a can and the contents of her head, her glistening blue-gray brain and one of her eyes, spilled out over her cheeks. Her full lips made a soft pomegranate O of disbelief.

I found my feet and pivoted and plunged out through the screen door to the porch.

"Thank you, Maggie," I heard Julie say. "The project will be in touch about the bank account."

Once down the driveway, I had to make Julie pull the car over so I could throw up the cake and coffee.

"Oh baby, oh poor you," Julie said. "I have some wet wipes in the trunk. Wait." She got them out and pulled a few for me, rabbits from a hat. I sat in the weeds and scrubbed at my teeth and the collar of my shirt. "We should have known it could be like this."

"I thought it would be more civilized," I finally said, trying to blink the black stars away from my vision.

"I guess I did, too. But this is awful stuff, Thea. We shouldn't expect it to be sanitized, should we? People process unspeakable loss in whatever way they can, to find the strength to live with it and go on. And this might be just the beginning. Roman is not a bad man. He's a decent man who made a bad mistake, something you know all about. But some of the participants we might meet after this, well, like Merry says, they may be Saul, not Paul. There's a good chance they will be bad-deed doers who want to change. But the bad stuff they did, they might have done on purpose. That's what the project will have to face. That's what the real making of this effort is about."

"The worst of them, though, they wouldn't be sorry. Right?"

"I don't know," Julie said, and shrugged. "I don't know that many people who have killed other people."

"You sound like my mother now. They're not our sort of crowd. Most killers don't know very many people who've killed other people."

"That's true."

"What I meant is that I didn't know how awful it could be… on the other side of tragedy."

"Well, that woman would have been a perfectly nice person her whole life, with a husband, daughter and two grandkids, if none of this ever happened. Right?" I got back into the car, gratefully accepting Julie's offer of a bottle of water and a sleeve of saltines that she found in the trunk. What else did she have back there? She intuited my look and told me, chocolate bars, baby wipes, blankets. "I knew someday I might get stuck in my car but I decided that at least I'd never die of hunger or thirst." I smiled at her and tentatively patted her hand.

What business did we in fact have here at all? What titer of hubris so possessed us to think that we could right wrongs, repair damage, offer compensation—this much for an eye, this much for a limb, this much for a mother's love and protection, this much for a life? Good purpose was no defense. What I was experiencing, and Julie could not, was the plain recognition of the role reversal that had begun like the distant sound of sirens and now come roaring up with lights ablaze and knocked me flat. For the first time in a long time I thought of Jill. Not the menacing Jill. But my once-upon-a-time friend Jill. Jill, grief-stricken, deprived of her lovely daughter. Her Bindy. Her only.

Then I said, "Maggie has a right to her hate. But in my mind, even though this isn't true, in my mind…"

"Roman is Stefan."

"That's right."

"So maybe Jill has to be the next recipient of The Healing Project. If she is open to it. Maybe it is time for Stefan to express his deep remorse directly to her."

If I hadn't already been sitting down, my legs would have gone slack with the immensity of the realization. "That's impossible." But even as I said it, I knew Julie might be right.

"It certainly will not be easy," she said.

"Julie! There's an ocean of distance between easy and confronting Jill McCormack!"

"You don't have to be the one to confront her."

"What else could Stefan's plan for renewal be?"

"Remember the rules call for no direct contact between the participant and the victim's family," Julie said. "So I'm thinking the clearest message of remorse and amends might be for Stefan to offer to support Jill's organization SAY. If she would have him. He would have to make the case why in his letter. After all, she formed it in honor of Belinda."

But how would that even be possible? Why didn't Julie suggest that he run the hundred yards in nine seconds...or cure cancer? The idea was so outrageous that it bewildered me to respond. And that was before considering whether Jill would even allow it. Besides, wouldn't Stefan joining SAY somehow be seen as an admission on his part that he had physically abused Belinda before her death, something Stefan categorically denied. It could be seen as evidence to corroborate the belief that he was a habitual criminal who simply didn't get caught until his crime escalated and he committed the ultimate offense. Something I knew was not true. And yes, it could be powerful, a boost more effective for the message of SAY than any public relations campaign could ever be. But it would also wipe out any hope of a good opinion of Stefan from anyone who knew about his past. It would keep his past alive to be judged all over again. By new people.

"Honey," Julie said, "let's go home so you can clean up and maybe have a nap. Then, if you want, we'll go out and get a nice dinner and talk about it."

I tried to force lightness into my voice, but the tears had a stranglehold. "Do you think he could really go through with that? Joining SAY? Would they even have him? Stefan shied away from any kind of violence. He flinched when someone hit a woman or a kid on TV. He really believes in that message, in that sense. The police told us that they tried to find evidence that he was violent with Belinda before that night, but they couldn't find any. They were pretty eager to charge him with whatever assault they could."

"Well, no one can charge him with anything else now. It's Stefan who clearly thinks he got off too easy. Remember The Healing Project was his idea after all," Julie said. "That's coming from somewhere. And maybe it will turn out to be enough." She paused for a moment and drained her own bottle of water, then handed me another one. "Did you ever ask him how they seemed when they were together that fall up there in Black Creek? Did you ask any of their friends who might have seen something? Knew something?"

"I didn't know any of their friends from up there. He was only there a week or so full-time when it happened. We had just seen Belinda for the holidays...afterward, I assumed the police did all that. I just concentrated on taking care of what was right in front of me. Stefan. First in rehab and then in jail. We didn't spend the time we had together talking about the...the past."

"Did you ever contact the detectives afterward and follow up?"

"No," I said.

Julie said, "Why not?"

Why not indeed. Since the night in the hospital when Detective Pete Sunday described the injury that the golf club had wrought to the back of Belinda's head—and in a blurt of new nausea I now realized that image was now twinned in my mind with the photo of Jessamyn we had just seen—I hadn't dared to risk knowing anything more. In fact, I made it a point not to know anything more. Who in my situation would want to? What good could it possibly do? Or was I just too locked in shock to question anything at all? I just knew I had to move forward.

Until Stefan came home from prison, unless I was at work or on my way to visit him there, I deliberately fuddled my con-

sciousness. There was no trial as such, just a judge who heard
Stefan's guilty plea and the lawyer's account of our son's lack of
intent and diminished capacity. When we heard the sentence,
we felt relieved, lucky even. After that, I had one purpose, keeping Stefan alive until he could come home. I didn't want to
know about the rest of the world. It worked alarmingly well, as
if I'd brought on my own early dementia. I even started losing
things, not just the customary car keys or folder of papers, but my
grandmother's opal watch and my first edition of *A Tree Grows
in Brooklyn*, Jep's gift to me when I completed my PhD. Being
a part-time eccentric during that period of time was a fair price
for a mind that was free from fomenting bad thoughts. But it
had its pitfalls. If it was late at night and I was vulnerable to in-
trusive thoughts, I could get comfortably foggy with two pills
or two fingers of Scotch, or both, until I was well on my way
to four pills and four fingers of Scotch and had to give that up
entirely. I still tried to keep Stefan's account of his vague memories of that night in the abstract—the screams and shadows and
then one terrible, dull sound, everything happening in the time
it takes to speak it, a twenty-second interval when the gleam-
ing train of Belinda's future slammed to a halt.

So why did I want to bring everything into sharp focus now?
I didn't, not at all. Yet how could I ever put this behind me if
I didn't first face it? I might finally need to muster the courage
I lacked before—to know more, to know everything, to know
the specifics of that horrific night that were as much a blur to
me as they were to Stefan, who'd at least had the courage to
face his journey of redemption.

The girl caller had repeatedly told me I didn't know everything about that night. Longing Esme of Belinda's poems, un-
shriven and suffering, now clearly thought she needed me. I had
her number. She came and went like smoke. Maybe my husband
was right, that she was no more than a fantasist or a creep. If she

was, she was a fiercely persistent one. It was time to call her back.
I reached down into my bag to grab my phone and texted her.

Please answer: I'm wondering if you're safe.

My phone brrr'ed right then, and I almost dropped it.
But it wasn't Longing Esme. It was Jep.
"I can't talk right now," I said, rushing into the gap after he
said hello. "We've just seen this woman, the first one..."
"Honey, are you on your way home?"
"Why? Did something happen to Stefan?" A new hot taste
of that damned cake rushed up my throat.
"Stefan is fine, and I'm fine. But something happened here."
"What?"
"Someone's apparently been in the house. And it's...not
good."
What someone had done was indeed not good; it was not really damaging, but it made my home feel like it was a haunted
house.
Jep met me and Julie at the door and said, in exactly the way
guaranteed to make you do just that, "Now, don't flip out."
As my father's daughter, I had an extravagant number of
his beautiful family photos, matted at the Papierie in identical
museum-quality frames. There was a lush image of me in a white
dress, sitting with newborn Stefan in my arms, among fabric-
draped knolls that looked like a collection of clouds. There was
Stefan, at twelve, hoisting a glistening bass on a line; Jep and
Stefan grinning at each other after the All-Conference football
championship. And an addition that my father recently took,
one with my stubborn hopefulness and my father's tenderness on
display, of Stefan in a torn tee shirt leaning out of the window of
his truck, the bed of which looked like a parade float, mounded
with barrels and baskets and clay pots filled with flowers. On
the wall nearby was one of Jep, Stefan and me on an expanse of

white steps above the blue, blue Aegean, taken in Santorini the summer after Stefan's sophomore year of high school, a trip my parents hosted for our whole family. To each of these photos, someone had taken a black marker and blackened out Stefan's eyes—not on the photos themselves, but on the glass covering the images. Whoever did this hadn't stopped with the photos in the living room. Blighted also was the photo of Stefan and Belinda on Stefan's nightstand. Circles as small as periods blackened out Stefan's newborn eyes; bigger blots canceled his eyes in the photo with the truck. Over those other photos—of my father's parents and of me and Alzy Hodge on election day, giant X's were drawn in black. My first move was to check my cherished photo albums, a parade of road trips, lost teeth, first days of school, the groundbreaking for the addition to this house five years ago, all lined up in dated order on the lowest bookshelf. But the photos in those albums were unmarked.

"I don't get this," Jep said. "But I do know now what they mean when they say people who are burglarized feel violated."

Julie said, "Is Stefan home?"

Jep said, "So far as I know, he's at work. No, wait. He left a note. He went to Milwaukee with Will for something."

"Did they break a lock or a window?" Julie said.

The moment she said it, I knew exactly how someone had gained entry. The sliding glass door that led from our basement onto a small patio was just a hair short of flush, and impossible to lock. I was always going to get it replaced; but it was expensive, and even with the protestors, I felt who cared? And as creepy as the hooded figure was, I never actually felt he would come threaten us in our home. It was Portland, Wisconsin, after all. And real crime in Portland was about as common as pineapple plants.

I told Jep about the glass door.

"And you didn't have it fixed? Despite what's going on. People throwing eggs at our house and walking around with hate signs."

"It didn't occur to me. I guess I always felt safe in our neighborhood. Besides, you live here too. Why didn't you have it fixed?"

"I have a few other things on my mind, Thea! I'm not on sabbatical, and my work demands…"

"What about my work? Writing a book and helping Stefan start an organization too…"

Julie said, "Guys, guys, don't take this out on each other…"

Ignoring her, I said, "Do you believe me now, Jep? This is a sign, it's a sign from them that they know how to get to him anytime they want…"

"From who?" Julie said.

Jep said, "I'm calling the police. Now."

I shouted, "No! What are the police going to do? Say it's harassment? Duh! Dust for fingerprints? I assure you, they won't find any."

"I'm still calling."

"Jep, just wait. Please, not now. Give me a little time to gather my thoughts. I think I know…"

Jep said, "You don't know."

"I'm going to find out!"

"And because you're Sherlock Demetriou, nobody will bother you, of course."

None of us noticed Stefan standing in the hallway arch until he said, "What fresh hell is this?" I couldn't decide whether to acknowledge the old Dorothy Parker reference or try to block the view of the pictures. I had been away all day. So had Jep and Stefan. Suddenly I realized this meant that someone had been watching our house. How else would they know when no one would be here? I thought of the menacing hooded figure; but every time I saw him, he kept at a distance. The unquiet yet personal nature of the attack was repugnant to me: Marking out Stefan's eyes was to make him blind—to the truth? To the future? It was a mutilation, and not just of the pictures. Our whole psychic space was polluted by the phantom presence of someone slipping through our own landscape, inspecting and handling our own things, ordinary objects rendered sacred by the breach.

Julie gave me a hug, then left quietly. Jep and I quit picking at each other, and the three of us huddled together. Then we made some tea with lots of sugar, the way they do in those BBC mystery shows. Half-heartedly, Jep suggested Jill McCormack might be behind this, and then the three of us exchanged looks. Jill hadn't occurred to me, but Stefan said, "It's just that, yeah, she hates me, but this seems a little bit…"

"Over the top," I said. "Even for Jill."

"Do you really think that Stefan's in danger?" Jep said. He suggested then that Stefan might want to go stay with his grandparents for a while. They were just across town. He wouldn't have to interrupt work.

But Stefan said, "I'm not going anywhere. Unless you want me out of here, which I would respect, Dad, since you've put up with a lot. But I feel like I have to stand my ground. It's like, this is my home. This is my place. Do your worst."

I would be lying if I told you that I didn't imagine, in that moment, what the worst could turn out to be, not ever reckoning that the worst would be beyond my imagination.

Stefan said then, "This is actually good. In some weird way, I feel like it gives me a new kind of energy. This just makes me want to send a message to the world, even more. About myself. About what I'm trying to do. With The Healing Project. Do I call Channel 15 now, or what?"

I struggled to take this in. The timing could not possibly be worse, given the threats that came earlier. What I wanted was to scream at him, Don't you dare! How stupid are you? You can't invite any more attention!

But I fought down my revulsion. He was pushing back, as a person should do.

It was then that I remembered the card the red-haired PBS

producer had handed me months ago. All this time, it was in the small wastepaper basket next to the door: It had become stubbornly lodged in one of the wicker plaits and it never seemed worth my time to pick it free. I got it out and handed it to Stefan.

"Do you trust this lady?" he said.

"I don't even know her. She's just another reporter. I guess I assume that public TV people have cleaner hands, which is stupid. She could just want to crucify you, like all the rest."

"Well, I need to try," he said and took out his phone. He looked so sad that it was as if he'd already accepted the tragic fate that was his, and I had to turn away from the sight. "Ms. Kessler? My name is Stefan Christiansen...yes, I figured you'd know... I wanted to know if you want to do an interview or something with me...sure, my mom would do it too."

I shook my head violently, but then closed my eyes and nodded and left the room.

My face in the hall mirror was as red as if I'd hiked uphill, and I stepped out onto the porch and hauled in lungfuls of air. As my eyes adjusted to the dim falling light of late afternoon, across the street nearer the corner, leaning against a bus stop sign, was the slight figure in the hoodie and aviator sunglasses. He raised his hand and pointed at me, making the gesture of firing a pistol. A scream beat at my throat like a trapped bird. Then the bus arrived and when it pulled away, he was gone.

7

If Stefan was seeking public attention for his cause, now he would get it.

"It will be okay. It's about something different," Stefan explained to me, anxiety carving his young face into sharp lines. "It's something positive."

I didn't want to damage his hope, but I knew the danger here.

"I do so want you to be part of this, too," the producer Deanie Kessler said when she called me back. "I think it will help Stefan feel more confident."

No punch pulled, no heartstring untugged.

"What could anyone want to know about me?"

"You could explain, as Stefan's mother, what it's like to be you."

"There's no sympathy for that. For the mother of the monster."

"Don't be so sure, Thea. How many other people do you think have stood in your shoes?"

I started to splutter out a further objection, but she went on.

"How many other people are broken because they have to live with the fact that their children have done something awful? Ordinary people, who tried to live careful lives. They always tried to do the right thing. They are terrified for their kids but also furious with them for dismantling their precious dreams. Maybe people need to see that other side. Maybe they need to understand it. Maybe they need to know they're not alone."

If she had given me the traditional something-good-can-come-of-this rap, I could have more easily turned my back. But now I thought of Roman Villera's mother and the grief in that brief glance. "You can tell your side. You're not really a woman who raised a monster. And maybe some people whose stories are even worse will feel better."

"Whose stories could be worse?"

But I knew there were worse cases. The lawyer who represented Stefan at his arraignment had a client who was all of fourteen when he killed his mother, her sister and her parents at Thanksgiving dinner: I would never forget the man telling me that Thanksgiving was apparently a favorite setting for these kinds of massacres. He was able to get the kid released into his father's custody after just eighteen months. I remembered, also, thinking at the time, how could his father want him?

How, indeed?

"Anyway," Deanie Kessler went on, "Of course the big focus is on The Healing Project to consider. It's been quite the thing, right? We talked with the Hodges and Roman Villera. Mrs. Slaney was definitely not interested! But maybe this way of focusing on it, Stefan can get credit for doing something really positive. And maybe more people will volunteer for the project. Maybe it can happen in other places."

"Do you think people who see this will really give him credit?" I said, even as I thought, do you think some crazy will kill him?

Deanie Kessler answered, "Those who will, will, and those

who won't have their own issues. Stefan's won't be the only story that's featured. The series is about the issues that face people re-entering the community after incarceration. We'll focus on four individuals over the two hours, Stefan, two young women and one very successful older man."

The series was called *In Our Times*. It was about people who found themselves in the middle of hot-button social topics. Previous episodes centered around hometown racism, animal activists and the crisis facing the family farm.

To his credit, Stefan had set stern guidelines: The story was to highlight Stefan's rehabilitation efforts and The Healing Project. It was not to be about his own case or dig deeper into the night of the murder; it was to be about the process of trying to reclaim his life. The show would comprise interviews with us in our home, or on a walk in the arboretum, in comfortable places, not in front of an audience. Deanie Kessler agreed to all the conditions.

The day approached. I got more and more tense. I thought of my university colleagues. I thought of members of my book club. It wasn't as though they didn't know what had happened, at least that Stefan had been released. But I knew there were people who would think he was trying to make excuses for his conduct or to distract from his crime. I knew there were people who might think the same things about me. And yet, if they were going to gossip, let them. I couldn't stop them, and, with everything else I had to worry about, there was no room for further unproductive stewing.

The night before, I asked Stefan again, "Do you really want me to be part of this? It's not my story."

"Well, it is partly your story, too, Mom. I would like you to, but it's not essential." Too quietly, he reminded me that I didn't have to defend him. I reminded him, in turn, that it would be myself I was defending; and he pointed out that I didn't have to do that, either.

Jep, who disapproved of the whole thing, went upstairs to
finish packing, tossing back over his shoulder that he was grateful he would be out of town and not to let anyone photograph
his hip-high pile of old jerseys that he kept on the floor of our
walk-in closet and kept insisting had "plenty of life left in them."

Deanie Kessler emailed us a sheet of tips for looking and feeling comfortable on camera.

For probably the first time in ten years, I overslept.

"This has to be some kind of psychological defense mecha-
nism," I said to Stefan from the hall. His door was ajar and I
pushed it open, to find him reclining on the bed in just a pair
of sweatpants. He snapped the laptop closed and sat up so fast
it almost tumbled to the floor. Porn, I thought, for a moment
irritated and then relenting, remembering being his age, when
you couldn't imagine that anybody could live without sex for
a whole day.

"Could you maybe knock?"

"Could you maybe trouble yourself to get dressed," I said.
"You were the one who wanted to do this and they're already
down there in front of the house." Filming the protestors, I
thought but did not say. I glanced out through the window at
the end of the hall and saw that some of Jill's girls were especially dressed up and dramatic that morning with brand-new
picket signs. Ready for their close-up, I thought.

Stefan rolled to his feet and said, "I am dressed, almost."

"You're not going to wear sweatpants for this."

"What should I wear, a tuxedo?"

"Not the time or the place, Stefan. Just wear something normal." A few minutes later, he came down in dark brown cor-
duroys and a caramel-colored long-sleeved tee shirt. He tried
to smile and so did I, but both of us were too anxious to fake it
effectively. Grateful that Stefan would be interviewed first, and
that his interview wouldn't start for at least an hour, I grabbed
my bag and headed to the local salon down the block to get my

hair blown out, bringing along the fifty dollars' worth of new makeup I had bought a few days earlier on impulse at the mall. The stylist had offered to help me apply it. I wasn't exactly virginal about makeup, but I had no idea how to make the "bolder eyes" and "outspoken cheekbones" that online videos assured me were necessary for a camera-ready look. When the stylist was finished, I was startled, if not displeased, by my own image in the mirror. It was as if I was impersonating myself, wearing a costume of an unflappable, regal Thea who did this sort of thing every day. Which sort of defines exactly what I was doing.

Back at home, I changed into tights and boots and a long tunic in a plain, cheerful color. Was it green? Was it plum? Though I would watch the show several times, then and since, I would have a hard time, for reasons that weren't clear beforehand, remembering details. I do remember being sick with nerves. I had never been on TV, at least not willingly, only captured in my own driveway or running into the courthouse in Black Creek—pictures that made me look deranged or drugged, the way actors look when you're watching a movie and you hit Pause.

As I came into the kitchen, Deanie Kessler said, "Don't worry, Thea. I'm not going to trap you." So many people were milling around that I felt like a guest. "I can't say that this will be easy, but it won't be as bad as you fear." She looked very young, and all those tumbled red curls were disarming.

"Are you going to trap Stefan?"

"Of course not."

"Are you going to make him talk about the night of Belinda's death?"

"I said I wouldn't."

In the end, there was no choice but to believe her.

Deanie Kessler went over some questions that didn't sound particularly threatening—about the experience of having a relative incarcerated, my feelings about the protestors and the reactions of family to Stefan's homecoming.

We decided to shoot in the backyard. From the hedge break, Charlie Ribosky watched as Stefan sat down at our patio table and the crew wired him up. I stood near the back door, appalled as several other neighbors drifted into Charlie's yard and lined up next to Charlie.

"If you can't hear, you can get closer, Charlie!" I called. The group pretended to disband but really just slipped behind a taller portion of Charlie's privet hedge.

Showtime!

Deanie Kessler told us that she had recorded a brief introduction to the series and this program earlier, thus it would be possible to get straight down to business.

"So we're not here to talk about the crime, Stefan. We're not here to talk about prison. We're here to talk about what comes after you did your time. What do you want people to know about you today, Stefan? What do you want people to know about starting over?"

"It's hard," he said. "A lot harder than you think. I didn't know what to expect but it can take your heart out. At first, it feels like no one will ever trust you again, and nothing you do can ever make you anything but a loser."

He talked for a few moments about incarceration. "The punishment you get doesn't take away the responsibility. I think there's a responsibility to do something good, too, not just survive prison and go on with your life. Like a counterweight, not that it would really have the same weight. That is my reason for starting The Healing Project."

"Now, this is like a platform for people to do something for their victims or their families. Are you your own first client, Stefan?"

"No, I'm not," Stefan said. "The first participant was a woman who broke into a summer cottage up north when she was a teenager and trashed it with her friends. She never even got caught. Those same girls are grown-up women now, and the owners of the cabin are grandparents in their eighties. To make amends, they went up there and fixed up the cabin and stocked it with all kinds of food and wine and stuff. I helped with that."

Stefan obtained permission from his parole officer to travel for one day to northern Wisconsin, outside his fifty-mile radius. Amelia wrote a letter of apology and her husband Andy and Stefan and a carpenter friend of Andy's fixed the porch, the roof and the door frames of the old cabin. Then my sister pitched in and they all cleaned it planks to rafters, laying in every manner of canned staple and delicacy for summers to come. The owners barely remembered the break-in but said afterward they were moved literally to tears. Amelia felt as though she'd lost twenty pounds. Stefan proffered Deanie long-ago Polaroids of the destruction, which the couple had given their insurance company, and of the renewed cabin. He also gave her a cardboard rendering of the official logo of The Healing Project, the silver arrow turning to gold.

Deanie laid both the photos and the logo aside, promising that the broadcast would feature them and the number to call The Healing Project. Something walked lightly across the back of my neck. I was like a dog that could feel a thunderstorm coming.

"So to be a participant in The Healing Project, the person has to state their remorse in writing. How about you, Stefan? Have you done that?"

"I have. My remorse was the inspiration for this program. My renewal was starting it."

"Can you tell the viewers what you said?"

"I said I was responsible for the death of the girl I loved. Belinda McCormack."

"You hit her with a golf club and killed her."

"Yes."

"Why?"

"I really don't know what happened. I really don't. I took a lot of drugs in the evening."

"More than usual?"

"Well there was no usual. At first, it was just that I took…well, methamphetamine to keep up…with school. With Belinda. She was so much smarter, and I was worried all the time."

"Worried about school?"

"Yes, worried that if I messed up school, I would have to drop out and I would lose her. Because she wouldn't respect me anymore."

"So," Deanie said, leaning in. "Why was this night different?"

"Well, I was upset. So I took a bunch of drugs. Different kinds. Whatever the person I was with offered me. Crack cocaine. Heroin. And I don't have any memory of anything that night except that I ended up in the hospital."

"You were upset," she said, in a level tone. Then she waited. It was fascinating to watch. She knew full well that no one could endure the silence for very long.

"I was upset because I heard… I knew that, well, for sure I was going to lose her."

"You were angry at Belinda."

"No. Not exactly. Not… I just wanted to keep her. I wanted to plead with her."

"You didn't want somebody else to have her."

Stefan pressed his fingers against his eyes. "Of course not. Nobody would want somebody else to have the girl you love, right? That doesn't mean I was some insane psycho…" He stopped. "Don't do this to me. Don't make me sound worse than I already am."

Deanie softened. "Okay, we won't use that last moment. I promise. Let's go on." She tapped her knee with her silver pencil. "So you are blaming your drug use for what you did?"

"No. Or in part. I just started to use drugs for the first time that fall when I was hanging out with Belinda's friends." He looked up, pleadingly. "I told you why."

I could feel doubt walk along my arms like an electrical pulse.

I knew Stefan was prepared for her to move on, past the death. This was supposed to be the kinder, gentler version? What about Deanie Kessler's promise? If this wasn't a trap, why did it feel that way?

"Was Belinda afraid of you?"

Stefan sat back and almost laughed. I gasped. He recovered as if it were a kind of cough and glanced around him. He said, "No. Not at all." But I knew that somehow, the camera could make a nervous grimace into a casual smirk.

"Why did she have a golf club in her apartment then?"

"Because she was a golfer. Her mom is a professional golfer. She gave Belinda a set of her clubs when she went to college."

"And so you served a couple of years in prison and then you came home. And you live right around the block from where Belinda lived?"

"I live in the same house I've lived in all my life. I'm glad to be home, for sure. I want to fit in. But of course, everywhere I look, I think about Belinda and I miss her. We were best friends all our lives, even growing up."

"Okay, let's break for a moment."

Stefan sighed, and pulled his shirt away from his chest as if to cool himself off.

"You're doing great," I told him, as the makeup artist descended with a huge powder brush. "You really are. Just keep it low-key. He's doing great, isn't he?" I said to Deanie.

"Yep," she said. I felt those electrical pulses again.

The crew took a break. One of the camera operators asked Deanie Kessler if they should get a dolly ready to film a walk through the neighborhood. I quickly put a lid on that idea.

"You're not going to walk him past those marchers," I said. By law, the protestors weren't allowed to gather before nine in the morning, so we tried to be on our way to wherever we needed to go well before that time. But if Stefan or any of us was late getting out, the group would chant. *Listen, Stefan! Stop Abuse Young! Save a Young Life!* And *Stefan, say, say, say her name!*

"No, I'm thinking," Deanie said. "We might finish with both of you at the arboretum later on. But let's just move to another setting out here. Maybe by the tree?" I brought a pitcher of iced tea. There were several takers. As they bustled about, I kept searching their eyes for clues about the way they felt; but when they took a break or moved things around, they were breezy and impassive, telling jokey stories to each other about their upcoming weekend plans. Someone asked if I preferred "Dr. Thea Demetriou" to "Professor Thea Demetriou," and I said no, professor was fine…and using no title at all was fine too. "We just have to write it on the files. Deanie will put it up."

It was time to start up again.

Deanie steered the questioning back to Belinda's death. "Stefan, you said you were desperate to keep her. Why desperate? You were still together when Belinda went away to Black Creek for college."

"I thought, the more people she met, the more just stupid I would seem. I couldn't think of her with someone else. I would have waited forever for her. But I was losing her. And my reaction was, I was putting pressure on her to stay with me."

"Did she say it was over?"

"No, but she needed a chance to see who she really wanted to be." Like all good interviewers, Deanie Kessler knew that sometimes, it was just better to wait, because people will plunge in to fill the silence. "She was my best friend. We loved each other enough that we figured that we could work everything out somehow and get married anyhow and have a family. She wanted that, too. I had to let her find herself."

"But you couldn't."

Stefan roughly struck tears from his cheekbones with the heels of his hands. "I could sense that she was with someone else."

"An older boy?"

"No, not that. It was a girl. I knew that Belinda was bisexual, but I thought she was just experimenting... I was just a kid. I didn't know."

My eyes blurred. The poems snapped into place like a gorgeous Scrabble word, like *quickly* or *maximize*, for which all the parts had been there but not in the right order. Perhaps Longing Esme was never just Belinda's persona, her alter ego, but a real person, her lover, her muse. So was the Esme of Belinda's poetry actually the girl caller? The voice who said she knew everything? Was that why she was so scared and so sad? Why would she think that the possibility of Stefan talking about her and Belinda would mean that nobody would love her anymore? In this day and age? Did the girl's parents not know, as I had to believe that Jill had not known? As I had not? Was that all there was to it? If so, why all the threats to our son's welfare? Sadness and fear didn't square up with repeated warnings about Stefan keeping his mouth shut if he knew what was good for him. I glanced back at the window, my living room transformed into a sound stage beyond it. So much for keeping his mouth shut.

In that moment, I almost wanted to go find Jill and put my arms around her, gentle, conservative, devout Jill. For her, this show might feel like another loss, a very public wound. All the cats were now out of the bag and rolling around on the carpet.

"What do you want people to know, Stefan?"

Pale, now clearly on the ropes, Stefan took a breath and persevered. "I want people to know that I'm not doing all this just to prove a point. I really want to make a difference in the world, however I can. And I want Belinda's mother, Jill, to know that I'm against dating violence too, and I will help with the mission of SAY. I'll talk about raising awareness and how girls can tell if they're in an abusive relationship."

"Do you think Belinda should have known?"

Stefan said, "I'm telling a truth that no one will believe. It makes it almost impossible for me to move along in my life. But truly I never abused Belinda."

Deanie just let Stefan's words sit there. She didn't respond. In a moment, she nodded crisply. The segment was over. Stefan took off the mic by himself and went inside.

Now it would be my turn.

Why had I given Stefan her business card? Why had I agreed to this? Why wasn't Stefan here, encouraging me, like I'd encouraged him?

I was still gasping from Stefan's revelation about Belinda. And I was shocked at myself for being so shocked.

The crew began by filming me supposedly writing at my desk, then moved quickly to my kitchen table where I had spread out the materials for my upcoming book. Deanie Kessler introduced me, then asked me to explain what the book was about. And I skipped right into a snare: "Women in literature who were obsessed, with men mostly but also with society and the dangerous amusements there, with their reputations..."

As if listening to a simultaneous translator, I reflected on how my words sounded—even as I spoke them.

Great. Just great.

"Don't use that part about my book," I told Deanie Kessler.

"Why not? It was really just a warm-up question anyhow but tell me what bothers you about it."

This was like therapy.

"Nothing," I said, guaranteeing that the quote would make it past the final edit.

From that moment, every word I said seemed fatuous. I *knew* my son. I *knew* that the awful event that happened was an aberration. How? He *told* me. I *knew* Stefan was basically a gentle person. He even chose not to play college football because it was too rough.

"Given everything, given what he did to this girl, can you say that your love for your only son has never diminished?"

"I...of course not. I love him. You never stop loving your child."

The final segment featuring me would last about eight minutes. The whole time the crew of *In Our Times* spent at our house comprised about eight hours, which felt like eight years. Finally, as I was watching the crew pack their gear and leave, they waved to the protestors, who waved back. Exhausted, I retreated upstairs to my bedroom.

Early one evening a couple of weeks later, I was in that bedroom again with my sister Amelia and Julie. We lay three across on my bed in a row, relaxed as kindling in a box, and watched the segment. Downstairs, Stefan and Jep watched the show with Amelia's husband, Andy.

Why was I surprised to discover they had interviewed Jill?

I should not have been surprised.

Why was I surprised when a third of our segment was devoted to her contention that the community was in danger when violent offenders were released, and that was why the work of SAY was more important than ever? Why was I surprised when she said that Belinda chose to go to college in Black Creek yes, in a youthful rebellion against her strict Southern Baptist upbringing, but also to escape Stefan's increasingly controlling behavior?

Dating violence wasn't even considered domestic abuse in some states, she said, and it was rarely reported—like rape a couple of generations ago. Jill's organization had grown and now hosted events at high schools and colleges. There was now a phone network, staffed by girls for girls, to say, yes, what you're going through is wrong and it has to stop. If Belinda could have spoken about what she was going through, Jill said, she might still be alive today. "I'm really proud of the young women of SAY. They're strong and beautiful. There are more than seven thousand SAY volunteers around the country, including some young men, because they get abused as well. If Belinda could see this, she would be so gratified. I hope she can see it."

Belinda never used drugs, Jill added. She understood why Stefan was suddenly offering to support SAY, but clearly, that would be inappropriate. Offenders like Stefan should not be allowed to come back to the places they lived before.

"But what if their support system is there?" said the host. "That's so key to staying on the right path."

Jill shrugged.

"Protecting the innocent comes first," she said. "Our whole society has failed to protect the innocent, and so our whole society has failed."

Chopin's "Nocturne in C Sharp Minor" accompanied a photo montage—a family Christmas before Belinda's father died, Jill and Belinda on a dock kicking droplets of water into the air, Stefan and Belinda swing-dancing, Jill majestic in black lace at Belinda's funeral, SAY protestors circling the state capitol, Jill unfurling a petition of thousands of names, then a photo of Jep and Stefan, forehead to forehead through the open car window the night he came home—the picketers and TV cameras a smeared traffic of light in the background...and the last one, of Stefan and Will in April on the golf course at Nine Springs.

Who had taken that? Who had been watching Stefan swing a golf club?

Amelia winced. She said, "Now that's subtle."

There was also a photo montage of our family, and I had no idea where those pictures had come from—of Stefan playing with Molly when Molly was a puppy, Belinda and Stefan dressed as playing cards for a school party, Stefan and Jep after a football game. Stefan's edited account of his time since prison sounded authentic, and even Maggie Slaney gave him credit for his effort with The Healing Project.

My own words closed our portion of the show: "A person has to be seen as more than the worst thing he has ever done."

Julie said, "I thought Stefan did just great. You too."

"I hope something good comes from it," I told her. "Or at least, I hope nothing bad comes from it."

We listened to the guys rattling around downstairs, the refrigerator opening and closing, a muffled laugh from Andy. We ventured quietly downstairs.

"...like watching a train wreck," Jep said.

"Not him, though," Andy said. "I was proud of him. He was direct and honest."

I stepped down into the kitchen, where all of them were eating slices of pastrami out of the butcher's wrapping, first dipping the slices in a saucer of mustard. If anyone felt a lack of composure, it wasn't evident from their food consumption. "I was the one who looked like a train wreck?"

"They meant Jill, listening to Jill, and I know what Dad means. It just rolls right over anything you have to say because she has the moral imperative," Stefan said.

I thought of all the other narratives, the girl who sold the drugs, the drugs themselves, all part of my quest to find another story, another part of a story, all part of that niggling sense that there was something I didn't know, something that was important, stoked by the caller with the sobbing voice, her assurances that she knew the truth and that Stefan was in danger. Was this all because, even after all this time, my own mind was incapable of fully accepting the one truth? And yet, I didn't know that Stefan was part of a love triangle. Why had Stefan never said so, in so many words? Or hadn't I given him a chance? I assumed that what I had heard was the truest thing, that Belinda was avoiding Stefan because he got too deep into drugs and she had no use for that. Even Julie wondered why I hadn't asked the police about Belinda and Stefan's friends, why I had never looked through the police reports.

I decided right then that I would do this. It was the last stone, but it was unturned. And then I would get on with my life, no more digging in the ashes. I would call the detective, Pete Sunday, tomorrow, and ask him to send me the files.

"I'm going to Will's. See you in the morning," Stefan said.

"Wait," I said. "Did this do what you wanted it to?"

He stopped for a moment and went into the kitchen cupboard where I kept a bin with spare toiletries, rummaging until he found a disposable razor and a toothbrush, which he put in his pocket.

"Mom, I'm going to go to church tomorrow. Meet me there?"

I swallowed hard, and nodded.

"I'll take the truck. The truck is behind you. So you can get out in the morning, Mom. I'm not going to hide."

Andy said, "Good man."

"I wish I hadn't done it though," Stefan continued.

"Son, you tried to express your truth and that's all you can ask of yourself," Jep said.

"But I looked fat," Stefan said. "I looked like I had three chins."

We all stood there flat-footed for a moment. Andy was the first one who laughed but eventually, uneasily, we all did. I mean, you're a twenty-year-old guy. What else would you notice?

Late that night I got a text: Curt Cowrie from The American Association of Mental Health Nurses (AMEN). Give me a call. I have an idea. Anytime is ok.

There was one more text, from the area code shared by Black Creek college and the prison nearby. It said,

Longing Esme/broken grace/passion buried/under lace.

She picked up on the first ring. "I didn't call you," she said.

"I called you. I have to ask you something. You said you were there that night. Were you Belinda's girlfriend?"

There was a long, slightly liquid pause. And then, with the

kind of little breath catch that a baby makes falling asleep, she said, "Why would you say that?"

"What is this truth you say you know?"

"You can't call me anymore. I can't talk to you anymore. Bad things will happen. I'm sorry."

She hung up.

The phone pinged again. I glanced down, no text. But a few moments later, a voice mail showed up. Was anyone asleep tonight? I put the phone on speaker, then decided against it and pressed the phone to my ear.

"Thea, this is Jill McCormack calling. This isn't over, Thea. But I've decided that there won't be any more protestors near your house. Good night."

Good night.

I lay back down and must have slept. When I woke up again, still feeling awful, flu-like, what I could see from my window looked like one of those lurid sunrises that make false promises for the beauty of the newborn day.

But it wasn't sunrise. I knew that when I heard Molly whimpering and growling and saw the rolling lights of the fire trucks and heard the banging at the front door. I ran down to open it and saw that the rosy glow came from the old Mitsubishi, which was now on fire in the driveway.

8

The fire demolished more than my sister's vintage junker. It wiped out Stefan's confidence too.

Heartbroken, I watched as he parked his truck and stepped onto the porch the next morning. He looked to the left and to the right, then ducked inside, glancing around him as he sprinted.

"I'm fine!" he snapped at me before I could say a word.

Jep said he wanted to install alarms and follow lights.

"Those are good ideas," said the young police officer who came. She went outside to scold the crime-scene investigators who'd left strips of sticky paper and sticks of blue chalk on the driveway ("Didn't your mom ever make you clean up your room?"). "But something like this is up close and crazy. It feels like a grudge, don't you think? The bad thing about a grudge, it's personal. The good thing about a grudge is that most wear out with time. I'm not going to ask if there's anybody who has it in for you. I know your story. The best thing you can do is exercise more caution than you ordinarily do, and we'll be watching, every night for a good long while, for anything that looks funny."

A good long while: This just suggested that more was on the way. Who was behind this? I was convinced that the answer wouldn't turn up on Washtenaw Street in Portland.

I called Pete Sunday that afternoon.

"I want to see copies of all the police reports from the night Belinda McCormack died. Not just the ones that pertain specifically to Belinda's death. I want copies of those too. But I want to see any copies of anything having to do with the drugs he might have been on—whether there were bad drugs circulating at the time that might account for Stefan's behavior that night. There must be all kinds of things I didn't see. From the…the autopsy. And the way that the…crime scene looked. I never saw all that."

"Mrs. Christiansen, why would you? You already had access to all of the relevant documents."

"I only remember hearing about the report dealing with the emergency call at the time of Belinda's death, and I'm not sure it was complete at the time."

Pete Sunday sighed, but somehow, I could tell that it wasn't from impatience or boredom. He actually didn't know what to say. It had been several years since that night in the hospital; but I could still picture him, a sharp-dressed man seemingly out of place in the Northwoods hamlet. Belinda's death had been the most shocking case of his career; to be fair, it would have been among the most shocking cases of anyone's career outside Baltimore.

"Mrs. Christiansen, there's a limit to what I can share with you."

"Okay."

"Okay what?"

"Can you make copies and mail them to me? Or email them?"

"I can't mail police reports. We can discuss what you need to see. You'd have to come up here and pick up any reports. The ones I can give you anyhow. Which I'm not sure what they are."

"I...don't want to," I told him.

He said, "Well, sure. That makes sense. But we don't mail copies of police reports. To anybody. If you want them you have to come up here and fill out a formal request form."

So that was how I ended up making the decision to go back to Black Creek, to make a journey I had formally forsworn, dragging the ballast of my own misgivings and my family's disapproval.

"Don't go," said Stefan. "The place is bad luck."

"Wait," said Jep, "for better weather, better timing, for me to come with you."

"I have to do it now," I told them both. "I need to know more now. I need to read everything they have on file. I don't remember what I actually saw and what the lawyer told us. And I just have to put my own mind at rest. I want to read the police report thoroughly now. And I know I never read any follow-up reports at all. I have to find out what became of everything after you were sentenced. I feel guilty that I never even asked..."

Stefan said, "Mom, I know you're doing this because you still don't believe you could raise a kid that could do something like I did. But there is no other story. There's only one story."

Jep said, "And what is it you're really looking for exactly?"

"Insight," I said, at the same moment that Stefan said, "Trouble." Stefan and Jep nodded sagaciously at each other, so alike that a wash of tenderness nearly swamped me.

"Look, this isn't over. At least for somebody it isn't over. Obviously! Are you both going to ignore the fact that there was an arson at our house? At our own house? Maybe the publicity spurred someone to act. It can still get worse. What about the calls, the stalker? What's next? The whole house itself? One of us?"

That silenced both of them. Jep said then, "I'm sorry for blaming you, Theaitsa. But we just need to move on as a family."

"Well I can't move on. Not until I know…whatever it turns out I need to know. I just need to do this. Maybe there is no puzzle. I just feel like there still is. And I'm missing a piece."

Then we all subsided to our corners like old soldiers hors de combat.

The morning before I left, I sat down with Stefan to ask if he had chosen the next candidate for The Healing Project. Dozens of suggestions had poured in since our appearance on TV. It would take a long time to sort these new ones into priorities and future possibilities. Since Merry was on a maternity leave, for the first time he'd be doing that entirely on his own with situations that were unfamiliar, related in no way to him or us. Even given his driving desire to make amends, he felt like he was underwater in heavy current.

Julie and I hadn't revealed the full scope of my own colossal flop at being a ministering angel to the survivors of Roman's victim. I hadn't asked Julie to lie, but I couldn't bring myself to tell the whole truth. I thought of myself, hands on my knees, heaving in the weeds. Still, it more or less all worked out in the end, hadn't it? I'd offered my help in sorting through the mail, but Stefan gently refused. Good for him, I thought.

More in the spirit of hopefulness than sage counsel, I said, "You'll do fine. Just trust your instincts. You have good instincts."

"Let the people figure out their own goals. You just be the listener and the facilitator," Jep said. "You don't have to influence. They know what they need. They'll tell you if you give them room and just listen."

I left them making coffee and went upstairs for my things.

By the time I came back downstairs with my overnight bag, Stefan was carrying his files into the den to spread them out on the big library table in there. He apologized again that he couldn't go with me. Jep kissed me like I was his best girl, and then slipped something into the pocket of my coat. When I reached for my gloves later on, I almost laughed. It was one of his big silver coaching whistles, the kind that lets out a blast that could stop a train.

Coming into Black Creek that afternoon after so long was probably akin to the experience of people returning to a place of their youth, to find everything a little smaller and more be-grimed than the way they were remembered by their smaller and more begrimed selves. As if my turning onto that very exit road animated a tableau of that night, the steely sky closed in and the snow threw down. I didn't remember that the drive from the highway to the hospital parking lot was literally seconds: The storm-gauzed lights from the hospital building, glimpsed from the top of the ridge road, were as terrifying to me as if I'd come upon an alien installation. I drove down there and parked for a moment in the lot. After seeing Stefan in the locked ward that night, I'd come back out here, and, laying my hand against the hot hood of the still-running car, I threw up in the snow.

There were things I hadn't thought about for years; how was that possible?

I remembered again the sticky red leather seat of the booth in the Denny's, where, that following morning, Jep and I sat across from Stefan's lawyer located quickly for us by a coach friend of Jep's. He sketched in the potential outcomes of our son's case. Some were bad; some were worse. "We don't want a trial. The best hope is a judge who'll see Stefan as a kind of victim too, of drugs, not a longtime user but a first-time offender; a judge who'll give him less than ten years, for manslaughter, maybe a spin in a mental health facility, even though those places are hellholes."

"And the worst hope?"

"Murder can mean a life sentence," he said. "Parole after twelve years maybe."

Worlds we never knew existed were smashing fists to our ribs.

I didn't want to remember that sensation. There was no profit in such recollections. It was getting late now so I slowly steered the car out of the hospital lot and headed toward the town.

Even though it was Thursday, and barely dinnertime, the main street had a frowsy feeling, as if the performance had already happened, and somebody had forgotten to tear down the tattered posters. The place would not have looked sinister to anyone but me; it was just an ersatz hippie little college street of no particular distinction. Cuddly single-story abodes of the cottage type sat a little back from the street, surrounded by patches of scrappy lawn, and the retail establishments that flanked them followed a nonconformist conformity—bagels, juicery, head shop, bookstore, repeat. The signs on the stores reminded me of the precious way some people name their cats: Gypsy Threads, The Exuberant Alternative, Mrs. Pennyroyal's Papers, Bagel Bountiful. Not in any particular hurry to get to the Glory Be Bed-and-Breakfast Inn, I decided to find myself a quick dinner first, then maybe do some scouting around.

The restaurant was called Mack The Cheese. It served only variations on macaroni and cheese. In a town filled with homesick college kids, I thought, this idea was a stroke of genius. Beside Mom's Traditional, there was Spinach and Artichoke Macaroni and Cheese, Macaroni and Cheese with Andouille Sausage, and Taco Pizza Macaroni and Cheese. As I ate my Macaroni-and-Gruyère with green peppers and sun-dried tomatoes, I thought helplessly of Jep and me, more than twenty years ago, before Stefan, "cooking dinner" in our wretched studio apartment, believing that Kraft Spaghetti Classics in a box was a real gourmet triumph, especially with a healthy side of iceberg lettuce. We had been so sweet and earnest: How could this foul luck have come snuffling its dark way through time until it found us? Only a fool believes that people who do good must then derive good from fate; but we're helpless in that belief. Why else do good? Why not teach our kids just to smash and grab in life?

When I finished dinner, it was still early, but I was exhausted. My plan was to go directly to the bed-and-breakfast inn, and, by eight o'clock, anesthetize myself with Valium and a slug of the innkeeper's sherry. Although the weather was moderate for this time of year in north central Wisconsin, it was no day at the beach, as it were. Still, I decided on a short walk, just a couple of blocks, before getting into my car, to shake down the pound of macaroni and cheese I'd eaten and to clear my head.

I thought of the time back then, when he had just gone into the hospital, I asked Stefan, where did you get the drugs? I was so naïve, I never dreamed he wouldn't just come right out with it. Thinking about it with the remove of time, I'm shocked that he did, knowing I could have tracked the girl down, knowing that I might well have given the police her name. I could have told the police, and I should have.

Why didn't I?

It honestly hadn't occurred to me that the drugs were a crime as well. And no one had asked me.

"Emily," he said. "Emily Lindquist. Or Lundgren. Or something with an L. Belinda's best friend up there."

"How did Belinda know her?"

"From…from before college. She met Bindy in cheerleading camp, I guess. I think she was from Chicago. But I didn't realize at first she was the same person she used to talk about from cheer.

"We weren't like insane addicts. It was just drugs like there are in a college town. Weekend drugs. Study drugs. It went fine, it was fun. Except for that night."

I walked along. Maybe it was what I knew about the place, but the town felt creepy. Human beings really do have animal senses. You can tell if you're being watched. I felt eyes on me from all those frowsy, closed, empty little places. Then my phone vibrated with a text in my pocket and I pulled it out.

I can see you, walking up Pottawatomi Street. What the hell do you think you're doing?

Abruptly, I felt cold, but not from the weather.

I texted back, Why are you here?

She replied, Because you're here.

Back when this girl told me that she wasn't involved with bad people, I believed her. Now I didn't. She was entangled in some way with a murder in a small college town. She was drawn back here. Or if she wasn't drawn back here, she was following me, and her reasons for doing that couldn't be pure. I found a little courtyard between two small brick houses and tucked myself into it.

How did you know Belinda? I texted her.

She texted, Cheer competitions.

So Stefan was right. Except he didn't know that Emily was Esme was Emily.

I texted back simply: Call me.

She agreed, but said she had to go somewhere safe first.

It grew colder as the evening drew in fast. I found a bench and sat huddled. At last, my phone vibrated.

"Hi," she said. "Please, I can't talk long."

She said she was enrolled in school that fall semester. She and Belinda were already making plans to study together in Paris for their junior year abroad.

I said, "Paris?"

"That was what we wanted. It was everything to us."

I couldn't stop thinking, Paris? What about Stefan, poor chump, who thought that Belinda just needed some time to stretch her wings before she settled down?

"I have to go now," Esme said. She sighed. "I shouldn't be talking about this. Just tell Stefan if he ever remembers anything, you know, to just not say it."

"What do you mean, anything?"

"He'll know what I mean."

"Stop this! You're following me even now. At least come see me."

"No," she said. "I'm scared."

She hung up. I stood and glanced around me. The only buildings were those one-story commercial affairs, all of them still. From where was she watching me? All the cars parked along the street were dark and seemingly empty. I got up and went to my car, stuffing my phone into my pocket as I hurried along. A door slammed and someone else was running, their soles slapping in time with mine, whether toward me or away from me, I couldn't tell. My keys were in hand: Another thing I'd always told myself was that I would never be one of those fumblers hauled out of her vehicle by the zombie because she couldn't start the car. I threw myself into the front seat, locked the doors and smoothly stuck the key fob into the ignition...but the car wouldn't start. It was that crazy gap that sometimes occurred as a result of good intentions, in this case, the anti-theft lock. Those painful prickles of bio-electric current raced up my throat and forearms. I wrestled with the wheel, jiggled the key.

Just then, the thin guy in the hoodie, his face obscured by a balaclava, rose up from the ground like smoke on the driver's side. His face was separated from mine by an eighth of an inch of glass, and I could see his breath and the level look in his pale blue eyes. Where had he come from? Was he the one running behind me? Was he under the car? I tried to scream, but my voice was as balky as the ignition. Then I reached into my pocket and found the whistle Jep put there and blew on it like all the sons of Aaron at Jericho. A car horn stuttered and then blared. But the hoodie figure didn't take off running. Horribly, he slid back down out of my sight and, when I glanced in the rearview mirror, he was nowhere to be seen. Did he drop down a manhole? Crawl into a yard behind one of the rows of picket fence, no more than two feet tall?

Suddenly, I was able to turn the key. My car roared to life. And then another lock clicked over as well, this one in my brain.

I blew on the whistle again, a sustained blast, and was relieved when I heard the whoop of a police car and the scoop of blue lights as a single officer approached in one of the little sport utilities they drive now. He made a motion for me to roll down the window, and I did, but just a couple of inches.

"You're the one with the whistle?" the man said. I nodded. "Can you step out of the vehicle, ma'am?"

"No," I told him.

"I need you to step out of the vehicle, ma'am."

"I'm afraid to," I said. "If you'll escort me to the parking lot of the B&B where I'm staying tonight, I'll get out of the car. Someone was just following me, and he came right up to my car. And he could still be here somewhere."

"Can I see your license and registration, please."

I put down the whistle and gathered them and pushed them through the narrow opening in the window.

"Do you know Detective Sunday? Pete Sunday?" I said.

The police officer looked up. He nodded. "I'm here in town for an appointment with him tomorrow. I'm here to get some documents…about a murder."

"A murder."

I gave him the short version of the story, but not my married name, and thus not Stefan's last name. I didn't want to see that particular lock click into place. He left and after an interminable time in his squad car, the officer came back and agreed to follow me to the bed-and-breakfast, which was called Connell's Glory Be Inn. There, I stood awkwardly in the gravel parking lot while the cop shined his flashlight into my car and under my car as the innkeeper watched from the porch, occasionally lifting her hand to flutter a wave.

"Do you mind if I look in the trunk, ma'am?"

"Actually, I do."

"Any particular reason?"

"I don't have to have a reason. I know that much. All I did was blow a whistle because I was scared. I don't have anything in the car except my overnight bag and my laptop."

"No firearms?"

"Firearms?"

"You said you were here about a murder."

"I'm looking into a murder. I'm not planning to commit one." I sighed then. "Go ahead and look in the trunk if you want to."

"Is everything okay?" the innkeeper called.

"It's fine, Sherri!" the police officer called back. "Just a mix-up!" To me he said, "You don't need to open the trunk, ma'am. You're good."

I was soon ensconced in a room where all the wall art and reading material and seemingly all the TV channels, too (although this was impossible) were concerned with fundamentalist Christianity. While I'm all for people's beliefs, the strangeness of the inn bled into my paranoid fantasy. As I locked the door, Sherri, who owned the place with her husband, Wayne Connell, a farmer, asked if I wanted a glass of wine or some cheese and crackers. "Our own cucumbers with that, and our own dill!"

"That would be nice," I said, agreeing to the cheese and cucumbers. But no wine, just water, I told her, and she said there was water and orange juice in the mini-fridge. I drew the shades and then the curtains, thanking god almighty, or whoever else might be listening, for letting me be here under this soft quilt in this warm room.

Jep's phone call wakened me. To my surprise, I'd slept all night.

"Are you okay?" he asked. "I tried to call you a few times last night." As I swam up from sleep, I recalled the sound of the phone boring into my consciousness several times, and ignoring it.

"I'm good, I'm good," I told him.

"What time will you be home tonight?"

"I'm not sure yet. It depends on what happens today."

Jep said, "I don't think you should drive home too late. Or do you want me to come up there now to go with you to meet Sunday."

"That's not necessary," I assured him. I chatted about the innkeeper's famous waffles I was anticipating for breakfast and an alluring claw-foot tub with bath salts that I invented on the spot. Eventually I hung up, only to see a deck of text messages.

Stefan had texted: U OK?

Jep had texted: U Still ALIVE?

Julie sent one of her customary long missives: I hope you find whatever you're looking for. I hope it doesn't end up costing you too much. You thought I didn't know that you took off for up there, but I did.

And then there was the one I'd been waiting for: No one hurt you? I saw the police. I was scared!

It seemed impossible that Esme had seen what happened to me last night, but clearly, she had. What kind of crappy game was this? Suddenly, I was furious with the caller.

I'm fine. I was scared too. Are you going to come see me today?

I waited, but she didn't answer.

I put down the phone, got up, then I did slip into a long bath—no claw-foot, but it was a deep tub with soothing salts—then hopped back into bed for another nap before breakfast, which would be served just after nine.

When I got up the second time, I checked my phone again. No reply from Esme.

I don't believe you anymore. I think you're making this all up.

The waffles with raspberry syrup the innkeeper prepared

were actually heavenly. I thought of telling her so, in just that way, but decided against any sort of hijinks. She was clearly a decent person, and she might think that I was trying to tease her about religion. Which would have been unkind. Maybe it was my mood, however, but the eldritch nature of the whole place was enhanced by portraits of children, the same boy and girl, that hung all over the dining room walls, old-fashioned colorized photos.

"My kids," she said affably.

"Grown up now?"

"Oh, no," the woman replied. But there were no sounds of children, nor any bookbags or boots scattered near the door. The place was prim and clean as a vault.

By the time I'd eaten and changed clothes, it was time for me to see Pete Sunday. I told Sherri I'd be back later on and that I probably would stay the second night—a possibility I'd left open. I was still exhausted.

The detective and I had arranged to meet at a coffee shop on Pottawatomi Street, where I fortified myself with a double-shot latte. He walked in, wearing a slim-fitting blazer in a Prince of Wales check over charcoal trousers and a striped shirt. We shook hands. He looked unchanged. After he ordered his own coffee, he asked me to follow him to the public safety building, just a few blocks away. When we got there, he settled me comfortably in his office.

"Why do you work here?" I asked him.

"Why does anybody work anywhere?"

"You dress like you'd work in a big city."

"Ah," Sunday said, spinning his desk chair and sitting down to face me. "People tell me that all the time." He went on to say that he'd recently applied for a transfer, to Dane County, and was starting to be afraid he'd actually get it. "I know that's hardly a big city. I want the challenge but not the change. I'd miss it here. I'd miss the quiet and the lakes and the trees and my mom and dad and all my brothers. Speaking of that, I heard from one of them that you had a little scare last night. Big whistle."

"That was your brother? You guys go all in for the fraternity of police stuff, huh?"

"No, that was my actual brother, Judson. Jud and Ross are both county sheriff's deputies, Jud here, Ross in Marathon County. My other brother lives in town here, too. He's a librarian at the university."

"What do your kids think about moving away from these north woods?"

"No children yet," he said. "No wife yet. Just small crimes and good suits."

"Not all small crimes."

"Mostly. Not all." As if apropos, he pointed to the banker's box on the floor beside him.

"I don't want you to get the wrong impression about our local cordiality. All the reports from Belinda McCormack's death are in that box. I copied them for you and I won't even make you pay the copy costs."

To my next question, he answered that he had never heard anyone mention the name Esme. He showed me a list that Jill McCormack had compiled of Belinda's close friends at the time of her death: Caroline, Celeste, Laura, Kilty and Anastasia. While he agreed that this was a notorious case, it was Pete's opinion that if Belinda had not been a beautiful blonde girl on campus, whose mother had the wit and determination to focus on dating abuse as an issue, there would be no echoes. Women in America died every day at the hands of the men they loved. They ran the gamut, from poor unemployed mothers, flight attendants to Broadway actors, advertising executives. They answered the phone at the water utility or taught second grade. When I told him that many of those very women had reached out to Jill's organization, he shrugged and said he hoped awareness would make a difference because many of the women whose lovers hit them felt oddly guilty, as if they deserved it. Your own side of that story, he said, might not be so popular; but there were plenty of people on the wrong side of the equation in a case of violent death—yet deserving of a certain kind of empathy too. There was no such thing as too much understanding.

I told him about the strange incidents at our house, not just the demonstrations (he already knew about those) but about the unexplained car fire and how someone came in when we weren't home and drew black dots over the eyes on our photographs.

"Ruined them forever..." he said, genuinely downcast.

"No, it was just on the glass. But whoever it was used some kind of oil-based marker, so it was hell to get it off."

I told him about the slender young man in the hoodie and the aviator glasses, his appearances on my street, on my campus, and now here. "It's probably one of the most frustrating things about something like this that yes, it's wrong and scary and creepy, but it's not a crime, not until there's some kind of threat."

"And then I bet it's too late most of the time."

"Once in a while it's too late, but not most of the time. Unless somebody is really nuts, a person will usually obey a restraining order. But it's the ones who don't obey it that worry you. Either they know the system, and they don't care about it, or they don't care about anything."

Why I didn't tell him more about Esme-or-Emily, right then, about her texts and phone calls, and what they seemed to entail, I'm not sure. I hadn't even told Julie everything about Esme. Until I had a fuller picture, it somehow seemed to be a risk.

I assured Pete Sunday that I didn't need help carrying the box to my car, but he carried it anyway. We shook hands and parted. I stowed the box in my trunk, thinking it would fit right there next to my nonexistent assault weapon. Lethargic now, as if all the docked hopes for what I might learn and what I might do with it were brewed into some kind of sedative, all I wanted to do was to crawl beneath my scenes-of-the-holy-land quilt at the inn and sleep the rest of the time before checking out and heading home early in the morning. Actually, I reprimanded myself. I would sleep for an hour and then read these reports, so I could call Pete Sunday on my way home if I had any more questions. Why it seemed easier to call him from my car than from my kitchen at home, again, I have no idea. I drove back to the inn, fell on the bed, and slept until the afternoon sun and my lunchless stomach teased me awake.

I'd passed a diner on the way to the inn. Maybe they had chili.

The diner was one of those pods that resembled an overgrown Airstream trailer. I ate my chili quietly. It wasn't half bad. When I was finished, I came out into a hushed street.

Did anyone really go to school here?

The temperature had soared into the fifties, which Wisconsin people think of as balmy. Shouldn't there be college kids rocketing around on bikes and skateboards, pushing the calendar to its limits? Across the street was a little pocket of a park, in the center a dry fountain and a few stone benches, ringed by a tiny labyrinth of paths. From the groomed evergreens hung suet balls studded with berries and birdseed.

I decided to sit for a moment, send a text to Esme, and savor the raw white sunlight. My arrival startled up birds. I looked down the street and realized I was near the police station. There came a piercing recollection of Belinda's love for Edna St. Vincent Millay ("Don't you think Vincent and William Butler Yeats would have been perfect for each other?" Belinda told me once, without a scrap of irony. "They had so much in common. Sad love, being Irish.") I thought about the lines, *Thus in the winter stands the lonely tree, Nor knows what birds have vanished one by one, Yet knows its boughs more silent than before.* Every girl who dies is canonized, of course; but Belinda's sweet hopefulness was latticed with the cheerful steel of a supermodel. She was National

Honor Society and Prom Queen—both things. With grueling practices and iron will, she pushed the cheer squad not just to compete, but to place first in state. She wrote op-eds about the fate of abused animals that raised thousands for the Humane Society. The plaque on the cherry tree that her class planted in Whitehorse Park read *She Always Had Time For a Friend*. Seeing her walk shining into a room of adults, Jep used to tease, "I'm Belinda McCormack, your senator."

And what might she have been?

Whether from the breeze or the sentiment, my eyes watered and I reached up, for just a moment, to cover them with my hands. That was when a feeling crept over me again. And I knew he was there. I knew he was watching me from behind those aviator glasses. I should never have come to Black Creek for any reason. This was the place where our future was revoked. And now someone who seemed to sense my every movement had followed me here, as well. No wonder I was a scream with a skin around it.

I jumped into my car and, within moments, I was on the highway. Esme called me. I refused the call. She texted me. I glanced quickly at her words. Where are you?

I pulled the car over into some murderous-looking little rest area, the kind with crumbling asphalt and a battered box the size of a phone booth meant for donating old clothes. My hands were shaking. I texted back: I think you're nuts. I came all the way up here to get a few pieces of paper that probably won't be useful for anything, but I was willing to see you. I really believed you wanted to help Stefan and me. If you just want to spy on me, then leave me alone. Esme, this is your last chance. Do you want me to meet you? I started the car and backed it up so that my way back onto the road would be a straight shot. No need to put the car in Reverse. I checked all the locks, turned the old Marvin Gaye song that just came on the radio up as high as it would go, pulled my coat around me and closed my eyes. Just then, I got a text from her. Tell me where you are. I'll be there in ten minutes, it said.

I typed in the mile marker sign and hit Send. Then I panicked. Who might she bring with her, to this lonely apron of concrete surrounded by a thicket of spindly trees cackling in the wind? I sat still, trying to breathe my mind and hands into a semblance of composure.

Then a car pulled into the rest area. It couldn't be Esme; I'd barely completed my last text message to her. The driver stopped, opened the door. Striding toward me was no slight college-age girl, but the androgynous young guy in the hoodie and aviator glasses who now stood next to my car. It was the same person, the same narrow shoulders, the same lanky swing of the arms. Slow, slow thoughts slid into my consciousness like syrup: Move, Thea. Move, for your life. I jammed the car into Drive, so wildly that I all but ran him down, and spattered gravel onto the highway right in front of an eighteen-wheeler whose driver sent out a blast of air-horn outrage as he hauled his rig into the next lane. I never even dared to glance in the rearview mirror.

I'd driven at least ten miles before I remembered that I had left my things in the room at Connell's Glory Be Bed-and-Breakfast. I should turn around, I thought. Nothing would make me turn around. I could call when I got home and ask the owner to mail them to me and add that to my bill.

When the fuel light blinked on an hour north of Portland, I did not even stop for gas. Let it run down to nothing. That was what the tow trucks from AAA were for.

It wasn't until I got off the exit closest to home, begging the indifferent universe just to let me get there, promising in return that this was really over, this time for sure, I would stop chasing shadows, willing myself into my house, into my own bed, imagining myself pressed against Jep's sturdy, warm, inert back, that I remembered Esme's text. I'll be there in ten minutes, she had typed.

I began to pant. I scrabbled for my phone.

Nothing.

I had left her there. I had left Esme to pull into that deserted scrap of pavement, all alone, looking for me, where he waited.

9

When I hit my own driveway, it was late. Except for a small light in the upstairs hall, one we always left burning, the house was dark. On a street suddenly as still as a canyon, I got the willies. I actually missed the protestors. When I called Stefan's cell, it went over to voice mail. Jep…same thing. Pulling into the garage, I let the door close behind me and summoned my courage, getting out briskly and opening the door to the kitchen, pushing my purse and the box of documents inside.

"Molly!" I called.

The dog didn't come running. She would have come running, acting as though she hadn't seen me in ten years instead of less than a day. This was the part in the scary movie when the person trips over the mutilated body of the dog. That did it for me. I slammed the door and turned on all the lights. If somebody had killed Molly, that somebody would reap the whirlwind. I heard her then. She was scratching at the back door. She was outside in the yard. Somebody had let her out and left her out there. I didn't know for how long, but she was thirsty, giving me only a cursory greeting before heading toward her water bowl.

Who had done that?

Jep or Stefan…never. Jep and Stefan treated Molly with more regard than they did most people, and they were nice to most people.

Who had left Molly outside? I knew the doors were locked. The fussy slider downstairs was long since fixed. Who had been in our house and how?

I sent Stefan a text, asking if he had let Molly out. Jep too. Jep answered that Molly was not outside, that must be asleep upstairs and our bedroom door just got closed on her. Let her out before she gets all excited and pees, he wrote. A second later, he wrote, U do ok? U ok now?

I told him I was fine.

Who put Molly outside?

What did the hooded young guy have to do with Molly? With our family photos? With the night Belinda died? His visits could not be a coincidence. And they carried a definite message, be afraid, presumably meant for Stefan. But Stefan had not been with me on my little fact-finding journey. So he meant to scare me. Why me? I didn't kill anybody. This was part of… something. It made no sense. Maybe it made no sense because you have to be crazy for it to make sense.

How could this guy creep around for months without anyone else but me ever seeing him, except for that one time on the highway on the way back from the prison?

But since then, it had only been me. Was there an image? I realized that I hadn't checked the CCTV across from the parking lot at Ferber Humanities Hall. I made a mental note to suggest that someone from campus police do that, if they preserved the surveillance tape that far back and didn't tape over it. What did I care if they thought I was nuts? They probably already thought I was nuts.

The other thing I thought about were those cases, maybe not even a dozen, but I'd read about them. All you had to do to find out about them was to open the trap door under human doings and drop down into the darkness. They were those cases in which the police had photos of a suspect, perhaps even video, even a few seconds of voice recorded on a victim's phone, and they still couldn't identify the person. They had eyewitnesses who could describe people well. The eyewitnesses watched as a short middle-aged man with cropped ginger hair sprinted across a picnic park to grab two fourteen-year-old cousins, by the shoulder and force both of them into a minivan (silver, with a tan interior, possibly leather). In yet another unsolved case, at least two observers heard an eighteen-year-old girl cry out for her father and the shriek of her personal alarm when it deployed. The witnesses saw two men, both of them wearing stocking caps with Chicago Bears logos, both of them wearing navy-blue quilted jackets. One of the women, whose big German Shepherd was roaring and straining at his leash, and who said she would regret the rest of her life that she didn't let the dog go, was close enough to heard a man's rough grumble instruct "Jerry" to "get her to shut up."

Yes, those witnesses told police; yes, that drawing the sketch artist made looked like the guy who was shorter. Yes, the guy who seemed older was over six feet tall. They would tell police about that summer evening near the old dam in detail—but not until two days after the teenager's body was found. They didn't come forward. They didn't want to get involved in somebody else's business.

The next day, I called Pete Sunday, knowing that I would sound at best paranoid, at worst institution-ready. I was sure the hooded figure was after us.

"If nothing was taken…"

"Nothing I know of."

"It's clear that somebody's trying to scare you, Mrs. Christiansen…"

"Thea."

"Thea, thanks. Still, I would say the same thing to you as the police down there told you about the car fire and the photographs. Yes, someone was watching you. Now, yesterday, you were alone, you were unarmed, so you were vulnerable. If…whoever it is wanted you dead, or badly hurt, you'd be dead or hurt now."

I'd thought of the same thing. If he wanted to kill me, I'd already be dead. He could have killed us that first time he harassed us on the highway. He could have killed me in the rest area. He could have killed me here in my own driveway. He didn't have to play games. That he was playing games meant he wanted something else, that there really was another story, no matter how adamant Stefan and Jep were. That guy had followed us down the highway from prison, and to my office, and then the cemetery and then to Black Creek again. He might even have been the one to set Stefan's car on fire.

"True, of course. But isn't threatening to scare somebody a crime?"

"Harassment is a crime. But it's hard to prove, like stalking, on the basis of just a few events. Menacing is a crime of assault. But nobody has attempted to directly hurt you, correct." He paused. "There has to be something else he wants and the big riddle is what, but the even bigger riddle is why."

I thought the same thing. "Why me? If my son is the one who's being warned, why scare me?"

"No idea."

I pointed out that hearing a detective say "no idea" was not reassuring.

"I assume it has something to do with the murder, but that crime is over and Stefan has been punished. So what is the loose end?"

"You're the detective."

"Yes, but not a psychic."

So I had to be content with wondering, for now. The question simmered in my mind day and night, leaving me restless, exhausted, snappish with everyone. I felt an odd foreboding, even as ordinary days slipped past, a sense of someone hunting something invisible that was hunting me too. I tried to banish the notion. It was so fanciful, so unlike me.

I found myself anxious at the thought of opening the box from Detective Sunday and so I avoided it. It left me gripped with fear. That was unlike me too. I could feel the box, under my bed, pulsing like the telltale heart.

Instead, I stacked and sorted reference materials for my new book.

I stacked and sorted them again.

My sabbatical would be ending soon and I had been thinking of extending it. I was happy with the progress I was making with my book and didn't feel ready to be back on campus just yet. I spoke with Jep about it and its impact on our finances. He told me to do what I wanted, that we would be fine. For tenured faculty at Thornton Wilder, there was an option to extend a sabbatical for up to another full year, if you were willing to do that extension without pay. So I called Keith to bring up the idea. I wasn't sure yet but promised to give him an answer very soon. He seemed glad to hear from me and equally receptive, maybe even relieved, to my keeping my return date open for the near present. Adoche was doing well with my classes, really coming into her own as a lecturer. I didn't particularly need to hear that part, but I maintained a cordial tone.

I didn't leave the house, or return calls, even as Julie's texts and phone messages crossed over from concerned to annoyed. I found myself paralyzed to move forward, but unable to go back and live in the space where I had blindly accepted Stefan's guilt. Stuck and on my own, I tried to distract myself.

A few nights later, I tried to make a fuss of Jep, pouring champagne and digging out a satin nightgown he'd given me one long-ago anniversary; but he could tell that my ardor was compensatory. Sweetly, he assured me that our life as currently construed left him feeling no more lustful than I did—with no offense to my charms.

"I can't find out anything about who is stalking us," I told him. "I can't protect Stefan."

"Stefan has to protect himself, Theaitsa. He managed to do that in prison; he told us how. He's alert and he's smart. How could he be in any more danger now than he was then?"

"I don't mean protect him like he was a child," I said. "I don't mean hold his hand, though I would hold his hand if I could. There's something more I'm supposed to know." This becalmed state was unprecedented in my life. There was a process, and when I followed my process, it always led to resolution—not always the resolution I wanted, but some resolution.

"If you don't know, it's probably something you're cooking up in your mind," Jep said. "You're like a dog with a bone. You can't let go. Probably all those threats were just a bunch of hot air and not connected to the car fire or the photographs. And I would bet that this radio silence is just another way for this sicko to keep you off balance, too. A sick way to get his kicks."

Maybe he was right. Certainly, Julie was right when she said that a crisis was by its nature an event of deepest challenge bracketed in time. What was a crisis that kept unrolling?

I caught myself striding around in front of my desk, unable to perch longer than the interval it took to write a sentence. I had received a modest contract for my book about obsessed women in fiction, now titled *The Haunted Lady.* My editor, who'd worked on my previous book, *Sad-Eyed Lady,* was effusive.

"I hope our Tess is among your subjects," she said, referring to Thomas Hardy's ill-used heroine—a murderer, no less, from the he-had-it-coming school of fallen women.

"She is indeed," I told her. "I'll be including her. All of the greats."

"You have such an engaging style, I can't wait to read the finished manuscript."

A few days later, I signed on the line. The advance was a chuckle, about what it would cost to spend on a weekend at a great hotel, but I had just paid off my car, now six years old, and the last of the radioactive credit card bills, and money still seemed to vanish like water into sand.

I thought of Pete Sunday it seemed all the time now. I wanted to contact him again, but what would I say?

This was a busy time for Jep. The season was in full swing, and Stefan had fallen into a somewhat busy routine, with his landscaping contracts and keeping The Healing Project going forward. Any commotion stirred by the public television episode seemed to have died down for now. Whether it had garnered the kind of attention he had been looking for remained an open question.

"Are you feeling good?" I asked Stefan.

"What you mean is, am I feeling suicidal? I'm not feeling suicidal. I'm feeling tired. Ordinary tired, Mom. The way people get who work all the time."

Finally, one day, I forced myself to go outside for a long walk with Julie. A new dusting of pristine snow refreshed the evil-looking plowed-up foothills that sat behind stores and dumpsters. Swaddled in fleece, we were powering to Lava Java when Julie said, "Thea, you're miles away. When I say you look like shit, I don't mean you've lost too much weight, although you have. I mean, you look weary."

"I never thought I would mind hearing I'd lost too much weight."

But it was more than weight. I'd stopped paying attention. These days, a pair of sweatpants with an old UW–Whitewater jersey was what constituted getting dressed. Not getting dressed was leaving my pajamas on, with a UW–Whitewater jersey. The day before, as if to provide me with a double handful of nothing, the nice young officer from the Portland Police called to say that there hadn't been a whisper about who'd burned up our car, though she said she'd expected some gossip, "this being a small town."

The universe doesn't exist to send you messages, I told myself. Things just happen. They're part of a pattern, but sometimes, you never get to see the pattern.

"You could try getting away from all this a little bit. You could go skiing with Jep," Julie said.

"We're just making it," I told Julie. "I mean, we're fine but no extras right now…"

This wasn't really true. We could afford a nice trip. My comment was just meant to break the chain of the conversation: People always seemed cautious about arguing with a financial motive. Even to my closest friend, I couldn't admit the truth. What if we came back to a tragedy? What if we were to be punished for relaxing our vigilance? The ineluctable urge I felt to watch Stefan like a newborn, to put the metaphoric mirror to his lips, was stronger than ever.

Jep and Stefan were going away, in fact, to a game in Utah. Since he would be with his father, Stefan applied for and received an exemption from his parole officer: He'd filed a travel plan and created a schedule to check in by phone every day. They would do some real skiing, as there was already plenty of snow in Utah, and a bonus was that Jep's travel costs were covered by the team budget.

Julie was no fool and she was no stranger to magical thinking.

"So if he goes away, that's okay but if you go away, that's dereliction of duty?"

"He won't be away from Jep," I said. "That's what makes it okay."

"And that's all there is to it?"

"Okay! Even if I could get away, I can't get really away. I carry this burden around, like a turtle carries its shell. You were right. I don't really know about Stefan's life in Black Creek. And I don't really even know the full story of that night. Okay, of course, it's too late for this to make any difference. But there's this sense, I feel like I let him down by just accepting whatever everybody said, even if Stefan accepted what everybody said. I need to find out the whole truth. I'm obsessed. It's like a reflex now." I sighed, feeling my rebellious outer thighs clench as we hit the steep part of the street. Hadn't I used to bound up this hill like a gazelle? Well, not like a gazelle; I'd never done anything in my life like a gazelle. But I had gone up this hill many times like…like a golden retriever. And not that long ago. Creaky middle age seemed to have swamped me in record time.

Julie said, "Sweetie, you will never be able to know the whole truth. You weren't there. Stefan can't tell you the whole truth either. You're chasing a ghost. It would make anyone feel weighed down."

"I thought when Stefan got out of prison, we would be able to move on. Our family. Instead, there's a sense of, I don't know, of menace. More intense than ever. When he was in prison, all I had to do was to focus on keeping his spirits up so he'd survive it. Looking back, it seems so easy compared to now. Now, this girl…"

"What girl?"

"This girl caller that keeps getting in touch with me and dropping hints about that night."

"You never told me about any girl. And you didn't tell me ahead of time that you were going back up there."

"I'm sorry. Jules, I'm sorry. I never keep anything from you. But I feel like this is a stain, and if I tell you, it will get on you, too."

I told her everything then, about how I felt an urgency to know more now, to uncover the whole truth, whatever it was, to make sense of that fatal night. About the guy in the hoodie, about the caller named Esme and her relationship with Belinda, about how I sped away spooked and in a panic before Esme arrived when we were supposed to meet.

"I'm sure she's fine," Julie said.

"But that guy..."

"Was there to scare you. If he wanted to..."

"He'd have done what? Shot me through my windshield?"

With a long exhale, Julie said, "I was going to say, if he wanted to hurt you he would have followed you and...and really run you off the road." The memory of that slow spinning slide to the edge of the river cliff on the way from prison silenced us both for the stomp home.

Just before we got there, I told Julie about the box of police reports Detective Sunday had given me, how I wanted to dig into them, how I was too terrified to dig into them, how I'd let the box sit under my bed since I came home, even though I could feel it pulsating, as if it were somehow alive.

"You know what? How about you and I go to the cabin? Right before Christmas?"

"Your family will be there."

"Not this year. Hal and the boys and my brothers' families are leaving early this year to go diving someplace warm. But not me."

"Well, I'd love to do that. It seems like years."

It had, I realized later, been years, four years, in fact. Julie and Hal customarily spent Christmas at her storied country home on the Door County peninsula, with her brothers and their families, and we'd visited for New Year's many times, the memories of those crepe breakfasts and midnight hot tubs still an arsenal against despair for me.

Some of the best times of my growing up were the three weeks in August my parents let me go to stay with Julie's family. The main cabin was a four-story, ten-bedroom spread that even I, as a child, understood cost serious change. None of the Bishops ever talked about money.

"We can ski cross-country. Or just hike. I'll get a chef," she said.

"We can buy frozen pizza."

"No, it'll be fun. Chefs love these little gigs."

I hadn't been anywhere alone with Julie in years. The idea was so appealing that I took hold of her shoulder and hugged her, there in the street.

"And here's the deal. Bring the police reports," Julie said. "You can look at them with me right there. I'll look at them with you."

"I don't want you to have to do that."

"I can't imagine you having to do something like that by yourself. You've already faced so much by yourself. And you managed to do your job and be good to your husband and son and friends and your sisters… I could never have done what you did." Trust sweet Julie to make grace of my disgrace. And yet her generosity was not by far the best thing about her: Only she had never, not once, flinched from Stefan.

When he arrived home, minutes after us, he made her come back outside onto the porch. And he switched on his lights.

Julie gasped at the glorious bower that Stefan had created at our house for Christmas, with all the fairy lights, garlanding and only-slightly-dinged British-inspired gewgaws left over from his jobs decorating lavish private homes, businesses and a country club or two.

It continued, outside to inside.

"You're a genius," she said.

"I am indeed, Jujubees. Whatever a person can do with some fourteen-dollar light strings and some baling wire, I am that genius."

"I mean it. This looks professional."

"I am a professional. I'm a professional landscaper."

"You know what I mean. I mean, it looks Hollywood, Stefano. It looks Hollywood."

She was right. It was still weeks before Christmas but we noticed cars slowing down to look at our house—not just for the customary reasons. In early November, Stefan banished me and Jep for an afternoon of shopping and a long dinner out. We were gone for five hours. Then, when he heard the sound of our car, he powered the whole thing on.

It felt as though we were entering a private fairyland. Jep said some of the same things Julie was saying now.

"You don't have to give me another thing for Christmas," he told Stefan. "When I was a little kid, you know I lived in England for a while with my parents. And this is what the village looked like…"

"Writtle," Stefan said proudly. "I know. I looked it up. I looked in your boxes of old pictures. They went all out for Christmas, like a Dickens story. I did this trying to resemble that. I can't believe you actually think it worked."

Jep had tears in his eyes. They were tears of pride, for Stefan, but I think also that he wished that he, and by extension Stefan, saw his parents more than a couple of weeks every year. His mom always wanted to come at Christmas; but his father always insisted on summers. I honestly didn't know why Paula went along with John when he preferred going to Italy or Spain for Christmas, although Jep's sister and her family usually joined them, at a time of year Jep simply couldn't be away. After his father retired, the Christiansens were planning on moving back to the States, but that wouldn't be for several years. Jep's dad and mom were hale in their sixties. I hoped that there would be at least one chance for us to go to see them there…to see the place in London they lived now, and also that village called Writtle… with Stefan, before they moved back.

After inspecting all the decorations, Jep added, "You know, this will be our first Christmas at home in a while."

Stefan looked downcast then. "I know, and I'm sorry I wrecked it while I was away, if I didn't wreck it forever."

It was Jep I felt sorry for then. The last thing he'd meant was to lace Stefan's contentment with guilt over the past holidays. While Stefan was in prison, we'd made the trek to Black Creek to partake with the prisoners of the only decent meal they were offered all year and from there, our dispirited progress to the home of a family member, there to try to escape the harsh sounds of the demonstrators and our stony solitary state. He fumbled to make amends. "I didn't mean that. Wait, son. Look. Take this as my clumsy way of saying, even if all we had was a wreath on the door, even if we didn't have a door, I would be glad you were home."

But it took a while for Stefan to smile easily again: His guilt was like a spring always close to the surface.

"This is gorgeous, it's exquisite," Julie said now. "You, lad, have a tremendous eye."

"I'm going to tell you how he managed this, because he won't…"

"Mom, I'm not fourteen years old."

"Indulge me," I told him. "What he did was go around and offer to buy all the leftover lights that his clients weren't going to use on their houses and businesses this year, but I think only one lady took money for them. The rest just gave them to him."

"So intrepid," Julie said. "Well, now I'm going to have to go home and settle for less. Next year, I'm your first client, is that clear? I mean, before Thanksgiving." Julie's mini-mansion was always decorated by a team of pros who came with their own cherry pickers and extension ladders.

"It's a date," Stefan agreed.

"I have something for you," Julie said now. She reached into her big leather bag and brought out a box. "Merry Christmas," she said. It was my name in Greek wrought in gold on a pendant, a diamond in the middle of the circle of the first letter. "Thea was a Titan. She gave birth to the sun and the moon and the dawn."

"I think she married her brother, though."

"It's a good thing you only have sisters, Mom," Stefan said.

"Details, details," said Julie.

Julie had a version of the same thing for Stefan, a charm of his name, in Greek, on a slender but masculine gold bracelet.

"I hate to think what that cost," I dithered.

"I don't," Stefan said. "It's very wow, Jujubees. But sleekly wow. Very much like I picture myself."

"That's what I told them. Go for sleek wow!"

Julie's gift from me, from Stefan and me, was a bright blue shawl of the softest cashmere, which Stefan had knitted. She marveled. It was a pretty marvelous shawl.

Stefan said then, "I got to scoot."

"Hot date?"

"Several, in a row tonight. I have to keep up my strength."

When he was gone, Julie said, "He still hanging out with that kid he knew growing up?"

"Yep, Will Brent, and Will's friends. You won't believe it, but they actually went winter camping last week. It was that one really cold clear night, last Friday. Stefan said it was one of the worst experiences of his life, that you had to keep anything you didn't want to freeze inside your sleeping bag, so you were cold even though you would have been warm." They got out pans to cook in the morning, but the eggs and milk were frozen. When the sun came up, one of the guys told them they could throw everything in his van, that it would probably thaw out by July, and they all went to the pancake house we had gone the day Stefan was released.

Julie asked, "Any of those friends girls?"

"I don't know," I said. "I would be surprised if they weren't. Will's a nurse, and a lot of the other student nurses are girls."

"What does he say?"

"I would not go to that topic with him wearing a bulletproof vest, Jules."

It wasn't as though I hadn't thought about that myself, but when I did think about it, it seemed like getting off a flight of stairs and climbing K2. I didn't even know how to bring it up with my son again, because any way I did would be border-line creepy. I also didn't know what the whole public revelation about his rival for Belinda's affection being a girl had wrought in his consciousness. It was one thing his knowing; it was another everyone knowing. And not for nothing, it spelled *motive* with a capital *M*.

That very night, speaking of synchronicity—which I was not and never would—Stefan came home early. "What did you do?"

"We went to Molinaro's for dinner and then back to Katie Molinaro's and played Ping-Pong."

"It's her family's restaurant?"

"It is. I didn't realize I knew her and her sister in high school. They live up on Wapheton. I mean, her family does. She lives downtown now. She's a nursing student. She has a very deluxe condo at Capitol Place, and the game room has like, a nickel bar and an Olympic-size pool and ten pool tables and all these big-screen TVs. They even have a sort of bar for kids where they can get milkshakes and candy and stuff. It's very nice. I would take Julie's son Ernie there sometime. He would think it was heaven."

"She's nice then. Is she going out with Will?"

"Will has sworn off other nurses for a while, at least until after January. He says they're exhausting, and yeah, he means like that. I realize that is a stereotype." He paused. "It wasn't Will she was interested in, though." I just waited. "She was flirting with me. But how can I, Mom? The elephant isn't just in the room, it's a herd of elephants. Of course, she knows. Anyone I meet around here will know, and I know she knows. To say this is awkward doesn't really begin to cover it. I don't know why she isn't running from me screaming and the fact that she isn't running from me screaming is kind of, like you would say, unsettling."

They had actually been having a great time when Stefan suddenly got so tense he was short of breath and had to beg off. "I'm sitting in Will's car in the parking lot, breathing in this old McDonald's bag from his back seat, which smells like pickles, because Will's right, I'm having a panic attack, and I think, this is great. This is what happens when a pretty girl flirts with me."

He further told me that Will directed him to A Deux, a dating site for Midwesterners, and when he put his picture up, he got a rainstorm of pings. "But then, we start to chat, and I hate the word chat, I have to tell her right away. How do I bring it up? I've actually never gone snorkeling, but you should probably know I killed a girl. It wasn't as though I embezzled, or even that I was in the car when some guys stuck up a convenience store. And what if they still like me? Like those women on visiting day at The Hill? I told you about them. That would creep me out. I don't want to go to any party where they'd want me as a guest."

He slumped back on the couch. I began flicking through channels. Everyone on TV seemed to be kissing or screaming. Did we have only the murder channel, like the Christianity channel at Connell's Glory Be Bed-and-Breakfast? Stefan went on, "Are there Greek Orthodox monks? Do you think I should become one? I could raise dogs in Switzerland or something." He went to get his yarn bag, which was overflowing with the beautiful gifts he was knitting for my mother and my sisters. "I could knit when I wasn't training the dogs or ringing the bells or something."

I didn't want to laugh, but Stefan grinned at me, and then I relaxed a little and grinned back. At least, he could still joke a little. We watched a decorous English murder mystery, only because I couldn't figure out how to turn it off without risking Stefan's irritation. He knew full well that, before all this happened, I delighted to the Edward Gorey montage that introduced the PBS series *Mystery*, and he would know I was switching leads because of him. We watched some story in which the new vicar was actually a former Scotland Yard inspector, and I was uncomfortable the whole time: I hadn't watched a program like this one for years. How had I ever been able to watch and forget these polite, cold-blooded crime stories? And if my flesh crawled, how did Stefan feel, seeing scenes of ersatz police peering down at a crumpled body, the actor-as-world-weary-coroner suggesting blunt force trauma…? How did he shrug off such dense, heed-less bruiting about by popular culture?

Stefan finally went upstairs. After another hour, so did I. Jep was having dinner with the team and would be home late. I didn't want to fall asleep without him being there, but some-how, I did do that.

Lately, I'd begun having new nightmares, in which I would wake up crying, sweating, my heart punching in my chest and all I remembered was that I'd been carrying something in my hand, but I'd dropped it, and now everyone would die. Julie suggested I follow Stefan's lead and get some really good ther-apy. "Forgive yourself or you won't be able to go on."

Stefan worked all day Sunday, but that night, as he was all but falling asleep over a plate of red beans and rice, I plucked up my courage and said, "You know, you're not giving them a chance. I'm sure there's a group, like a social group…"

"This isn't Parents without Purpose, Mom. There's no group for My Violent Offender Valentine." He went on, "I don't need a dating service exactly. I need a dating intervention."

"There's got to be that girl out there who would understand."

"That's what I'm afraid of, Mom. I told you this."

He was restless, though, and motioned for me to follow him outside. It was the weird weather that persisted all that year, today was not even cold enough to need a coat. We stood on the porch, in the beautiful winter night, a gentle dry cold, a soft breeze that occasionally shook snow from the trees with a shower of sparks, all a necklace of colored lights that seemed to run along one continuous roof on our street. When I turned to ask him something, I saw that he was crying. He remembered how much Belinda loved Christmas, how she'd start making gifts in September, and four different kinds of cookies. And after Christmas, she'd say, don't get depressed, it's almost spring. "O wind, if winter comes, can spring be far behind?"

"Ode to the West Wind," I said.

"I'm already forgetting her," he told me. "I can't remember how she smelled. Her cologne was like cookies, I used to think. Like cookies and tea."

"That's human," I said. "That's how we survive."

I should have been happy, and I would have been, if it hadn't been for the nagging knowledge that some befanged fate was waiting. Nothing had changed.

Not long afterward, the night before I was going to go away with Julie for a few days, Stefan casually mentioned that he'd been talking to a girl, online. His voice was tight; clearly, he wasn't going to answer questions, but he offered that she was a junior in college, at a private school near Milwaukee. He hadn't yet told her the truth about what he had done, but had revealed that he'd gone to prison. She expressed surprise, but remained interested.

Stefan said he was trying to hang in there this time, even though it made him sick.

"Of course, I want somebody to love," he said. He described again the women in the visiting room at The Hill, how they seemed to actually like knowing that their men couldn't leave them or cheat on them. "I'm sure some of them were normal people, like Roman's wife, or they got involved from a prison ministry or something. But most, no. There was one girl who stood out. This girl was gorgeous. She was as beautiful as a movie star, but you took one look in her eyes and you could see she was so crazy, and the other women were afraid of her. Trina told me the word was that one time, to prove to her husband that she loved him, she used the edge of a metal chair to cut her arm open, right in the visitors'. I'm not making that up."

I said nothing. Stefan noticed the silence. He continued on. "Like, I'm a grown man and I've never had sex. People thought, you know, at Portland High, that I'd been getting it regular since I was fifteen, but how Belinda was…"

"Sorry, Stefan, but I can't hear this. Talk to your father or Will about your sex life."

"I have to be perfect, Mom. I have to repent, every day, forever. I can't need anything. My whole life is just being sorry for..."

"Please, Stefan..."

I went back inside and ran up the stairs. A few moments before, my son and I had been having a decent chat about something toweringly difficult. This was evident proof of just how much further south a situation could go even when you thought you were tied up at the McMurdo Station of scenarios. Closing my bedroom door behind me, I took refuge in my bed and flipped my laptop open to begin the march through my neglected emails. A text message from my phone popped up on the screen, then another.

It's Esme, are you there? It's Esme. Could you message back?

Is this Professor Demetriou? It's Esme. Are you mad at me for Black Creek?

She gave me her new gmail address. Everyone had one, if not four. Hers was LongingEsme.

I answered her. I'm sorry I didn't wait for you. I couldn't. I feel guilty about that. I know you are scared, Esme. But I truly need to know what exactly you know or saw that night to understand what we need to fear. I know you loved Belinda. I trust you're trying to help Stefan.

About an hour later, I got a reply.

Is Stefan okay? Did you warn him?

I wrote, I did. I have. He doesn't know what to believe. Stuff has happened. You know it has. And he was not really okay before. He's still pretty depressed and now he's scared too.

Another hour passed. Then a ping. I have to tell you what happened. But I don't know if I'm doing the wrong thing.

You have to trust me, I wrote back. I squirmed a little when I wrote that last line. I wasn't really looking for her trust or her friendship. I wasn't really offering mine. I just needed answers. But forget her; all this was her idea. She could take what she got.

Stefan was knocking at my door. "I'm sorry, Mom." I didn't answer. "Okay, anyway. I'm sorry. I'm not perfect. Not even close. I'm weak. Maybe I'm not even good enough. Maybe this whole thing is a waste of time."

I opened the door. He looked blotchy, stubbled, like the kind of college kid who had a beer in the morning.

"Take a long hot shower, hon. You'll feel better. You are good enough. You have talent. You have compassion. You have plenty to offer the world."

"Maybe not."

"Like you said, it's too late to give up. It's got to get easier. I know it will get easier."

Stefan shrugged. The cant of his eyes seemed to mock me, or at least to betray the essential mistrust of a child for a parent, the doubt that rose along with the accumulated years, to replace the tender adulation. Your child had to reject you. You had to suborn it. But it was a brutal process in the best of circumstances. And these were not the best of circumstances.

The next morning Julie showed up at our house in a new Volvo, her present from Hal, and I put my overnight bag and the file box into the trunk and said goodbye to Stefan and Jep. I felt guilty leaving Stefan after our talk, or nontalk, the previous night, but I knew I would feel just as guilty if I stayed home. Then I snuggled into the new-brew scented glove-y leather and slept all the way to Sister Bay.

The cabin was alight in the afternoon shadow of the woods, and a young chef, slim as a pleat, with red-and-purple hair, already had a soup with tomatoes and garlic bubbling on the stove.

We skied. Moving is like cooking. It helps everything. We came out of the birch forest panting, to the edge of a broad-shouldered cliff and the lake frothed below, vasty as a sea. Worn out afterward, we took long baths, with absurdly expensive soaps and unguents.

"You're so lucky," I said.

"I am," she said. "You'll be lucky again, Thea."

An ugly-faced cutworm gnawed me. My sweet best friend Julie—considerate companion, sane soul, gracious giver of gifts and good counsel—would her face glow with such unlined purity, if she were me? There were very few problems that money couldn't solve, but, to be fair, ours was one of them. The more I chewed on that thought, the sicker I got of myself. This was patently as whiny as anything Stefan had come up with. Julie was rich, and toned, and well-married, and good. I'd stopped going to my book club when this same thing happened, because I couldn't face my old friends' good lives. But surely, they had their problems too. Some of them must wake up crying at times and not know why. Even Julie.

I filled her in on a recent development. We had agreed to do a lecture, Stefan and I.

"Really?" Julie said. "How did that happen?"

When I finally got another message from Curt Cowrie, I had forgotten everything but his name, and I only remembered that because it was the name of a shell.

As it turned out, he didn't really work for the American Association of Mental Health Nurses (AMEN). What he did was to match speakers with events. AMEN was hosting its annual national meeting in Milwaukee in just a few weeks; the main speaker had just pulled out. The organization was going to sub in a panel discussion on the topic of criminality and the duty of care. "But I told them I could book an even better speaker than they already had."

"I don't know anyone," I told him.

"I mean you. And if he wants to, Stefan. I'll get you both top dollar, forty minutes tops, then a question and answer session, in and out. No social duties, no reception. It'll start at six and you can stay over that night at the nicest hotel in town, and I don't know what that means in Milwaukee, have a great dinner after the talk, and in the morning you are on the road back home."

I said, "There's not a chance that I would do this. I'm not a speaker."

"You were pretty great on that show."

"That was...a fluke, a one-off..."

"Thea, you've been giving lectures for years. You're a professor."

He described the audience. Professionals, doctors, psychiatric nurses, social workers, some representatives of advocacy organizations. I said that there was really no way I could talk about my own life in a lecture. He mentioned a figure that was less than half my annual salary, but not much less. I took a deep breath and refused.

"Why don't you ask Stefan first?"

When I did, to my horror, Stefan was definitely interested. He was interested in the money, because who wouldn't be? But more importantly, he saw it as an extension of his quest to bring more attention to The Healing Project. We talked over what this speech might look like—that is, Jep and I talked it over while Stefan ate a whole family-sized bag of taco chips and texted his friends. Curt Cowrie had advised me to make my talk a narrative, a story. Tell what happened, and how we felt then and how we felt now. What was learned? What do you wish you'd known? These audiences would want news they could use in their professional lives. They would also just be curious. They would have questions.

Stefan said he wanted to do it, for sure.

So we'd agreed.

"Well, how bad could a bunch of psychiatric nurses be?" Julie said, and then both of us burst out laughing.

"There will be all kinds of people there, Jules. You know and I know. Some will just be people who want to feel better about themselves. They want to know they're better parents than we are. But the trap door opens for everyone. Nobody gets through life without it happening, not like for me, but some way."

"Would you want it to open for everyone?" Julie said.

"No," I said. Yes, I thought. I told her, "What if it draws somebody out in the open?

"If Stefan talks about that night, maybe it's like a challenge. Don't hang back like a little coward. I have a right to know who's after me. Stefan has a right."

"What if it draws somebody out into the open but this time that person doesn't just stop with burning up a car? It's a risk," Julie said. "You can't control a big lecture like a little story at the local public TV station."

"Jep said that. But Stefan said he couldn't hide forever."

"That's true."

"I don't know if I'm brave, but Stefan is. He's dedicating part of his life to letting people know he repents. He's helping other people repent. He's not even letting this threat stop him. Even though he's scared to death sometimes."

I remembered Curt's words. "To be honest, I didn't know if I really could feel much sympathy for Stefan. My wife was the one who brought the show to my attention, because she's a psychiatric nurse. She told me, unless this kid is really sincere, what's in it for him? Now that I've seen it, I agree with her. I don't think I could have faced up to it so publicly, the way he did."

"It's a lot of needless exposure, honey," Jep said. Community leadership covered a whole bunch of ground and a whole spectrum of politics. And there was no avoiding that the gallery of ghouls, the kind of people who slowed down to gape at car accidents, would probably be there too. "Let things die down a little."

"Dad," Stefan said. "I can't wait my whole life for this to die down."

Between two old friends, lay not only bottomless love and irritation, but the allegiance of soldiers. I knew that, when Julie was first married, she inexplicably fell in love with her younger sister's college boyfriend and was tempted to run away with him except that, before she could, he ran away from both of them. She knew that I had changed the order of the stack of vitae in Keith's office so that it looked as if the committee had put my name on top instead of Steve Ngobe's. We were smug in the possession of each other's murderous secrets.

It got late.

There were fourteen other beds in that cabin, but when I asked Julie if I could stay in her room with her, she said she was hoping I would, just like when we were twelve.

Then she told me, "I think it's time to open that box now." It still sat under the dining room table, where we'd left it when we carried it in. Now we brought it into the bedroom and sat it between us on the bed. Carefully, I began to take out the contents, one envelope and file folder at a time.

Julie asked, "Do we have to make a list so we put them back in order?"

"These are just copies," I said. "I don't have to give them back."

One of the padded envelopes was marked CLIP. Expecting a file of newspaper articles, I ran my nail under the seal. A small plastic bag fell out onto the quilt. Inside was a single blond curl, one of its strands darkened, as if with a messy dye. It landed between us, a grim artifact. The label on the bag read, B. McCormack. Like one of my Victorian ladies of fiction, I clutched my throat.

"Julie, wait," I said. "That's real."

She said nothing. When I looked up, I could see she was crying. She reached out and took my hand. I wanted to punch Pete Sunday. What was he thinking? Was he that sloppy, to include real evidence in a box of copies? Quickly, I opened another envelope.

These were photos. They were of the crime scene in color, both lurid and washed out. At first, I couldn't determine what exactly I was seeing...a close-up of something that looked matted...

I told Julie, "We shouldn't be seeing these. He must have given me the wrong box. I was just supposed to have copies. Documents. Police reports. Not all this."

Julie was up then and running to the bathroom, retching into her hands. I followed her, holding her hair back as she threw up in the green marble toilet. I sat on the edge of the beautiful tub, also green, with satin-nickel finish. The soothing luxury of the setting, the low caramel lights, the spatter of fairy-tale snow against the narrow floor-to-ceiling bathroom windows, all in sharp contrast to the violent contents of the box. "We don't have to look any more," I told Julie. "The detective must have made a mistake. He would not have done this on purpose."

"We should go through everything while we are together," Julie said. "You don't want to have to do it some other time alone."

"I don't have to do it at all," I said. "There's not going to be anything in this box that will tell me anything I don't really know."

Was there even a chance that Pete Sunday's choice to give me this box was no error? What if my visit had unsettled him? What if it stirred up some doubts he still had about Stefan's case? Maybe he wanted an excuse for some fresh eyes on the evidence. Police did that all the time on television. As if examining again the real photos, the lock of hair might reveal motivation or something else that was previously overlooked. Or what if he just wanted to rebuke me with the facts, for my nosiness?

"We have to be brave," Julie said.

I fanned the photos out like a deck of terrible tarot, pushing the first and most terrible picture of Belinda's skull aside with one finger. The next photo was of the golf club. In general I didn't know one golf club from another, but I knew this was an iron, a black shaft with a chubby foot, shiny with blood. Here was a picture of Belinda on the floor, her legs as disjointed as a doll's, ringed in chalk, then photos of the splattered ceiling, walls, lampshades, couch cushions. Stefan's stained, pale blue sweatshirt on the floor next to Belinda's head; the dark, impossibly huge pool of blood on the gray carpet; a man's rugged fist, index finger extended, pointing to a bloody footprint.

Julie and I sat back. I was panting like I was in labor. Julie went to the kitchen and brought back big mugs of tea with lots of sugar a few minutes later.

The big clock from the church at the edge of the lake struck twelve midnight.

We went on.

INCIDENT REPORT: At approximately 8 p.m. 2000 hours on the evening of January 20, I was contacted by Detective Sergeant Dashelle Lamartine to report to the Covered Bridge Townhomes, 100 Tamarack Road, Black Creek, Wisconsin, Apartment 216, pursuant to the report of an individual found bludgeoned in her living room. I arrived at approximately 8:11 p.m. and was briefed by Detective Sergeant Lamartine. (Prior to my arrival Black Creek County Fire and Rescue responded to the scene including Captain Purvis, Captain Tran, and Fire Medic Probacyzk and Fire Medic Lucarelli.) I observed an injured individual lying facedown on the floor in front of the couch, head pointing north, feet south, a very large pool of blood surrounding the individual's head and shoulders. Upon observation, this appears to be a woman between the ages of 18 and 25. A single large wound to the back of her head, the size of a man's fist, seems to be the only visible injury. The skull displays a fracture, from which there is bleeding and bloody serum that have issued from the wound. The victim is wearing black stockings or tights, and a long sweater, probably white in color originally…on the floor adjacent to the body at a right angle is a

Callaway Big Bertha Women's Flex 9 iron golf club with
what appears to be significant hair and tissue on the
face of the club. Also present are a number of bath
towels, also soaked in blood, a bowl containing what
appears to be popcorn, a set of electric hair rollers,
and a pillow in the shape of a pineapple.

Fire Medic Lucarelli had assessed that young woman did
not have a pulse or any respirations. Sophia Smith,
Black Creek County Coroner, confirms this.

Presumed perpetrator Stefan Paul Christiansen, 17

AUTOPSY PERFORMED by	**Assistant:**
Sophia Smith, M.D.	**Brian Bello, M.D.**
55 College Avenue	
Black Creek, WI 53575	**Full Autopsy**
Name: McCormack, Belinda Lowell	**Coroner's Case #:** 2004-277
Date of Birth: 10/31	**Age:** 18
Race: White	**Sex:** Female
Date of Death: 1/20	**Body Identified by:** Caroline Jackworth McCormack—aunt
Case 001294-23E-2004	**Investigative Agency:** Black Creek County Sheriff's Department

EXTERNAL EXAMINATION:
The autopsy is begun at 8:30 a.m. The body is presented in a black body bag. The victim is wearing a long white-appearing sweater, size S, black tights, size S, and pink ballet shoes, size 6, a bra size 32B and underpants size 5. Jewelry included two smooth-textured silver hoop pierced earrings, 1-inch diameter, one in each ear, and one 1-inch wide silver expandable wristband on left wrist with two charms, one in the shape of a cross and one in the shape of a star. Fingernails and toenails are painted a pale pearl pink. The body is that of a normally developed and nourished white female measuring 67 inches and weighing 119 pounds, and appearing generally consistent with the stated age of eighteen. The body is cold and unembalmed. The teeth are native and in good condition. The genitalia are consistent with a normally developed adult female. The eyes are closed. Irises are gray. Pupils are fixed.

INJURIES:
The neck is fractured at the C3 vertebra. There is a depressed skull fracture of five centimeters of the occipital bone. Extruded brain tissue is observed. An abrasion of four centimeters to the left cheekbone appears sustained post-mortem.

I shifted through more papers.

The alleged perpetrator, Stefan Paul Christiansen, age 17, of 11 Washtenaw Street, Portland, Wisconsin, is unable to stand, walk or answer questions. He explains his arms are on fire. He asks for his mother. He tells this interviewer, "It is all my fault." (See video recorded statement.)

Then this:

REPORT OF THE IDENTIFICATION DIVISION

To: Detective Sergeant Peter B. Sunday, cc Detective Sergeant Dashelle Lamartine
Black Creek County Sheriff's Police Department
55 College Avenue
Black Creek, Wisconsin 53575
Specimens delivered by Louis Torres

60 negatives

60 photographs of latent prints, including tips, sides and lower joint series of fingers, palm prints and footprints of Jillian Rae McCormack, Belinda Lowell McCormack, Stefan Paul Christiansen, unidentified fingerprints and palm prints.

Photographs of household surfaces include TV, nightstand, coffee table, lamps, presumed murder weapon golf club. Prints of all three individuals distributed throughout the living area of the apartment 216, Covered Bridge Townhomes, 100 Tamarack Road, Black Creek, Wisconsin. Prints on the shaft of the golf club include palm, tips, lower joint prints consistent on examination with those of Belinda Lowell McCormack, Jillian Rae McCormack, Stefan Christiansen and two unidentified others.

I was wondering now whether some of the unidentified prints might belong to the caller Esme. Maybe she had been there, as she claimed, and left before the EMT arrived? Why would she have touched the golf club? What possible reason?

"Wouldn't an autopsy report have the contents of the victim's stomach?" Julie asked.

"That's what happens on TV."

"It's what happens in real life too. There's nothing like that here. I don't see a toxicology report of any kind for Belinda or Stefan."

We wrote down two questions for me to ask Sunday when I called him:

Where were the toxicology reports done on Stefan and Belinda?

How many hours after the murder was Stefan's first interview? Was he still under the influence? Did that happen at the hospital or the police station?

After all this distress, I still didn't feel that I'd learned anything new. I'd just been forced to look at disturbing images. Forced? I wasn't forced. No one forced me except my own demons, unleashed by me. Maybe now they would get back into the box.

"We need to get some sleep now," Julie said. So I gathered up all the files and envelopes and carefully replaced them. Then Julie said, "I'm glad we are here together, in case you have nightmares."

We lay back to back, as we had for thirty years. The melony smell of Julie's hair was as familiar to me as my own palm, the slight lift in one of her shoulders from a broken clavicle sustained by falling off the handlebars of my bike as known to me as Stefan's eyes.

"I have to let go of this," I told her. "Julie, put a spell on me. Make me stop ruminating. I'm sick of this cat-and-mouse game, like waiting, waiting, waiting, for what? For that one fact, that exists only in my mind? Or for the big climax? Is somebody going to shoot him from ambush? Or shoot me? This has to end."

"Maybe it has ended already. Maybe it's over and you don't know it."

"Maybe. Jep said whoever has been calling might just get bored and move on to some new craziness."

I drifted off, with my brain for once off its customary red alert. Only a few times over the past several years had I gone to sleep when it was dark and awakened when it was light. Most often, I itched and twisted until I was nearly on the floor with my pillows or lay awake trying to convince myself that I really didn't have to go to the bathroom. Once I was up, I had to repeat nonsense, *Fee Fi Fo Fum*, to the bathroom and back, or I would be quietly watching BBC reruns on my computer until the sun came up.

Physical and mental exhaustion can have their uses, and the light that awakened me was red dawn.

Sleep had also sent a letter to my subconscious, as it will. What I kept searching for was a way back to normal. Not just for Stefan, but for me. For Jep. For us as a family. The Healing Project, the TV interview, I wanted them all to do—to do the work of stain remover.

But there would be no return. No one in my family had any "before," anymore, only after. The "before" was forfeit. Before Belinda died, not much in my life had prepared me for anything except moderate good fortune. I had good parents, good health, good teeth, a pretty good job, really good hair, an astoundingly good son and a very good marriage. My bad luck was customary bad luck, the kind a life contains, a miscarriage, a broken wrist, a coveted job that went to someone else, the rear-end smashup of a new car.

After Belinda died, the good days were the ones when I didn't want to die. Stefan's future was shunted onto a broken track where the stops were no longer mortarboards and first real jobs, wedding boutonnieres and champagne toasts, but sobriety tokens and perhaps a street to walk down quietly without being threatened or shunned. And that was my future too, at least, my near future. Only Jep seemed somehow absolved, and how could I be sure he wasn't just sparing me his complaints? How did I know what kinds of looks he got, what comments broke off when he entered the room?

I had never allowed myself to consider how much I resented this pressure. How was any of it my doing? The notion that good parents could raise bad kids was increasingly out of favor. Nothing comes from nothing. So what had we permitted or forbidden that thousands of others had not permitted or forbidden without consequence?

Perhaps the worst truth was the one I failed to admit even to Julie, and barely to myself. Certainly, I was wildly grateful not to be Jill. Four years was a long time to have a pain in your tooth, but not in your heart. For almost four years, she had been without her girl. Jill's pain was just beginning. Jill had only Belinda's past. But I had Stefan's past as well as his present and future. Within him, cached inside him like the rings of a tree, was still the chuckling baby with enormous feet or the six-year-old who liked his eggs sunny-side up and called me his "sunny-up egg." I might have to contend with everything I hated about the situation, which was wound around everything I loved, but the fact remained, I could still hug Stefan, my only, my child.

And yet, to do that, I had to accept not just the child I had loved, but the man, with blood on his hands. I hadn't accepted the fullness of his crime. I stopped just short of it. I sat up and quietly made my way to the window, looking out on a stereotypical postcard of forest majesty. I had to truly see that man and forgive him, just as the people in The Healing Project strove to do. It was time to express my remorse, and to seek renewal. I loved Stefan, but if I was honest, I had not forgiven him. Now, for his sake and mine, I would. And that would be the final step to ending the long night that had begun over three years ago, so that the rest of our lives could truly and cleanly begin, I thought. We could look toward a time when this awful time was a memory, fading slowly away.

It was too early to get up.

I slipped into the bathroom, brushed my teeth and, as the red fingers of dawn worked their way around the edges of the blinds, I got back into bed and curled up in the warm hollow next to Julie's back.

It was in that sweet bath between sleeping and waking that the realization slammed into me like a truck through the side of a building, shoving aside or flattening everything in its path, and I sprung awake. I saw it, the reason I kept combing the riverbed for one nugget, another story or at least an additional story. Here was the meaning of all those sobbing phone calls and texts from Esme, her confession to what she had done that stopped just short of confessions, her oversized concern for Stefan's welfare, her guilt over Belinda, the agony that went beyond loss. Here was the reason that the unidentified fingerprints on the golf club had to be hers.

Esme had killed Belinda.

And, somehow, she had set Stefan up to take the blame.

BOOK THREE:

Redemption

10

I couldn't wait until morning so that I could call Pete Sunday.
I glanced at the clock.

It was 6:20 a.m.

What kind of person would awaken her peacefully sleeping
best friend on a cold morning to say something that could easily
be said two hours from then? I would wait until eight o'clock.
That resolve lasted three minutes.

"Wake up, Jules!" I said. She grunted, snuggled deeper into
the plushy mattress. Sleep was another of the gifts I envied her.
"Julie! Wake up."

"Huh? What the hell, Thea."

"I have to go home right now. I'll take a bus if you don't
want to go back."

"Wait, what?" Julie said. "Go home why? What time is it?
Is it morning?"

"It's morning."

"I haven't even had coffee."

"I have to make a phone call. It's urgent."

"Thea, there are phones right here."

"I have to call from my house."

Julie sat up with a reluctant sigh and a stretch.

She said, "No, Thea. No, you really don't. This phone connects to anyone on earth you need to call. Why don't you tell me what's going on? What happened in the past six hours that I've been asleep?" She swung her feet to the floor. "No, don't tell me yet. Wait, I'm going to make an espresso for me and one for you. That will take less than ten minutes, and then you can tell me."

I said, "I figured out last night that Stefan didn't kill Belinda."

Julie would sooner have held her hand to a flame than disrespect me, so she kept her face neutral as she made the espresso and put butter on my raisin toast, peanut butter on hers.

"So so so…" she said. "I clearly missed out on some key life moments."

I said, "Julie, I'm serious."

"I know you are," she said and hugged me briefly but firmly. "Thea… I don't know what to say."

I laid it out for her then, all the clues in the phone calls, the unremitting inquiries about Stefan, the warnings about "remembering" too much.

Finally, Julie said, "It's all very compelling. But…why didn't you think of this before now? Why didn't Stefan? For that matter, why didn't I?"

I didn't know why. The best reason I could think of was that all of us believed the same story to be true; Stefan had confessed. Not one of us had a complete picture of that night. I hadn't wanted to remember. Stefan couldn't.

A few months earlier, I'd suggested that he consider being hypnotized to remember more of the events that night. His reaction was pure fury. "Do you not get that I want to put this behind me, Mom? Not keep going back and back and back and

back until I'm a complete emotional cripple who just sits in the
closet chewing on my raincoat? I'm done, Mom! I want a life.
I suggest you get one too."

"I have to tell him."

"Well, you don't have to tell him before breakfast. I imagine even detectives don't get started until after they have coffee.
Particularly on a Sunday."

I said, "What? I mean Stefan. I have to call Stefan right now."

Julie literally took hold of my shoulders then. "No, Thea, no.
Not until something real comes of this…"

"But what if it's all true…?"

"If it's true, it will be wonderful beyond anything and awful
beyond anything and it will all happen very soon. But imagine
if you told Stefan and then this theory came to nothing? This
isn't like not getting a job, Thea. It's like having your life held
out to you after you'd thought you lost it and then losing it all
over again." She sat down and closed her eyes, inhaling the smell
of the espresso. "I won't let you do that to my godson. I don't
even want you to tell Jep."

"I have to tell Jep."

"Okay, maybe, maybe you're right. Think that one through.
Let's take this one world at a time, Thea. One world at a time."
She began to run a bath.

I tried to force myself to settle and when I couldn't, I threw
on my wraps and went out for a hard solo hike to the edge of
the bluff. My brain was like dolphins racing, silvery beams of
light in a deep blue abyss. The list of questions I'd written down
after examining the contents of the box didn't matter now. Well,
they did matter, but if Esme's fingerprints turned out to be one
of the unidentified fingerprints on the golf club, it would just
be more proof that she was guilty. She'd been there, or so she
kept insisting, and she must have wrapped Stefan's hand around
the handle of the golf club to cover her own guilt.

What if the reason they couldn't ID her was she didn't have any fingerprints on record?

I wouldn't worry about that now: Everybody had fingerprints on record these days—kindergarten kids, teachers. I did. All the Thornton Wilder instructors had been fingerprinted. And if she didn't, she would be fingerprinted when they arrested her.

As it turned out, I had to leave a message for Pete Sunday, who was on his honeymoon. The colleague who answered asked if this matter could wait until Friday. "No," I said. "Well, yes. But please tell him it's urgent."

Unknowing, I had waited years. I could wait a a few days more. I would think and make lists. I would go through all the texts and make a list of everything she said, and a list of her myriad phone numbers. I would put together a case. The important thing was that Pete Sunday believe me. I didn't have to prove that Esme did it; he would have to do that. All I had to convince him of was that this wasn't just a mother's natural protective instinct coming up again after so many years.

Which, of course, it was.

And yet, if it were not for that instinct, I might have given up, long ago. Then there would be no answer. There would be no justice. There would be no other story.

11

Jep and Stefan were at work when Pete Sunday called me back. I was prepared to give an impassioned speech if Sunday didn't take me seriously. But before I said anything, he pointed out, "I gave you the wrong box."

"There are no mistakes," I said.

"Well, other than this one. It was an honest mistake. I probably broke a law or two. I wanted you to see the evidence but I didn't intend for you to see those crime-scene photos, Mrs. Christiansen."

"Thea."

"Right, Thea."

"And it's okay. You didn't force me to look at them."

"What's up?" he said.

Then I plunged in, racing to reveal the whole jigsaw of suspicions and suppositions so that he would see this was more than just a mother's longing. I explained how the mention of the fingerprints on the golf club in the report contained in the evidence box, unimportant as this seemed, was the final puzzle piece.

"Okay," he said, as if talking to himself. "Okay. Say this girl, this…"

"Emily. On the texts, she calls herself Esme, which I guess is the name that Belinda called her. But if she's the same girl that Stefan knew, and I know she is, her name was Emily Lindquist or Emily Lundgren and she came from Chicago."

"Did she live in Black Creek?"

"I think so. I think she went to college there."

"Did you ask Stefan if she was in school with Belinda?"

"I, uh, I haven't told Stefan about this theory I have. I don't want him to get his hopes up…or hate me…or think I'm crazy."

"That makes sense. Do you have a picture of her?"

"I never saw her in my life. I have no idea what she looks like. Stefan might."

"So you could ask him for a picture of her."

"I could, but I don't want to tell him. And maybe him having a picture is a long shot. There's no reason he would have kept it, unless… I don't know, the picture included Belinda too."

"Why don't you think that over?" Pete Sunday said. "As for the box, you can't just pop these things in the mail, as you know. I'll come to get it myself. Would that be okay?"

"You could just send someone else, someone junior. It's a long way."

I heard a beep and a shuffle. "From what I see here, it looks like about…mmm, twenty-two miles."

"It's nearly two hundred miles, detective. It took me three hours."

"Well, I'm driving to work right now, it's about a half hour drive, pretty drive, we live right on Red Cedar Lake near the winery. That winery is a beautiful place. Wine isn't bad either."

He was having some kind of chuckle at my expense. This seemed odd, and a little out of character, until I typed "Red

Cedar Lake" into my phone. He really was twenty miles away.
"You moved," I said. "You took the job in Dane County…"

"Just a few weeks ago. Changed jobs. Got married."

"Do you like it?"

"I never realized how simple and easy my job was before. The
things I did once a year up there, I've had to do in my first week
here. People here seem more determined to harm each other,
you know?" he said. "They're not all cases like Belinda McCormack. But people are bashing away at each other every night."

"True thing that," I said.

"It's exciting for sure, but we'll see."

I put on makeup, ground beans for coffee. I went back upstairs to bring the box down and restore it to pristine order.
Literally, all I could do was to hope for the best, and that was
never a problem for me. All the while I was wondering if this
situation gave me permission to do something that would have
been unthinkable even a year ago. Then, I did it. I still vacu-
umed under Stefan's bed, and I knew he kept a boot box down
there filled with photos. Slowly, I drew them out. The whole
top layer was made up of lavish photos of his work, gorgeous
evidence of his ability. There was a photo of a series of stone
shelves that formed a waterfall, all hung about with thick, flowering vines and backed by a stand of sunflowers. It looked like a
feature from the garden of a king. Another garden was laid out
in a series of concentric circles around a fountain, three rings
forming masses of yellow and purple perennials hugged tightly
by small, shiny evergreens trimmed to the shape of big beads in
a string. These had clearly been taken by Stefan with his phone
and made on the photo printer in our house, which sat on the
corner library table that was Jep's makeshift desk.

A thick pocket folder held all the family photos that my sister
Phoebe had sent to Stefan in prison. I slid those back and fastened the envelope. Beneath those, there was a plain, thinner
envelope marked SUMMER. I opened it.

There were a dozen photos of Belinda, brandishing a wooden spoon as she cooked, her hair piled up artfully, Belinda sleek as a seal at a lake in her bikini, Belinda on a stone bench reading, several of her in the pool at her own house, and of Belinda asleep on her bed (that chilled me). The scene shifted then. There she was with a group of girls in front of that restaurant in Black Creek where I'd eaten macaroni and cheese. And then there were a clipped batch of photos of Stefan and Belinda, her in a shiny top and jeans, him in a soft blue denim shirt. In several of those photos, they were with another girl, a dark-haired girl with a cap of short feathered hair, very slight but almost as tall as Stefan. They were all miming firing a gun at the photographer. In another photo, it was possible to see Belinda's image in a mirror, as she snapped a picture of Stefan and that same girl, sitting on a cream-colored couch. I had seen that couch, in the crime-scene photos, splashed with Belinda's blood and tissue. In a third photo, the girl and Belinda were wearing witch's hats. They held up a sign between them that said, BOO! STEFAN. That one would have been taken before Stefan moved to Black Creek. Some of these photos were of different vintage. They were all relatively recent, but in some Belinda's hair was shorter, in some longer, at least one dated back to junior prom.

There were twenty photos, and I wondered with a shock if Stefan had these with him in prison. But who would have sent these to him? Were they part of his belongings from the hospital? Was a murderer even allowed to have photos of his victim? On the other hand, how would anyone sifting through mail have known that this particular girl was Belinda?

Or who the other girl was.

It had to be her.

I was looking at her.

I put all the photos back except two. If my luck was extraordinarily bad, Stefan would notice what I'd done and hate me for the violation. If my luck was extraordinarily good, he would see what I had done as needs must and his relief would subsume all his qualms.

Pete Sunday rolled up to our house about twelve.

Pete praised the coffee. I offered him an egg salad sandwich and, to my surprise, he accepted, since he'd forgotten breakfast.

In passing, as if I were a heavyweight warming up for the title bout, I mentioned the contents of the box, my questions in brief. The fingerprints all made sense now, and he said he didn't know why the toxicology reports were not included, but he did remember them well. Stefan's blood revealed a high level of stimulants, opiates and alcohol. Belinda's tested positive for the antidepressant sertraline, sold under the name Zoloft, as well MDMA, or 3,4-Methylenedioxymethamphetamine, known as ecstasy.

I thought of all the years that I would never have believed that Belinda used drugs.

Just so that I could see everything fully, I asked about the things Stefan said when he was interviewed that night. I also asked why he was interviewed when we weren't there, because he was a minor, but just as quickly, I remembered the lawyer telling us that with a crime this serious, the age of seventeen was a presumed adult.

By the time Sunday entered the apartment, he said, paramedics were going through the motions on Belinda, and Stefan was on the floor, groggy but alert enough to already be in handcuffs. The coroner showed up about the same time as Sunday did. The first time Sunday talked to Stefan was at the hospital ward: "He was pretty incoherent, just crying and moaning. I tried to ask him what happened but he didn't really seem to get it. The only thing he said to me was, will Belinda be okay? He didn't realize she was dead."

The second time Pete Sunday interviewed Stefan, he'd been processed, allowed to shower and been given a huge pair of surgical scrubs and a robe to wear. He was shivering so fiercely that Sunday went to the nursing station to get him a blanket, which our son looped over his head like a Bedouin's robe. Wearily, then, Stefan confessed to breaking down the door by kicking it and hitting Belinda with the golf club. He didn't recall doing it but he had been told that was how she was hurt. He did remember getting into a physical fight and screams and blood. He remembered things that hadn't happened, however. For one thing, upon examination, the door was in perfectly good order. Pete Sunday had written down what Stefan said. "He said, I guess I just went in and then I hit her. Why would I do that?"

I sat across from the detective, delicately deconstructing and reconstructing my egg salad sandwich, but my thoughts went to Stefan. Abruptly, the sight of my food, soft and soaking into the bread, suddenly revolted me. I got up to tip it into the trash.

"You see why he was so confused now," I said.

"Maybe. You're thinking this girl, this…"

"Emily. Or Esme. Emily Lindquist. Emily Lundgren."

"You're thinking that this girl just told him all this before the police got there and he heard it somehow and believed it. As much as he could understand."

"Something like that." Then I asked, "Are you going to arrest her?"

Pete Sunday blinked. "Arrest her? I don't even know who she is yet." If only I'd heard from her recently. I personally had called every one of those numbers and every one of them was disconnected. Could Pete find out who'd used them and how, in previous months? That depended, he said, on what kind of phones they were.

"This is important," I insisted, just north of a whine.

"It is, but, Thea, it's an old case, and yes, it's a priority, but I have other cases. A guy who just robbed and beat up six women who'll get away if I don't find him. I don't even work for that jurisdiction anymore, so I should just hand this box and your

thoughts over to them. I just can't bring myself to do that. So
I'm going to have to ask my boss here if I can use my own time
to chase this down."

Frustrated, I asked him how long this would take. Conser-
vatively, days if not weeks, he said.

The speech we were to give was in two days' time. What if
it wasn't relevant at all anymore? Why should we do this?

Pete Sunday asked the substance of what we were to address
and I told him that it was the challenges Stefan faced coming
out of prison.

"Well, that's still something you faced, right?" he said.

It was. With a promise to try to speed things up, Pete Sunday left, the box tucked under one arm.

It's really almost over, I told myself. Almost really over for
good.

We arrived at the hotel in Milwaukee early in the morning
that weekend, although the speech was not scheduled to start
until that night at six. I was practically teen-like in my relief
when Jep was able to come with us. Curt Cowrie met us in the
lobby of The Nines, the very kind of hotel I'd dreamed of last
January when Stefan came out of prison, with a rooftop restaurant where we lunched on Thai barbecue until my stomach
literally protruded. He said we were welcome to stay overnight
in the suite booked for us, dine out, have brunch the next day,
whatever we wanted, and we agreed to take him up on that.
We went to the theater and did a sound check. How many seats
there were, how long it took to walk from the back of the theater to the stage, these things literally nauseated me, or maybe
it was all that barbecue. Forty minutes, an hour with questions,
I told myself. It couldn't last forever. Be brave and be seated.

After lunch, a stylist showed up to do hair and makeup. Stefan looked like old money in a slate-blue Marc Jacobs sport coat
over a gray checked shirt with a dark green tie. He told me that

he'd gone swimming in the indoor rooftop pool and then took a nap. At four, we showed up at the theater. We sat side by side on the stage in big wing-back chairs. The sound technicians inserted the mics, clipped them and turned them on. When it was time for each of us to speak, we would get up and stand in front of a slender podium on which we'd set our notes.

An hour until the curtains would open. A half hour. Five minutes.

As the lights went down, I looked out over the crowd, which was startlingly vast, and reminded myself not to think too much. I began, "Today, you're going to feel the whole range of emotions, from outrage to pity. When you leave, I hope that you will also feel understanding and compassion, even if that surprises you. I can assure you that this whole range of emotions is something that everyone who knows me and who knows my son Stefan has felt..."

Suddenly, a line of bright lights flipped on, along the first row of the mezzanine. A whole row of young women stood, fifteen? Twenty? Some were holding large flashlights, others leaning out over the railing, unfurling a canvas the size of a putting green, imprinted with the morgue photo of Belinda's face.

"Say, say, say her name," they began to chant. "Say, say, say her name."

For twenty minutes, the rest of the audience watched aghast as extra security grappled with the girls, who were modestly attired in red or pink jumpsuits so that they could fall limp to the floor. Each time the guards gently wrestled one of them into the aisle, she ran back and began chanting again. Finally, using zip ties, they secured the young women's wrists to the railings so tightly that it was necessary for police to turn on the auditorium lights and use delicate surgical scissors to free them.

As soon as police were able to get the girls out of the auditorium, we went on, probably less shaken by the familiar chants than the rest of the audience was.

I finished up by saying, "People always ask, how could you not have known your son was in so much trouble emotionally? What kind of parent are you? That's a legitimate question. Until this happened, I would have said that I was a good parent, raising a loving and responsible son. I would have said that my son was the last person to be violent or to have a serious struggle with depression or mental illness or drugs. So I wasn't really looking for any other possibility. And maybe that's the only lesson I can leave you with.

"Each of us owes the people we love and the people they love, or the people they could hurt, the responsibility to look without favor or prejudice. Maybe there was a sign in my son's propensity to fall in love so madly he couldn't see anything but the girl he loved. Maybe there was a sign in the way he seemed to cut off almost all communication with us when he went to college. We just thought he was trying to experience himself as a young man who didn't need to report his every move to his mother and father, and we didn't want to interfere with that. We weren't with him every day, as we had been when he was younger, and we definitely would have seen changes in him if we had gone up there, or cajoled him into a visual phone call.

"We second-guessed our impulse to reach out. We should have reached out. I'm not suggesting that you have to question every move someone makes, but then again, it doesn't hurt to question. The worst that could happen is that we irritate or offend someone, and that seems a very small price to pay. We loved him, and we knew that he knew it. You know, if love alone was enough to prevent a suicide, almost no one would ever die by suicide. If love alone was enough to deter someone from violence, there would be a whole lot less violence in our violent world."

Stefan spoke then, briefly. "I never imagined myself to be the kind of person who could violently hurt someone I loved, and it doesn't matter that it was an accident. But I had to go on and I still want my life to matter for something, which is why I started The Healing Project." He talked about its aims and goals. "Everybody has the obligation to do good, like John Wesley said, as much as we can for as many people as we can. But if you've done wrong, you have even more of an obligation. It's the most important thing."

Then we took questions. One woman, not unkindly, asked me how I coped with the inevitable shame:

I told her, "I wanted to hide away. I wanted to die at first. But like Stefan said, the most important impulse you have, along with the guilt, is you want to do something good. It wouldn't do anybody any good if I just hid away. I really didn't want to even do this speech, not even for money, since it was too painful to even think about. But I became convinced that there was a good reason to do it, that maybe at least it would give somebody the insight to help another family along."

An older man raised his hand and got up. He turned to Stefan. "What about you? You paid your 'debt to society.'" The sneering quotation marks hung invisible and heavy in the air. "Do you feel like you should go on and just have a jolly life now?"

"No," Stefan said. "I don't. But even people like me have families, my grandparents and my parents who need me too. I'm all they have, and maybe I don't deserve for them to love me, but I want to try to deserve it."

When we finished, there was a sprinkling of applause, then a great boom of applause. I could see Jep in the back, making the clasped-fists signs of congratulation, and then gesturing to let us know he would go to get the car.

We walked out through the lobby, where several people stopped us to murmur approval for the talk and for our grace under the pressure of the protest. As we neared the door, I heard someone behind me, "Wait, dear, just a moment!"

A small, elderly woman was quickly bearing down on us, using her cane to propel her along. It was only when she got so close that I could study the way she moved that I realized, too late, she doesn't really need that cane…but by then she had slugged me, a strong right to the jaw that knocked me to the carpet on my rear end. Stefan jumped to help me, while one security guard and then another pinned the woman's arms behind her back. "Why don't you kill yourself?" she screamed as they dragged her away.

Then it was a few minutes of first aid from a nurse practitioner who'd been in the audience, followed by an ambulance ride to the closest emergency room, with Jep and Stefan following behind, where I got stitches and painkillers. We decided to forgo the hotel stay that night so it was not until nearly midnight that we were finally home, and I let Jep tuck me in, and bring me hot milk with honey and cinnamon.

The next morning, I played back the voice mail on the answering machine, for some reason on speaker. There were a few random remarks about the attack on me at the speech, which had been mentioned on the news, one from a personal injury lawyer offering to sue the assailant. At the last message, Stefan and I froze, as if a tiger had just walked into the room. "Thea, this is Jill McCormack. I need to speak with you. Please give me a call as soon as you can."

12

"Ouch," Jep said that night when he inspected my luridly swollen lip. "Theaitsa, that little old lady packed a punch."

"She wasn't even old," I said.

The details turned out to be ludicrous: My assailant, a veteran nurse certified to counsel rape victims, was only fifty, but she dressed up to look at least twenty-five years older to divert suspicion. Since the organizers picked up my medical costs, the stitches for my lip, the cost of my ruined white wool jacket, she ended up only paying a fine of $100. I declined to press further charges for assault.

I spent the next couple of days feeling sore and spent and feeling really sorry for myself. There were calls from virtually everyone I knew, even the cousins I only saw every few years at my aunt Helen's family reunion. I slept long hours, often from dinnertime until ten the next morning, waking disoriented from blank, cavernous sleep that was the gift of the robust painkillers. If only such great medicine weren't also so dangerous, for such sleep was not only my wish generally but specifically right now. I just wanted to sleep until Pete Sunday located Esme and questioned her.

Dithering about whether to tell Jep was a torment. There was almost nothing I didn't confide in him, particularly if it was important. Whenever we were together, I felt as though I was cheating on him. And yet, when I pictured the pained look that would steal over his face at my latest piece of detective work, as he tried to understand how my own hunches and the text messages had combined to concoct this cataclysmic conclusion, I just couldn't bring myself to say anything. Julie was right; everything would be revealed in time, if it turned out that there was anything to reveal.

I did tell Jep about Jill's message.

"Should I call her?"

"Don't ask me." He put his hands up in front of him. "I'm just a simple guy. I don't know about the protocol for this tortured emotional stuff."

"Right, okay, draw the old Disney movie football coach card."

"Why do you have to get so bitchy? Go or don't go. She's not dangerous, Thea. She's not going to kill you."

"I'm scared to go. Will you go with me?"

"I absolutely will not go with you," he said. "I'll drive you and wait for you, but I'm not going to face off with Jill McCormack." He went to the refrigerator and began getting out ingredients for about four kinds of snacks, plus the chia seeds he was now obsessed with sprinkling on everything. My tension was so great that I wanted to smack him. A moment later, he muttered, "You should have thought of this before."

"Before? Before what, Jep? Before The Healing Project? Or before I had our son, because it doesn't come from your side of the family, huh?"

Why would I say such a thing, particularly at that point? Was it just pure spite? When I look back, I suppose it was superstition. Much as I rejected it, the accepted narrative, however awful, was safer than a far-fetched theory. Immediately, contrition replaced anger. Jep and I never went at each other with verbal broadswords, and it was a miserable, lonely feeling. That mood had to be popped; one of us had to do it. When I said, "Let's stop, now. We're better than this…"

I expected that Jep would immediately cross the kitchen and take me in his arms. But he didn't. He nodded, and gave me a tight little smile, and then carefully made a plate of salami and cheese on rye toast. These last months had been so filled with event, by contrast with the past couple of years of leaden sameness, anyone would be at a loss. Under enough relentless stress, even steel breaks.

"He's going to leave me," I said to Julie on the phone. "I have to tell him about Esme, but then he'll really leave me."

"Thea, he is not going to leave you. You two have just been jumping from one rock to another for years, trying not to fall into the river and drown. You need to go to a family therapist. I have a…"

"A list, oh sweetie, of course you do."

"Hal and I have gone to counseling."

"How could you possibly ever need counseling? Your life is blessed!"

But she was right, there were always things in a marriage—not so lurid as the things that beset us, but all kinds of petal-tender doubts and lacks.

I told her, "The truth is, I can't do anything until this is over."

Julie asked then, "Have you heard from Esme?" I hadn't and it was driving me mad to have to wait on her whim. "She'll call," Julie went on. "When she does, you'll be ready. And maybe the detective has already found her. He could be talking to her right now. You don't know. So just keep on with whatever you're doing."

It took me another entire day to find the resolve to call Jill.

She answered on the first ring. Fear sizzled along my forearms. She told me not to worry, she wasn't bringing out the picketers again, but she had something to talk over with me. Could I meet her tomorrow at the Lava Java? I imagined the visual of Jill and me in a booth sharing a chat over our mocha lattes. Making noises about people who could be too curious at such a popular spot, I suggested somewhere more private, a place I frequented, the apple orchard at the university arboretum. The weather had been temperate; it would probably be good enough to sit outside on a stone bench for a very brief time. And I fervently hoped it would need only a very brief time.

Tomorrow, then, Jill said, about three?

The next day, there I was. As I waited, snow began to fall, of course it did, first lacy lazy flakes that gilded the darkening grove of squat, skeletal, snow-buffed trees, as the late afternoon sun pierced the cloud bank. There were eight hundred apple trees of different varieties. We used to come here often when Stefan was small. The arboretum allowed visitors to gather apples free on two specified weekends in the fall. There were signs urging everyone to share; but there were always a brigade of aggressive Mennonites armed with rakes and baskets the size of baby strollers menacing the rest of us with the force of their virtue.

Jill pulled in exactly at three.

We were the only ones there.

It occurred to me that I hadn't told Jep that today was the day, and I hadn't told Stefan anything at all.

Despite the snow, it was not really cold, and we got out and slowly walked toward each other like gunfighters, advancing on some imaginary middle line. I didn't reach out to touch her, to shake her hand or hug her—although that would have happened in the movie. I didn't say she looked well. She didn't ask if I was teaching. She smiled then, a clear message of rapprochement; and I recalled with a pang how decent and gentle Jill had always been in the before times.

"Yikes, Thea," she said, reaching out and nearly touching my lip before she caught herself and held back. "What does the other guy look like?"

"I'm sure you know what happened."

"I do. That must have been awful."

"It was scary. I was scared."

"Now you know how scary it would be to have someone hit you," Jill said. "First, I should say thank you, Thea. Thank you so much for coming."

I said, "Do you remember that time we baked mini-muffins for the kids' soccer game and, on the way, I went around a corner so fast that we spilled them all onto the floor mats? And we kept trying to pick the dog hair off them? For like ten minutes?"

Even Jill smiled. "Then we wouldn't let Belinda or Stefan eat them? And we just watched all the other kids scarfing them down? I wanted to throw up." She said then, "I need to ask you a favor."

"What is it?"

"In recent months SAY has gotten involved with the forgiveness movement, not quite like your... Stefan's thing that you're doing, I mean the one that's been around for years. And while I'm not at that point, I have learned a few things and one of them is that you're supposed to ask for what you need, if that is possible."

"You know Stefan would do anything to take your pain away. But that's impossible. How could he and I help...?"

"I don't really know," Jill admitted. She had recently heard from an old friend, a pastor who had been at seminary with her late husband and was now, like our Merry Betancourt, a part-time prison chaplain. He encouraged her to come to one of the meetings he was brokering with a family in the process of forgiving a man who'd shot a grandfather of five in a home invasion. She did, and left both moved and confused. "It really didn't have that much to do with the person who did it and everything to do with the victims. It really gives the victims a feeling of power over their own lives. And, Thea, I need that. I really feel like a pebble that's getting kicked around on the ground."

I was surprised. I said so. "You founded an organization, Jill, a good one. It's changing young women's lives. I don't agree with it in the case of my own family, but its intentions are really good, Jill."

"But me, personally. I still feel lost in the world." Which made heartbreaking sense, but which was something I would never have suspected. There was nothing I could say, so I just waited and listened. "Now as for the perpetrators. A lot of them feel new hope when they're forgiven. But other ones, they apparently actually feel pretty awful when they're forgiven, worse than before. I guess they're the sensitive ones, right? I guess even some of them feel better after some time passes, like they're more able to go on, like a burden is off their shoulders."

"Stefan told us all about that. There was a guy he knew who, well, he killed himself. And for Stefan, his regret just got worse for him when he was free. That's why he wanted to try to do something like what he's doing."

"Do you think I should explore forgiveness more?"

Why was she asking this of me, of all the beings in the known universe? In concept, it sounded like the absolute pinnacle of civilization, the best humanity could hope for. How would it work out in reality? The more I thought about it, the more I thought that it might be a gesture that could free Stefan from the endless cycle of genuflection, something he could point to—at least privately: *If she of all people can forgive me, so can you, and maybe even so can I.*

"Does it feel like time for that?" I said.

"I think so. I don't want to be held back emotionally. It keeps you from other chances in life."

"Are you getting married again?"

Jill shook her head, startled. "No," she said, almost with a snort. "I'm not seeing anybody. I think about it sometimes, though. I think about it more than I used to."

"I thought maybe that was why you wanted to see me. Although now that I say it, there's probably no reason on earth you'd want to share that information with me, of all people."

"Well, no, it's not." She turned her face to the failing sun, and I saw how beautiful she was, how like Belinda, clearly something I didn't want to think about every day. "But it's kind of like that. I wanted you to know that I'm thinking of adopting a child."

"You are?"

"Yes. This prison chaplain I met, he said something that really got to me. I was talking about how all the love that I had for Belinda, I poured love into Belinda, and that it was all gone now. And he told me not to think that way. He said no love is ever wasted. No love is ever wasted. I didn't ever really think of it like that."

She shrugged her shoulders and walked a few paces away from me, looking toward the dappling light around the trees. She told me about some of the research she had done, looking into adopting from Uganda or Jamaica, a slightly older child, five or six years old maybe, a girl or maybe even a boy. It was difficult for her to think about learning to love another child, but the adoption social worker she'd spoken to said some initial fear was normal, especially for someone who had suffered the kind of losses Jill had suffered. It would be strange, in fact, if she didn't feel some worry.

"That's probably true," I said, still wondering why this particular chat was something she felt moved to share with me, although it might once have been something she would have brought up, on those occasions when we would sit on her porch and drink coffee, when we were friends. Perhaps it was part of her attempt to open her spirit to forgiveness. I asked her then, "Are you still a golf pro?"

"I took two years off, but yes, now I'm doing that again," she said. "Why?"

"You're just so, ah, fit." She was fashion-model slender, her pants and top fitted to defined, shapely arms and a flat belly.

"For a while, I was just too thin. But I'm getting strong again. Slowly. You…you're thinner, too, Thea. Not that you were ever at all overweight. The truth of it is, I just should eat more." She paused and said, "I have trouble eating these days, for obvious reasons."

"I don't understand."

"Because she can't."

"Can't?"

"Because Belinda can't eat. Beet salad or macaroni and cheese or bean enchiladas or twice-baked potatoes or rum raisin ice cream."

I thought of Stefan eating rum raisin ice cream in that horrible hotel on that horrible winter day. "Oh, Jill, oh Jill, I'm so sorry."

She said, "I know you are. That's the real reason I wanted to see you. I want to ask a favor of you. I want you and Stefan to stop speaking about Belinda in public."

Again, I was caught flat-footed.

"You got so much attention, and it puts Stefan in the position of being kind of, I don't know, familiar, a decent guy who made a big mistake, like somebody anybody could understand. This whole thing is making Stefan and you look very sympathetic. It's breaking my heart, Thea, it feels so unfair to the memory of my daughter. And the girls and women who work with SAY are outraged, Thea."

"I saw that for myself. But the interruption of the evening, that really wasn't fair, Jill."

"I had nothing to do with that. It's their right to peaceful protest, their right under the constitution."

"But so was the talk."

"You're trying to make it like there are two sides to this, and there aren't."

"And Stefan said it was his intention to try to support SAY. He still wants to do that."

"And I said that was impossible, Thea. Even you must see why."

I finally told her that it was only one speech. I said, "I won't accept any another invitation. I promise."

"You should not, and maybe even for your own good. I read about what happened to Stefan's car recently. Aren't you worried that something worse could happen to him or to you?"

Is it her? I thought then. Is it Jill who's behind all that cautioning from Esme? Jill got to her and converted her and now she's using her as her mouthpiece to shut us up. Jill probably paid that guy in the hoodie to stalk us too. Maybe even set Stefan's car on fire.

But in the same moment, I thought, that is ludicrous. Jill might be fanatical, but she wasn't crazy. You didn't break into someone's house or terrorize them in the parking lot at their work and then have a chilly but civilized chat in the arboretum. Jill's whole life these days was predicated on non-violence. Still, I studied Jill's face as she stared me down. The way she looked nearly frightened me: Her eyes seemed to recede into her head and the contours of her face had sharpened, although I am sure that could be my imagination or a mere trick of the light.

"So I have your word that you will stop," she said.

"You have my word."

"If you don't, I think you will regret it."

Was that a threat? So maybe it was her. Or maybe, more likely, she meant her words as an ordinary phrase people said all the time in an ordinary way, that I would regret a sort of egregious disregard for a bereaved mother's feelings.

Then, as she was walking back to her car and unlocking her door, I spoke up.

"Jill, wait. I don't want us to part like this."

"I don't either, Thea. But there is no other way to part for you and me."

She didn't say thank-you or even goodbye. Why should she have? She just gave me that unblinking hooded look once more and then nodded, once. Before she started the car, I asked her, "Do you know a person named Esme?"

Jill glanced upward, the way people do when they're thinking, then looked away. "Hmmm. No, I don't. I don't think I've ever met anyone named that, actually. Now, if you asked me if I know somebody named Kayleigh, I know fifty. If you asked me if I know someone named Brianna, I've got a list of ten."

"Okay," I said. "Goodbye, Jill. I'm sorry. I'm sorry for all this suffering and I'm sorry that what I did felt like making it worse."

"Not sorry enough," Jill said.

After she left, I sat huddled in my own car, overtaken by the desire to just fall asleep there in the front seat. I had writing to do at home, and the day was closing in fast, but instead of keeping to my planned course, I stopped to get the ingredients for eggplant parmigiana, which the family loved, but which I rarely made because it was so labor-intensive: peel the eggplant, drain the eggplant, bread and crisp fry and then layer the eggplant to bake with cheese and sauce. When I got home I went straight to the kitchen and the dish and made tsoureki, too, and a custard to serve with the sweet almond bread, for dessert. When Jep walked in and sniffed the fragrant air, he looked concerned.

"Wait, was today the day you saw Jill? Is this some way you're trying to...I don't know...make it up to me because we had a little spat? You didn't have to do that. You had a right to do whatever you want, Theaitsa."

"I didn't!" I told him. "I mean, I didn't do it to make up to you. I just needed to busy my hands and stifle my head."

Stefan walked into the kitchen, and I told him about Jill, and told both of them what she wanted. Jep only shrugged, and we sat down to eat. Stefan was distracted during dinner, only vaguely noticing a main dish he usually complimented extravagantly, and he was quick to clear off the table and slip away. Not long after, I saw him head out to his truck. Jep wanted to watch an old Alfred Hitchcock movie. I went to my desk and sank down into *The Haunted Lady*, then realized after a while that I was boring even myself. Nine o'clock. Then ten. Just after ten, Stefan came back, driving very slowly, dousing the lights at the verge of the driveway, parking conspicuously slantwise across it. Curious, I met him at the door, and he reeked like a brewery.

"You're drunk," I said, more curiously than accusingly.

"So what," he said, nearly comically trying to stare me down first with one eye, then the other.

"You can't drive drunk. Are you nuts?" Jep said, pounding down the stairs. As someone who had spent his professional life trying to channel the passions of young men, he was not only a single-beer kind of drinker, but a fanatic about sobriety behind the wheel. Ten years earlier, he'd lost a star player in one of those hideous black-road country crashes that killed all four people. The car rocketed so far off the road that police didn't even find it for three days.

"I didn't, Dad. At least not all the way. Will drove us to his place, so just from there. I'm sorry," Stefan said. "But the fact is I feel like shit anyhow. Booze is its own punishment." He followed Jep upstairs and I heard the tinny sound of cheering on TV. But then Stefan came back and sat slumped on the landing. I made him a cup of tea, which he drank like a man on Everest. I made him another, more sugar, please, Mom?

He asked me if he would ever meet anyone normal he could love. I knew that the key word was "normal." I didn't say anything, just made myself a cup of tea and sat down on the bottom step. The girl he'd been talking to online apparently for months now was finally ready to meet him in person. They had arranged to go to The Priory Dance Hall not far from Wisconsin Dells, a fabulous place that had been a convent but was now a restaurant, bar and dance floor on three levels. Stefan brought Will along for moral support; the girl said she had a girlfriend who was single and would like to meet Will. The girl had sent Stefan a photo, although not a very good one, and said that she and her girlfriend would be wearing bright yellow UW–Milwaukee jerseys and waiting for them near the reservation desk at the restaurant.

They waited for two hours.

At first, they thought, did we get the time wrong? And then they thought, did we get the meeting place wrong? Had the girls gotten in some kind of accident? Stefan tried to call the girl, who'd just the day before given him her number, but after the sixth time he'd heard the greeting *Nothing new, just do what you do!* he got fed up. A half hour later, the girl texted him with a profuse and qualified apology. She couldn't leave her friend. Her friend wouldn't agree to meet Stefan and Will.

What? Why? he asked.

Her friend was afraid of Stefan.

So Will and Stefan got hammered, which for Will was not uncommon and for Stefan was only the second time in his life. He confided that even being a passenger driving home along some of those serpentine roads, he was terrified. He felt like he was seeing some kind of contracting and colliding nightmare world where lights stretched and shivered and roads signs leaped out of the darkness like rabbits. When Will dropped him off, he got into his truck and slept for a few minutes, then woke up terrified by a guttural howling nearby he was sure at the time (not so much now) was human in origin.

"Party party party," I said.

"So yeah. Alcoholism is definitely not in my future."

"If this is what it took, as long as you didn't kill yourself or

Will or anybody else then I guess…" My words snapped in the air between us. "That's a figure of speech. It's just a figure of speech that people are going to use all your life and it doesn't mean that. It does, but it…"

"Mom, okay, okay. Don't worry about it."

"I didn't mean it."

"I know you didn't. I just feel like this is the best it's ever going to be. I sort of opened up to this girl. And what, did her friend think we were going to kidnap them from the dance place or something?"

"I don't know what people think, Stefan." I got up and touched his shoulder lightly. I didn't know what to do. He was an adult. I couldn't sit him on my lap. I wondered if he would ever have a child and have to understand this delicate dance of the years, of approach and retreat, offer and hold back. I wanted to say, she's shallow and a coward and she's not worth it. But I'm a zealot. What, I thought, would Julie say? "I'm sorry that such an unkind thing happened to you. You must feel awful. I hope you won't let the way you feel about this thing set the tone for all the other things to come." I then made myself get up and pass by him where he sat, huddled and ashamed, up the stairs to my room, closing my door behind me as tears streamed into my mouth and every muscle fiber in me tensed with the desire to go back to him and say, I will make it better. Mom will make it better.

He was on a road where I couldn't follow. He was on it alone.

He texted me the next morning from his truck. I am an advertisement for aspirin. Sorry. Really sorry.

Right after his came another text, an angry one. YOU WENT AND TALKED ABOUT IT AGAIN IN FRONT OF A WHOLE AUDITORIUM OF PEOPLE. I SAW IT IN THIS STORY ONLINE. WHY DON'T YOU LISTEN? DON'T YOU REALIZE THE REAL DANGER STEFAN IS IN? DO YOU THINK I'M LYING OR SOMETIHNG?

She made it sound as though we'd spoken earlier that day in-

stead of weeks before. At last, I could give Pete Sunday a number
I knew was current. I looked at the phone as if a genie would
emerge from its bland face and then I called Pete Sunday and
sent him a photo of the phone number and the message. When
I called the number on my own, though, it was disconnected.

I made some more tea and then walked outside, into our
backyard. I'm not sure why. I certainly didn't hear a sound that
summoned me. But when I glanced over at my rose garden,
the many-legged creature of fear walked along my neck. All
the roses had been uprooted and lay tangled on the soil, like a
miniature forest after clear-cutting. After the shock, I made my
feet scamper to the back door, and only when it was closed and
locked behind me did rage flush my face and chest.

It was a modest plot of suburban real estate, not Buckingham
Palace or The Cloister Club…but it was my real estate and the
thought of someone plundering it for malice while I slumbered
a mere dozen feet away was just one more ugly sin.

Then for a moment, as if from nowhere, something Pete Sunday had said in passing went through my mind like the sound
of a coin rolling across a wooden floor above my head.

He was talking about suspects, and he said that the way that
you could tell a person was lying was if the answer included too
many details, like the way Jill answered when I asked if she knew
anyone named Esme, when she brought up other popular names
for young women. And there was something else, and maybe
that didn't mean anything at all, except perhaps that Jill didn't
care much about me. She didn't ask why I wanted to know…

13

I promised myself I would wait until after Christmas to contact Pete Sunday again. Even police work must diminish at
the holidays, I thought, even bad guys must take some time off.
This, although Christmas and Thanksgiving were notorious
dates for family massacres.

We spent Christmas Eve at home quietly, just the three of us.
The next day, we went to Amelia's for brunch and an evening
gathering with relatives. Stefan delighted in his godson, Gus,
for Phoebe and Walker, who were staying with my parents for
the holiday, had figured out a way for him to have the honor
in absentia. This was the first time we'd seen the baby since he
was born. We gathered around the extravagant tree, Stefan ea-
gerly showing my sister pictures of our outside décor.

"Will you do this for me next year?" Amelia asked. "I'll pay
you anything."

"Consider it done," Stefan said.

He then gave each of my sisters a scarf he had knitted by hand,

and for my mother, he'd made a shawl in bands of rose and gold. He had taken up knitting to calm himself when he felt stressed, at the suggestion of his therapist, and he had taken to it. My mother held the shawl carefully up to the window light, and for a moment, I thought she was going to say something about how this was no work for a man, but when she looked up, her eyes were brilliant with tears.

"This is something you have not heard me say so very many times in my life," my mother said. "And here it is. I was wrong." She stopped for a moment. "I was wrong about Stefan coming back home. Father Kanelos sings out his name in church. All my daughters' friends praise him for his hard work and his kindness. For the wrong he did, I will always cry, as he will cry, the angels cry. But I am proud of my grandson. I am proud of the man he is becoming."

She could not have given Stefan a better present.

I forced myself to do the things that ordinary people without morbid obsessions did. One of those things was forcing myself to put in some hours every day on my book. To my surprise, the book, which really amounted to a knitted-together series of my class lectures, was nearing the home stretch. My thesis was that in life and in fiction, women who'd lost someone—a child, a husband, a sibling, a love—felt incomplete, in ways men in similar straits did not, and were therefore vulnerable to desperate and even doomed adventures. Whether raving or retiring, desperate women make for a dramatic narrative and soon, their familiar stories captivated me all over again. Only two chapters remained unfinished, then I would give the whole thing a polish and it would be ready long before the summer deadline.

Inevitably, I thought of Esme, recently silent. What if I was wrong about her? Well, I thought, things would then be no worse than they already were. We would go on. I knew that I would always be drawn back and back and back to the night Belinda died. Whatever we knew, we could never know enough, we could never forget enough. What if Pete Sunday never found Esme? What if Stefan remained in danger, our never knowing its source? Back then, I wished for safety; he wished for peace. Neither of us knew then that we were wishing for the wrong thing, and I could include Esme in that too. By the time Esme next reached out to me, her fate had already begun to overtake her. One day, there Esme was, her text jumping up on my phone screen, again with the strange familiarity, as if we'd just spoken an hour before.

How is Stefan? Is he okay?

I replied, He's fine. Very busy.

Good. As long as he never tells!

I think we should get together, I replied. And then she was gone. Infuriated, I called Pete Sunday and gave him the latest in Esme's string of phone numbers.

When I saw Stefan later that night, I said, "That girl. That girl who texts me. Esme. If she ever contacts you, tell me. The police think she might be part of this harassment thing. I think she's just barking at the moon. But let's be safe anyhow."

"I could not care less about your whacked-out callers, Mom. I'm trying to move on." While he still missed Belinda, that was something he had accepted he would always feel. So he was filling his time with his business and getting ready to start school this coming semester, reading letters for the next Healing Project, seeing Will and Will's friends. "I'm the person who only looks forward."

That night, I got a text from Esme. It read simply, I am going away. I will call you.

My sleep was restless afterward. My phone didn't ring, but

I dreamed that it had, and I quickly answered, noticing that it was Esme's number. But when the caller spoke, it was Belinda. I woke up fuddled, and stumbled through my days.

I don't believe in ghosts. But now, with what I hoped would be a reckoning so near, Belinda was everywhere. A figure walking away from me on a quiet street transformed as if made of water into Belinda, her spine neat as a viola, her stride, her long bright hair. The TV picture faded to a shadow but the outline of her face seemed to waver in the dark glass. A voice in a crowd set itself apart from the others, raised in a cry. Was that how Belinda cried out when Esme attacked her? My mind shied from the thought. There were nights when she seemed especially close, when small strange things happened. A curtain of shells that hung mostly forgotten from the porthole window in my room began to clatter and shiver, without the breath of a breeze to stir it. I lay down in the gloaming to read and I felt a warm breath at my cheek. Portents are another thing I don't believe in, but it was as if Belinda herself wanted something from me. I knew full well that this was a delusion. I also knew that it felt true. And it scared me.

It reminded me of when I was a new mother, going through a phase of being afraid of the dark. Jep and I traded sides on the bed so that he was nearer the door and could protect me from what he teasingly called "the black rectangle of doom." Now, two decades later, I shamefacedly asked him to do the same thing, not sure why it made me feel better to know that an assailant would have to take three extra steps to cut my throat, not certain why the assailant wouldn't just cut Jep's throat instead. I didn't ever want to see that slight young guy in the hoodie again. But I wondered what he was up to if it wasn't scaring me.

"I keep waiting for somebody to do something else to us. What are they waiting for?" I asked Jep one morning, as we ate our oatmeal. "But I guess, it makes sense, if you were going to really hurt somebody, would you do it while that person was on guard or when that person was confident that the worst was over?"

"May I ask what you're talking about? And could you please talk about it in English?" Jep said. "You brought this up as if we were in the middle of a conversation, not as if one of the things on your mind suddenly came out of your mouth."

"I'm sorry. I thought we *were* having a conversation. I was just having both sides of it."

"They have medicine for that, Thea."

"Come on! Did you even listen to my question? Do you think if someone wanted to hurt you, he would wait until you were all relaxed and thought that..."

"If I was this stalker, I'd just wait until the person died from the bleeding ulcer he got worrying about it."

"Gee, thanks for taking this all seriously," I said.

"I've got you for that."

He finished his breakfast, tossed Molly the last bite of toast and disappeared up the stairs. But he came back down promptly with a garment bag in hand.

"Where are you going, Jep?" I asked. "Are we getting a divorce?"

"Gee. Hadn't planned on it. I'm just going to Tulsa for the same meeting I go to every year. And I'll be back tomorrow night. If you want a divorce, we'll have to find a way to synchronize our calendars."

He leaned over my chair and hugged me and kissed me on the back of my neck. He sat down, whistling under his breath, checking his phone, going through his departure ritual. I thought about how, for years, I looked forward to Jep's short absences. When he was gone, and Stefan was up to his own devices, it was freeing to stay up late reading and eat roasted beets and panzanella salad, what Jep and Stefan called "girl food," instead of having to baste slabs of steer. Now I wanted Jep near, more than when we were newlyweds. I didn't want him away from me. It didn't feel safe, for him or me, for him to...well, fly so much. And...what if my visions of Belinda persisted?

"Please don't go this time, Jep," I said.

"What's wrong Theaitsa? Are you not feeling well?"

"No, I'm fine. I'm fine." I kissed him.

"You don't seem fine. You're fretting yourself into the ground, honey."

"You go, I'm really fine," I said and hugged him briskly. "No, don't go this time. I have a bad feeling."

He looked me over, as if assessing my balance. All our lives together, with a few exceptions, I'd been sturdy, right there, upbeat rather than given to agitation or angst, even in the valley of the shadow, I was sturdy, not liable to capsize. All that seemed to leak out of me, all at once, as if my hardy emotions were hemorrhaging, leaving me husked, shivering in the heat.

"Mom!" Stefan yelled, pounding his way down the stairs. "Don't we use heat anymore? It's like forty degrees in here and I'm dying."

I'm dying.

After Jep left, I went upstairs and lay with my head back to staunch the tears which kept coming, wetting my hair, wetting the pillow. The ceiling was a pristine pale peach cove, but I could see bloodstains all over it.

Jep was right. Maybe I needed some medicine.

"Mom! Are you okay?" Stefan was standing in the doorway of my room.

"Sure, sure," I said. "You know, in truth? I don't feel so good. I'm going to...to take a nap, okay?"

"Do you want some tea, Mom?"

"No, no..."

"I'll bring you a glass of water anyhow."

"Oh, okay, thanks, sweetie."

He was so sweet. It was on my lips to tell him right then.

What if I could baptize him innocent? What the hell was wrong with Pete Sunday? How long could this take?

With Molly at his heels, Stefan pounded back down to the kitchen. For perhaps only the third or fourth time in my life, I decided to pretend to be asleep. I just couldn't trust myself not to spill everything about Esme. I heard Stefan quietly set the water down on the leather mat I kept on my nightstand, smelled the scene of his lavender aftershave…nausea boiled up my throat again. I must have fallen asleep.

Thea, she called. Thea? Where are you?

I had thought I didn't remember her voice. But I did.

The wrought-iron fence, the heart-shaped headstone.

Beautiful Dreamer…

I woke up, stumbled to the bathroom and rinsed my face. Whatever changed in the coming days, the fact of Belinda's death would endure. I could not imagine ever being free of the dark bloom that shadowed everything else, chilled everything else, every graceful moment, every clear-eyed glance, laced every laugh with a suspect syrup.

Damn it.

What was going on with Esme? What was going on with Pete Sunday? I promised myself I would call him first thing to-morrow.

Finally I lay back down, but I shook and sweated in my sheets. I slept and woke, exhausted. The house was dark and chilled. I didn't dare go back to sleep. Yet, sleep overcame me, hauling me down. When I awakened in the dark, she was sitting in my chair near the window, her back to me. I could see her plainly in the silver light from the streetlamp. She didn't turn around. "Thea," she whispered. "Thea, you are the door."

I snapped on my bedside lamp. Then, I stayed up the rest of the night, drinking so much tea and eating so much cinnamon toast that my stomach washed side to side like a water balloon when I walked.

When Jep came home, I climbed and clung to him, voracious, unable to wait even for him to shower the road off him. "What did I do right?" he asked me afterward, naked and streaked with new sweat.

"Don't leave," I pleaded. "Don't go to any more camps. Don't even go down to get a snack. I'll bring you pie. I'll bring you coffee. Stay up here, please. Remember when we were going to put a little refrigerator in our bathroom?"

"And then we decided it was too decadent?"

"Why did we decide that?"

"Because it is too decadent. We're people with limits, Theaitsa."

"Just stay by me."

"What's wrong tonight? What's gotten into you? Not that I mind."

"You're right about everything. I'm up on the ledge. I have to find a way to vacuum my mind."

While Jep was in the shower, I put on one of his shirts. He did go downstairs to make a sandwich. He did go down again, for pie. But he held me as I slept. Normally, I wouldn't have craved this: I'm not a cuddler. Be skin to skin with me while we're going at it, but afterward, you don't have to prove anything else: Let me sleep unencumbered on my own little island of cotton and feathers.

In the middle of the night, I heard a crash and Molly's frenzied growling. She wasn't yapping, as she did to annoy the UPS guy; she was trying, in her aging, Australian-shepherd-lady way, to warn somebody off her turf. I paid attention, because Molly would have welcomed the ghost of Genghis Khan if he'd brought liver treats. Jep was on his feet, but I was faster, throwing my robe around my shoulders like someone in an English ghost story movie. Stefan was in the kitchen...with, to my horror, a sledgehammer in his hand.

"He was out there," Stefan said.

"Who's out there?"

"The guy," he stammered. His eyes were pits. "The stalker from the road, Mom. The Unabomber." Stefan said he was up late, working on some sketches for a Whole Blooming World project for which he'd been recommended by Luck Sergenian, a big job with a big budget, doing all the landscaping and plant-ings for a new college-prep school for girls. He had headphones and some raucous music on, but through it, heard Molly whin-ing and scratching at the patio door. He came out of the library where he'd been working and switched on the light over the back door. He very nearly screamed.

The stalker was standing there, not six feet away, perfectly at rest, his arms by his sides. He wore black tennis shoes and that black sweatshirt with the deep, voluminous hood Stefan re-membered from that icy day on the highway back from Black Creek. Stefan couldn't see his eyes, but he knew the guy was watching him, watching for him, that it was the same person: Something about the slant of the shoulders and the stance had branded itself on Stefan's memory during those awful few sec-onds after we spun down the embankment. Stefan didn't move. The figure didn't move. Stefan felt that if the stalker rushed the door, he would die—even if the door was double-locked, even if the glass was reinforced, he would die. What should he do? Turn off the light? Call the police?

Just then Molly threw herself against the door, growling and scratching, and Stefan almost let her out, his only fear that the guy had a weapon and would hurt the dog. But instead, he turned and walked away, unhurried, out of the silo of light from the patio fixture. But where had he gone?

Stefan ticked over the locks, basement, front door, garage door...and gasped aloud when he thought of the side door of the garage which we sometimes left unlocked, that led out into the backyard. Forcing himself, knowing that the guy might still be in earshot, Stefan sprinted into the garage, grabbed the mallet, slipped back inside and locked the side door.

I generally hated phrases like "the new normal." They were slick the first time you heard them, but quickly facile. But this time I could not avoid its apt quality: This was our new normal, in which nothing would ever be normal. What, I wondered now, was this creepy guy's part in all this? Was he another vigilante, entirely separate from Jill and her minions, with his own dire purposes? Standing around, I well knew, was no crime. So would he ever be stopped?

I was never a particularly timid person, and I resented this welter of small paper cuts that slowly undermined me.

I thought back to when Stefan was two, my sister Amelia watched him while Jep and I set out on a long-delayed week-long honeymoon, part of which was our attempt to hike Angel's Landing Trail in Zion National Park, which was one of the most harrowing and distressing experiences of both our lives. We were both strong, young and fit. And yet nothing could have prepared us for mincing our way along eskered spines of rusty rock with drops hundreds of feet on either side. At first, Jep cheered me on, telling me to trust my strong legs; but then, halfway up, he suddenly stopped and said, "Thea, are you terrified?" I told him I was. He said, "I am, too. I'm not one of those people who gets high off being terrified. We have a kid. We have a future. Let's go back down."

So we did just that, and I was never more secure in what a wise decision it was to marry Jep. That whole idea, of a limited hardship, a finite exposure to danger, was what some people thought of as adventure. If I ever got past this, I vowed never to seek out another risk. From now on, my idea of an adrenaline rush would be ice-skating. In the middle of the night in my living room, I vowed never to do anything, not for any reason, not for any goal, that put me or my family in danger.

There were no more interruptions that night. Stefan gathered his sketches and went to bed. With a few snuffles and wheezes, Molly settled down to her aged-girl sleep.

The next morning, the same young police officer who we had called when the garden was uprooted, who'd come after the house was invaded and the photos were violated, and after the car was set on fire, the one who took milk and sugar in her coffee, showed up and listened to Stefan's description. After Stefan left for work, in a hurry, she lingered.

"What do you think is really going on here?" she asked me.

"Well, like before, harassment. Somebody's still trying to scare us. I guess, scare us into leaving. Scare us into going away and living somewhere else. But how did he know Stefan would be awake?"

She considered her coffee mug carefully, turning it in her hands so that the Wisconsin Book Festival logo went around and around. Finally she said, "You don't want to hear the answer to that."

"How so?"

"Well, he's watching you. He's looking in these windows or he's got a long-range lens somewhere in a tree or in a stand of bushes and he knows what you're doing. And maybe he didn't know that Stefan was going to be working in the library, because the only window in there faces the front. Maybe he didn't know Stefan would come to the door. That raises a possibility that's more troubling. What was he planning on doing that he didn't get to do?"

"I'm not feeling very reassured."

"My job isn't just to reassure you, ma'am. It's to inform you. This other event was…what, eight or nine months ago? That's a long time for a peeper to stay interested in one family, if it's even the same person, but I would have to say that if I was a betting woman, I'd bet that it was. Something's going on here, and I don't like it, but the fact is, nothing's been done. Nothing's even been taken that we know of. No one has been hurt."

She added, "Most of the time, the motive is sexual. Maybe this is, too. But I'm not getting that kind of vibe."

It was more or less the same thing Pete Sunday had told me. Being a creep wasn't a crime. Simply terrifying someone wasn't necessarily a crime. It wasn't even a threat. It wasn't even mayhem. Trespassing was a civil offense. The worst that could happen might be a lawsuit for invasion of privacy.

Before she left, the officer tried to come up with a plan. Though it was a long shot, she would make sure that there would be the extra presence overnight of an unmarked car, parked or driving by, for the next couple of weeks. There would be a log and photos of any late-night strollers who seemed to linger a little longer near the house. Keep the windows locked, she told us—as if anyone with our history would not lock the windows—especially on the first floor.

The next day, I was alone at home and restless.

I wanted to see Julie, but she was off on a dental mission. I opened my laptop to start a video chat with her but she was too busy. Her recent emails told me of her fury over a recent dustup: Not once, but several times, she'd been called an "evangetourist." Global Smiles had been fixing kids' teeth in developing nations for forty years and had no religious connection of any kind. They'd worked for decades in Haiti and talked their way into rural India where people had no access to dental care—in the country that trained the best dentists in the world. It was Julie's first time in Africa. At a big UNICEF gathering in Addis Ababa, Julie was confronted by the co-founder of an anti-colonialist organization called BanWhiteSaviors, who told Julie that her organization was more invested in her own smiles than in those of African peoples.

"You come, you fix a few things, and you're back to your Southern California lifestyle," the woman said. "We're committed. We stay."

"She's the wannabe, not us," Julie wrote to me. "I was so mad

I had to walk away. We're giving people healthy teeth and teach-ing them how to keep them that way. It's not a hill of beans."

"You can't eat your hill of beans with no teeth," I wrote back.

"I wanted to knock HER teeth out," Julie responded.

She then sent me what she described as "the strangest selfie in history." After her Global Smiles project ended, she had been traveling with a small group of doctors, all but one a woman, hiking into Bwindi Impenetrable National Park, along the mountain trail. There was my pal, down on her haunches among a thicket of shrubs, while yards away, a gorilla studied her with magnificent patience. I tried to imagine myself into such a breathtaking moment.

"Do you think it gets old for the gorillas?" I wrote to her. Her being away so much must get old for Julie's sons, I thought, not for the first time, for I knew that Ernest and Miller missed their mom when she was absent, even though Hal was a generous, deeply engaged dad. While Jep traveled with his team, I'd been righteously on the scene every night at dinner with Stefan—and look where that got me.

Oh Julie, I thought, *take me away with you*. Though she worked very hard, all those storied destinations raised the canopy of her mind, while my mind scuttled about like a bug trapped under a water glass. She had invited me, often, to accompany her. Why didn't I when I could? Before our lives were changed forever? Before I'd lost sole custody of my own life. But I had plenty of time left, didn't I? People my age were starting new careers, hav-ing their first children. That kind of boldness felt extinguished in me. But that was okay.

The next morning, I asked Stefan if he heard periodic re-ports from any of the people who had been involved with The Healing Project.

"I just heard from Rebecca in fact," he said. "She's so great. She's like an inspirational person living the way people should live. I'm going to have lunch over there next week. Rebecca might want me to do some landscaping and I just... I'd like to see her again."

Becky was a good ten years older than Stefan. "Do you like her, like a girlfriend?" I asked.

"I don't think so, but what if I did? Not everybody has to be twins like you and Dad."

On an impulse, to kill time as much as anything else, I decided to call Rebecca Broom myself. My cover would be that I was just checking in to see how things were going. The reality was, I liked her. She was also a tie to my past, in a certain way. She didn't pick up, but I left a message, and then I felt uneasy about that.

At dinner that night I asked Stefan if he thought there was any professional reason I shouldn't have called her.

"I don't know," he said. "She called me about some landscaping work. Could you imagine ever calling any of the other people from The Healing Project just to have lunch?"

He rightly said it was like him wanting to get together with Roman Villera just to hang out. Even though from time to time he thought about taking Trina Villera up on her offer of a massive puppy, he was reluctant to reopen that book. I could only guess why. Edging up on a year later, Stefan's principal reality had shifted: He was more of home now than he was of prison. He might have to admit that his and Roman's friendship, despite its very real emotional import for both of them, was also provisional, bracketed in time and space.

I thought about it more and half convinced myself that my wanting to see Becky Broom was different. Because of my family's relationship with the Hodges, I felt a greater obligation and thus perhaps a greater permission. The next day, I told Stefan this.

He shrugged and said, "I can see that. If you do, tell her I was asking about her and will see her soon." He was busy packing his truck: He and Will Brent, along with Will's new girlfriend, were hosting a blowout weekend at Julie's cabin. Julie had emailed him directly with the suggestion, and he was clearly pleased with the idea. Luck Sergenian was coming, with her fiancé, plus her younger sister. It made Stefan feel good to be able to host for once these now good friends and mentors who had helped make him feel normal.

"What's her sister's name?" I asked Stefan. "Chance?"

"No," he said with a sly smile. "It's Snowy."

"Is her sister a pet rabbit?"

"Mom, cut it out." But he was laughing. "Her name is Snowy River. It's awful, I know. It's after this place in Australia where her parents were when she was, ah, conceived. But she's a really nice person. Luck thinks I should ask her out. She's my age."

I knew better than to do anything except nod briefly. I was glad to see him planning something that was purely social, with people who accepted who he was now. It wasn't until very late Sunday night that he got home, and I heard him whistling as he came into the house. Then he was on the phone, assuming we were sleeping the sleep of the deaf and aged. "So what time do you leave?" he said. "I really don't mind driving you. Well, that depends. How much luggage would I have to pick up? I shouldn't even come over, since I should be offended that you want to go to Paris for some reason instead of hanging out with me."

A few days later, he was asleep on the couch when I came in. Some horrifying punk rock music video from about 1988 was splattered across the screen, blaring. I flipped the TV off. "I was watching that," Stefan said ritually.

"You were snoring."

"Fine, I'm an exile," he said. "I meet a girl I like and she goes off to junior year abroad. Do I have good luck or what?"

"At least you know it's possible."

"Maybe for one in five hundred, if I have a pre-introduction and family members to vouch for me."

School would start soon. Stefan had been accepted to UW–

Madison to study in the Department of Landscape Architecture. He'd worried about the process every step of the way. If he did get in, he wouldn't fit. But he probably wouldn't even get in, it was so competitive. And finally, he said, "I'm really worried that somebody on the selection committee will know who I am."

"If they didn't admit you because you have a criminal record…" I began.

"No one would ever know that was why I didn't get in, Mom! You know better. You're part of the secret society of academic snobs."

"Look, universities fancy themselves to be egalitarian beams of light," Jep said. "I don't think that would be a factor, either way. Just don't try to keep it from anybody who asks, but don't volunteer either. Anyway, how could they turn down Father Nature? I bet you have more experience than most of the people who already graduated from that program."

Now that he was in, he had gone right over to worrying about how he would manage it. The program would be a heavy load, because he was unwilling to give up his best clients, plus the work for Rebecca if it happened, though he would have to work only part-time, mostly on weekends, with the help of two high-school kids he trained and trusted. Jep and I had faith that most of the time-management stuff that would be new to the other students was already Stefan's daily bread.

At least, he said that day, he wouldn't have time for the steady girl he didn't have.

Stefan finally roused himself to go back to work, and I waved goodbye as he pulled away, then went in and finally called Becky. As it turned out, she was glad to hear from me. She begged me to come to dinner at the big house that very night… yes, it was kind of a free-for-all, but the women competed to outdo each other in the culinary arts and tonight was Cuban night, not to be missed. So I agreed.

When I got there, Rebecca gave me the tour. Inside, the

place looked gorgeous. Each of the four renovated "pods," two bedrooms separated by a lush shared bath, was decorated in a different, vibrant shade—peach, tangerine, eggplant. The big rooms downstairs were equally pretty and comfortable with wide welcoming sofas and scattered rocking chairs, built-in shelves crammed with books and whimsical ceramics, islands of plants, including a huge lemon tree festooned with fruit, and stereo speakers that piped music all over the first floor. Just the environment itself could hardly fail to lift a person's spirits. From there it would be easier to motivate the residents to take better care of themselves and their peers. One corner was given over to Alzy's grand piano, and a painting of her took pride of place on the wall behind it. She was seated on a porch swing, barefoot but dressed formally, I realized with a shock, in the dress she had worn in her coffin.

We sat outside on that same porch swing, as the setting sun dragged away the day's heat. Then Becky told me her news: She was pregnant, eight months.

"What? You can't even tell!"

"I know you can't. People just think I've gained some weight. This is the gift of being five feet ten and, as my mom so delicately says, big-boned."

"I mean you really can't tell."

"Well, you haven't seen me without these artful garments." She pulled back her long tunic, and yes, she most certainly was quite convex.

"Are you sure you have your dates right?" I asked and then added, "I didn't even know you were in love."

"I am, with this guy right here," she said, pointing to her belly. "But I must admit I never met the papa. I picked him out of a book for his great brains and curly hair. So I know I have my dates right, down to the hour. I'm thirty and I know that's not old for having a first kid, but it just seems like the right time for me. If I ever meet my grown-up prince, he's going to have to consider little boys value added."

"You already knew you were going to do this when you came to Stefan with your idea."

"I was pretty sure I was going to do it. That was a big factor in why I wrote to him. I wanted to make myself right with the universe before I welcomed my son into it."

"You'll have lots of aunties to fuss over him."

"I didn't count on that part! They already fuss over me! I gained no weight for the first few months, but twenty-five pounds in the past two months. I may not show much, but I feel the size of a sumo wrestler. I feel like my body gets across the room before my brain catches up to it."

"Are you going to stay here after the baby is born?"

Becky said, "Of course. This is my house, and it's my home. And it's my job. I'm going to have someone help me with the day-to-day for the first few months."

"Are you worried about living with...?"

"With addicts? I'm not. Are you worried about living with Stefan? Of course you're not," Rebecca said. "But don't feel bad for wondering. It's a legitimate question." She added, "None of these women was ever violent, Thea. The only ones they hurt were themselves."

We ate ropa vieja, black beans and rice with tomatoes and corn fritters with the residents with crema Catalana and espresso to follow. These women could cook. Seeing them sitting there in the candlelight, the youngest a freckled twenty-two-year-old, the oldest in her fifties, with a froth of silver hair that fell past her shoulders, it was difficult to imagine any of them so desperate for a drink that they had lost families, careers, homes. It hadn't occurred to me when I called Becky that we would be having dinner with them, and that all of them would know my son's role in The Healing Project and its establishment of The Alice Hodge Safe Home. About that part, they could not have seemed more grateful or complimentary. A couple of them were local, and knew about Stefan's history. A few had watched the public television episode we had shot at our house. Another had seen a photo of Belinda with Stefan as part of the Mother's Day broadcast of *Say Her Name*, a PBS special last year about college girls killed by their boyfriends, including Belinda, and Jill's activism against domestic partner abuse.

"It must be so hard," said the beautiful woman with the cloud of silver hair.

"It is," I admitted. "It's getting better, but it will never go away."

"You probably feel so guilty. It's not your fault."

I didn't know where to look or what to say. The expectant silence stretched. I half expected Becky to jump in and throw up some kind of conversational diversion. When she didn't, I realized that this was a house where banter had no place and deep revelations were everyday fare.

"I struggled with that. We both still do. I felt remiss for not knowing everything my own son was involved in."

"But you raised him," said Margo, one of the younger women, a kindergarten teacher who had nearly died from liver damage. "As a mother, wouldn't you ask yourself, what should I have done? If he was abusing her all that time."

Should I correct her? I knew how it would sound. These were AA women, who knelt on the Twelve Steps like stations of the cross, and they brooked no excuses.

"He didn't abuse her. That is what some people believe. That is what Belinda's mother believes. But I believe that whatever violence happened that night, however it happened, happened just that once."

"What did happen?" asked Margo.

Again, their blunt inquiry left me speechless. I glanced at Becky, who made the slightest gesture of a shrug. "Belinda died from a blow to the head with a golf club," she said. "Thea, do you want to add more about that?"

"Well, I wasn't there. I don't know all the details," I said, thinking, what will they think when they find out that it was really Esme? Please, I thought, please let there be a chance that it was. And then, shamed, I was reminded that, if it was true, another family would be devastated, as mine had been. "Stefan has no memory of that night. Some impressions but no clear memory. He was…he'd taken a cocktail of drugs."

"He blames the drugs. Your son."

"It's not that simple."

Margo said, "But he's right to some degree. Drugs wreck lives. Booze wrecks lives. This poor girl's death, another gift of substance use. My kids are only five and seven, and I can't see them except for a couple of hours on the weekend with my ex present. I'm not there for them. They need me. I was sober for five years. Why didn't I try harder to think? Before I went out?"

"You're thinking now," said another woman. "Margo, your best thinking got you here."

Margo turned back to me. "Alcoholics are professional blamers. I blamed everything and everyone else for drinking myself out of a great job and a great family and a great marriage. It sounds like your son's blaming too. And you? You're probably mortified by your own actions. But the first step is to admit that you were at fault."

"I don't feel we were entirely at fault. At one point I did. But I'm not my son. I'm myself. I didn't put him in that situation. I didn't make him kill his girlfriend. I saw that Stefan was obsessed with Belinda. He loved her almost too much. But I didn't see other things. Stefan was an athlete. He didn't even drink so far as we could tell. So we didn't see that coming. As for him, he has admitted he was at fault. He's admitted he had no power over the drugs he used."

Becky spoke up then. "There were definitely things with

Alice I didn't let myself see. Because if I let myself see them, then things would have had to change. I would have lost my job. I would have lost her. I tried to convince myself that she would get better."

Feeling undressed before these strangers, I gripped my cold cup of espresso and gazed down at my shimmering plate of lush custard, the spicy food I had so enjoyed now scalding my guts. I took a bite of the flan. Then I got up and smiled at them all. "You know, I think I need to get going now. Thank you all for a lovely meal. This place is fabulous. I'm tempted to move in!"

"You don't have the résumé for that," another of the women said. I didn't know how much more awkward it could get.

Becky got up with me. "Want to take a little walk before you head home, Thea? I could use some exercise."

We headed down across a few streets to the Lakeshore Path, where dozens of strollers and bikers were ambling along under the benign moon. After a short while, Becky said, "You know, they were hard on you. I'm sorry, I should have warned you. These are women who have not had the easiest time at the hands of men, as you might imagine."

"Not for nothing, but The Healing Project *is* Stefan's idea. He's the one who created the charter. He's the one who picked out your letter. He didn't even realize how close I was with Alzy. He didn't make the connection until I told him."

"When we have our lights-out meeting, I'm going to make the point again about Stefan being behind the idea that's helping all of them."

We walked, and talked about Becky's excitement and hopes for her baby, whom she wanted to name either Julian or Patrick.

"Name him both," I said. "Let him pick. Patrick Julian. Julian Patrick. Patrick Julian Broom. Those are both names that have gravitas and music."

"Unless they call him PJ or JP."

"Are you having that hallucination that makes you think you

have any control over your child's destiny? You need to let that one go."

Becky put her hand on my arm, then linked her arm through mine and said, "I didn't realize you don't really know exactly what happened to Belinda that night, do you?"

"Bits and pieces, but no. Stefan had no memory of that night. He needed our help to navigate the grief, the judgment, the overdose, the addiction, being incarcerated. We thought rehab and prison were the hard work. But it was when he got out that he needed us even more, to overcome his demons and find a way to accept himself and feel accepted. And now, I've been over the police reports and..." Should I tell her? I didn't even know her. "There's something else. There's this girl, Stefan's age, and she's been calling me for months, on and off for years, really, and she kept saying she was so sorry. She kept saying she couldn't live with the guilt of what she did, that she was there that night and she knew the truth."

Becky eased herself down on a corner bench. "You think she's involved with Belinda's death?"

I nodded. And I had to reassure her—and myself—that it wasn't just because of Stefan's nature. "I mean, he's just not violent, except once, when he just got out." I told her about the lumberyard and the fight there.

Rebecca said, "That could have happened to anybody." But she looked thoughtful for a moment. "Women aren't usually physically violent. It's pretty rare. So you think this girl was violent by nature?"

"No, not necessarily," I said. What did I think? It was no more likely that Esme snapped than that Stefan snapped. She probably didn't go around battering people. On the other hand, if she let someone else go to prison for her sin, her crying and wailing were all show: She had no conscience at all. "It all just seems to fit together, it makes sense. She was Belinda's lover, and she was just like Stefan, terrified of losing her."

Maybe, by that point, any way was better than facing the wide span of life without her. How could I know what drove Esme? How could I know how people had treated her in her life before? I'd never even spanked Stefan. I hadn't struck a person in my life, not since I was nine and slapped my sister Phoebe for stealing my ten silver dollars from my jewelry box. What cyclone of emotion could whirl someone into such rage as evidenced by the photos in that box was beyond my ken.

"It's an interesting hypothesis. Is this just a thought you've been having? Have you told anyone?" I told Becky about Pete Sunday and his promise to find Esme. While it might be a slim chance, even the detective seemed to think it was worth investigating.

I told Becky, "Either way this turns out, the guilt they brought up. I really don't feel that way."

"That's good."

"It was the drugs, just like it was the drink for Alice."

"I'm glad that's how you feel." There was a reserve in the statement that snagged my defenses.

"Wait, am I missing something? You don't think that Alzy would have frozen to death in a snowbank unless she was drunk, do you? I know Stefan wouldn't have hit Belinda or anybody else unless he was so messed up he didn't know what he was doing. That isn't just me rationalizing things. The judge thought the same thing, or he would have sent Stefan away for murder."

"I know," she said. "But it's not the same as with Alice."

"Do the Hodges feel guilty, like they could have done more or something different?" I asked.

"I don't know," Becky said. "They're political people. They put up a brave front. And they're also actually brave. But Alice didn't do anything to...anyone else. Both of these things are tragic. Tragic mistakes. But not the same."

She was correct about that too. But no matter what the outcome, if this was as good as it ever got for us, would I exchange our fate with Stefan for the Hodges' fate with Alice? No, I would not. A thousand times, I would not. Especially not now, I would not. For that, maybe I should have felt guilty.

I told Becky that the reason Stefan got parole on his first application was because he didn't describe his actions as "a mistake." What he had done was wrong, he went on, much worse than the things violent criminals did, because he wasn't a violent criminal. He wasn't raised to do wrong. He had no excuses. He could never atone for what he had done. But he swore he would never hurt another person as long as he lived.

"I think he means that, and I believe him," Rebecca told me.

Finally, having put way too much out there already, I told Rebecca about the threats Esme had made.

"She keeps saying that if Stefan ever remembers more about that night, someone is going to get him. I know, it's crazy. But doesn't it really stand to reason if she's the one who would get him? If she already killed one person, might she feel like what has she got to lose? I'm sorry for bugging you with this. This wasn't what you meant by taking a little walk."

"Just go on. Tell me the rest."

"Well, she was livid because Stefan wouldn't back down from talking publicly about Belinda's death. He wanted to take responsibility. But when he did talk openly, nothing happened. I mean, I'm glad nothing happened…but was it all a hoax? Or was she afraid that he would reveal details he didn't know about at first, because his memory was blocked? I thought she was trying to protect Stefan but was she just trying to protect herself? She must have hated Stefan."

"You could ask her now."

"I can't find her. She goes through these times when she doesn't answer. And I keep thinking, what if she knows the police are looking for her now? We'll never find out the truth. She'll just vanish into thin air."

"Well, she will call you eventually. She wants something from you. She's addicted, in a sense. At least from what you tell me. And when she does, just casually suggest getting together because you were never able to pull it off that other time. She'll either agree or she won't. Call the detective as soon as you set a plan."

I told her that was exactly what I was going to do.

When we parted that night, Becky thanked me again for calling her. She had been surprised to hear from me and asked me why I reached out just then. I confessed that I wasn't really sure. She told me then that she'd almost called me, to ask if we might have lunch or coffee, and wasn't sure why she felt that way either.

"Destiny, I guess," she finally said, and asked if she could hug me. There was something about her, a straightforwardness and complete lack of cant, that was so appealing.

Two days later, Esme texted from yet another phone number. I'll tell you the truth. I promise this time.

Quickly, I texted back: All this time you've wanted to see me. You wanted to warn Stefan he was in danger. You wanted to tell me something big. Then you just disappeared. I know you are afraid. But if you know some surprising truth about that night, just tell me.

She texted back: It's not just about that night. It's other things, too. If I tell you the truth, you can't tell anyone else.

Not even Stefan?

No one else. Don't talk to Jill. Don't talk to the police. No one. Things could happen to me. I could get killed.

No one's going to kill you.

You don't know. You don't understand!

And then she was gone again. I nearly threw the phone across the room. Sleep was lost to me now. I finally got up and paced

until the sun rose. I wondered if I would ever be able to see a
sunrise again and think only about the weather. With Molly at
my heels, I desultorily inspected our raised garden, the wreckage
of the tomatoes I planted every year, determined every time to
give the tender plants my most valiant effort, an effort which I
then, at least for the past several years, abandoned by July. As if
reproaching me for my desertion, many fat fruits hung heavy on
the vine. Others were regrettably smashed on the ground. I made
a pouch of my sweatshirt and began to fill it... I would make
myself busy, I would make marinara sauce and freeze it. I had
once been a devout gardener; I used to have ordinary pursuits.

It was when I was making my way back heavy-laden to the
patio that I noticed something: Footprints in the mud around
the rosebushes Stefan had replanted were just a few feet from
the back door. It had rained a few nights before, washing the
snow nearest the house to mud. Then the mud had frozen. So
that meant...night before last or the night before that, someone
stood there, yet again, facing the windows to our family room,
forty inches of air and an eighth of an inch of glass from our
vulnerable lives. The shoe prints were running shoes, but with
a different pattern from the Nike Air Max I wore when I took
walks. How did I know the pattern on the bottom of my running shoes? I knew because I often used a garden tool to dig
the dirt and gravel out of them before I put them in the washing machine. And these prints were not my size. I set my foot
heel-to-heel within one print. They were noticeably larger, by
perhaps almost half an inch.

Fifteen minutes later, Esme called me. It would later seem like
something that would happen on TV, my struggling to extract
my phone from my pocket, spilling all the tomatoes onto the
patio flagstones, where they lay seeping like small organs. Was
she out there, watching me? Or did only the hoodie figure do
that? Was privacy the most ridiculous of illusions? She said softly,

and to me chillingly, "I still remember the sounds. Stuff hitting the walls. Yelling. I should tell you. I have to get it over with."

"And so you should. You have to get this off your chest. We should really meet, now, before you go away."

"I've waited too long," she said.

"Tell me more," I said, and listened to her breathing. "Tell me the rest."

Silence. Breathing. Then not even that.

I was the one who finally disconnected. Then I stood with my hand on the phone receiver. Did I understand just what I was asking for? If Esme was indeed as sick as I believed that she must be, was she the one drawing me close, then pushing me away, in a game intended to entice me to throw away caution, to come to her, on her terms?

Was it not really Stefan she wanted to hurt, but instead me, to punish Stefan by taking away yet another person he loved?

Of course, if she and I did meet, there would be police at the ready, but would they be close enough and quick enough to save me? Dire things happened in seconds. They happened every day.

14

I finally spoke with Pete Sunday and we met at a local coffee shop.

"I wish I had better news," he said. "We basically came up
empty. I don't know who this girl is, or if she even exists and
I can't find anyone who ever saw her. We'll have to ask Stefan
what else he knows."

Before I agreed to that, he told me there was no Emily Lundgren or Lindquist in Black Creek anywhere near to Belinda's
age. There were six with similar names, but five were women in
their forties and fifties, and one was a three-year-old girl. There
were also plenty of female students from Chicago at the school, at
least a couple of dozen in Belinda's year, more in the year before
and after, but none of them, to my surprise, was named Emily
or Esme, and a search of their records showed that none of them
looked anything like the girl in the picture I'd shown to him.
Among that number were also several girls named Emma, but
the only one from Chicago was Emma Doll, an Olympic speed

skater who was African-American and whose face was famous around the world. Pete had spoken with Emma Doll, now a senior, and though she knew about the case, she had never met or seen Belinda before her death. There were girls with the surname Lundgren or Lindquist. One of them was called Caroline Lindquist and she had, in fact, known Belinda fairly well, she told Pete Sunday. In fact, she had been so shaken by Belinda's murder that she had taken the semester off. Caroline was a name on the list Jill made of Belinda's close college friends. Had Stefan somehow confused the first and last names?

Of course, it was possible that Esme was not the girl in the picture.

Pete wanted me to know that he hadn't given up.

He thought that my suggestion to Esme that we meet up in person was spectacular, and we created a plan. As soon as a place was set, I would inform him and he would find a way to be there as well, undercover, with other police to back him up. He promised that I would be safe.

As for the solitary figure in the hoodie, who somehow felt bold to haunt and despoil our lives according to his whim, a few rosebushes one time, maybe next time a piece of wire strung at neck height in the dark, Pete had no idea. Did he know Esme? Was he sent by her? All we knew was that he watched, and that he bided his time.

I had put way too many hopes in a basket that turned out to have a hole in the bottom.

I went to bed.

For once, nothing was required to shove me down into sleep and keep me there.

When I woke to hear Molly scratching at my bedroom door, the clock said 3:00 a.m. Molly didn't ordinarily fuss to go outside in the middle of the night; but when she did, there was a reason, and I hoped it wasn't a skunk that she wanted to harass.

I reached out to nudge Jep so he would go down and I

wouldn't have to face the literally rude awakening of the first raw blast of winter dawn, then remembered he had gone on another overnight trip. I got up, wrapped myself in my old robe, shoved my feet into slippers and followed the dog downstairs, ruefully waking myself with every step. I let her out through the patio door, leaving it cracked so she could come back in when she'd done her stuff, and shuffled into the kitchen to put the electric kettle on for a cup of chamomile tea.

The kettle boiled and I turned it off. Molly whined at the door, somehow having managed to close it. She followed at my heels, whimpering a little, the way she did sometimes. Back in the kitchen, I turned on the countertop light, got out a mug and a tea bag, filled my mug and flipped Molly a freeze-dried chicken treat, which she let fall at her feet. She ignored it. Molly wouldn't let a rabid raccoon stand between her and a chicken treat. I should have known then.

When I looked up, the figure was standing in the corner of the room, ten feet from me. His hoodie was drawn down over his slender face, and his hands were jammed in the pockets of his sweatpants.

You wonder all your life what you'll do if something like this ever happens, and you try to prepare. You talk to yourself about the pros and cons of running or fighting. You ask, will I open my mouth to scream and nothing will come out except a whistle of air? Will I advance, rage lending me unwonted strength, or submit to the inevitable, like a goat in the tiger's jaws? I roared, grabbing up my electric kettle and throwing it at him, sending boiling water across his chest. He was the one who keened, some sort of strangled syllable, and took off out of the room, falling in the kitchen over a chair, rolling to his knees, as Molly growled and barked wildly and I heard Stefan come pounding down the stairs, just as the man burst through the patio door to the yard.

"Don't, don't, don't!" I shouted at Stefan, as he shoved his feet into his shoes and bounded after him. "Just let him go! What if he has a gun or a knife?"

But there was no stopping Stefan. The young guy was fast, but Stefan was faster, and bigger by a foot. Turning on the porch lights, I saw him hit the guy with a textbook tackle before he could gain the alley of aspens that ran along the back of the yards. I grabbed the first thing that came to hand, a fireplace poker, and ran out after Stefan. I heard the "whuff" as he pushed the guy down on his stomach, and Stefan yelling, "What do you think you're doing in my house, asshole?"

But the next voice I heard didn't match.

It was small, tearful. I recognized it from a dozen phone calls.

"Please don't hurt me," she said. "Please. It's Esme."

15

Up close, she was so slight. The stuff of all my nightmares was just a girl, a tall girl, but so slender that her head looked too big for her body, her face shielded by her hood and the dark glasses.

Stefan pulled her to her feet and awkwardly brushed off the snow.

"What the hell is this?" he said.

She was crying hard by then, and the two of us stood there as she wrapped her arms around her thin chest and rocked back and forth, her knees slightly bent, as if she couldn't support her own weight.

"Please let me come inside," she said. "I'm scared."

"You're scared?" Stefan bellowed. "You're the one who's scared? Why are you stalking us? Who are you?"

A light flicked on at the Riboskys' house. Saying nothing, I gestured for Esme to follow us inside. I needed to call 911 and fast, but if I said nothing, the police would just assume it was an accident and text me to confirm it.

"Are you hurt?" Stefan asked her, none too gently. "If you have broken ribs, you deserve it."

"I know," she said and pulled the hood back. Her dark hair was artfully shorn, no more than an inch long, her blue eyes strangely transparent. With her dirty cheeks and pointed chin, she looked like some medieval panting of Saint Joan of Arc. "I would deserve it. I'm so sorry. I'm so sorry."

Stefan looked at me, his face wide open and guileless. "It's you!" he said. "It was you all along. There was no Unabomber. It was just you, the famous Emily. Do you know what she did? Do you even know what she did?"

"I do," I said.

It was the girl from the pictures in Stefan's room.

Stefan kicked one of the chairs over. It landed six inches from Molly, who yelped and jumped to her feet, before it skidded across the room, crashing into the wall. He pointed a shaking finger at Esme. "She…she…"

I had to get control of the situation long enough to find the phone, whatever Stefan thought he knew, whatever I thought I knew. And what if she was dangerous? What if I went upstairs to get my phone off the nightstand and came back to find Stefan with a kitchen knife in his ribs? Why didn't I have some of those zip ties that criminals always seemed to keep at hand?

"I'm sorry, Stefan. I'm so sorry. I loved her so much…"

"And *she* loved *me*, you sick psycho!"

I had never seen Stefan like this, stupid with rage, tears and snot coursing down his red face.

"She did love you. She never loved me the way she loved you." Esme straightened her spine. "I wrecked your life, Stefan. And I wrecked hers. It was my fault. If there was anything I could do to change it, I would do it. I wouldn't care what happened to me."

Stefan swung out of his chair and Esme half rose, I put my hand on her arm and she sat back down. I heard Stefan swear as he slipped and went down hard…*why is there water all over the*

floor? From the kitchen, I could hear the sounds of Stefan filling a glass with ice and water, then unspooling paper towel to
clean up the spill from the electric kettle.

"Are you hurt?" I said. "Are you burned?"

She said simply, "Yes." She raised the hem of the hoodie and
the pink tee shirt beneath it, to reveal an ugly mountain range
of welted red flesh. She said, "I really only wanted to talk to
you before I left, and I was just going to knock on the door.
But it was the middle of the night and so I thought I'd just sit
on one of the lawn chairs and wait until it got light. But I was
freezing cold."

Stefan came back into the room. "So what do you want with
us? That you keep following my mother and breaking into our
house?"

"I need to go upstairs and get my phone," I told Stefan. I
mouthed, call nine-one-one. But he didn't seem to understand
what I was saying. "Okay. I'll wait here and watch her."

Upstairs, I got my phone, pulled on a bra and some sweatpants and shrugged back into my nightshirt. And I almost called
the police in that moment. But I knew that when I did, they
would take over. I would never be able to ask Esme anything on
my own. Rummaging in my medicine cabinet, I found the last
couple of painkillers I'd been given after the woman split my
lip in the lobby of the lecture hall. I got out a kit with first aid
cream and a bandage roll. When I got back downstairs, I dabbed
a thickness of the cream on the girl's stomach and wrapped the
bandage roll around it, tying it securely.

"How do you even know her?" Stefan said sharply to me.
"You act like you know her. How do you know who she is?"

"I do know her, kind of. I've never met her, but, well, it's a
long story. Just give me a minute to talk to her."

"Talk about what? I know why she tried to kill us on the
highway. I didn't know it was her, but she tried to kill me once
before, Mom. And I really am aware that I didn't need her help

to fuck myself up with drugs, but she did help, Mom! She was the supplier! Always. For Belinda and me. She made it easy for us to get wasted. She hated me. That night, what she wanted was for me to die."

"I know for a fact she wished you would die. She was obsessed with Belinda, but so were you, Stefan! So were you! It was like a bomb waiting to go off, the whole situation."

"I loved her," he said.

"I loved her too," said Esme and then, "I'm going to throw up. Please."

I stood quickly and ushered her into the bathroom. We could hear her retching, water running, more gagging.

"Wait," I said, in a low voice I hoped would still command him. "Look at me. I have to tell you something."

But just then Esme came back out into the kitchen. I gave her one of the painkillers with a glass of milk. Then I made her a piece of toast to eat so she wouldn't throw up the medicine.

Finally, I sat down. "If you loved Belinda, why did you kill her?"

"Kill her?" Esme struggled to her feet, gasped at the pain and fell back down in the chair. "Are you serious? Why did *I* kill her?"

"I'm completely serious."

Stefan said, "What the fuck are you talking about, Mom?"

Esme cried out, "I didn't kill Belinda! I would never have hurt Belinda!"

"Then who did kill her?"

"Are you out of your mind? He killed her."

"Were you there when he killed her?"

"I wasn't in the apartment. You know he killed her. Look, I came here to say how sorry I am. I came because it's my Healing Project, right?"

Stefan said, "How do you know about that?"

"I saw it on TV, like everybody else," Esme said. "And I

thought wow, you're doing such a good thing. So I wanted to do something good, too. I wanted to admit it. It was partly my fault. I got him into a frenzy. I told him that Belinda was breaking up with him. And everything else, since he got out, that was my fault too. I just came to tell you that it wasn't my idea. It wasn't my idea to scare you, ever."

"If it wasn't your idea, whose idea was it?"

"It was Jill's."

"Why did you...why would you..." I stammered. "How do you even know Jill?"

"Jill is like a mother to me," Esme said. "She doesn't know about me and Belinda. Our relationship. She doesn't know about me giving Belinda and Stefan drugs, I hope you never tell her. It would break her heart."

"What?" I still couldn't comprehend all this. Esme knew Jill, but Jill didn't know who Esme was to Belinda?

"She just knows that I was one of the first volunteers," Esme said, with a lilt of pride she couldn't seem to suppress. "I helped her with it from the beginning."

"Are you really from Chicago?" I asked her. "Did you come up here just to torment us?"

"I was born there. My dad is still in Chicago."

"Do you live in Black Creek now?" I asked then.

"I did," she said. "Not now. I live with Jill. Or I did, until tonight."

Trying hard to get a good breath, I looked down at the phone. Then I thought, ten more minutes won't matter.

I only wanted a moment to see the night Belinda was killed through the eyes of one who was there. I owed Stefan that much. I owed Belinda that much. I owed myself.

"Tell me how you knew Belinda," I said.

"Why do I have to hear this?" Stefan said. "Why does this matter at all?"

"Stay here," I told Stefan. "I am going to call the police. I still think that there's a good chance she really did kill Belinda. She has every reason to lie. But I need you to be here too."

Softened by the painkiller, Emily, for she said this was her real name, told us that she met Belinda at a cheer camp in Wisconsin Dells. One day, they took a picnic to Kettle Pond. They kissed. The power of their connection scared both of them. Emily had known all her life that she was gay, but she was not out, not even to her family. Belinda was the first girl she ever loved, and Belinda confessed she had a deepening crush on Emily, as well. Belinda called her Esme when they were alone and wrote poetry about her.

But then Emily found out about Stefan.

"If I had left Belinda alone right then, she would still be alive." Instead, she pleaded; she threatened; she cajoled. Belinda, though conflicted, maintained her loyalty. They didn't see each other for a while. Slowly, though, Emily wore her down and they started up again. Emily pressed her hard: Did Belinda want to live a lie? Did she think that loving a girl was something to be ashamed of? Did Stefan deserve more than a limited love? At last, Belinda agreed at least to be frank with her mother and with Stefan about her new love entanglement.

"Did you know then?" I asked Stefan.

"I had already guessed as much," Stefan said. "But I wasn't going to give her up without a fight."

Abruptly, Belinda switched from her plan to go to Thornton Wilder for college. She needed space, away from everything familiar to explore all the feelings she was experiencing for the first time, or so she told herself. Suddenly, she wasn't just Jill's daughter and Stefan's girl. Stefan panicked, then he despaired. How could he face losing his Belinda, I thought? She was his light, his only. He told me as much now.

"I knew that if I pressured her, it would give her an excuse to break up with me," he said. Much as his purloined heart drove him to grovel for her affections, he didn't want to betray how much more he needed her than she seemed to need him. Stefan decided to pretend to be more tolerant of Emily than he ever felt. What we thought was exhaustion from the endless commute was something much more serious.

Teetering on the edge of despair, Stefan never let on to us or to Belinda.

"I had relatives in Black Creek. When I was a little girl, after my mom died, I went there summers to stay with my aunt and my cousins. I talked her into going there. I said I would go there, too. I promised not to pressure her. I never went to school. But Belinda didn't know that."

She lied to Belinda, too. August came, and Belinda fell into Emily's arms. If Belinda had believed she was going to Black Creek for needed space, she now knew that wasn't true. The space between Belinda and her storied Esme was the space of a breath. The next weeks were a euphoria. First they were ardent, then completely abandoned, then consumed and consuming. Their love was like a tropical disease. While I didn't doubt then, and I don't doubt now that Belinda still loved Stefan, it was in Emily that she first found the fullness of sensual delight. First freedom, first rebellion, first sexual passion; there was no more flammable a brew. Emily couldn't eat or sleep or breathe, either. There was nothing she wouldn't do.

Only Stefan stood between them.

"They had private jokes," Emily said, wincing at the memory, if not the burns on her belly. "She would say, green peppers or something and they would just crack up for half an hour. He had her in the way I really wanted. But I guess I had her in the way that Stefan really wanted."

Still, Stefan reasoned that history was on his side—not just their history as a couple but Belinda's history as a conservative Christian. Jill would never approve. He had to wait for this passion to burn itself out.

After all that passion went up like gas lightning that awful freezing night, Emily's rage and grief found their natural target in Stefan.

"I wanted him to pay for what he did," she said. Prison could not be cruel enough; she hoped that some evildoer would slash his handsome face. She hoped he lived in fear, as she did. Consumed with the notion that Belinda would come back to haunt her, she took to sleeping in a sleeping bag on the floor of her bedroom, so that the bed was between her and the door. She made me remember Stefan's early weeks at home, the way he slept on his bedroom floor. She forgot to eat. Sometimes, she forgot to breathe and had to remind herself that she wasn't at the bottom of a pool. "I lost maybe thirty pounds."

When she read something about Jill's dating violence protest group, SAY, it was the key to her lock. She reached out to Jill who took Emily under her wing. "I knew Belinda, so it was like I knew Jill. I guess I adapted to her. And having me around made Jill feel closer to Belinda. At first I would just demonstrate with the other SAY members back when Stefan was still in prison. Then it got to be like I would have dinner with Jill and sometimes sleep over. And then I moved in."

Emily started to cry then. Her own mom died in a terrible road accident when she was six, ruining her dad so utterly that he no longer even seemed to know that Esme was there. With Jill, there was again some of that barely-remembered state of refuge—a text asking if you were okay when you were fifteen minutes late, soft carpets instead of cast-off throw rugs, someone who knew you liked brown sugar but not raisins on your oatmeal. And so Jill sharpened Emily into an instrument of her own wrath. She made her do things she hated doing. She did them because she wanted Jill's love.

"It was all you, then," I said. "Every bit of it."

"It was all me."

Emily egged our house and wrote threatening messages on our garage doors in red paint. She tore up our roses and scat-

tered the contents of our mailbox in the street. Jill once suggested that she poison our dog, but she refused. It was Emily
who broke in and blacked out Stefan's eyes on our family photos, who entered our house surreptitiously half a dozen times,
stealing small things, my grandmother's opal watch, my tiny
marble bust of Pallas with a raven on her head and the inscription, *Nevermore*, my first edition of *A Tree Grows in Brooklyn*.
She stole my dark pink Pauline Saucedo scarf, the one Jill was
wearing in a news photo I later saw. I had never quite figured
out why I kept staring at that photo like those drawings of hidden pictures from my childhood. Can you find the teaspoon,
can you find the mitten…

Before she could go on, Stefan spoke up. "What if you had
killed us on the road that time?"

"It was never supposed to go that far," Emily said.

Following Jill's orders, Emily disguised herself as a male figure in a hoodie, with mirrored sunglasses. "Just to scare you."

"But you couldn't control something like that! In a blizzard!
You could have killed yourself too. Would Jill have wanted
that?"

She dropped her face in her hands.

"She got totally ruthless," Emily admitted. "She didn't care
what happened to Stefan. She pushed me. She wasn't as nice
anymore." When Emily balked at trying to hurt us on the road,
Jill said such niceties shouldn't really matter to someone who'd
already attempted murder.

What did Emily mean by that, I thought?

Knowing that she was betraying Jill, but unable to bear the
shame any longer, Emily assumed the Esme persona and started
texting me, warning Stefan to keep quiet. Insinuate yourself into
Stefan's life, was Jill's next mandate. But that backfired: It was
during those months spent chatting online with Stefan under
a fake name and profile, pretending to be a college junior and
trying to con him into liking her, that her compassion for Ste

fan's true grief overtook her. She felt rewarded by his trust and protective of his broken vulnerability.

Stefan said, "You were that girl? You were the one who stood me up?"

"I was." The pictures she sent Stefan were of her friend Olivia. To me, she said, "I called myself Stephanie, just so I wouldn't forget the name. But he thought it was funny, us having almost the same name."

"You're pitiful," Stefan said. "You're a vile human being."

He got up and stepped over the back of the chair to stand at the kitchen window, where sleet now spattered the dark glass with a sound like the tsk of disapproving tongues.

He added, "It's not because you stood me up. I would hope even I could do better than you. No, it's because everything you did, you meant to do. It wasn't an accident."

"That's not true," Emily said. "I probably am a vile person. But you have no room to talk."

Which face of Emily should I believe in? I could recall the cocky scolding attitude of the hooded figure, who tried to run us off the road and then kept coming back to haunt us. Or was this shamed, fragile girl the real Emily, no more than Jill's pawn? Jill's motives, if deplorable, were at least comprehensible. Further, all Jill had to do was to conceive of those things, not carry them out. So who was really the more ruthless? No matter who coerced her, what she had done to us on the road a year ago was attempted murder. She belonged in jail, and she would go to jail. I thought of Jill, that arctic morning outside the prison gates. Jill, there to make sure that her handmaiden was ready to perform as instructed. Jill, there to make sure her will be done. What would become of Jill, if this whole tale turned out to be more than just a ruse? What was Jill's culpability here? Should I call Jill, right now, bring her here? Didn't she deserve to be in on this? Should I wait a few minutes after I called the police and then, when they were almost here, summon Jill, so that Emily believed that I would give her into Jill's hands?

Maybe.

Still, there was no reason to alarm Emily, at least for the next few minutes.

Whether or not I called Jill, I was nearly ready for that other call—to the police. Emily was relaxed, almost drowsy, her cheek resting on her open palm. She seemed to trust that I would not really turn her in. Or, maybe she didn't care if I did. Maybe that was what she wanted all along. I was the one who said there were no accidents. Did Emily already know when she knocked on our door that the only place she would be going tonight would be the police station?

"Okay," I said. "I need you to go back and tell me about that night. Every single thing that happened."

Stefan said, "This sucks. It's sick, Mom. I don't want to hear this anymore."

Early in the evening, Emily asked Stefan to stop by her place so they could go to Belinda's together.

"It was too cold to walk, and I told him I scored something special just for him. Something different."

I got up quickly, banging my knee on the kitchen table. Just to get away from her, I crossed to the living room and sank into the couch. A blast of wind shoved the back door open and I heard the pulsing growl of thunder. Emily followed me and sat down gingerly across the room, on the small caned chair next to the fireplace. "I got what we usually got when we'd go out dancing. Molly and some coke and a little meth, too. But I also got an eight ball for Stefan."

"An eight ball?"

"Heroin and crack. I wanted to give it to him before we picked Belinda up. It might make him sick, but it would definitely make him act crazy and that was something Belinda would really hate. She was still scared of drugs. Every time she did them was going to be the last time. She said they made her feel like her head was filled with glitter. But Stefan really liked them. He never said no. I knew he'd try anything."

Anything, I thought? I didn't know Stefan at all.

"Why that night of all nights?" I asked.

Emily sighed and gently touched her stomach. "I couldn't stand it, back and forth, back and forth. He would come up, we would go out dancing, he was a really good dancer, and he would be so nice to me. I would put up with him so Belinda didn't hate me, and Stefan would say how nice it was that Bindy...he called her Bindy..."

"I know what he called her," I said.

"That she had a best friend. He was sweet about it. He was so nice," she said. None of that, however, mattered. As October rolled over into November, then December, Emily's own world rocked with Belinda's indecision. "When he would leave on Sunday night, then we'd be back together. Stefan would head out and I would move back in. She would make me leave in the middle of the night, but she didn't make him leave. I knew they didn't do, you know, everything, because she had this Christianity rule about being a virgin when she got married. But they did lots of things in bed. Almost everything, including things we did together. I would go nuts thinking of her with him, like that. I would rip her sheets off the bed. I would pray he would get in a car accident on the way back and die."

Stefan's eyes were terrible. I could only imagine the blistering effect of such intimate talk, from this girl's mouth, in front of his mother—and how it must have brought back unbidden images of Belinda, fearsome in their sweetness.

Right before Christmas, Belinda told Emily that Stefan would soon move to Black Creek full-time. He was going to start school, with one class, then a full load in spring. Now Belinda would have to make that long-deferred choice. If Stefan thought he would win in the long game, Emily thought she would lose.

How could she lose Belinda? Her lover-angel-best friend, Belinda's cologne on her palms, Belinda's strong athlete's legs and
hips, her voice singing off-key in the morning light as she boiled
water for tea, how could she lose all this? She decided to wait.
She decided to do something to stop him. She said, "He's right.
I did want to kill him, Thea."

"And you mean, really kill him?"

"Not bomb his house or something. But he wasn't an idiot.
If he died, it would be his own fault. It would be because he
was too big a dope fiend to turn anything down and take care
of his own life."

And that was when Emily said, she stepped over the wire.
She began to make her plan.

How could I sit here with such a creature in my home? Yes,
she was also a victim, if only of Jill's consuming obsession; but
this did nothing to stem my revulsion. I tried to remember what
it was like to be eighteen years old and desperately in lust, truly
believing that your sole umbilical cord to joy was attached to
one person. I loved Jep but I had never felt like that about anyone—not until Stefan was born and my helpless love surrounded
him like a nimbus.

"So then he was always at Belinda's. We would do things together, all three of us. We would go out and dance. He was really a good dancer. I would bring over stuff for when we hung
out. Usually Molly."

I glanced at our dog. She recognized my confusion.

"Molly. The drug. Ecstasy. Stefan just took what I gave him.
So that would be how I would stop him. That night, the townie
girl who sold me the drugs said, you can't mess around with this
stuff. It kills people. I didn't care."

"You heard her now, Mom," Stefan put in, his fist slamming
into the paneling.

I jumped up. "Don't make it sound like she forced you, Stefan. You made that call yourself."

I pictured my son as he had been that first night in the hospital jail ward, turned away from me, the back of his head soaked in blood, then turned toward me, his eyes sunken in dark pits, his fingernails crusted, spittle and blood dried on his lips.

That night, she first gave him the Molly, and only pretended to take some herself. "Then I told him he had to use a different way to take the other stuff. We went to my room and I boiled some water in my teakettle. I had those vitamin C packs you use for your immunity, so that was good. I could mix that with the drugs and some bottled water, and I did. Then I heated up the mix a little so it dissolved, and I got out a syringe and showed him how to shoot up because he had never done it before and he was afraid. You have to be really careful."

"I can't hear this crap," I said, leaning forward to grip my knees, trying to control the spurt of bile in my throat. By now, I would have thought I would have the emotional equivalent of alligator hide, but I could still be shocked by the grim details.

"You said you wanted to hear every single thing."

I took a long breath. "Okay."

She went on, "You have to make sure the bevel of the needle is facing the right way. You start with the veins closest to the wrist. But at the last minute, I said, Stefan, don't. That stuff is too much for you. But he did it anyway. I saw his eyes roll up in his head. After, he wanted me to drive him to Belinda's. I called Belinda and she picked up. I said, I need you. She said, I need you too, but don't come, don't let Stefan near the place, because her mom had just called and Belinda hung up on her and Jill was going savage."

Jill had found Belinda's small leather portfolio, in which she kept her special things, apparently kicked under the bed and left at home by mistake. When Jill picked it up, a single photo fell out in a thin delicate silver frame. It pictured Emily and Belinda under a waterfall. "We were kissing and our bodies were sort of covered by the waterfall. You couldn't see my face, but you could see we didn't have any clothes on. We took it by setting the timer on the camera one morning at Blueberry Park. There were letters too, bound with pink ribbon."

Emily didn't think that was really any mistake, for how could Belinda not have noticed that folder was missing for days? Belinda was crying, asking Emily, what should I do? What should I do? The time had come.

Emily hung up and turned to Stefan.

"I'm so sorry, Stefan, but she says it's over," she told him. "He said I was lying. I said I wasn't lying. I was lying, but Belinda and I, we talked about running away, going to another school." So, as if saying so would make it true, Emily told Stefan that she and Belinda were going to run away. "She doesn't want to see you."

His head was already swimming with the toxic drug cocktail, Stefan started to cry like a little kid. He said he thought he was dying. He kept passing out and waking up.

I asked, "What did you do? Were you frightened?"

"I just watched him," Emily said. And shrugged. She knew he would insist on going. So let Belinda see what kind of feeb she was involved with.

I glanced over at Stefan. He was crying now, silently. It occurred to me that this might also be the first time that Stefan had heard a full account of the next fatal moments. While I wanted to get up and go to him, it seemed disloyal to treat him like a child now, in front of this girl.

"Then suddenly he grabbed his car keys and ran out of the apartment to the parking lot and I went after him. It was like, zero out. We were freezing because we didn't have any coats. He promised he wouldn't do anything crazy, but he had to see Belinda. He just wanted to talk quietly with Belinda. I tried to grab the keys and said he was too messed up to drive. He said he'd give me the keys but only if I'd drive him there. Otherwise he'd take me out of town on a lonely road and leave me there."

So she did. When they got to Belinda's building, he jumped

out. But Emily couldn't find a place to leave the car, even an illegal spot. It took her ten minutes and she was still half a block away. As she finally made it to the top of the stairs, she stopped across the hall from Belinda's apartment door, out of breath and courage. She heard voices, but couldn't make out the words. Finally, she pushed open the door. The room was dark and quiet. Esme fumbled for the hall light switch, and tripped over Belinda's cell phone. From somewhere inside, she could hear Stefan moaning, almost growling.

"What came next?" I said.

With all my might, I did not want to know. "What did you do?"

Emily crept into the living room.

She leaned to one side to snap on the lamp she knew was there.

She said that Belinda and Stefan were lying on the floor, in front of the couch, their bodies half on top of each other, almost in an embrace. A golf club, thickly coated in blood, was propped like a sword against Stefan's leg. He was stirring, his head thrashing a little, but Belinda… Belinda's head was broken in the back like a pumpkin after Halloween.

"There was nothing I could do, Thea. I knew she was dead."

Emily breathed in slowly, then out. She said she went into the bedroom then and found the little satin bag she and Belinda were using to save cash for their plan of running away together. They'd put together a few hundred dollars.

"Then I just ran, Thea, I just ran. I didn't want to go to prison. Because now you get it, right? You see what I mean when I said I knew the truth. It was really all my fault." She glanced up and reached for her backpack. "I have to go."

"Wait," I said. "I'll drive you to the bus."

Stefan slapped his hands on his thighs and got up. I heard him going up the stairs, then the bathroom door slamming. Didn't he realize I was just bluffing?

Esme said, "I'm going far away. Because things happen to people. Something could happen to me. In a deserted place, and I would just be there until I was a skeleton, all alone." She added, "Things could happen to Stefan too." She snapped her fingers. "Like that! That easily. If he remembered the wrong thing, he would tell you, and you would tell the police."

If he remembered the wrong thing? *There is only one story...*

"What wrong thing?" I said. "Are you talking about Jill? Is this tied up in some weird way with Jill's reputation? With vengeance?"

Emily said, "No," and then, "Yes." Then she said, "Trust me. You don't know the side of her that I do."

And I didn't. If nothing else, what Emily-or-Esme told me proved that Jill had a capacity for petty vengefulness that she concealed very well.

I left her briefly and followed Stefan upstairs to quietly call the police, and as I got to the landing, I heard him turn on the shower.

When I told the Portland Police dispatcher that there was an intruder in my house, he said, are you safe, can you go to a safe place? I told him I was safe, that I knew the intruder. He paused. Then he asked if there was a domestic dispute in progress. I told him no, there wasn't, not at all, but to come quickly.

"A car is on the way," the dispatcher said. I looked out through the porthole window. The stars were beginning to fade into the dark gray sky. It was five in the morning. Then I called Pete Sunday, on the cell number he gave me. I expected him to sound muffled, like one of those people who knocks the phone off the nightstand.

"You have her in the house? Is she restrained?"

I almost laughed. "Uh, no. I wanted to use those zip ties, but I ran out. She's downstairs, she, well, I spilled some boiling water. She startled me, in the kitchen. She has a burn, but it's not very bad."

"Seriously, Thea. I'm on my way. Did you call the police?"

I told him I had, they were on the way, and added, "She denies killing Belinda."

"What did you expect?"

"I thought she was coming here to confess to me, but what she confessed was that giving Stefan that whole brew of drugs was wrong. She just admitted inciting him to rage over Belinda."

"Do you believe her?"

"I don't know. I know she thinks I believe her," I told him. "She's the Unabomber."

"What?"

"She was the guy in the hoodie. The one who kept following me. That was her all along."

"I thought it might be."

"Why didn't you tell me that?" It seemed strange, to say the least. "And she is also that girl in the picture, the tall, dark-haired girl. She says her name really is Emily."

I hurried back down to the living room. Our dog Molly was happily chomping on liver treats, which were scattered everywhere. The empty bag lay on the floor in front of the open door.

Emily was gone.

When the police arrived, they immediately called for more officers and began a neighborhood search, on foot through backyards, in vehicles that sent cones of light into every dark passage.

Pete Sunday said, "We'll find her."

But they didn't find her. They never have.

We were no worse off than we had been, and yet, I couldn't deny that the conclusion felt worse.

I felt like some credulous, desperate hag; but at least, I didn't have to feel foolish in front of Jep or my family. No one beyond Stefan and me—and Julie and Rebecca Broom—needed to know about the ultimately doomed, possibly fanciful attempt to exonerate Stefan, which I still believed was based on truth, even if Stefan didn't.

What he finally said was this: "What if she did kill Belinda? I didn't save her."

We knew all we would ever know. And still, a curious peace settled over us. We had finally changed our landline number, so most of the calls we got now were from people of good intent—I counted among those even people selling timeshares. No one was going to be crouching in the kitchen anymore or marching up and down outside chanting hymns of hatred for me and mine. Tomorrow, I might wake up as a person whose life perhaps contains ordinary sorts of trials and triumphs—a person who could spend hours worrying about mole holes in the backyard or my mother's hernia surgery.

I stood in the cold, huddled in my parka with my mug in my hand. How long had it been since I'd felt free to stand alone outside in the dark?

Did I think I would see Longing Esme? No, I knew she was gone. Did I think that I would see Belinda's sweet shade in starlight? I walked around to the red-carpet walk of chokeberry Stefan had made of our driveway, the rock walls and turrets crested by azaleas in frank purple to shadowy lavender, swirled round with painterly waves of phlox, bluebells, bleeding heart and trillium. All those blooming decks were fast asleep now, but they would surge back in the spring. I felt that when she left, Emily-or-Esme took with her the night that lasted four years.

The next day, we didn't talk about Emily.

We didn't talk about Belinda.

When Jep came home, Stefan showed us some of the real estate sheets he'd been collecting. We'd agreed that he might want to stay on at home until he got through his first year of school, but he wanted to see what was out there in terms of a house. He had plans to be an eccentric bachelor in his own pad.

A few days later, Rebecca called Stefan, all excited. She had indeed arranged that big commission for him to do a full landscaping of the parklike lawn that surrounded The Alice Hodge Safe Home and thereafter maintain the garden and the green space adjacent. The weather stayed open, more springlike than polar, so he did some planning over there, laying out strings and doing digital drawings of where he might set lavish herbaceous borders, then adding artful ornamental trees, like holly and hemlock, maybe an unusual blue ceanothus and an apple tree like the one we'd planted when he was born. He hauled paving brick, taking advantage of the strangely warm weather, and set to work constructing a small central piazza with rubbled stone benches and a huge old cement birdbath at its center, surrounded by sentinel arborvitae. So that the women residents could grow their own vegetables, he was thinking to build raised box gardens and he sketched how the succession gardens, separated by winding paths, would start with spring peonies, poppies and irises, followed by midsummer lilies and late-summer irises and asters. When he showed me and Jep the plans, the very names made me tipsy.

Becky and I met for coffee again and she told me Stefan received a lot of attention from the ladies, who competed to bring him hot cider and hang around to watch him heft the bags and stones. I tried to see Stefan as they might see him, a quiet, polite, hunky guy with an ephemeral smile, and got a kick out of the image. One day, I dropped by to view the progress. Becky, who'd popped like a plum in recent days and was now enormous in girth, was sitting outside on a folding chair with a big blanket over her lap. In the late afternoon sun nearby was a small older woman bundled in a vivid red padded coat and hat. Her grandmother, I thought; but no, to my surprise, it was Stefan's grandmother, my own mother. To see her there filled me with delight, because, of course, her connection to the Hodges was even stronger than mine. "Look at all this," she told me proudly, gesturing with the black lacquer cane she only affected, because my mother could outwalk a peasant farmer. "He has a gift, Thea."

Becky got up, with difficulty, and pulled me aside then. "I should have asked you this sooner."

"What?"

"Would you be with me when I go into labor, Thea?"

"Rebecca, that should be your own mom."

"But it's up to me," she urged me. And her mother also lived out of state, and what if this all happened suddenly? So I agreed. Everything was on track, Becky told me. The baby was due any day. Her doctor said Becky just had to follow along. I knew she would remember that comment ironically someday.

I finished my book and turned it in. Stefan got ready for school to start in a couple of weeks. Jep began his quiet season, with hours at home with me, big meals, movie nights together.

All the other shoes had dropped. All the cats were out of the bag. We had lived innocently in Beforeland and suffered our sins in Afterland. Perhaps, this new land, Tomorrowland, was where we would live from now on.

16

At first, the snow on Greek Orthodox Christmas spun down in big lacy pinwheels that looked like something that would taste of pineapple. Then afternoon brought in a rock wall of weather, and the world disappeared. We ate early, with candles, the kind of meaty, stuporous meal that rightfully should be followed by two hours of baling hay. Instead, we topped it off with the ekmek kataifi that Amelia made to perfection and drank Greek coffee from demitasse cups. We would then ordinarily do something antique and embarrassing with the kids, like team charades, but Phoebe and Amelia wanted to leave for home earlier; and my parents decided to stay overnight. We had celebrated what my aunt Elena called "American" Christmas like most of the secular Christian world but Greek Orthodox Christmas in January was still a religious holiday for my parents, like "Greek" Easter, with its red-dyed eggs baked into tsoureki. It was celebrated when Americans celebrated The Feast of the Epiphany, if they celebrated it at all, the day when the three kings finally

arrived at Bethlehem, after all those days of GPS-ing by that
one outrageous star. I loved Orthodox Christmas, especially this
Christmas—which I thought of as the first Christmas out from
under—and it was especially thrilling because what Stefan had
done to our decked-out house made me feel like I was living in
a Viktor&Rolf perfume bottle. So after American Christmas,
I might have been downcast when my sisters left, drawing all
the chatter and teasing after them like a crown of ribbons, had
I not known we would be together in a short while for another
groaning meal and more presents. After they were gone, the five
of us left broke holiday protocol by turning the television on,
not to the Vienna Boys Choir but to 13 AccuWeather. By four,
the front door was so drifted that Jep couldn't open it.

"I have to plow," Stefan said regretfully. "I should be ahead
of it. What did I think it was, Christmas?" He told us he understood now why people worked in offices.

"I'll come with you," Jep said. "We can share father and son
bonding. I can tell you lore from Christmases of old, stories of
ancient Scandinavian drunks who are your forebears."

"No, Dad, I'm not dragging you out in this. You nap by the
fire, elder, with your new suede slippers," Stefan told him. "I'll
be back in a couple of hours. The big issue is Luck's apartments
and her new condominium complex. People are always outraged by snow. It's like they think they live in Miami." Most of
his regular landscaping clients needed him, and I didn't think
a couple of hours would do it, but he assured me that, except
for a couple of places, he would leave the hand shoveling to
his teenage helpers after all that snow was down. It was only
his third or fourth time driving the new truck—a massive red
Ford only a few years old that came with a tough heavy-duty
blade, a splurge he allowed himself because we were covering
his schooling. The Whole Blooming World design burst from
the doors. The first few snows of the year were sugary flirta-
tions, but they'd taught him how to operate the plow. I could

tell that he was eager to put his truck through its paces against some elements. He filled the biggest thermos in the house with hot sweet tea and set out, first scraping our own driveway to perfection. Jep and I geared up and tackled the walks with more will than success. Since it wasn't cold, it was exhilarating to be out in it, such a dramatic storm with lightning that seemed to shatter among the stars. You could see how people would be tempted to read in it the message of some epic event. There were strange sights. A woman all in green fleece went power walking through the drifts. Two houses down, a white owl sat mythically on a mailbox. The neighbors across the street were toasting marshmallows near one of those free-standing fireplaces. Burly as buildings, the municipal plows roared down the street.

Two hours passed, then three. Feeling like an ass for doing it, I called Stefan and texted him. No response...because of course, he was busy. There were cars piled up all over, a four-car wreck on Highway 51. He didn't really understand the physics of driving that big rig. The sharpest pity was reserved for people whose kids died on Christmas, on their own birthdays, on their wedding day...but I was being an idiot. The sharpest pity was reserved for people whose kids died just when they'd survived their worst challenges, when the sky was big and brilliant. I was being an idiot, driving myself nuts. Another hour passed, a slower hour marked by eight-minute increments, the most I could force myself to wait between bouts of checking my phone. Jep got out the ham to make a sandwich.

"How could you eat anything?" I snapped at him.

"It's been three hours since my last feeding," he said, one of those expressions his sister used to infantilize men, which drove me nuts.

Instead, I decided to join the devil. I ate another huge slice of the dessert, just to keep from checking my phone. When I picked it up, it rang, as if my touch had brought it alive. The number was unfamiliar. Hadn't I asked for an ordinary life, with ordinary fears? This was ordinary life in a Wisconsin blizzard. Black ice on a road, on a frigid night. The paramedics would say he was breathing on his own, which was good...stop, Thea, I said. Stop it. But the universe was talking. There was no shutting it up.

It was Stefan. And he was calling from someone else's phone because he'd left his in the truck.

"What happened, Stefan?"

Jep set his second sandwich down and came to stand next to me.

"It's Rebecca. She's in trouble here. The baby is coming. It's awful. I'm taking her to the hospital."

I pulled on my coat and Jep grabbed his.

"You don't have to drive me," I said. "You know I'm a better driver than you are."

"Please," he said. "Don't disgrace the holy day by lying through your teeth. Anyhow, it's more that there will be two of us if we get stuck."

We got stuck within fifteen minutes, the car having spun like a figure skater and nosed into a snowbank. I was stunned by the amount of snow that had fallen, easily twenty inches. By then, I could see the lights of the hospital, like watch fires through the snow. "I'm going to walk," I told Jep, who just shook his head. A few blocks on, I realized that the lights of the hospital were the urban equivalent of being able to see the Rockies from western Kansas. I was unavoidably reminded of the night Belinda died. Even my eyeballs were wet. A Jeep pulled over just ahead of me. In it were two boys, maybe eighteen years old. "Do you need a ride, lady?" one of them said. It crossed my mind that this was how murder podcasts began. It was the driver saying "lady" that convinced me to risk it, that and the fact that I had about four steps left in me by that point. When I got inside, I looked so woebegone that the person at the ER desk asked me the nature of my injury.

There were so few people in the hospital that someone from the information desk volunteered to personally walk me up to the OB floor, probably to have something to do. "She'll remember this blizzard, huh?" the woman said, and I thought, Rebecca would be hearing this for the rest of her life.

Stefan came running the minute the elevator doors opened.

"Mom! Oh god, you have to help her, something awful is going on. She's in terrible pain!"

While we waited for the nurses to finish Rebecca's check, Stefan told me what happened.

The Alice Hodge Safe Home was the last house on his plow list. He promised Rebecca he would check on her. When he finished plowing, he texted Rebecca twice. No answer. The lights were on in the kitchen so he glanced inside. To his horror, he saw Rebecca on all fours on the kitchen floor.

"I'm coming!" he shouted, fumbling for the big blue-collar key ring on his belt. When he got inside, he asked, "Are you doing exercises?"

"Exercises? I'm trying to get my phone out from under the cabinet so I can call an ambulance."

"You don't need an ambulance. I'm here."

"Great. What a relief. Can you help me up?"

Stefan lifted Rebecca to a standing position.

Within minutes, he had her in the truck.

"The pains are just minutes apart," the nurse told us. "Are you her family?" She nodded to Stefan. "Dad?"

"Yep," he said. We looked away, so as not to laugh and then were whisked into gowns and caps.

In the labor suite, another nurse was telling red-faced Rebecca, "Okay, my dear. We're going to have a birthday. What's his name going to be?"

Becky said, "Jesus." The nurse didn't laugh. "Not really! Patrick." She gathered herself again, her yell guttural and sustained. The nurse whisked a pile of bedding under Becky's rear.

"Okay, Becky, I'm right here," I said. "Squeeze my hand as hard as you can."

She did, and in minutes, literally no more than four minutes, there he was.

"What a pretty baby," the nurse told Becky, as she cradled him close.

"It's you and me, fella," Becky said to her son. He was beautiful, rosy and big with masses of dark hair. We each took turns holding him, Stefan in the stereotypical stiff comic panic, as if Becky had handed him a bundle of burning rags.

Weakly, Stefan said, "I'll always be grateful for those tires."

I told Becky that I would be back to give her a ride home in the morning and that I would bring a change of clothes.

"But wait," she said. "Wouldn't you two like to be Patrick's godparents?"

"We're Greek Orthodox," I told her. "Wouldn't we have to be whatever...you are?"

"I'm not anything. I was Catholic as a child. Patrick can be Greek Orthodox. I think that would be colorful. And I have this great baptismal gown I shouldn't let go to waste. Do you know a priest who'd baptize him? It's all superstition anyhow. We just need all the luck we can get."

"Mom, please don't say true thing that," Stefan warned me. "It's becoming a tic."

"True thing that," I said.

"As for me, I am a veteran godfather," Stefan said, referring to my sister Phoebe's baby Gus. "I would be happy to do it. I'm not sure I can offer guidance but I intend to excel at that one day. I'm very good at presents."

Stefan also agreed to lean on Father Kanelos, who got so many compliments on the landscaping of the church that he would be helpless to refuse.

"You're supposed to have family for this," I reminded Becky. She said, "Maybe that's my choice. And maybe I do."

That night, just days before the anniversary of Belinda's death, Jill called out of the blue and asked to meet with Stefan and me, because, after much thought and prayer, she had decided to forgive him, and how could we refuse?

After her call, I stood on my porch in the dark and thought about where life had taken us, which felt something like a circle.

As Iris Murdoch said, human arrangements are nothing but loose ends, and time, like the sea, unties them all.

17

So what did I think would happen, people ask me. I don't know the answer to that; I only know that, if you had given me ten tries to predict what did happen, not one of them would have come close.

When I talked things over with Julie, two days before we were to meet Jill, she implored me to stop thinking of this event as momentous. It was a formality, putting a frame around feelings already experienced, like marriage put a frame around love. After this meeting, nothing in Stefan's life or mine would change. For his part, Stefan thought the request was impressive. He remembered, during his first nights out of prison, the strong desire he had to see Jill and talk to her—the desire that had led, in part, to The Healing Project. For Jill to do this, it seemed to him, was exceedingly brave and benevolent.

The date she set was the fourth anniversary of Belinda's death, a Monday at three in the afternoon at the cemetery. It wouldn't be dark yet, but, she said, and I agreed, a Monday was best because none of us needed an audience. Don't share any of this with the press, she cautioned me, and I said that of course, I would not. "I don't want there to be any perception that I don't believe in the work of SAY," she said. "I believe in that work more than ever, and I hope it goes on."

I said, "I think it will, Jill."

She said, "I am not so sure."

I had mixed feelings about meeting at Belinda's grave. It was not that I didn't understand or consider the place appropriate. But what could be more upsetting and poignant? I wanted to suggest the cherry tree planted for her in Whitehorse Park; but I was in no position to suggest anything. Only Jep wholly disapproved. He wanted to come with us, only because he thought he might be able to bring the thing to a speedier conclusion. "This can't go on forever, Thea," he said.

"It's going on forever for her," I told him.

"I know but..."

"This feels like an ending, Jep. She's trying to take the steps for what they call closure, these days."

On the way, Stefan and I stopped to buy a dozen pink roses. Unavoidably, we remembered the last time we had come here, so long ago. I was still surprised that Stefan didn't ever come here privately, on his own, and yet, this was perhaps the most complex of mournings, snagged at every corner with shadows. At the appointed hour, the winter shadows already thickening, Stefan and I parked as close to the grave as we could. We walked up toward that knoll as scarves of mist swirled up off the lake. I was surprised not to see Jill's car. I saw her, then, though, sitting quietly, wearing the heavy maroon-and-gold varsity coat that Belinda had given us, the one she'd been wearing that day I saw her outside the prison, the day that Stefan was released and Esme tried to terrorize us. I had never asked her why she was there that day, perhaps it was to give Esme the go-ahead. On her lap, Jill held a big leather folder, almost like a small briefcase, and she turned to the sound of our footsteps.

She stood up.

Her face was awful, a bony pale slash, her eyes, untended and reddened, sculpted downward. "Thea," she said. "Stefan." It was a greeting that felt foreshortened, without the customary attendant movements, without a handshake, an embrace, or even a wave.

"Hello, Jill," Stefan said. "I hope we can help."

She sighed. "If you two would sit there."

We sat down on the bench. "As you know, I have not really been able to move on successfully from Belinda's death. I think it's a combination of things. I don't have a partner to share this with me and, losing a husband and then my only child, it's too much."

"But maybe in time..." I said.

"I don't have time, Thea. What do I have? Really?" She gestured to Stefan. "You have him, so you have a future."

"The work you do..." I began.

"Oh, who cares? I started that because I had to make it matter. Didn't I?"

She was confusing me. I didn't dare glance at Stefan. There was nothing he could say at all. If I sat quietly, she might go on and at least I would know what was expected of the next few minutes. Jill began pacing up and down in front of the bench. The lights of cars from far down the hill, on the street below, searched the trees, up where there was still full daylight in the sky. At our level, objects at a distance near the thickest hedges were becoming indistinct, the graves and small mausoleums at Angel Oak blurring into a kind of miniature mountain range. And it was cold. I started to shiver, and felt Stefan move closer to me; but I stiffened so he wouldn't come nearer. I was afraid of that. It would underscore her loneliness. We would walk away from here together. She would walk away alone. In my warm kitchen, in the light, even now, Jep was pulling out the makings of four or five meals. I wished I were there, the cube of light a shield around me.

Finally, I had to speak: "Do you mean, to make Belinda's death matter? Or make domestic abuse matter?"

"Yes, both. I had to make something matter: I had to go on living with myself. You know, Stefan. Like your Healing Project? First the remorse, then the renewal?"

What was she talking about?

Jill swept in front of us again, clutching the leather case to her chest. She stopped and faced us then, as if surprised to see us there. "We should get on with this."

She opened the small briefcase. Now we would see the certificate she brought, or a candle.

She took out a gun. It was so big and military that it looked fake.

You wonder what you will do, at a time like that. You rehearse it, although not as much as you rehearse what you would do if someone broke into your house. Rush a man with a gun, they say. Flee a man with a knife. Both of those people are lethal. One of them is crazier. Run, always run. The person is going to shoot you anyway. Never believe anybody who says if you just cooperate, nobody needs to get hurt. Run, say the self-defense mavens. Run crookedly, side to side and bent over. Be a bad target. Yell. Yell at the top of your lungs and blow a whistle.

A whistle.

I still had mine.

Was it still hooked to my purse by that little chain? Or...no, I had taken it off. Which coat was it in, and in the inside or the outside pocket? I stood up and patted the sides of my trench coat. Something was in there. The rectangle of my phone. Something else. My keys. Something else.

"Listen, I've done the research," Jill said. "I know how to make it look as if you killed him and then killed yourself. I stud-

ied the forensics. What would be on your hands. What would
be on his coat. How you decided to do it here."

With every drop of resolve in me, I willed Stefan not to move.
I couldn't look at him, I couldn't signal, but I tried to speak to
him with my brain.

"You're going to shoot us? Both of us?"

"Him first," Jill said. "Stand up, Stefan." Instead, he slouched
forward, his hands capped over his head. I could hear sirens.
Wouldn't it be rich if somehow, Jep was suspicious, and sent police? If Stefan had found a way to reach into his pocket and dial
911? But no one knew where we were, back out of the view of
the main roadway through this place, under the tree. Far back,
behind the cemetery, there were houses on a ridge, but blocks
distant from where we stood. Marines in assault gear could be
standing at the gates right now, and they would not be able to
get here in time.

"You don't want to do this, Jill."

"That's what they say on TV, Thea, before the person jumps.
I've thought about all of this. For months. Maybe for years. You
have no idea how much I want to do this," she said.

"What about forgiveness?"

"Oh, I fully intend to forgive him. But the only way that I
can forgive him is if he's dead."

"Jill, listen. I get that you're in despair. I get that it never goes
away. Anniversaries are the abyss. Let today pass. Then see..."

"If I can get you to come back here another time to kill you?"
She added then, "You get it theoretically. You get it in one of
your storybooks."

"How can you think about this clearly? Is this what Belinda
would want? Is this what justice for Belinda looks like?"

"It's not what she would want. It's what I want. Bindy is with
our Lord. The sufferings of men are not her portion. You don't
feel what I feel, Thea. Maybe I should just hurt you so badly
you'll never walk again, or you'll never see again, and let you

live. So you can live the rest of your life without him. So you can see him die."

There was always an even-worse, and Jill reached down into the well of her madness and brought it up squirming in her old hand. I said, "Jill, that's your portion too. You have lived as a woman of faith all your life…"

"Oh yes, even as my piece of trash husband embezzled money from my father's church, the church my father founded, and dragged his name through the dirt," she said. One of the first things Jill confided in me, when she moved to Wisconsin from North Carolina was how it took every ounce of spiritual strength she had to go on believing after Lowell's death. In the shadowed gully where he'd fallen hard, fallen sixty feet down from the slope where they were skiing a sunset run, the two of them alone together, Jill held Lowell's hand and sang to him as he died, knowing she couldn't leave him even to summon help, his spine was severed, she couldn't let him die alone. She waited until the light went out of his eyes, and only then did she make her way back up onto the track. She was an expert skier. What had really happened to Lowell McCormack? Was this Jill now or Jill always?

"If you're going to do this, you don't have to do it right this moment. There's nobody here but us. Don't I at least get to understand?"

"You're stalling for time. In a story, this would work. But this isn't a story. You don't have any options."

"But you do. Jill, think. As of right now, nothing has happened. You got hysterical, and who wouldn't, and you made some threats, and nothing happened. This can stop, right here. Nobody has to know. It's a mistake, not a tragedy."

"So how do you suffer then?"

"Don't you think he suffered in jail? Maybe not as much as you wanted him to…"

"And you? How do you suffer now, Thea?"

"I have to live with knowing what he did, all my life. I have to live with wondering how I raised a son who could..."

Jill lowered the gun so that it was nearly touching Stefan's hair. I heard his breath catch, as it had when he was a toddler trying not to cry.

"Okay, you don't have to live with that, Thea."

"What do you mean?"

"Are you stupid?" Jill said, lower now. "I know Emily told you. I know she came to see you. I know she left town."

"Told me what?"

"Everything! About the fight I had with Belinda that night. After I found that photo of them, their disgusting photo, their love letters. I was begging her, how can you do this? How can you choose to live in such sin? And Bindy was crying and she said she loved Emily but she loved Stefan too."

"Jill! Stop this! You weren't even there that night."

"Oh yes I was! You know I was. I came to bring her home, to get her away from this...thing, whatever it was, their three-way thing...and she shouted in my face, I'm not your little doll, Mom. I'm not your little robot!" The gun in her hand bobbed and shook. It was a miracle that it hadn't gone off. "And then *he* barged in. He tried to grab the golf club. He missed. I was so angry, I couldn't even see. I just hit out. At her. At him. Everything was out of control. Everything was gone."

"What happened?"

"Bindy stepped between us. She stepped right between us."

"What are you saying?"

"Come on, Thea! You don't have to live with it, for the few minutes you have left to live! He didn't kill her. I killed her. I killed my little girl."

With a guttural cry, Stefan ducked down and lunged for Jill, grabbing her around the knees but impossibly, she was too quick, stumbling back but never losing her footing. It was Stefan who went down hard. Fueled by some malevolent syrup, she kicked

Stefan in the chest, knocking him backward, off balance, so that he had to reach for the bench to try to get up.

Haltingly, as if his voice were an instrument that needed tuning, Stefan began, "You...evil, you..." and then went on, "You let me think that I killed Belinda when I didn't? You knew all along, and you let me go to prison?"

"Who cares about you? You belong in prison, you sick piece of trash. You were out of it. I put your hand on the golf club. Then Emily dragged it away and dragged me out of there."

"How did you convince Emily to lie?" I asked her. She held the gun in both hands, leveled at Stefan's chest, so I fought down my desire to shout.

"Her name's not Emily, by the way, Thea. Convince her? She was a pervert. She couldn't wait to do all the stuff I wanted her to do. She knew I would take her down too. If Belinda never went to Black Creek, she would be an accomplished woman of grace. Look what Emily did for her. The first sin is hard, the next one is easy. Why should I go to prison? After everything I've already lost? At least I had something to give. What did she have to give? What did he have to give? Nothing."

"Jill, stop. You don't know what you're saying."

"I won't stop, Thea. Or maybe, okay, I won't kill you. Maybe I'll do what I planned. I'll shoot Stefan right in front of you and let you go on living, like I had to do." She began to cry and her hands shook. "Who cares what happens to you? Who cares what happens to me?"

She stood up straight then and put the barrel of the gun under her own chin.

This, I had never rehearsed this in my mind. This wasn't something I ever imagined my way into doing. I took a step forward and slugged Jill in the side of the face. She fell to one knee and the gun went off with a crack so loud that I saw lights flip on in several of those distant houses. I felt the thud of the discharge in my side, as if I'd been holding an M-80 under my

arm when it went off. I stood back and pulled the whistle out
of my pocket and blew the whistle, over and over. More lights
went on. Stefan scrambled for the gun, pushing Jill down and
kneeling on her so that she couldn't move. "What do we do?" he
said to me. "We can't tie her up or anything. What do we do?"

"Use her sweater to tie her up. Tie her hands behind her and
tie her to the bench."

I called the police and reported someone threatening people
with a gun. It was clear that we would have to be the ones to
guard Jill with the gun. I'd never used a gun in my life; I didn't
know if Stefan had. But they had to be pretty self-explanatory.
Stefan handed me the gun, while holding on to Jill's arm, trying to get her sweater over her head and round her wrists. She
thrashed and kicked and leaned over to bite his hand. "You
nutcase!" he yelled, and pulled both her arms behind her. Jill
jerked her head back and hit Stefan in the mouth. "That does
it," he said. He kneed Jill in the back hard enough to knock the
breath out of her and jerked her arms up over her head, tying
the sweater around her hands. Then he pulled off his own shirt
and tied it around her feet.

We saw flashlights approaching and I realized I hadn't even
noticed it was full dark. We could have been lying here, like
Esme said, all alone. As three officers arrived, their own guns
drawn, I thought of Esme then, saying, *You don't know her like
I do...* How right she was. And how wrong. How pitiless. She
had known everything, all along, far more than I realized.

"Okay, ma'am," the officer said to me. "Put the gun down.
Now. Step away. Slowly."

I said, "Gladly. It's not my gun. I mean, I wasn't the one
with the gun, she was, although yes, technically now I have the
gun..." I set the gun on the ground.

"Now turn and face the bench."

"What? Why me?"

Stefan said, "Mom. He'll figure it out." The officer spoke into his radio. "Yes, send him up. We're just getting started here. Can somebody get some lights?"

Twenty minutes later, Pete Sunday arrived at the grave site, explaining all our roles to the other police in a few sentences.

"When you're wrong, you're wrong," I told him.

"I couldn't agree with you more. Although I think that if I was faced with the same facts again, I'd make the same mistake again." He rubbed his hands together. "She was very convincing."

"She thought she was on the side of the angels."

"I just don't get the motivation. Your kid is dead. You know it was an accident, you didn't mean to hurt anyone, the worst thing has already happened, no horrible consequences for you, but instead of fessing up, you decide to hurt someone else's kid, and you wait until years later?"

Someone flipped on a spotlight, and Pete Sunday's face gaped in horror. "Get an ambulance!" he yelled, whipping off his really great trench coat and pressing it to my left arm. "You didn't tell me she shot you!"

I looked down. My arm was swollen, purpling and covered with blood, and for the first time, I experienced a hot ache, just above my elbow. Stefan was sitting on the bench and I glanced down at the whorl of his dark hair and then suddenly I was looking down on my own dirt-smeared face, my tangled hair, as if from a perch on a tree limb. I knew all about hypotensive shock and the blessings it confers on mortally injured creatures, but along with the surcease of pain came a pleasing sense of rightness and goodness, as if currents from the earth were joining currents in my veins, linking me to all the plants and grasses and even the people under this quiet ground. The new universe winked at me.

Stefan yelled, "She's hurt, this way, help us!"

Her hands cuffed behind her, Jill was being hustled away. She glanced back over her shoulder and said, "Oh, Thea! I'm sorry."

It was the last thing I heard. I remember waking up next to wonder how really sick people even managed to survive ambulance rides, much less their injuries, because the one I was in was bouncing like a carnival ride. The young paramedic on his haunches next to my shoulder said, "Well you can stop bleeding anytime you want, ma'am. You're giving us a little too much drama here."

I said, "Don't put in one of those tubes. I'm even afraid of blood tests. It hurts too much." He gently held up my hand for me to see.

"Already did it. I'm the hero of all IVs. Got one in an eighty-four-year-old gentleman the other day. My crew bet me three days of breakfasts I couldn't do it."

Then it was too much work to talk. At the ER door where I'd been so recently when Rebecca had her baby. I was deftly wheeled through the secret swinging doors and into a cubicle bristling with gloved and gowned people. "Not every day we get a GSW," said someone. "Since this isn't the Wild West, we'd probably better get that hunk of lead out of your arm, Mrs....?"

"Demetriou."

"Okay, let's just get an X-ray in here..."

I heard Jep before I saw him, *where is she? Is she being operated on?* When he was ushered past the curtain, I watched his face as he engaged in a titanic struggle not to say, *didn't I tell you so?*

"Let's just have a little bit of...ten milligrams diazepam, get you all comfortable while the numbing medicine takes effect."

Jep took my other hand and said, "You're the only person I've ever known who's been shot."

I said, "I'm the only person I've ever known who's been shot. Sheltered lives we've led."

"That's one way of looking at it." He went on, "Stefan told me everything. This changes our whole life. But I confess I'm having a hell of a time wrapping my head around it. Why would she do this? How could she do this? Do you think she's making it up?"

That hadn't even crossed my mind. I considered it briefly.

"No," I said. "I'm sure she's not making it up."

"I'm glad I called the police."

"You were the one who called the police?"

Jep smiled and kissed my forehead. "I had a hunch."

"Okay," said the doctor, holding up the X-ray. "You got lucky here, as far as being shot-wise goes. Didn't hit a bone, and muscle tissue pretty much takes care of its own healing. You're going to feel this for a while though. Maybe quite a while. It'll feel like a bad bruise. Right now, you're just going to feel some pressure while I get this thing out. We'll keep you overnight and give you some antibiotics IV."

Jep went on, "How could she carry this on so long and wait so many years?"

When he said that, suddenly, I got it. I got the whole thing.

18

Stefan did buy a house. It's that ramshackle copy of a tiny English cottage where he lives with Molly and Figaro, the absurdly huge Neapolitan mastiff puppy given him by Trina Villera, who is Molly's obedient servant. Julie loves the place. It's a refurbishing project with a capital *P*. Her boys love it because they can throw stones out the upstairs windows and try to hit the ducks in the creek nearby. All I can see are hot-and-cold running mice. Still, Jep and I relish our born-again solitude, this one such a different tenor than when Stefan was in prison, and I have a second…well, a second second career too. In part I'm sure because of all the spicy elements—murder, betrayal, dating violence, the spectacular fraud of Jill's activism—and probably because Belinda was beautiful, white and middle-class—the news engine roared to life… I was nonplussed by such events as hearing the familiar gentle voice of Anderson Cooper on my answering machine. Of course, the developments sparked Curt Cowrie to approach me again with a whole new idea for a series of talks, and this time, for sure, a book. ("This is a dilly," he said in the message he left.) Were we interested in such things, now that we could slip back to our quiet private lives? You bet your ass we were interested…show me the money. We wanted everyone who saw us broken on the rocks to hear how hope—which a Japanese philosopher once called "that which prolongs the torments of man"—pays off once in a while.

Or so we first thought. As it transpired, never did those talks. There was no joy left in a circus of self-righteousness. The pure jubilation I thought I would taste was spiked with such bitter sadness. Stefan felt the same way. It was time to draw a curtain in front of our lives.

Stefan still has his business. He's in college and should finish in a year. The Healing Project has seven volunteers and sometimes, Julie and I still help out. The stories just get sadder; but the healing always helps. For a while it seemed like Stefan and Luck Sergenian's younger sister, Snowy, who got a stomach virus and ended up coming home early from Paris, would be a thing. But then, one day, he told me that was over. Hesitatingly, I asked why? He said, "I liked her a lot, but she liked me more."

"Isn't that good?"

"I guess it could be unless…"

"Unless?"

"Unless you like someone else that way." He stopped for a moment. "And I do. I like Becky." All those days of working and then hanging around for dinner at the safe home, playing with the baby, his respect for Rebecca grew, for her competence, her quiet beauty, her matter-of-fact vision of the world.

"She's so much older. She has a child. Does she like you that way?"

"I didn't ask yet. Not in so many words. But I think she does. She said one time that her mom was five or six years older than her dad. I'm going to win her." The hundred objections I could have mounted melted in the sun of that courtly phrase. This was none of my business, at least not yet.

In the meantime, Stefan is wildly overcommitted, with school and with work and night classes in fire science at the community college. He longs to become a volunteer firefighter, and perhaps eventually do that as a career if he likes it. It's as if he's wheeling in space, looking at all the doors opening to him, the former felon. It's as if he's making up for lost time.

I have my own business to attend to. Paradoxically, I am writing another book; in fact, it's finished now, but not yet published. It's not about the case, exactly, but about something I never thought I'd tilt with. Forgiveness, it transpires, is not just a slogan on a coffee mug. It's the hardest work a human being can do, or at least that this human being can do. It controverts both your instinct and your intellect. I initially thought I would write about the experience of lives kidnapped by one woman's malevolence. But Aeschylus was right—and how could I have doubted such a wise and voluble Greek? Wisdom, if a human being ever can be said to achieve wisdom, comes through pain, drop by drop, in our own despair, against our will. The deeper I dug, the more I unavoidably understood. The universe has its own forces.

A force for good, dialed up many notches, can do harm. Jill's obsessive love for Belinda was the perfect twin to my love for Stefan. Stefan's love for Belinda…Emily's love for Belinda…they made up a hall of mirrors, each reflecting back the love that pushed them to obsession. But if those obsessions led to terrible acts of wrongdoing, the love itself was never wrong.

Jill was charged with felony assault with a deadly weapon, obstruction of justice, malicious prosecution, filing a false police report and contempt of court. She was sentenced to five to eight years. We sued her for defamation of character and her insurance was ample. Stefan received a small settlement from the state of Wisconsin, which has a lousy reputation for parsimonious compensation, but settled with Black Creek County for much more in a lawsuit for wrongful conviction.

That is the shining side of my personal planet. There is a dark side.

I don't work at Thornton Wilder College anymore. Jep is so wholly beloved at UW–Whitewater that the powers somehow found me a tenured faculty position there; but for now, I teach only one of my literature seminars, a couple of sections of creative writing, and (my penance) remedial writing for athletes. I could have stayed at my beloved school; but it never felt right after my sabbatical. Then, after our life reversed when Stefan was vindicated, it felt even more awkward to slip back into the slot where I'd spent such a long time genuflecting to my shame. I should not have done that. I should not have been allowed by my colleagues to feel that I should do that. They should have embraced me and borne me up—instead of sighing and simply suffering my presence.

When I showed up to tell Keith the news, he had both a flowering begonia and a long-suffering expression. "Thea, of course I apologize..." he began.

"But you shouldn't have to apologize," I told him.

Keith's face softened. "I'm glad you see that."

"I mean, you should never have treated me in a way that requires an apology. And of course, even that would have been understandable, if not commendable, because of all the many times you called me when I was on sabbatical, and returned my calls."

He hadn't called me once. When he returned my calls, he left a brief message and pleaded about how "crazy busy" things were in the English department of a college with 845 students.

People are usually good when it suits them, and often some will make a special effort to be good when there's a special need. But most people aren't naturally inclined to goodness, particularly if it gets in the way of something they want. And what they want doesn't have to be a palace or a person or a promotion. What they might want is the kind of power that comes from having front-row seats at a tragic drama or the immense emotional satisfaction of feeling luckier or more competent than someone else. That power was what my colleagues got from me, and I wanted it back.

"You judged me, Keith, like the kids say. You and Frank and Robin and almost everyone else. You judged me and you felt justified in doing it. You judged Stefan too, not that there was any way around that really."

"What would you have done, Thea?"

"Maybe I would have done the same thing. I hope I wouldn't have. I certainly would not now. Whether or not I would have done it, that's not the issue. It's that we can't go back to before it happened, and I don't mean Belinda's murder, I mean what happened to me, here, where I should have been safe."

"I really hope you don't feel that way, Thea."

"I love the work I do," I said. "But not here."

And so, I was changed. I would not have wanted to be changed; still, I cannot go back to before. We are annealed, but not restored. It was against my will that I learned what Jill had to teach me about love and loss, and about myself. Am I better for learning it? Probably, but only because I have no choice.

Now I know that, when you lose a child, it's not the same as losing a contemporary, even a beloved husband or wife. When you lose a child, you grieve as a child grieves, which is to say, you grieve backward. You don't get better as time passes, you get worse. Time does not take you closer to acceptance, only further from the one you love. Day by day, Belinda slipped away from Jill. Season by season, the clothes in Belinda's closet were no longer the current style; the music on her player was not the music other kids listened to anymore. Year by year, other people's daughters and sons, once the same age as Belinda, grew up; and they did the things that Belinda would have done: They graduated college and started medical school or graduate school.

They joined the Peace Corps. They backpacked across Europe. They found their first jobs. They learned to sign contracts and leases and health-insurance forms. Some of them got engaged. The more of those milestones that passed, the more meaningless the world became. Jill did not get stronger, she only got older—older without Belinda. The very good memories—silly small things, the way Belinda cried when a dog died in a movie, the gleam of sunscreen on her small shoulder when she was a child at the beach, the color of the Christmas wrapping paper she stamped by hand, the way Belinda hummed as she made her oatmeal, the way she wrapped her long hair in an old tee shirt to dry...these began to lose their sharp edges. The sound of a laugh that was like Belinda's, the sudden burst of a song Belinda loved when Jill turned on her car radio, the smell of freesia, a scrawl of words on an old grocery list in the bottom of a drawer, BUY STRAWBERRIES, all these had to be wrenched out of her mind and compacted like trash until they were no longer familiar or even recognizable. Those very good memories once scalded Jill like zinc in her eyes; but she realized that the scalding was better, much better, because at least it was feeling and feeling had washed off her like sidewalk chalk in the rain. The scalding grief was better because it was the dark twin of the stupefying love you felt for your child when you had your child with you, a passion so much bigger than anything you expected to feel, so much bigger than any other parent's love, so magnificent you had to keep it secret, lest the bored gods notice and knock it out of your hands. Jill's love for her only was a second sun. And as the sun disappeared, minute by hour by day by week by month by year, so did her reason. She would have been the last person to be aware of the awfulness of her crime. To the end, she would have considered Stefan responsible for Belinda's death, as he does, and now, as I do, in a sense, as well.

I comprehend all this because I comprise it. Not everyone is constituted this way. I think that I exist for myself in part by ex-

isting in the eyes of others, especially those nearest to me. Some
people have a robust sense of self independent of parenthood. I
don't. If Stefan died that way—in all honesty, if Stefan died in
any way—I would lose my reason. I would want to. I would be
diminished, minute by hour by day by week by month by year.
I wouldn't do what Jill did. But I would want to cast a killing
frost on the world. Sometimes, I would try to seem brave or
enduring—even inspirational. That would all be a show and
eventually, I would stop trying.

I sometimes think of Belinda. I think of Belinda and say to
myself, I will remember her forever; I will never let her depart;
I will keep her locked forever in the round-tower of my heart.
But every day, she is further out of reach. I can no longer hear
her voice, I can only hear my own voice repeating words I know
she said, and my loss is not a hundredth part of Jill's. Stefan has
put it all behind him. He doesn't want to remember. Youth is
programmed to go forward. For him to recover does not make
him cruel. It makes him healthy.

One weekend a month, when I'm not with Julie or my family, I drive north, not to Black Creek, but to a place high up on
a barren fan of land in Iron County. With my small overnight
bag, I check in at the little roadside inn where they now know
my name and my errand. I lay myself down on the stiff mattress and try to sleep. Every time I make this journey, I think
this could be the last time. Nothing is promised. Nothing is
expected. Just after the sun comes up, I drive a couple of miles
to a park where a small waterfall froths over a chin of granite
and crashes into a little creek with surprising force. One sizzling day, I walked right in and stood under it, still in my linen
pants and tee shirt. Afterward I was dry within ten minutes.
One brutal winter morning, the waterfall was frozen in flight.
Sitting there, I drink my coffee from a Styrofoam cup. Then, I
drive one more mile. I park my car outside the gates. Inside, I
hand over my big leather purse and submit to the wand and wait

while they flip through the books and magazines, the pretty stationery and stamped envelopes that are so important for sending letters out, in the hope that letters will come. There is a list and mine is the only name on it. I fill out a form. On the line that specifies RELATIONSHIP TO INMATE, I write, *Friend*.

★ ★ ★ ★ ★

BREWSTER, MA, 2021

This is a story that I wrote alone but not on my own. I owe a debt of gratitude first to my agent, Jeff Kleinman, who always settles for more, and the kind hearts and sharp minds at Folio Lit, and then to my editor, Kathy Sagan, whom I feel I knew before I met her, and all the team at Mira/Harper-Collins. I can never repay The Ragdale Foundation, home of my writer's heart, where portions of this book were written in 2019, especially Amy Sinclair, Linda Williams, Regin Igloria and Jeff Meeuwsen. I also wish to acknowledge the Turkeyland Cove Foundation on Martha's Vineyard, where I wrote the first words of this story a year and a month ago today. To my friends and colleagues at Miami University of Ohio, especially Keith Tuma, Laura Van Prooyen and Hoa Nguyen, to my boyfriend, Chris Brent, my beloved sis, Pamela English, my best pal, Ann Wertz Garvin, my true friends Moira McDermott and Holly Robinson, my brother Bobby, all my love for bucking me up when I thought all was lost. Oh brave old world, that has such people in it. Always, there is my own darling crew, Rob Allegretti, Dan Brent-Allegretti, Martin Brent, Francie Brent, Mia Brent, Merit Brent, Will Brent, Marta Brent and Atticus Brent—as well as my fab daughters-in-law Kat Hodge Allegretti and Olivia Brent, and my brand-new grandson, Henry, with a special hug for Merit and Martin for the forty-two times I made them listen to parts of this book, and for my little Marta, who thinks everything I do is really very good. Each one of you is my only. There is one more person I wish to mention. I don't know her name. Years ago, I was standing in the coffee line at a hotel where I was giving a speech when the woman in front of me dropped her book. I picked it up and asked if she was at the convention but she said, no, she came every week, to visit her son at the nearby prison where he was serving a long sentence. In a drug-induced psychosis, he'd killed the only girl he ever loved. This mom was a lovely person. He was her only child, her only relative on earth. And I wondered, could you still love the one you loved most in the world after he had done the worst thing? Then I realized, you would be the only one who could. How many times I thought of that woman I cannot say, but I put off writing a story so anguishing. Finally, however, it wouldn't let me alone. But in this story, I exercised the artist's right to correct history, as I wish, for her, I could correct life. Finally, this is a work of fiction. All the people and places in it, even the ones with real names, are portrayed here not as they actually exist, but as I imagined them. There are certain to be plenty of errors, and all of them are mine.